Books by Judith Miller

The Carousel Painter

The Chapel Car Bride

The Lady of Tarpon Springs

FREEDOM'S PATH

First Dawn

Morning Sky

Daylight Comes

BELLS OF LOWELL*

Daughter of the Loom

A Fragile Design

These Tangled Threads

LIGHTS OF LOWELL*

A Tapestry of Hope

A Love Woven True

The Pattern of Her Heart

POSTCARDS FROM PULLMAN

In the Company of Secrets

Whispers Along the Rails

An Uncertain Dream

THE BROADMOOR LEGACY*

A Daughter's Inheritance

An Unexpected Love

A Surrendered Heart

BRIDAL VEIL ISLAND*

To Have and To Hold

To Love and Cherish

To Honor and Trust

DAUGHTERS OF AMANA

Somewhere to Belong

More Than Words

A Bond Never Broken

HOME TO AMANA

A Hidden Truth

A Simple Change

A Shining Light

REFINED BY LOVE

The Brickmaker's Bride

The Potter's Lady

The Artisan's Wife

www.judithmccoymiller.com

*with Tracie Peterson

JUDITH MILLER

BETHANY HOUSE
a division of Baker Publishing Group
Minneapolis, Minnesota

Published by Bethany House Publishers
11400 Hampshire Avenue South
Bloomington, Minnesota 55438
www.bethanyhouse.com

Bethany House Publishers is a division of
Baker Publishing Group, Grand Rapids, Michigan

Printed in the United States of America

Library of Congress Cataloging-in-Publication Data
Names: Miller, Judith, author.
Title: The lady of Tarpon Springs / Judith Miller.
Description: Minneapolis, Minnesota : Bethany House, [2018]
Identifiers: LCCN 2018002378| ISBN 9780764231063 (trade paper) | ISBN
    9781493414741 (e-book) | ISBN 9780764232060 (cloth)
Subjects: | GSAFD: Christian fiction.
Classification: LCC PS3613.C3858 L33 2018 | DDC 813/.6—dc23
LC record available at https://lccn.loc.gov/2018002378

Scripture quotations are from the King James Version of the Bible.

Cover design by Kirk DouPonce, DogEared Design

Author is represented by Books & Such Literary Agency.

18 19 20 21 22 23 24   7 6 5 4 3 2 1

This book is dedicated to:

Karen Huntley, Nancy Smart,
Annette Baum, and Beverly Parker.
Four special ladies, four special friends.

CHAPTER 1

TARPON SPRINGS, FLORIDA—1905

Zanna Krykos closed her eyes and offered a silent prayer for God's direction. This was going to be one of the most difficult conversations of her life.

The bell over her law office door jingled. She opened her eyes, swallowed hard, and waved Lucy Penrose toward one of the threadbare chairs in the sparsely furnished room. She forced a smile, tucked a stray lock of ebony hair into her fashionable pompadour, and turned her eyes toward the stack of papers on her desk. The sun had begun its ascent over the Anclote River and created a golden hue that shone through the early morning haze.

"Good morning." She attempted a warm smile. At least this conversation could begin on a pleasant note. "I asked you to come by early because I know that once you begin seeing patients, there's no telling when you might be available to visit with me."

"I knew it must be important or you wouldn't have been so insistent." Lucy traced a finger of her gloved hand across the worn fabric on the upholstered chair before sitting down. "You really should do something about this office furniture, Zanna. If you expect to attract clients, you need a well-appointed office." Her forehead creased into wrinkled concern. "They have a good selection of fabric at Alderman's. I'd be happy to go along and help you make a choice, and I can vouch for Henrietta Armstrong as an excellent upholsterer."

"Thank you, I'll keep that in mind. However, I'm afraid the upholstery isn't my primary concern right now." Zanna placed her palm atop the stack of papers on the center of her desk. "Your late father's contract with the Greek divers is what has kept me awake at night." A knot tightened in her stomach. "I fear my news isn't going to please you, but I've been unable to find any way to nullify the contract."

Her friend's bright blue eyes darkened several shades. "What do you mean? You told me you would find a loophole in that contract. That I need not worry. That everything would be fine."

Zanna shook her head. "You've embellished upon what I actually said. I told you I would look for a flaw in the contract—one that would permit you to have it set aside. Unfortunately, the agreement is ironclad. The contract was drawn by a knowledgeable lawyer in New York City, a Mr. George Moskatos. Believe me, I did my best to find something—anything—that might provide you with an escape, but there's simply no way to have it set aside. You're held to all of the terms. Even though your father is the one who signed the document, the contract contains a provision that his designated beneficiary is obligated to uphold the terms and conditions of the agreement." Zanna met her friend's forlorn stare. "That is you, Lucy."

Lucy leaned forward until the lapels of her dark blue jacket touched the desk. "But you're a lawyer. You're supposed to find a way for me to avoid this obligation."

"I know. And I tried." Zanna sighed. "Look at it this way, Lucy. You're a doctor, but you can't heal all of your patients. This is much the same. Surely you know I feel terrible giving you this news." Zanna retrieved a letter from the stack of paper work and extended it in Lucy's direction. "I've been in direct contact with the lawyer who prepared the contract between your father and the divers. I received this letter yesterday. The divers will be arriving here in Tarpon Springs next week."

The letter fluttered onto the desk. "Next week!" Lucy pushed up from her chair and paced the short distance between the front window and Zanna's desk. "I shouldn't have waited so long to have you look at this, but I simply didn't want to accept my father's death and deal with the paper work involved. Now look what's happened. My procrastination has made things much worse." The wide-brimmed hat that had been carefully balanced atop Lucy's mass of blond curls shifted sideways. She yanked at the hatpin, pushed the hat into place, and forced the pin into the taffeta and chiffon fabric that surrounded the crown.

Zanna watched in amazement. "I'm glad you didn't jam that hatpin into your head." She grinned and hoped her attempt at levity would ease the tension that now filled the room.

"I doubt I'd feel any more pain than this news has caused me. I don't know how I'm going to handle any of this, Zanna."

So much for easing the tension. Lucy hadn't directly blamed her, yet Zanna felt a weight of responsibility. She'd been certain she could help and had given Lucy false hope.

Zanna inhaled a breath. "I know you don't think I've done enough to help you, but I've spent countless hours poring over the contract as well as your father's will. When I could find nothing on my own, I wrote to Mr. Burnside and asked for his advice. He agrees that you are bound by the terms of the contract. I trust what he's told me. After all, that's what he does each day—prepare and examine railroad contracts. Once I heard from him, I wrote to Mr. Moskatos and asked if he would contact the Greek manager who signed the contract to see if he would be willing to release you from the agreement. He said it was too late. The men, their boats, and the diving equipment had already sailed from Greece. Yesterday I received his letter saying they'd arrive in Tarpon Springs next week."

Lucy dropped into the chair, her lips drooping in defeat. "What am I supposed to do with fifty men who can't speak English and spend most of their time underwater looking for sponges? Why did my father do this to me?" Her final question was a mere whisper.

"You know it was never his intent to burden you. His death was sudden. I'm sure he expected to live many years more. I think your father wanted to remain productive, and he found a way to increase business here in Tarpon Springs. The Greek divers are how he planned to accomplish his goals."

"I still can't understand why he didn't tell me about these plans before he died." Pain shone in her eyes when she looked at Zanna. "You must agree that having this dropped into my lap without any forewarning isn't fair."

Zanna angled her head. She'd never known Lucy to be a woman who insisted things should be fair. Truth be told, her friend usually railed against such complaints. "I know it's a bitter pill, but if you'd brought me the documents a week or two after your father's death, there would have been time to contact the divers and attempt to nullify or renegotiate the contract. They might have considered a request due to your father's death." She reached across the desk and gave Lucy's hand a gentle squeeze. "Even if they hadn't already set sail, I'm sure the funds your father advanced for their passage and to transport the diving equipment and boats would have been exhausted—not to mention the cost of building the sponging boats. They likely commenced construction of those as soon as the money arrived."

"Boats?" Lucy's voice cracked. She waved toward the docks. "Your father builds boats. My father could have had them constructed right here. None of this makes sense."

"If you would have reviewed the paper work, you'd understand the boats used by the Greek divers are specially built to accommodate the diving equipment. They have some sort of different equipment that lets them breathe underwater. They can go deeper, stay down longer, and retrieve better sponges." Zanna shifted in her chair and rifled through the stack of papers. "There's a lengthy description of the equipment and boats attached to the contract if you'd like to read it." She extracted the page and offered it to Lucy.

"I don't have time to go through all those documents." Lucy sighed. "That's why I gave them to you. Yet, I am curious how my father became involved in all of this. His interests always revolved around land acquisition and construction, not boats or the Gulf waters."

"From what I've read, it seems your father became acquainted with Adelfo Pappas, a sponge buyer of Greek descent who lives in New York. I'm not sure how they met, but Mr. Pappas has been coming to Florida for a number of years to purchase sponges for New York retailers. The sponges currently available are harvested from dinghies or rowboats in shallower waters by hookmen and scullers. However, the best sponges are found in much deeper water. At least that's what I gather from all this." Zanna tapped the stack of papers.

Lucy frowned. "So, my father decided this would be the perfect business and he requested help from this Mr. Pappas."

"Exactly. Mr. Pappas helped with the correspondence and acquainted your father with several contacts in Greece. Pappas helped translate the correspondence, but it seems he had neither the interest nor the available funds to finance such an operation. However, in one of his letters he stated there was a great deal of money to be made in such an investment."

"And Mr. Moskatos, the man who wrote that binding contract? Is he a friend of Mr. Pappas, as well?"

Zanna hiked a shoulder. "There's no way for me to know that, but since Mr. Moskatos's office is in New York and Mr. Pappas lives in New York, I can only assume they are acquainted. But that doesn't mean there's any sort of collusion. Your father may have requested Mr. Pappas locate a lawyer familiar with Greek practices so that matters could move forward with greater ease."

11

"I suppose most anything is possible, but as a friend of my father, it seems Mr. Pappas would have contacted me about this on his first visit after my father's death."

"Perhaps, but once your father began to work with the lawyer, I don't know how much contact he had with Mr. Pappas. Besides, he didn't know you were unaware of your father's plans. And the contract is with a Nicolas Sevdalis, not Mr. Pappas."

Lucy glanced at the cabinet clock sitting on a table near the south wall.

Zanna followed her gaze, then cleared her throat. "I know you'd rather be discussing anything but the particulars of this matter, but . . ."

"I have patients to see this morning. You know I pride myself on being punctual." Lucy tugged at the decorative embroidery that edged her cuff.

"I understand, but there's little time to decide what you're going to do. As I said, the men will arrive soon. You need to develop a plan."

"I'm a physician, Zanna. I've been called to the healing profession, just as you've been called to the legal profession. I don't want to devote my life to anything beyond caring for the sick. Other than sending the divers back to Greece, I have no plan." Lucy pushed up from the chair. "All my hopes were pinned on you and your legal training. I was certain I could be released from the contract. Since you tell me it's impossible, I suppose the only thing to do is send the men back to Greece. Perhaps you could check into the arrangements for me? I simply don't want to deal with this."

Zanna stared at her friend. She'd always known Lucy to be a compassionate and reasonable person. Granted, she'd been handed difficult circumstances, but she couldn't bury her head in the sand. Lucy was the one who had delayed going through her father's papers for almost a year. On more than one occasion, Zanna had suggested Lucy locate her father's will and go through his business documents, but to no avail. Lucy was always too busy, but now she expected

Zanna to find a solution. While Lucy's grief and unwillingness to review her father's papers for a period of time had been understandable, she'd pushed everything aside for far too long.

Zanna leaned forward. "After making an ocean voyage and then traveling from New York to Florida by train, I truly don't believe those men are going to board a return train to New York and sail right back to Greece. They've left their homes and families to come here. No doubt they all hope to make a better life for themselves. If you want them to turn around and go home, you had best be prepared for the fight of your life."

Lucy shook her head. "I have no interest in a sponging business, and I certainly don't want to become involved in an argument with anyone." She backed toward the door. "I'm going to leave all of this in your capable hands, Zanna. I know you'll find a way out of this misfortune before the men arrive."

Before Zanna had a chance to reply, Lucy disappeared out the door. Zanna stared at the jingling bell and leaned back in her chair. If there was an easy remedy, she would have presented it the minute Lucy arrived. Did her friend think a resolution would merely drop out of thin air?

Using her thumb and the tips of her fingers, Zanna massaged her forehead and bowed her head. "Since Lucy has dropped this on me, Lord, I fear I'm going to have to place it before your throne. I don't have any answers for her, but I'd be forever grateful if you would send a solution my way."

CHAPTER 2

Zanna pored over the paper work long after Lucy departed. She prayed she would find some phrase or clause buried deep within the pages that would permit an annulment of the contract. When that failed, she turned to the letters exchanged between Mr. Pappas and Lucy's father, but all seemed in order. The letters between Mr. Pappas and his contacts had been written in Greek, and she searched for some error in her translation of each one, yet she could find nothing out of order. Even the terms of her father's will provided no escape. An ache settled deep within as she returned the documents to their folder and placed it in her desk drawer. She'd been certain the Lord would hear her silent pleas and she'd miraculously find something—anything—that would prove she was a competent lawyer worthy of her friend's trust. But that hadn't happened. No matter how hard she tried, it seemed she would disappoint Lucy—and herself.

She pushed back from the desk, retrieved her no-nonsense braid hat, and adjusted it atop her massive pompadour. She looked into the mirror that centered the oak hall tree near the front door and tipped her head to one side. "So much for today, Zanna Krykos.

15

You may have a paper that says you're a lawyer, but you and that paper didn't do much to help your friend today."

A sigh escaped Zanna as she dug into the pocket of her skirt to retrieve her key, locked the office door, and turned toward home. The heels of her dove-gray boots clicked on the wooden sidewalk like a clock marking off the minutes until the men arrived. She continued onward, her eyes skimming a display of anchors, cordage, and ship chandlery in the window of G. W. Fernaldo's & Son, the store whereher father occasionally purchased supplies for his boat-building business. She passed the Tarpon Springs Drug Store, the Royal Palm Café, and Carvainis & Co., where a broadside boasted a new supply of men's and boys' wear, but it was the fabric swatches in the window of Alderman's Dry Goods Store that caused her to halt.

One particular pattern caught her eye. Lucy was right. It would look wonderful on the chairs in her office. The ache in her stomach tightened as she stared in the window before forcing herself to move. She didn't need another reminder of her failure as both lawyer and friend. If she didn't begin to win cases for her clients, she'd never be able to reupholster the furniture in her office. Truth be told, she wouldn't even be able to pay the rent.

"Zanna! Wait up! I'll walk with you."

She turned at the sound of her brother's voice. He hoisted a bundle of canvas onto his broad shoulder and hurried toward her. Forcing a smile, she gestured to the canvas. "That looks pretty heavy. Why didn't you bring the wagon?"

Atticus's boisterous laugh filled the early evening air. "You think I'm a weakling? Even you could carry this." He raised his hands toward the load.

She stepped away from him. "Don't you dare, Atticus. I'm not about to carry that canvas."

As he readjusted the load, several strands of dark hair fell across his forehead. He swiped them away and matched her stride. "I'm sorry. You must be tired after all that exhausting work you do at your office every day." He grinned. "Am I right?"

On most occasions, she found humor in her brother's jibes, but not today. She pinned him with a hard stare. "Work doesn't have to be physical to be exhausting. Using one's brain can be every bit as tiresome as shoveling dirt or sanding the planks of a boat." She lifted her gaze to his shoulder. "Or carrying a load of canvas."

He blew a long, low whistle. "What's wrong with you today? You can't joke with me anymore?"

"I'm sorry. It's been a long day and I feel like a failure."

"You? How can my smart sister who has her own law office be a failure? If you're a failure, then what am I?"

"You're an assistant boat builder—and a very fine one. Judging from my success over the past eight months, you chose the more profitable profession. Right now, I think I should have gone into business with Papa." She tugged the brim of her hat to shade the setting sun from her eyes.

"You think our father would permit you to work alongside him like a man when he still won't admit to himself that you passed that test and you're a lawyer the same as old Mr. Burnside?"

Zanna furrowed her brow. "I don't think that's true. I think he believes I'm a lawyer, but he's still unhappy because he believes I deceived him."

"Well you did, didn't you?"

"I did not. I merely remained silent about what I was doing, which isn't a lie or deceitful."

Her brother shifted the canvas to his other shoulder. "You can tell yourself that if you want, but you didn't tell anyone Mr. Burnside was helping you study to take that law test because you knew Papa wouldn't approve. Isn't that true?"

She lifted her nose in the air. "You're the one acting like a lawyer with all your ridiculous questions."

"And you're doing your best to avoid answering my question. I'll bet that's one of those maneuvers you learned from Mr. Burnside. Right?"

There would be no winning this argument—not that she truly cared. Sparring with Atticus about taking the bar exam was in the past. They both knew her father would never have agreed had she requested his permission to sit for the exam. They both knew that was why she didn't tell him until after she'd passed it. And they both knew he wanted her to marry and have babies—not practice law.

They continued toward the family home adjacent to her father's boat-building shop that fronted the Anclote River. "The river's higher than usual. I hope we don't get any more rain for a while." She caught sight of her father standing atop the bow of his most recent project and waved.

He called out a welcome and then gestured to her brother. "Hurry, Atticus! I need that canvas. You should have been back long ago. You always spend too much time visiting with Mr. Fernaldo."

Atticus tipped his head close to her ear. "No matter how soon I return, he says I spend too much time visiting."

"Maybe I wouldn't want to build boats, after all." Zanna smiled at him and turned toward the house, where her grandmother was sitting on the front porch winding a ball of bright blue yarn. She leaned down and kissed her weathered cheek. "What are you making, Yayá?"

She shrugged her shoulders. "I'm not sure. Maybe a wrap to keep you warm when we sail for Greece?" Her eyes brightened with mischief. "You would like that?"

"I would like you to make me a shawl, but I'm not planning a trip to Greece." Zanna tried to keep her voice even. "I'm sure Mama would consider making the journey with you."

Her grandmother cackled. "Your mother isn't the one who needs to find a husband." She pulled a knitting needle from her basket and pointed it in Zanna's direction. "But you! You should have been married long ago. If your papa had his way, we would already be on our way to Greece."

Zanna gave her grandmother a patronizing nod and hurried inside before the talk of husbands, Greece, and marriage could go any further. She removed her hat and stepped into the kitchen. "Do you need any help with supper, Mama?"

Her mother's graying hair was in the usual large knot at the nape of her neck. The older woman shook her head, the knot swaying like a melon preparing to break loose from the vine. "If you would bring in the wash from the clothesline, that would help."

Zanna picked up the large woven basket and made her way to the lines her father had strung from the side of the house to a tall palm tree. The sagging rope bounced as she lifted the weight of the shirts, work pants, cotton dresses, and aprons from the line.

The scent of her mother's fish stew, laced with fennel, thyme, and saffron, wafted through the open kitchen window and created an enticing incentive to move with speed. Both her mother and grandmother could produce lavish meals in the blink of an eye. Or so it seemed to Zanna, who still couldn't use the briki and make her father a cup of his morning coffee.

Her father and brothers were seated at the table when she returned inside with the laundry basket on her hip. Capturing her mother's attention, Zanna nodded toward the basket. "I'll take this to my bedroom and fold them for you this evening."

Her father pointed to the tureen of fish stew now in the center of the table. "You need to spend more time in the kitchen so you can learn to cook good Greek food."

Zanna strode into the bedroom, longing to tell her father she had no desire to prepare Greek food—or any other food, for that matter—but of course she held her tongue. Any retort would only evolve into yet another discussion of her need to marry and have babies.

While removing clothes from the line, she'd momentarily considered speaking to her father about the arrival of the Greek spongers and Lucy's predicament, but his recent remark was enough to erase that idea. Any mention of difficulty in the law office or her inability to solve a client's problem would only add fuel to her father's deep belief that his daughter should already be married. She'd keep Lucy's predicament to herself. If help was going to come, she'd need to depend upon the Lord.

As morning dawned, Zanna awakened with a start. An unexpected surge of excitement pulsed through her veins. She had a plan. And not just any plan, but one that had come to her in a dream during the night. Giving little thought to anything else, she donned her clothes, rushed down the stairs, and hurried to the door while calling out a quick good-bye. Her grandmother's admonition that Zanna should eat breakfast before leaving the house trailed after her as she scurried from the yard.

Her breath came in gasps as she pounded on Lucy's door. When she didn't immediately answer, Zanna danced from foot to foot, then knocked again. "Where is she? Surely she's not still asleep." Zanna cupped her hands around her eyes and peeked through the decorative triangle of tinted glass in the front door. Her heart plummeted. Maybe Lucy had been called out to care for a patient. She inhaled a deep breath and turned to leave when the front door opened.

"Zanna, what's wrong? Is someone ill? Your grandmother?"

"No, everyone is fine, but I . . ."

Before she could complete her sentence, Lucy stepped away from the door and waved Zanna inside. "From the way you were pounding on the door, I was sure there must be some emergency." Lucy's brows puckered, and her lips tipped into a wry smile. "My goodness! Did you get dressed in the dark? You're wearing the jacket to your brown suit with a skirt that doesn't match."

Zanna glanced down and felt the heat rise in her cheeks. "I can go home and change later. This is important."

"It must be." Lucy chuckled and stepped to the side. "Do come in and tell me what it is that would cause you to leave home in that terribly mismatched attire."

Zanna grasped Lucy's hands. "I have a solution to your problem."

"You do? Then I won't say another word about your outfit. Tell me everything. Did you seek help from another lawyer?"

"No. I don't think any lawyer can find a way out of that contract, but I had a dream last night. I had prayed and asked God to help me find some way to help you, so I'm sure the dream was His answer to my prayer."

Lucy pursed her lips and dropped back in her chair. "You know I believe in prayer, but I'm not—"

"Don't become skeptical before you've heard what I have to say."

"I'm sorry, Zanna. It's difficult to believe your dream is going to solve my problems, but I promise to listen with an open mind."

Zanna pressed her palms down the front of her skirt and nodded. "I am going to take charge of the sponging business for you. You will remain the owner, of course, and I'll seek your permission before making any major decisions, but you won't have to worry about any aspects of the diving operation. I know how to keep proper accounts. I managed Mr. Burnside's accounts when I clerked for him, and I understand the proper methods of bookkeeping. I read and write Greek, so I can communicate with the men who will be arriving next week. There may be a few who speak some limited English, but the majority will likely speak only Greek."

When she stopped to inhale a breath, Lucy scooted forward in her chair. "That's your solution? That you're going to manage fifty Greek spongers who are coming here expecting to go to work for my father? I'm sorry, Zanna, but how can you think that is God's answer to my dilemma?"

Zanna's mouth dropped open. She'd been so excited, so certain Lucy would be thrilled with her plan. Instead of listening with an open mind as she'd promised, Lucy had immediately been dismissive.

Zanna crossed her arms across her waist and frowned. "Unless you have another solution, at least let me tell you why I think this will work."

"I'm sorry, Zanna. I said I would listen." Lucy waved her hand in a circular motion. "Please, go on."

"Although you still want to believe there's some way to get out of the contract, you need to accept that you are legally bound by its terms. With that in mind, you must have someone manage the business for you. Since you have no interest in the sponging operation and want to continue with your medical practice, I believe I'm the best choice to assist you."

"And is that because you believe you failed as a lawyer?"

Zanna shook her head. "No. I've already told you that this came to me in a dream last night."

"Oh, yes. The dream. I'd forgotten." Lucy hiked a brow. "Do continue."

Zanna's stomach clenched in a knot. She hadn't missed the lack of belief in Lucy's tone. Maybe the dream wasn't God's answer to Lucy's problem. She fought off the niggling thought and continued. "As I said, I can read and write Greek. I'm a lawyer, which should give me an advantage in dealing with the sponge buyers and when legal documents are needed. In addition to working for Mr. Burnside and in my own law office, I've helped my father with the accounts for his boat-building business. And though you may not consider it an asset, I have two brothers I've been able to boss around with great authority, so I think I can handle the spongers just as handily."

Her friend waited a moment. "Is that everything?"

Zanna leaned forward. "No. In truth, I've saved the biggest reason of all for last."

Lucy's eyes widened. "And what is that?"

"My father is threatening to send me to Greece with my grandmother—on a matchmaking journey to find what he considers a proper Greek husband." Zanna reached for Lucy's hand. "Surely you can understand my plight. You've told me you don't want to marry unless you find a man who will permit you to continue your medical practice. And maybe not even then. If you let me do this, we would be helping each other. I'd relieve you of the day-to-day responsibility of operating the business, and you could continue with your medical practice."

"I know you have the ability to do what you've offered, Zanna, but—"

Zanna shook her head. "There is no other option. Those men and their equipment will be here soon. Either you take charge now or you arrange for someone else to do it for you."

"I wish I could simply put them and their equipment back on a boat and send them home, but I don't have the funds to do that. This entire disaster has stripped me of everything." A tear slipped down Lucy's cheek.

"Only for the time being. I believe it can become a sound business venture." Zanna hoped her assurance would finally convince her friend. "You wouldn't even have to pay me anything until the business is solvent."

"That's kind of you, Zanna." Lucy pushed up from the chair. "But perhaps I can find a buyer even before the business is solvent."

CHAPTER
3

Lucy's final remark squelched Zanna's earlier enthusiasm like water on a campfire. She stared at Lucy and briefly attempted to understand the comment. Lucy hadn't been herself since discovering her inheritance had been invested in sponging boats and diving equipment. She'd become annoyed at every turn. Zanna was doing her best to cope with Lucy's irritation, yet she longed for the return of the kind and good-natured friend she'd grown to love over the years.

Silence hovered over the room like a funeral pall until Zanna could bear the quiet no longer. "Exactly what do you believe you can sell, Lucy?"

Pinching the bridge of her nose between her thumb and index finger, Lucy sighed. "The business. Isn't that what we've been discussing?"

"Don't you see that there truly isn't any business yet? Until the crews arrive and begin diving, we won't know the quality or quantity of sponges to be found in the Gulf. This entire endeavor is a gamble."

"My father was willing to take a chance with his money. Surely there's someone else who would do so." A spark of hopefulness shone in her eyes.

"If you believe you can find someone willing to do so before the men arrive, then you can ignore what I've suggested. However, I believe your idea is akin to offering fifty experienced railroad workers and a coal car as a business, so I would argue you don't own anything of value to an investor. You have the crews, the boats, and some equipment, but there still isn't any proof this will be a profitable venture." Zanna shrugged. "The decision is yours."

"I'm not sure I agree that there's nothing of value to sell, but I know I won't find a buyer or even an investor on such short notice." Lucy's shoulders sagged in defeat. "On the other hand, I might be able to secure a loan to send the divers home. Under the circumstances, I think they'd prefer a return to Greece, don't you?"

"You're not thinking logically, Lucy. Why would you want to incur a large debt to send them back? The bank would require security and you'd have to pay interest. Do you want to place your home and land in jeopardy? Besides, how would you repay the loan?" Zanna drew in a deep breath. She needed to approach her friend with calm assurance. And while she wanted to offer support, what Lucy needed most right now was for someone to look to her best interests in the long run. "I told you before that I don't think the men will want to return home. I'm sure they have dreams of earning a better wage and eventually sending for the wives and families they left behind. If you attempt to default on the contract, they would likely be heartbroken. And they could possibly sue you, as well."

"I hadn't thought of that." Lucy's expression softened for a moment, but as quickly as it had appeared, it was gone. She squared her shoulders. "I don't believe any court would hold it against me. Any sound judge would see that my father was the one who intended to see the contract to completion."

"That matters not a whit, Lucy. You are the sole heir of your father's estate, and he made it quite clear that his heir would be bound by the terms of the contract."

"Perhaps, but he didn't think he would die soon after he'd signed that contract." Lucy's voice trembled during her brief rebuttal.

"I know, but that argument won't hold water in any court." Zanna sighed. "Any judge worth his salt would point out that nobody thinks they're going to die. Folks believe death will come to others, but most never consider their own mortality. Besides, any attorney for the opposition would argue the fact that your father stipulated the terms of the contract should pass to his heirs, and that is proof enough to bind you to the agreement."

Lucy sat down and stared out the front window for a long moment. She finally turned and looked at Zanna. "How long before the business is profitable?"

Zanna gulped. "Surely you realize that there is no way for me to give you a definite answer to that question. Since the Greek divers can go much deeper, they may be able to find sponges that are as large and lovely as those being harvested from the Aegean Sea. If they locate sizable beds of quality sponges and can reap large harvests, I would estimate the business could repay you within two to five years. But that's only a guess. There's no way for me to be certain."

"That's a long time, Zanna."

"Not when you consider the divers must receive wages, the cost of upkeep on the equipment, and the need to rent storage space for trimming, sorting, and storing the sponges until they're sold."

"I don't understand any of this. I'm a doctor. It's all I've ever wanted to do. This is far more complicated than I anticipated and only heightens my desire to rid myself of the entire matter."

"I completely agree, and that's why you should permit me to take charge. I'm willing to step in the minute you tell me to do so."

"I know you're worried about me." Lucy massaged her forehead. "And there aren't many options. Let me think about it. Right now I need to take care of my patients."

Zanna nodded. "Just remember. There isn't much time. There will be a group of Greek immigrants arriving in the blink of an eye."

That evening Zanna strode toward home. She had hoped to hear from Lucy before day's end, but that hadn't happened—at least not yet. Given their earlier discussion, Zanna was confident she would be appointed manager before week's end.

Her brothers and father had already taken their seats at the supper table. After her mother, grandmother, and Zanna had joined them in a prayer of thanks for their meal, Zanna filled her plate with a small helping of moussaka.

"That's all you're going to eat after I prepare one of your favorite dishes?" Her grandmother's tone was a blend of sorrow and admonishment.

Zanna forked a bite of the eggplant and lamb mixture and swallowed. "It's delicious, Yayá, but I'm not very hungry. I've had an exciting day. My stomach feels like it's tied in knots. If I eat too much, I don't think it will settle well."

"What are you saying? You think Yayá is a bad cook?"

"No, of course not. You're a wonderful cook." Zanna touched her hand to her stomach. "I have butterflies. Understand?"

"Instead of my moussaka, you want butterflies?" Her grandmother touched her finger to her temple. "You are going mad?"

Zanna closed her eyes for a second. "No." Deciding it was going to take far too long to explain, Zanna translated her comment into Greek. "You understand now?"

Her grandmother shrugged. "I still think you should eat more moussaka."

"Let her be, Mama," her father said, obviously weary of the conversation. He pinned Zanna with an inquisitive look. "So what is it that has caused you all these butterflies in your stomach? Have you been thinking about marriage?"

"No, but I have been thinking a lot about fifty Greek men."

"What's that you're saying about fifty men?" Her mother dipped a piece of crusty bread into olive oil. "I think one will be enough, Zanna."

28

Zanna chuckled and then confided there would be Greek diving crews arriving by train next week.

"What about women? Any wives and children? I would love to have some other Greek families living here." Her mother leaned forward to capture Zanna's attention.

"For now, just men, but if all goes well, they will likely send for their families." Before they could ply her with a host of questions, Zanna explained what she'd discovered upon examining Mr. Penrose's documents and will.

"So, all the money Dr. Penrose expected to inherit is gone?" Atticus spooned another helping of moussaka onto his plate. "I'll bet she's unhappy. What's she going to do? I mean, I can't imagine her down at the docks haggling with buyers and taking charge of sponging crews." He swallowed a gulp of water. "That's sure going to be a change for her. Who's going to take care of her patients? You think another doctor will come to town?"

Zanna drew a deep breath. "She's going to continue her practice. I'll be the one down at the docks taking care of the sponging business."

Her father's fork dropped from his fingers and clanked against the china plate. "You'll be doing what?" His voice boomed like an exploding cannon.

"Jurek!" Her mother waved a napkin in the air. "We are not deaf. Please lower your voice."

Her father leaned forward, his broad chest heaving. "Did you hear what your daughter said, Halina? She's talking about working on the docks—like she's a man. Your only daughter! And all you have to say is that I shouldn't shout?" His jaw dropped, and his bushy black eyebrows wriggled like frightened caterpillars attempting an escape.

Had the matter not been so serious, Zanna would have laughed aloud. As it was, she stifled a threatening giggle, covered her mouth, and feigned a cough.

"She isn't going to work on the docks. You're exaggerating." Her mother arched her brows and shot Zanna a warning look. "Tell your father he has misunderstood. You plan only to help your friend and you will be working in your law office like always."

"I heard what she said, Halina." Her father shook his head. "First you go to work in that lawyer's office as his clerk—and I never approved of that—then you go behind our backs and take that special test to become a lawyer. And then when Mr. Burnside leaves, you have your name painted on the front window and announce to the world that you are a lawyer." He heaved a sigh. "'Zanna Krykos, Lawyer' in big gold letters. How do you think that makes me feel? My daughter, doing a man's job."

"It isn't a profession for only men, Papa. Maybe in Greece, but not here. I don't understand why you want to cling to the old ways. You came to this country when you were ten years old, a little boy. But you still think we should act like we are living in the old country."

"There's nothing wrong with the old ways. Even in this country, most women are married and having babies by your age."

Zanna tipped her head back and closed her eyes. "I don't want a husband or babies, Papa. At least not yet. Maybe someday, but not now."

"You see how she is, Halina? She thinks like a man instead of a woman."

Before Zanna could utter a retort, her mother gently grasped her hand beneath the table and smiled at her father. "Now, Jurek, let's not ruin our dinner with all this angry talk. Zanna is a good girl who wants to use her mind and learn as much as she can before she takes a husband. She will marry one day and give you grandchildren."

Zanna glanced across the table. Her older brother was grinning from ear to ear. He was loving every minute of this exchange. She returned his smile before turning toward her father. "Yes, Papa, one day I will do as Mama says. But if it is marriage and babies that concern you, maybe Atticus should be looking for a wife. He is older than me."

Her brother's smile faded. "Don't pull me into this, Zanna. Papa is talking to you." His grin returned as quickly as it had disappeared. "Maybe one of those Greek divers will be looking for a wife. Right, Papa?"

Her father shook his head. "I want my daughter to marry a man who makes a good living and is home every night. A husband who is out to sea all the time is not for Zanna."

"Well, thank you both for deciding upon my future for me." She narrowed her dark eyes and sent her brother a look that told him she'd get back at him.

Atticus leaned back, a look of pleasure creasing his face. "It will be nice to have some other Greeks living in the area. Do you think those men will take orders from a woman, Zanna? I don't know how you think you can give them direction when you know so little about sponging. Will you be going out on the boat to show them how to dive?"

Her younger brother, Homer, joined the laughter. "I would like to see that, Zanna."

"Well, I would not!" Her father's tone brought a halt to her brothers' laughter. "I want you to forget about this silly idea. The docks are no place for a woman."

"This isn't about giving orders, Papa. I'm a lawyer and Lucy is my client. She hired me to help her and, as her lawyer, it's my job to do whatever is necessary to assist her."

"Baah!" Her father waved his hand. "I never saw Mr. Burnside working at the docks. He helped his clients from behind that big desk of his. But you want me to believe that for you to be a lawyer, you have to go down to the docks to conduct your business."

"If Mr. Burnside was still here, he'd do exactly what I'm doing. Lucy hired me to take care of her business, and that means going wherever I must to accomplish the task. If I could pass the exam and become a lawyer, I can do this, too."

Her heart pounded in her chest. Never before had she spoken to

31

her father in such a determined manner. She now realized it would have been better to remain silent until after the men arrived—until she was already embroiled in the business—just as she'd done with the bar exam. Being forthright with her family was going to do nothing but compound her problems.

Her father folded his napkin and dropped it across his plate before clearing his throat. "I know you think you know everything, Zanna, but let me tell you this: The philosopher Socrates once said that the one thing he knew was that he knew nothing; and that was the source of his wisdom." He tipped his head to one side and pointed his finger in her direction. "But you, Zanna, think you know everything. I hope you are right."

"I don't know everything, Papa, but Lucy needs my help."

He pushed away from the table and stood. "I will discuss this no more. I've told you what I think. You are a grown woman determined to set your own path. I hope you don't make a mistake."

Her father's parting words remained in her thoughts as Zanna prepared for bed. Had she made a mistake? Should she have ignored Lucy's plight? Would she have the strength to manage fifty men and make decisions that could impact their lives and Lucy's fortune? She should have remained silent until Lucy had given a definite answer.

She slipped between the sheets and adjusted her pillow. Perhaps her idea to take over and operate the business was far more than she could manage. Once again she drifted off to sleep with a prayer on her lips—a request for direction.

The night was fraught with nightmares of Lucy being left penniless and sued by the bank. When Zanna attempted to represent her friend, a beak-nosed judge ordered Zanna to jail. He declared she was a fraud who had never received a proper license to practice law. As morning dawned, she awakened gasping for air and clutching her damp nightgown, recalling her latest horror of the night: The Greek divers had organized a mutiny and thrown her overboard.

Zanna's hands shook as she slipped on her single-breasted suit jacket. "It was only a dream. It was only a dream." She continued to mutter the words until she descended the stairs and entered the kitchen. "No breakfast for me, Mama. I have an appointment and I don't want to be late."

"You look pale. Did you sleep well?" Her mother's eyes darkened with concern.

"I'm fine. I'll see you for supper this evening." She wanted to speak with Lucy before her first patient arrived. Between the disagreement with her father and the nightmares she'd endured, Zanna feared she'd made a mistake. One that could prove tragic for both Lucy and her. She rounded the corner and caught sight of Lucy exiting the front door of her office.

Zanna waved her parasol in the air. "Lucy!" When she didn't immediately stop, Zanna called again. "Lucy! I need to speak with you."

Lucy turned and waved her forward. "Hurry! I need to call on Bessie Rochester. She's not feeling well. Her sister came by and got me out of bed this morning."

Before Zanna could speak, Mr. Markley shouted Lucy's name and came running in their direction. "Got a telegram for ya, Dr. Penrose." He huffed for air and waved the telegram in the air. "Just arrived. You need to see it." He thrust it toward Lucy.

She unfolded the paper and read. Her head jerked upward. "This can't be correct."

Mr. Markley frowned. "It is, Doc. I took it down exactly."

Lucy paled and looked at Zanna. "I'm accepting your offer. The Greek crew boarded an earlier train and will arrive this afternoon at three o'clock. You're in charge."

CHAPTER 4

Nico Sevdalis signaled to the conductor, who was navigating his way down the aisle of the swaying train. The man stopped and was now visiting with one of the finely dressed female passengers. This journey would have been much easier if Nico had learned more English before he and the other men boarded the ship from Greece. The voyage hadn't been so difficult. There had been two Greek crew members on the ship who had been quick to assist them and answer their many questions. But once they'd disembarked to begin the final portion of their journey by train, they hadn't been as fortunate.

His attempts to locate the proper train in each of the depots along the way had been close to impossible. He couldn't read the names of the cities and times of departure posted on the large boards, and every attempt to make himself understood by other passengers or railroad employees had been problematic. The railroad agents had proved less than helpful, most of them ignoring him while they attended to passengers purchasing tickets—those able to speak English.

He'd managed to learn only a little English from an American he'd met in Greece, and the phrases he memorized didn't include the necessary skill to communicate their needs throughout the journey. When the conductor had finally finished his conversation, he glanced down the aisle. Once again Nico waved to him.

The man's lips tightened in a thin line as he approached. He stopped beside Nico and arched his thick brows. Nico tapped his pocket watch and pointed to his ticket.

The conductor removed a watch from his pocket and pointed to the three before lifting three fingers in the air.

Nico nodded, then stood and gestured to the men traveling with him. "We will arrive soon. Do your best to look presentable. We want to make a fine impression on Mr. Penrose and get off to a good start."

Nico was pleased to see several of his men pull combs from their pockets as he picked his way down the aisle and crossed the platform into the adjoining car. After delivering the same message there, he returned to his seat. He'd felt the weight of responsibility throughout their journey, but even more so with their destination drawing near. Perspiration beaded his forehead and upper lip. He dropped back into his seat and swiped his damp palms down the front of his pant legs.

He was the one who'd convinced these seasoned crew members to leave their homeland; he was the one who'd offered assurance they would soon earn enough money to have their families join them; he was the one who said Mr. Penrose could be trusted as an honest businessman who would honor his promises. And he was the one who'd said they would have a better life in America. In truth, he had hoped all of what he promised would come true, yet he couldn't be sure the men would earn enough money to bring their families in the near future—it could take years. And he'd never met Mr. Penrose. He'd relied upon correspondence from Adelfo Pappas, a Greek sponge buyer living in New York who had written to the director of the Greek Sponge Exchange. As for a good life in America, Nico had relied upon stories he'd heard from visitors, but he couldn't be certain he and his men would discover anything better than what they'd left behind.

The conductor made his way down the aisle and came to a halt beside Nico. He pointed to Nico and then gestured toward the door. Nico smiled and nodded, then stood and instructed the men to collect their belongings and disembark before he strode into the adjoining car to advise the remaining men. The weary group congregated on the platform near the baggage carts while Nico surveyed the few people waiting on the platform. He didn't see anyone who looked like he might be Mr. Penrose. There were two ladies and a young man, in addition to two or three trainmen.

He turned toward his fellow travelers and forced a smile. "I don't think Mr. Penrose has arrived just yet. Perhaps he didn't know we would arrive today."

"You told us you sent a telegram telling him we were arriving early." There was a note of accusation in the comment that came from the back of the group.

Nico stiffened. "I did, but there could have been a problem."

"Like maybe they couldn't understand your English and the telegram said we weren't coming at all." The remark was enough to cause a low murmuring among the men.

"This is not the time to argue. We have safely arrived at our new home, and I'm going to see if I can locate someone who will direct me to Mr. Penrose. Just remain right here. Mr. Pappas told me there would be an interpreter at the station when we arrived."

Nico attempted to tamp down the fear mounting in his chest. There was no way for him to know the size of Tarpon Springs, but he doubted he'd be able to locate the home of Mr. Penrose. There was a possibility Mr. Penrose might be waiting inside the station. One thing was certain: He needed to do something before his crews considered a mutiny.

Straightening his shoulders, Nico strode toward the station with a determined step. He hoped an air of confidence would lessen the murmurs of dissatisfaction among his men. Before he arrived at the depot door, one of the young ladies he'd noticed earlier turned and stared at him. He tipped his hat and flashed a smile. Surely two unescorted women hadn't been sent to greet a group of fifty Greek sailors. The thought amused him, though he had to admit she was lovely. Her dark hair and eyes reminded him of the beautiful Greek women they'd left behind. She stepped toward him. He'd heard that many women in this country possessed an unexpected boldness. Was this an example of such behavior? They would approach a man without proper introduction? He shook off the thought. He didn't have time to worry about women right now.

Zanna stepped into the path of the dark-haired Greek who had glanced over his shoulder as he walked toward the depot. She was directly in front of him when he turned around, and had she not taken a backward step, he would have plowed her down. He gestured to the depot door.

She nodded and spoke to him in Greek. "I'm here to meet you, Mr. Sevdalis." When he didn't immediately answer, she continued. "You *are* Nicolas Sevdalis, are you not?"

He nodded. "You speak Greek." He blew out a long sigh.

"Yes. Do you speak any English?" She guessed he and the other men hadn't encountered many Greeks along the way.

He held his finger and thumb apart a short distance. "A little."

She smiled. "Then it will be easier if we speak in Greek."

He nodded his agreement. "I am to meet Mr. James Penrose." Using his thumb, he gestured over his shoulder. "My men and I have come from Greece to work for him. You are the interpreter?" He gave her a generous smile. "I could not ask for anyone who speaks better Greek. It is a relief to be understood. The journey has been difficult since I speak only a little English, as I said. I didn't know there were already Greeks living in the city."

"Only my family, Mr. Sevdalis."

"Nico. Please call me Nico. I promise to be on my best behavior so I can keep you as my interpreter."

Zanna smiled and waved Lucy forward. "I am Zanna Krykos and this is Miss Lucy Penrose, the daughter of James Penrose."

"Ahh." He bobbed his head, then shifted his attention back to Zanna. "Her father has sent her to meet the train and take us to our lodgings. I am sure Mr. Penrose is a very busy man, but I look forward to meeting him very soon. We are eager to begin our work, and I'm sure he will want us out in our boats as soon as they arrive. I think it would be good if we could meet him later this evening. After we are settled."

"That won't be possible, Mr. . . . ." Zanna hesitated a moment. "Nico."

Lucy leaned close to Zanna. "What did he say?"

Zanna glanced back and forth between Lucy and Nico. "He wants to meet your father."

"Well, that's impossible."

Zanna sighed. "I know, but you interrupted before I could explain."

Lucy shrugged. "Then I won't say another word."

"I didn't mean to insult you, Lucy, but it's going to be difficult enough attempting to explain to him without stopping to repeat everything to you. I promise to give you a full report once he understands what has happened."

Lucy nodded and folded her arms across her chest.

Perhaps it had been a mistake insisting Lucy come along to meet the train. Before she could give the matter further thought, Nico tapped her shoulder.

"Then I will meet with Mr. Penrose in the morning. You come along to interpret so there are no misunderstandings between us. Such a thing could make for a bad working relationship."

Zanna shook her head. "I'm sorry to tell you this since I understand you and your men are likely very weary, but Mr. Penrose is dead."

He stared at her, then slowly shook his head. "This is a joke you decide to play on us, am I right?"

The train whistle hooted three short blasts as a conductor circled them and shouted, "All aboard!"

Zanna glanced toward the departing train and held a finger to her ear. "No. It isn't a joke, Nico. Mr. Penrose is dead." She raised her voice as the train chugged down the tracks.

Nico continued to shake his head back and forth. "You are testing me to see how I would react in a dangerous or stressful situation. You can be sure I am not a man who is easily flustered." He shoved out his chest. "I have weathered many storms, and I am still alive to tell about them." He leaned toward the women, a grin on his lips. "Next you will tell me that one of you lovely ladies is going to operate the sponging business."

"How did you guess, Nico?" Zanna smiled. "That's exactly right. I speak and write Greek very well. And since I am a lawyer, I understand the intricacies of business. I have lived in Tarpon Springs all my life. For those reasons, and a few others, Dr. Penrose decided I was the best choice to become manager."

He appeared to listen intently as she spoke. At first he frowned, but when she mentioned Dr. Penrose, his smile returned. She hoped he was warming to the idea. After all, it hadn't been easy convincing Lucy this plan would work.

"I'm interested to hear more." He smiled and gestured for her to continue.

Bolstered yet somewhat confused by his change of attitude, she continued. "I plan to do my very best to guide you and your men through the many difficulties that have arisen due to the untimely death of Mr. Penrose. I'm sure we'll encounter a few obstacles, but nothing that can't be overcome with cooperation between me, you, and your men."

For a moment, he stared at her as though she'd delivered a hard blow to his midsection. Then he tipped back his head and released

40

a deep belly laugh. Zanna glanced at Lucy before pinning Nico with a glare. "Why are you laughing?"

He pointed at Zanna. "At everything you have said. Your humor delights me, but my men are weary. While I'm sorry you had to bring me the sad news of death, I think it is time I meet the Dr. Penrose you mentioned a short time ago. I believe he would be the best choice to operate the business."

Her lips tightened in a thin line. "You've already been introduced." She nodded to the woman beside her. "*This* is Dr. Penrose."

He coughed and sputtered before finally gaining a modicum of control. He gestured toward Lucy, but his gaze remained fixed on Zanna. "Her?"

"Yes, her." If the matter wasn't so serious, Zanna would have laughed at his expression. "Dr. Penrose doesn't understand Greek, so I will interpret for her if you wish to ask any questions I can't directly answer for you."

"I have many questions. First of all, I do not understand why she has employed a woman to manage her business. It is not proper." He raked his fingers through his thick black hair.

Zanna sighed. How many times would she need to repeat herself? "As I told you, she chose me because I understand business dealings. I read and write Greek and—"

"What about your family? You have no father or brother?"

"I have both."

"Why didn't she hire your father or brother to manage the business? That would make more sense. A woman can't manage diving crews and a sponging business."

"My father owns a boat-building business, and both of my brothers work with him. My father couldn't afford to give up his business to manage one that belongs to someone else, and neither of my brothers has the ability to keep books, negotiate contracts with buyers, and manage employees."

"And you think you do?" He laughed. "This will never work."

Zanna arched her brows. "Except for your divers and the three of us, there is nobody else in sight. If you want assistance, I suggest you accept the fact that you and your men will be managed by a woman."

Zanna watched the changing emotions play across Nico's face. If he was the one who had convinced these men to leave their homes and families, he likely wouldn't want to tell them a woman was going to manage the company. Of all the things he'd told them about coming to a new country, Zanna was certain answering to a woman had not been included. Would they blame him? Would they ignore her when she issued orders? Would they revolt when Nico revealed she knew nothing about sponging? Her stomach churned at the thought. She clenched her hands together. These negative thoughts weren't going to serve her well. She needed to remain positive and reassuring. The men would more likely accept her leadership if she approached them with confidence.

As he shifted away from her, she saw a glimmer of thoughtfulness in his eyes. "I recall a letter from Mr. Pappas where he mentioned there were fleets of hook boats harvesting sponges in this area. Surely some of them must be Greeks?"

Zanna bristled at the question. He was still trying to find some way to avoid her control. "I've already told you, the only Greek men in Tarpon Springs are my father and brothers. There are some Bahamians, but no Greeks. If you plan to work for the Penrose Sponge Company, you are stuck with me."

"And it seems you are going to be stuck with me—and forty-nine men who won't look kindly upon working for a woman." As if on cue, one of the men shouted to Nico that he should cease his flirting and locate Mr. Penrose. Nico quickly waved him to silence, then looked at the women. "Are the lodgings you secured close to the dock?"

Zanna swallowed hard and whispered his question to Lucy, who merely shrugged. "I have no idea what to do with them, Zanna."

Before the two of them could discuss the matter further, Nico tapped Zanna on the shoulder again. "You could maybe visit with your friend after you have shown us where we will be living? My men are tired and hungry."

Zanna attempted to recall the terms of the contract. She was sure she would have remembered if there had been something about food and lodging. Nico was obviously attempting to take advantage because she was a woman. She folded her arms across her chest and met his gaze. "Nothing in the contract states Mr. Penrose will provide food or lodging for your crew. I can escort you to the hotel, but I doubt they'll have enough vacant rooms for all of you. I'm not sure what they charge as their weekly rate, but I'll be happy to inquire."

"And who is to pay? My men don't have money to pay for hotel rooms. The director of the Greek Exchange told me our food and lodging would be provided. The contract you have is written in English. I can't read what it says, but I know what we were promised." He took a step closer and bowed his head. "Unless you want to be the one to tell the men you have no place for them to sleep, I suggest you do something, Miss Krykos. You have told me you are experienced and able to manage a business. This is the perfect time for you to show me just how good you are."

CHAPTER
5

Zanna had never refused a challenge, but locating accommodations for fifty men when neither the men nor Lucy had sufficient funds was more of a test than even she could accept. The lawyer in her decided the only remedy was to take the offense.

She squared her shoulders and cleared her throat. "As I told you, there is no obligation to provide housing, Mr. Sevdalis. The contract is silent on that issue. I don't doubt someone may have told you that Mr. Penrose would supply living quarters and food—"

"Not just *someone*, but the director of the Greek Sponge Exchange. He is a man of virtue. Why would he tell me this if it is not true? He stands to gain nothing."

"But his name isn't in the contract—only you and Mr. Penrose signed this contract, and there is nothing that says anything about food or housing. I don't know why the director told you such a thing. I don't have any idea how he came to that assumption."

"The director was involved." Nico's dark eyes flashed with anger. "He is the one who came to me with a letter from Adelfo Pappas, who lives in New York and is a friend of Mr. Penrose. Mr. Pappas was the one who translated the letters that were sent to the director.

Maybe in those letters there was an agreement about food and living quarters." He hiked his shoulders and held them there for a moment. "How am I to know anything except what I was promised?" His voice grew louder. "What you are doing is not right. Should we lie down and sleep right here? Or maybe go inside the depot?" He balled his hand into a fist and pointed his thumb toward the building.

Lucy nudged Zanna. "What's he saying? I don't understand what's going on, but I can see he's become angry."

Zanna quickly explained, then bowed her head close to Lucy's ear. "We're in the right to deny lodging since the contract is silent, but if you have any suggestions, I'd be pleased to hear them." She forced a smile. "We're not off to a very good beginning."

"There's the land not far from the waterfront that Father purchased years ago. He never did anything with it, and some fishermen constructed huts they used for a period of time. Do you think they can make do down there? They'd be close to the docks, although some of them may need to camp outdoors." She arched her brows. "Do you know the area?"

"Yes. My brothers and I used to go down to the docks and fish when we were young. I recall seeing fishing shacks not far off, but we never went near them. Papa said there were snakes and alligators. That was enough to squelch any ideas about exploring."

Lucy smiled and nodded. "I don't think there are any alligators, but there may be a few snakes. I haven't been down there for years, so maybe the lean-tos have been torn down. Other than that, I don't have any ideas. You can take them down there and see if they'll agree to stay."

Zanna didn't miss Lucy's final comment—if the men were going to be escorted to the unoccupied land, Zanna would be the one taking them. She didn't particularly relish the idea, but the offer would reveal a good-faith effort. At least that was her hope.

Before she could discuss the possibility with Nico, Lucy gently touched Zanna's arm. "I have patients to see, and I have every confidence you'll have this matter well in hand before nightfall." That said, Lucy hurried toward the depot door and disappeared.

Nico glanced at the depot and then back at Zanna. "Miss Penrose is leaving before we have settled this matter? She is coming back?"

"Dr. Penrose has placed me in charge. She has patients who need her attention. However, she did advise me that you and your men may encamp on land she owns. It's located close to the docks, and there are already some shacks on the property—at least I hope they're still there. They were constructed by fishermen years ago, so I can't vouch for their condition. I'm sure you and your men have adjusted to difficult living arrangements in the past."

"Yes, but—"

"My father has often told me that men who make their living from the sea are men of great substance who can adapt to any circumstance. He's seen proof of that time and time again."

"My men and I don't need flattery, Miss Krykos. We need a place to sleep and food to eat."

Food. She'd forgotten about the food. "First, let's get you and your men to the encampment area. We can discuss the food once we're there."

He frowned. "Seems it would be easier for you to purchase food in town so we can take it with us. I don't believe a little thing like you could carry so much food. And this way you won't have to walk back and forth several times." His smile didn't quite reach his eyes. "Unless you weren't intending to return with food?"

"I'm going to help with food, but I don't have a plan just yet. As I said, food was not part of the contract, and I'm sure your men are able to fish."

He folded his muscular arms across his chest. "They can fish, but we did not travel with fishing equipment. Maybe your father and brothers could let us use theirs?"

"I'll see what can be done, but we can't go and purchase food at the market. Miss Penrose doesn't have the money to advance for food. Her father's estate was depleted by the funds he sent to Greece. Her medical practice furnishes her only enough money to meet her own living expenses. I'm sure you can understand her predicament."

He rubbed the back of his neck. "No more than she understands mine. She ran off without doing anything to help."

"That's not true. She's offered the land where you can live. If you'd quit arguing, we could go there and you could get settled before nightfall." When he didn't respond, she met his gaze. "Shall I take you there or shall I go home? The choice is yours. I truly want to forge a good relationship that will benefit you and your men as well as Dr. Penrose, but I have nothing more to offer you, Mr. Sevdalis."

"Nico." He turned to the men and waved them forward. "Follow Miss Krykos. She's going to take us to a place where we will set up camp. We're going to be sleeping outdoors. No complaints. Be thankful we are in a place where the weather is warm and it is not raining."

"Maybe she can keep us warm if it turns cold." The comment was shouted from the rear of the group.

"Be quiet, Peter. That was rude and insulting. And just so all of you know, Miss Krykos is Greek. She understands every word you say."

"So that's why she is so pretty. She's one of us," another man called.

Nico wheeled around on his heel. "I told you that is enough!" Nico came to an abrupt halt. "I will not have such talk about any woman, Greek or American. You all know this. If you do not agree, you can find work somewhere else or return to Greece. Do you understand?"

"We were only joking, Nico. You don't have to become angry. We're tired and hungry." The rest of the men murmured their agreement.

Nico waved them to silence. "Then stop talking and follow us."

The men's murmuring continued as they walked through town, most of them expressing interest in the stores as they passed by.

Zanna led them out of town and onto a well-worn path that eventually neared the acreage. She pointed in the direction of the water. "We need to go down this way. There's no path." Though she would have preferred to have one of the men take the lead, she was the only one who knew exactly where they were going.

Once off the path, overgrowth slapped at Zanna's skirt and a wayward branch scraped her cheek. Her gaze flitted about as she attempted to plow through the mass of tall grasses and palmettos. The oak, bay, magnolia, and mangrove, adorned by yellow jasmine and Spanish moss, created an illusion of security, but her father's warning of snakes and alligators plagued her at every turn. Gulls, cranes, and herons signaled the nearness of the river, and she heaved a sigh when at last she spied a small hut in the distance.

She glanced over her shoulder at Nico. "There's one of the shacks." She pointed in the distance. "See it?" He didn't appear overly impressed by the sight. She forced a smile and pointed to the left. "There's another. It appears they're all still standing. That's a good sign, don't you think?"

"We'll see once we get closer. They look to be in poor condition."

After leading them through the boggy land, she'd expected a little more enthusiasm. Then again, they'd been expecting hotel rooms with soft mattresses and fresh sheets, so a few crude huts weren't likely to garner much fervor.

When they arrived at the first hut, Zanna shaded her eyes against the setting sun that shimmered through the fluttering palmetto branches. "I can see five huts, but there may be more down closer to the water."

Nico leaned forward and peered into the opening, then stepped back and stood upright. "These are made to sleep one person. There is little space." He pointed to the opening. "See for yourself."

She didn't care to plunge her head into the hut, but she needed to appear strong and confident. After a quick look, she straightened and attempted a smile. "It will keep out the rain." When he didn't respond, she said, "Even though there is only one bunk, two men could sleep on the floor, don't you agree?" She took a backward step. "Why don't we see if some of the others are any larger?"

The men were already inspecting the remaining huts, and murmurs of discontent had begun to rise among them. "From the sounds of my men, I don't think those other shacks are any better."

"I have nothing else to offer. For now, they can sleep in the huts and on the ground. I know Dr. Penrose won't object if they want to cut down some of the trees and construct additional lean-tos."

Nico called to the men. After they'd gathered round, he explained that they would have to make do at the encampment. "You are welcome to use anything in the area to make more shelters, and some of you should make a fire at once. Miss Krykos and I are going back into town to purchase food."

Zanna jerked to attention and hissed through pursed lips until he looked at her. "What do you mean we're going to town and purchase food? I've already explained—"

He lightly grasped her elbow and steered her back toward the path. "I have been thinking about the food, Miss Krykos, and I am guessing that things in this country are not much different than they are back in Greece."

"I'm not sure what you mean." She had no idea what he had in mind, but she knew she didn't have enough money to purchase food for fifty hungry men.

He smiled. "Then I will be happy to tell you. Back in Greece when we go to the market and maybe we haven't yet sold our sponges or a fisherman hasn't yet sold his catch, we have the owner make a ticket we sign that says how much we owe. And later when we have received our money, we go back to the market and pay. I think it must be the same here in America."

"Well, that's somewhat true. There are people who have an account at the general stores, but my papa has always taught us that unless we have the money to pay for something, we do not need it."

"If your papa had hungry children, I'm sure he would change his mind, don't you think?"

"He would not let us starve, but . . ."

Nico held a branch back so she could pass. "I want you to think of those men out there as my children, Zanna. They are hungry and they need to eat." He pointed his finger back and forth between them. "You and me, we are going to find a way to feed my hungry children."

Her mind raced as they strode back to town. Nico remained silent when they passed the dressmaker's shop and the drug store, but then he came to a halt in front of a food display in the window of Alderman's. He arched his brows. "Let's go in here."

While she wasn't certain whether Mr. Alderman would consider Nico's idea, she decided not to argue. As soon as they had stepped inside, Nico went to a barrel of potatoes and began to fill a sack. Zanna grabbed his hand. "Stop. We need to first speak to the owner and see if he'll agree to sell on credit."

She'd barely uttered the words when Mrs. Alderman approached. "Hello, Zanna. How may I help you?" Her gaze wandered toward Nico, who had taken a position directly behind Zanna.

He nudged Zanna's arm. "Tell her we need food."

A hint of fear shone in the older woman's eyes. "Is this man bothering you, Zanna?"

"No. This is Nico Sevdalis. He and forty-nine other men recently arrived in Tarpon Springs. They're from Greece." The remainder of her explanation was given in fits and starts. First Nico would interrupt with a question, and then Mrs. Alderman would make another inquiry. When Zanna had finally explained that they wanted to purchase groceries on credit, Mrs. Alderman's shoulders sagged.

"I do wish you would have said that in the very beginning. My husband doesn't sell on credit to anyone who hasn't lived in Tarpon Springs for a least a year. I'm so sorry, but you could try Mr. Wharton. He might consider opening an account for Mr. Sedalis."

"*Sev*dalis. Nico Sevdalis," Zanna said. "Thank you for your time. We'll go over to Mr. Wharton's before he closes."

She tugged on Nico's sleeve as she conveyed Mrs. Alderman's refusal and their need to hurry to Mr. Wharton's store. He yanked loose of her hold and turned to Mrs. Alderman. "I am an honest man who pays. You should let me buy food for my men."

"She doesn't understand you, Nico, and we don't have time to argue. Come on." Zanna marched out of the store and hoped he would follow.

She'd taken only a few steps when he came alongside her. "You should have told her what I said. That's what interpreters are for. Am I right?" He arched his brows and pressed his forefinger against his chest.

"Yes, but she wouldn't have changed her mind, and we didn't have time to argue." She marched forward and remained silent until they arrived at the store. Her shoes clicked a steady rhythm on the wooden floor of Mr. Wharton's grocery. The balding owner approached from the rear of the store and glanced at the clock above the door. "We close soon, Zanna."

She nodded and hurried to explain Nico's need to purchase on credit. Mr. Wharton hesitated, but then agreed to a five-dollar credit limit. Zanna gulped. "He needs to purchase enough food for fifty men, Mr. Wharton. Five dollars won't be enough. Please, won't you help?"

He frowned, then shrugged. "I'll tell you what I'll do. If you agree to be responsible if he fails to pay, I'll raise the limit to twenty-five dollars. What do you say?"

The thought of being accountable for the debt didn't sit well, but she could think of no other solution. The men needed to eat. She dipped her head in a faint nod. "Agreed," she whispered.

Mr. Wharton opened his arms wide and looked at them. "Pick out whatever you want, bring it to the counter, and I'll tally it for you."

Zanna decided it would be unwise to give Nico an exact recounting of the store owner's offer. She didn't want him spending any more than necessary. "You need to make wise choices. Don't select anything other than what is necessary. Remember that you and the men will be able to fish. We can purchase whatever you need to set lines tonight."

While Nico surveyed the shelves and began to gather items, Zanna remained close on his heels. Whenever she thought an item extravagant, she returned it to the shelf. On a couple of occasions, he attempted to argue, but she won out. If she was going to be partially responsible for the debt, then Nico was going to have to be frugal.

When they finally returned to the campsite, the men had a fire going and had drawn lots to see who would sleep in the huts and who would sleep outside. Several of the men volunteered to set fishing lines while others inspected their purchases.

Nightfall would soon be upon them and Zanna needed to get home. She drew near to Nico's side. "I'm going to leave now. If I don't return home before nightfall, my papa will worry."

He grinned. "I wouldn't want your papa to worry. I'll escort you."

She shook her head. "I'll be fine. You need to help your men get settled." In truth, she didn't relish the idea of walking back through the overgrowth by herself. Yet if she wanted to gain the respect of these men, she couldn't appear weak.

"So how did you enjoy your first day as a manager, Miss Krykos?"

Nico's question drifted on the breeze as she pushed her way through the underbrush, heading toward home. She didn't answer.

She was determined to make this work.

CHAPTER
6

Burdened by the day's events, Zanna plodded toward home with her stomach growling, a reminder that she hadn't yet eaten. That morning she'd rushed out of the house without breakfast, and with the arrival of the telegram, she'd remained deep in discussion with Lucy when noonday arrived. She would surely eat more than her share at dinner tonight. The thought was enough to slow her step. A warm meal would be waiting for her, but those men out in the marsh—would they be able to concoct something palatable in that large iron kettle Nico had included among their purchases?

One thing was certain: They wouldn't be eating anytime soon if they cooked in that huge pot. It would take an hour simply to boil water in the thing. Zanna had encouraged him to purchase several smaller kettles rather than one large pot, but he'd ignored her—likely because she couldn't tell him how to make fish stew.

His words rang in her ears. *"A Greek woman who cannot cook should not give me instructions about what size cooking vessel I will need."*

She had been quick to tell him that he was too filled with pride to take any woman's suggestion. That remark had ended their discussion. The gigantic kettle was the first thing he had placed on

Mr. Wharton's counter. She hoped the men wouldn't suffer because of her remark—or because she couldn't recite a recipe for fish stew.

"Zanna!" Her father's voice pulled her from thoughts of Nico and his chiding remark. Taking long strides, her father loped toward her with the agility of a man half his age. "When those Greeks who are coming to work for Dr. Penrose get here, they should be happy."

"Why is that, Papa?" She wasn't yet ready to tell him they'd already arrived and were encamped out in the marshes, or that she'd accepted the position as their manager. A long and heated argument would ensue when she divulged those facts, and she was far too weary for a quarrel with her father.

"Their boats are here—three of them. They're at the main dock. I saw them earlier today but only from a distance. I talked to Frank Rudman at the coffeehouse. He says they are fine boats, different from the ones I build. Dr. Penrose should go over to the docks in the morning. She will need to hire someone to look after the boats until her crews are here."

The news startled Zanna. She attempted to recall what Nico had said about the boats when they were at the train station. Did he know the boats were arriving today? "Maybe I should go and tell Lucy now. She may want to have someone go to the dock before morning."

Her father shook his head. "They will be fine. Frank's a good night watchman. He won't let anyone damage or board those boats."

Nico would likely prefer some of his own men sleep on the boats, but she wasn't going to return to their camp—not tonight. She'd trust her father's advice and hope Frank kept a close watch on Lucy's investment.

During supper she weighed her earlier decision. Had the boats not arrived, she would have remained silent. But to say nothing of the men's arrival after hearing her father's news would likely lead to future problems with her family. Besides, she'd already accepted the position as manager, and once the men knew the boats had arrived, they would swarm the docks, eager to board and make certain they were seaworthy. Weary or not, she must speak up now.

"I have something I must tell you. I'm worried you won't be pleased, Papa."

Her brothers leaned forward, their eyes dancing with expectation. Homer liked nothing more than listening in on a family conflict that didn't involve him.

Yayá pushed from the table and held a finger to her lips. "No talk until later. All day I worked to make *ekmek kataifi* for dessert. I will not have it ruined with unhappy news." Her grandmother placed a serving of Zanna's favorite dessert in front of each of them, then sat down. "Eat!"

When Zanna attempted to speak, Yayá silenced her with a look that the grandchildren referred to as the "evil eye." She cut through the creamy top layer, then pushed her fork into the crispy, golden kataifi dough. The sweet dessert lodged around the words that stuck in her throat. Until now, she'd never wished for an evening meal without dessert.

When they'd finally finished their dessert, her father poured strong dark coffee from a briki into the small cup in front of him. He leaned back in his chair. "Now, what is it you need to tell me, Zanna?"

"The Greek crews arrived earlier today. On the three o'clock train. It was very unexpected. Lucy received a telegram only hours before the train arrived. I was at her office when she received word. As you can imagine, she was completely unprepared."

Atticus chuckled. "She wouldn't have been prepared no matter when they arrived."

"Don't interrupt." Her father shot a warning look at her brother. "Continue, Zanna."

"I know you weren't in complete agreement with my desire to help Lucy, but under the circumstances . . . I mean, with the men arriving early and her being totally unprepared . . . I told her I would take charge." She watched her father's face for signs of anger. Instead, she detected disappointment in his eyes. "I didn't want to disobey you, Papa, but Lucy is my friend and she needed my help." She inhaled a quick breath. "I know you don't approve, but I've given her my word."

Her father rubbed his palm along his stubbled jaw. "You are right that I don't approve." He took a sip of the steaming coffee. "You are a smart young woman. Sometimes too smart for your own good, I think. You must know you will face great opposition. Those Greek divers will not be pleased to learn a woman is in charge, and I don't think the buyers coming here from the big cities will want to do business with a woman, either. Your challenges will be far greater than my disapproval."

"I don't expect you to give me your blessing, Papa. I only seek your approval to let me try."

"Here is what I will agree to, Zanna." Her father glanced at her grandmother. "I will do nothing to stop you from helping your friend. You have given your word and you should keep it."

"Oh, thank you—"

"Let me finish." He pushed his coffee cup aside. "You know your mother and I want you to marry and have babies." She opened her mouth, but he waved her to silence before she could speak. "You want to help your friend and manage her business. So, here is what I propose: You help your friend until it is clear the business will either succeed or fail. At that time, Dr. Penrose should be prepared to step in herself or else hire a successor."

"But why? If the business succeeds, I'd want to continue. And if it is a failure, she will need a lawyer to help her dissolve the assets."

He shook his head. "I will agree to what I've said. Once the business is either a success or a failure, you and your grandmother will sail for Greece where she will find you a good Greek man, and you will marry."

Everything within Zanna railed against the condition. Was this the only way to gain her father's approval? She searched for an alternative. Lucy, for all the trouble she'd been recently, was her dearest friend. She had to help her. She had to concede. At least for now. By the time the business was operational, perhaps she'd find some way to change his mind.

"You agree?" Her father arched his bushy brows and waited.

"I'll agree as long as you know it's not what I want to do."

He hiked a shoulder and let it drop. "I don't want to agree to let my daughter take charge of fifty men and work on the docks, either. It is up to you, Zanna."

She nodded. "Whatever you say."

Atticus whooped and slapped his pant leg. "I didn't think I'd ever hear my sister agree she'd travel to Greece to find a husband."

She glared at him. "Don't get too excited, Atticus. I haven't boarded a ship just yet."

He bobbed his head. "That's true. And you might even find a husband among those fifty spongers. Any of them look promising?"

She longed to reach across the table and pinch his arm as she'd done when they were children. Instead, she kicked him under the table where no one could see. His eyes widened in surprise, and she curved her lips in a sweet smile when he leaned down to rub his shin.

"My daughter is not going to marry a man who goes out to sea as a fisherman or a sponger. That is no life for any woman—always waiting and worrying if he would be among the men lost at sea during a storm." Her mother grimaced. "I don't want that for my child. In Greece, Yayá will find her a man who can be at her side every night."

Atticus grinned. "That will be nice, won't it, Zanna? A husband at your side every night?"

She leveled him with a hard stare. "What about Atticus? He's older than me. Why isn't Yayá taking *him* to Greece to find a wife?"

"I need him here to help with the business." Her father's curt response was enough to curtail further exploration of the subject, but Zanna considered his reasoning rather one-sided. Why was it so important she find a husband, yet Atticus could remain single?

The following morning, Zanna was up before the sun. She donned a tailored white shirtwaist and a dark-brown gored skirt trimmed with covered buttons and satin tabs. Instead of her patent-tipped shoes, she chose a pair of serviceable low-heeled boots and hoped her appearance would signify she was prepared to work.

She stopped by Lucy's office to inform her that the boats had arrived, but her friend wasn't interested. While Zanna remained in the center of the room, Lucy rushed about the office in search of one medical instrument after another. "Did you hear what I said, Lucy? The boats are here now. Do you want to go down to the docks with me to make certain everything is in order?"

"What?" Lucy stopped and stared at her. "No. I don't want to look at boats. I thought you said you'd take care of everything for me. I can't possibly go to the docks. I'm on my way to deliver the Faraday baby."

"I'm more than willing to take care of it, Lucy, but I wanted you to have an opportunity to assess the boats if you'd like. The boats were a large portion of your father's investment."

"You don't need to remind me." Lucy closed her black doctor's bag with a snap. "I trust your judgment, Zanna. You don't need to include me in any of the business decisions." She patted Zanna's arm. "You're the one who grew up in the home of a boat builder. I don't know one boat from another, so I couldn't render an opinion even if I wanted to. And I don't want to." She smiled and stepped around Zanna. "I'm off to the Faradays'. I don't know when I'll be back to town. Do whatever you must to keep everything afloat."

Zanna smiled at her friend's choice of words. She had hoped Lucy would at least inquire how the reminder of yesterday had unfolded and whether the men had encamped on the Penrose acreage. But she hadn't. In some respects, Lucy's lack of interest was a good thing. Having to seek her approval at every turn would only delay the process.

A branch snapped, and Zanna started. "Nico! I didn't see you."

"You should watch where you're going. There are all sorts of creatures out here, and I think most of them visited our camp last night."

She shivered. "I came early to tell you that the boats have arrived at the docks. As soon as you've had breakfast, we can go and inspect them."

He cocked an eyebrow. "We?" He gestured toward the crew. "You mean me and some of my men."

She jerked at his response. "No, I mean you and me. If you want to bring some of the other men, that's fine, but I'm the manager and I want to inspect the boats."

A crooked smile played on his lips. "So you'll know if something is wrong with them?"

She shook her head. "Probably not, but you will. I know how to file a request for reimbursement if you discover any damage." She folded her arms across her waist. "Do you know how to file for reimbursement?"

He shook his head.

"Then it seems we need each other. Shall we go to the docks together, or would you rather join me later?"

He grimaced. "I don't want you going on the boats without me. Give me a minute to tell the men I'm leaving."

"You're not going to bring any of them with you?"

"Not if you're going. They wouldn't go near a boat with a woman on board—whether tied to the dock or not. Sailors are a suspicious lot. If they discover you were on any of the boats and we have problems when out to sea, they'll believe it was because of you."

Zanna shrugged. "I suppose they can believe whatever they want, but I'm not going to allow their suspicions to keep me from doing my job. Shall we go?"

"Do I have a choice?" His tone was lighthearted, but she didn't miss the look of trepidation in his expression. He didn't want her setting foot on those boats, either.

She tipped her head to the side and met his eyes. "You always have a choice. I've discovered the difficulty lies in making the proper one."

He matched her gait as they trod the distance to the docks. His shoulders squared, and he shaded the sun from his eyes as the boats came into view. "Those beauties are quite a sight. They look good from a distance."

For the remainder of their trek, his attention remained fixed upon the three boats. It was a wonder he didn't trip and sprawl in a heap before they arrived. The wooden boards creaked beneath her feet as she followed him along the dock.

He stretched out his arm and traced his fingers along the curves of the word *Anastasi*, which had been painted on the bow in royal blue. "She is the oldest, but my favorite." He gestured to the next boat. "She is the *St. Nicolas* and the third boat is the *Crete*. She is the newest, and most of the men like her the best."

"Because they believe the *Crete* is safer than the other boats?"

"Who can say? The divers always want the boat with the newest diving equipment, but all boats are safe if they are repaired when needed."

"Have any of these boats required repair?"

He frowned. "Of course. All boats require repair. I thought your papa was a boat builder. Surely he repairs boats, does he not?"

"Yes, but . . ." She hesitated, attempting to recall the exact wording of the contract. Why hadn't she brought it with her?

"But what?" He arched his brows.

"I seem to recall the boats were to be new."

Nico slapped his palm on his forehead. "You are a difficult woman, Miss Krykos. I think you look for trouble at every turn."

"That is not true." She jutted her chin. "I do not look for trouble. I'm merely doing my job. It is my duty to ensure the terms of the contract are met, and I recall the contract stating the boats were to be new."

"And I recollect it saying the boats were to be in 'like new' condition." He waved at the boats. "These boats are as good as any that slide into the water from the builders' blocks."

"Zanna! Zanna!"

She turned and shaded her eyes against the bright morning sun. Her chest deflated at the sight of her father, Atticus, and Homer rushing toward her and continuing to holler her name. She gave Nico a sideways glance. "My father and brothers."

"Ah, that is good. Your father will confirm what I've told you is true. These boats are the finest diving boats any man could hope for."

"But they aren't new." Why didn't he listen? Did she need to stomp her foot like a toddler to make her point?

Rather than respond, Nico circled her and extended his hand toward the approaching men. "Mr. Krykos, it is good to meet you." His grin was as wide as a half-moon on a clear night. He turned toward her older brother. "And you are Atticus?" After Atticus nodded and shook his hand, Nico grasped her younger brother's hand. "And Homer, am I right?"

Homer bobbed his head and glanced at his sister. "I'm surprised you told him about us, Zanna."

Zanna forced a smile. "Why would you be surprised? I'm not ashamed of my family, Homer." The hem of her skirt caught on a loose board and she leaned down to free the fabric. "Why are you down here, Papa? I thought you were behind schedule."

"Only a little. Besides, it is more important to meet new friends from the homeland." Her father patted Nico's shoulder. "My family is pleased to have more Greeks in Tarpon Springs. My wife and mother are hoping your women will soon arrive."

"I don't have a wife, but some of my men are eager to bring their families once they are sure they can earn enough money. Everything depends on the quality of the sponges we find—and the quantity, too. If the beds are small—"

"First things first." Though it was rude to interrupt, this conversation could go on all morning. Zanna smiled at her father. "We need to inspect the boats, Papa." She hoped he would take the hint and escort her brothers back home.

Instead, he nodded and moved toward the *Anastasi*. "She is a real beauty." He turned his attention to Nico. "I'm eager to take a look. You don't object, do you?"

"Of course not. I am honored to have any qualified man inspect the boats."

Zanna didn't miss the emphasis he'd placed on *qualified man*. "I'm sure that includes any qualified manager, as well."

Nico didn't answer, so she proceeded to lead the way.

CHAPTER 7

Zanna listened while the four men talked at length about the structure and seaworthy capabilities of the diving boats. She considered the topic somewhat boring, but she understood the need to learn all aspects of the sponging business—and that included the necessary equipment.

"Your boats are different from any I've seen." Her father's gaze settled on the stern of the *Crete*.

"In Greece, they are known as *salcoleve*." There was a hint of pride in Nico's response.

Her father nodded. "They resemble the Turkish boats known as *takas*. My grandfather told me about them."

Nico gave an enthusiastic nod. "The stern and forward topside flare are a little different, but you are right. The salcoleve and taka are both full-bodied and smooth-planked. We will see how these beauties sail in the Gulf waters. I am hopeful they will do well."

Zanna tugged on her father's sleeve as they prepared to board the *Crete* for inspection. "The other two boats are much the same, Papa, and there are matters I need to discuss with Nico regarding the contract. I'm sure you need to return to your work."

"I value your father's opinion and would prefer he stay—if he has time, of course. You may be able to help settle the contract matter your daughter speaks of."

She hadn't realized Nico was standing directly behind her. She wheeled around to face him and was met with a broad grin.

"I would be happy to help." Her father rubbed his hands together. "What is this problem?"

Atticus nudged her arm and leaned close to her ear. "I think you have met your match, Zanna. He's as shrewd as you are."

Her breath quickened. Why did Atticus take such pleasure in taunting her? No doubt he was the one who'd convinced her father they should come and look at the boats. She'd pretend he wasn't here. Atticus hated being ignored. She quickly stepped away from her brother and drew near her father's side. "I understood the boats were to be new construction, while Nico—Mr. Sevdalis—says they were to be in 'like new' condition. I believe that if the terms of the contract say new, Mr. Sevdalis is going to have to return a portion of the money sent by Mr. Penrose."

Nico's nostrils flared, and his face reddened. "What? You never said one word about returning any money. These boats are in sound condition. Better than new. Even if you are right, you know there is no money to repay you." He reached into his pocket and pulled out its empty lining. "You see? Nothing."

"You need to remain calm, Mr. Sevdalis." Her father turned to her. "And you need to choose your battles very carefully, daughter." He lowered his head closer to her. "I don't know what the contract says, but these boats appear to be fine seaworthy vessels. I can't judge the hand-operated air pump in the amidships hold, but I don't think you should argue with Nico. You need to remember that the men will refuse to go out to sea if they think the boats or equipment are faulty."

"But, Papa—"

"Hear me out, Zanna." He lowered his voice. "You must think of the consequences if you reject these boats. These men have no money

66

to pay you, so will you wait for newly constructed boats before you let them begin sponging? You're being unfair. If the boats were in poor condition, I would understand, but do not force a battle until you are certain you can win." He placed his arm around her shoulder. "Besides, you don't even know for sure what the contract says."

"I'll do as you say, Papa, but once I read the contract . . ."

"Zanna." Her father shook his head. "Heed my words and seek God's counsel before you do something you will later regret."

"Fine." She exhaled a long breath. "Now will you take Atticus and Homer back to the shop with you?"

He chuckled and shouted to her brothers. Atticus turned toward them and waved. "Wait, Papa. I'm talking to Nico about going out on the boat."

Zanna's eyes widened, and she hurried toward her brother. "No! Absolutely not! Neither of you is going to sail on these boats." She pointed back and forth between her two brothers.

"No worries about me, Zanna. I don't want to go underwater in one of those diving suits. That's the last place I want to be when I draw my last breath." Homer shuddered and hurried toward their father.

She pulled her older brother's shirtsleeve. "You need to leave, too, Atticus. These boats are not for visitors or sight-seeing. They're working boats, and the only people sailing them are the spongers."

"Well, who says I couldn't learn to be a sponger? Maybe if I go out with the crew, I can learn to dive. Right, Nico?"

Zanna leveled a warning look at Nico and was thankful when he shook his head. "Can't promise to take you out there, Atticus. I wouldn't want to get in more trouble with your sister."

When her brothers and father were finally out of earshot, Zanna paced the dock running alongside the *Crete*. "In the future, please don't take my brother's side against me, Nico. Creating problems in my home will only make it difficult for us to get along."

He laughed until a tear escaped his eye and rolled down his tanned cheek. "And what have we had so far? Smooth sailing?"

He was still chuckling when she headed toward the office. Maybe he wouldn't be laughing so much once she reviewed the contract.

Zanna leaned back in the creaky office chair and sighed. He was right. The contract said the boats should be new *or* in like-new condition. He'd probably have another good laugh once he discovered she was wrong. She longed to talk with Lucy. She needed someone who would lend a sympathetic ear.

After tucking the contract back into the file, she pushed away from the desk. Perhaps Lucy was in her office, and with a modicum of good fortune, she might be free for a visit. She'd not gone far when she heard her name being called in a high-pitched, warbling falsetto.

She turned to see the Rochester sisters scurrying toward her. Bessie, a buxom woman who was the eldest, waved her parasol like a soldier entering battle. Zanna cringed at the sight. Had Viola not ducked, Bessie would have landed a direct blow to her sister's head. "Be careful with that parasol, Sister." Eugenia frowned at Bessie as the threesome came to a halt.

Bessie ignored her sister's reprimand and pointed the tip of her parasol at Zanna's midsection. "I'm pleased to see you. I didn't know if you'd received notice the library committee was meeting today."

Zanna shook her head. "I don't know anything about a meeting. I was on my way to have a chat with Lucy."

Not to be deterred, Bessie grasped Zanna's arm. "Well, she's not in her office. I know for a fact that she's tending to Florence Morgan. Seems she's ailing again. And, knowing Florence, the doctor will likely be there for hours." She leaned closer. "Florence is a real complainer."

Viola peeked around her sister's ample body. "Bessie was sitting on the front porch when the doctor passed by a little while ago."

Zanna nodded. Putting the pieces together didn't take much thought. "So you inquired where Lucy was going and she told you Florence Morgan needed medical care."

Viola beamed as though Zanna had solved a deep, dark mystery. The older woman's gray curls bobbed beneath a large feather-bedecked hat. "Bessie likes to keep abreast of what's happening, you know."

Bessie glowered at her sister. "Only because I want to lend a helping hand if it's needed, Sister."

Viola ignored Bessie's retort. "Mrs. Knapp is hosting us at Crescent Place today. I do love going to her home. I believe it's the loveliest home in all of Florida, don't you, Sister?"

Viola didn't indicate which sister she was addressing, but Bessie agreed. However, Eugenia frowned. "It may be the loveliest house in Tarpon Springs, but I think there are a few others in St. Augustine and Jacksonville that outshine Crescent Place."

"Now, Sister, don't say that loud enough for others to hear." Bessie pointed a gloved finger at Zanna. "Don't you ever repeat what you just heard or Mrs. Knapp will never again invite us to Crescent Place, and we don't want that to happen, do we, Eugenia?"

"No. But I'm just speaking the truth, and there's nothing wrong in that."

Bessie clucked her tongue. "Do quit prattling on, Eugenia." She squeezed Zanna's arm. "I think you should come with us. Reading is important for young and old alike, and we want to make everyone happy with the choices that are made."

Zanna squinted against the late-afternoon sunlight. She couldn't possibly sit through a meeting with ten or twelve women as they attempted to choose what books should be purchased for the library. "I'm sure we'll all be pleased with the books you ladies choose. I certainly trust your judgment." She shaded her eyes with the palm of her hand. Was that Nico running toward them? She turned to Bessie. "Would you ladies excuse me? I see one of my clients in the distance, and I believe he wants to speak to me."

The ladies all gazed into the distance. Eugenia was first to speak. "I don't recognize him. Is he a fisherman?"

"No, not a fisherman." Zanna's stomach churned. She didn't want a prolonged conversation with the three sisters. They'd repeat every word she said, and most of it would be incorrect. They took umbrage if anyone accused them of spreading gossip. The Rochester sisters believed it was their civic duty to share news with others. Zanna wasn't certain there was any distinction between gossip and sharing news, yet she didn't share that view with the Rochester sisters.

"Tell the committee members I'll do my best to attend the next library meeting." Before they could question her further, Zanna hurried toward Nico. She was breathing hard by the time they met each other. "Is something wrong?" She gasped for another breath.

He shook his head. "No. I saw you with those ladies, and I was going to tell you that I would come by your office before going to your house for supper."

"Supper? Who invited you to supper?"

"Your brother, Atticus. Is that not all right? He said your family would be pleased to have me."

Atticus! Always meddling where he didn't belong. Always taking enjoyment in her discomfort. He was the typical older brother. She constantly tried to best him at his game, but he always found one more way to taunt her. She'd refused his wish to go out with Nico on one of the boats, so he'd invited Nico to supper. He knew she'd be uncomfortable. She also knew he'd do everything he could to embarrass her throughout the evening.

"I'm sure they will. Especially Atticus."

Disbelief shone in her brother's eyes when Zanna and Nico arrived in the family kitchen. She edged close to her brother's side. "Sorry to ruin your surprise, Atticus."

He chuckled. "I thought this was so well planned, but there's always another day."

Zanna ignored his remark and introduced Nico to her mother

and grandmother. Yayá looked him up and down, then shook her head. "Why you want to spend your time underwater? You can't find anything better to look at on land?"

"I won't be diving as much as I did in Greece, but the men in my family have been spongers for as far back as I can remember. When my grandfather would dive, he carried a sponge net and stone weighing as much as a small child to help him go deep to find the best sponges. He could hold his breath for almost three minutes." Nico shook his head. "I could never do that."

Yayá stirred a pot of bubbling *fasolada* soup. "I know about those divers. When I was a young girl, I would go with my friend Selia and watch for the boats to return. Her father was a diver." She turned and stared at Nico. "One day he didn't return. Selia was never the same."

"You are right. Many men die at sea. But death is part of life, is it not? There is danger in many places. I do not live with fear when I go to sea."

"That is good. But if you had a wife and children, they would live the fear for you." She shrugged. "Maybe is best for seafaring men to remain single."

Zanna winced. "Why don't you sit down over here, Nico?" She directed him to a chair between her brothers.

"My father mentioned you and Zanna were having a disagreement over the condition of the boats. Did you two get that settled?" Atticus shot a grin at his sister.

Nico bobbed his head. "On the way here, your sister told me the boats meet the requirements set out in the contract, so we hope to begin sponging soon."

"Hard to believe you gave in, Zanna. I know how much you enjoy a good argument."

She extended her leg beneath the table and ground the heel of her shoe into her brother's foot. If her grandmother and Atticus continued with their barbs, she was going to be on edge the entire evening. With any luck, Nico might decide to leave immediately after supper. He must feel as though he was being attacked from all sides.

When her brother grimaced, she offered a sweet smile. "Unlike you, I argue only when I know I'm right, Atticus."

Her grandmother filled their bowls with the steaming bean soup while her mother cut two meat pies into thick slices. The aroma of seasoned lamb and zesty tomato sauce filled the small kitchen.

"That's enough from the two of you. I'm weary of your childish bickering. We have a guest in our home who is new to this country. Let's make him feel welcome. He has much to learn about America. After listening to the two of you, he will want to return to Greece."

"This food makes me feel like I am at home, but I am not yet ready to leave." He took a bite of the lamb pie and swallowed. "I am interested to learn about Florida and the spongers who are harvesting from the hook boats I've seen in the area. I would also like to know more about the sponge dealers. Mr. Pappas wrote that there are sales conducted twice a week. Do you know if this is true?"

Her father nodded. "There are eight sponge dealers working at the docks in Tarpon Springs. They sell the sponges harvested by men using the hook boats. Years ago, the sponges were sold at Bailee's Bluff, but a hurricane in 1896 wiped out the area. Since then, the dealers have held the sponge auctions near the docks." He helped himself to the feta cheese and sprinkled it on his pie. "Can never have enough feta."

Homer dipped his spoon into the soup. "Did you ever harvest sponge from a hook boat, Nico? I don't think that looks as dangerous as diving."

"I went out with a friend one time and fell in the water. He told me to look through the glass in the bottom of the bucket until I saw some good sponge and then hook it. When I leaned over the side of the boat to get a better view, that's when I fell in. My friend was the sculler and he didn't balance the boat. I think he did it on purpose so I would fall in." He laughed. "I never went out with him again."

"I'd like to learn how to use one of those diving suits. I think it would be exciting."

Yayá pointed the tines of her fork at Atticus. "You can stop all that nonsense talk. You are a boat builder, not a diver." The older woman looked across the table at Zanna's father. "Isn't that right, Jurek?"

"That's right. Atticus needs to keep his head above water."

Zanna grinned at her older brother. This was one disagreement he wouldn't win.

The following morning dawned bright and clear. Zanna was surprised to see the men at the docks so early—all except Nico. She'd passed by all three boats and he was nowhere in sight. She approached Markos, one of the divers who usually remained close to Nico's side. "I see you're checking the equipment. Has Nico said when you're to go out?"

He shook his head but didn't look up.

"Where is Nico this morning? I haven't seen him on any of the boats."

Markos shrugged and continued wrapping a length of air hose. He turned his back as she continued to quiz him. She knew he understood every word she was saying, yet he refused to answer.

Well, if he wouldn't talk to her, she'd find someone who would. She marched the short distance to the *St. Nicolas*, where she approached several of the men. Perhaps she needed to begin with a friendlier approach. "Good morning. It's a beautiful day, is it not?" One of the men nodded. "Are you preparing to set sail today or tomorrow?" When they didn't reply, she continued, "I wasn't certain if you'd completed your inspection of the equipment. I'm eager to see the diving suits and have you show me how they work."

They stared at her as though she'd been speaking to them in English rather than Greek. She was doing her best to help these men. Didn't they understand she only wanted to help? She inhaled a deep breath, determined to elicit a response of some sort. "I am curious, where will you store the sponges while you're out in the Gulf?"

They stared at her for a moment, then turned and boarded the boat without a word. Anger swelled in her chest. She cupped her hands around her mouth and shouted, "Where is Nico?" Her question echoed along the river like the wail of a mythological siren.

Moments later, she saw him emerge from a storage shed used by owners of several hook boats. He sprinted toward her. Even at a distance, she could see the deep furrows creasing his brow. "What is wrong?" His eyes darted from boat to boat. "There is some trouble with the boats or one of the men?"

"The boats are fine, but the men are not."

He frowned and gestured toward the men scurrying about the boats. "They do not look sick, so what is the trouble?"

"They won't answer any of my questions. They wouldn't tell me where the sponges are stored or if you're going to sail today or tomorrow. They wouldn't even tell me where you were."

"To these men, I am the boss. They will not answer to a woman. If you have questions, you need to ask me."

She glanced toward the men. They were listening to everything that was being said, yet they wouldn't talk to her. "I want to know how far out you plan to go on your first sailing and when you'll return."

"There is no way for me to answer that question. I don't know these waters. Until we go out into the Gulf and dive, I cannot be sure of anything."

"You're as bad as your men. You don't want to answer my questions. Maybe I should go along on your first trip. That way I can see for myself how things are done."

The men shouted a chorus of objections. If a woman set foot on the boats, they would not sail.

"The decision is yours, Miss Krykos. Either you remain behind when eventually we sail, or we remain tied to the docks."

CHAPTER 8

Lucy clicked the latch on the front door and trudged into her office. It had been a long night, but the end result had proved worth the loss of sleep. Delivering twins had happened only once before in her career, only this time both babies were healthy. She rounded her desk, dropped into the leather chair, and traced her finger down the appointment book. Good! There was no one on the schedule until this afternoon. Barring an emergency, she could go home and take a nap.

After locking the door, she slipped the key into her pocket and headed off. The sun was ascending on the eastern horizon, and she stopped to admire the bold mixture of orange, gold, and blue. There was nothing more beautiful than a sunrise over water, except perhaps a sunset. However, the mood was soon broken by shouts of activity along the docks. There were auctions on Tuesdays and Fridays that always produced a flurry of activity, and yet it was far too early for the arrival of buyers.

She tipped the brim of her hat to shade her eyes and gain a better view. Uncertain what was going on, she crossed the street and walked to the end of one of the piers. Those looked like the boats Zanna had pointed out to her—the ones purchased by her father. What were those men doing? There was no sign of Zanna. Her heart pounded beneath her bodice. Had the boats been left unsecure? Were the men stealing them? She quickened her step and then stopped short.

What could one woman do against so many men? If they wanted to take the boats, she would have no way of stopping them. By the time she could get help from the sheriff, they'd likely be out in the Gulf. Hoping to hear their conversation, she edged closer.

"Dr. Penrose! What are you doing?"

Lucy gasped, spun around, and clasped a hand to her chest. She narrowed her eyes and let out a whoosh of air. "Oh, Atticus! You frightened the wits out of me."

He gave a lopsided grin. "I'm sorry, but why are you hiding behind that piling?"

Though her explanation came in fits and starts, she gave him a brief narrative of the morning's events. "I couldn't be certain what was happening, so I wanted to take a closer look. I believe those are my boats."

Atticus nodded. "They are, but there's no need to worry. They're preparing to take the three boats out to the Gulf for a short time. Nico wants to have a few divers go down in some different areas to see if they can locate some good sponge beds." He gestured toward the boats. "I'm going with them."

"That's nice. Has Zanna hired you to help look after things?"

He shook his head. "I wouldn't want to work for my sister. She's too much of a taskmaster. I've got an interest in those diving suits—I want to learn how the men stay underwater for so long. I've promised Nico I'll stay out of the way if he'll let me go along and observe this one time." His brow creased. "Have you met Nico? I can introduce you."

"We met at the train station when he arrived, but thank you. Now that I know everything is fine, I believe I'll go home and get some rest. I had a long night."

She'd meant what she said, but the unfolding sight held her

attention. Perhaps because Atticus had been so excited, or perhaps because the boats that belonged to her were going out to attempt something new in the waters off the Florida coast. The exhilaration caught her by surprise, and when the boats finally pushed away from the dock with their blue-and-white Greek flags flying alongside American flags, she experienced a sense of pride. She wasn't certain why. She'd had nothing to do with any of what was happening, and yet she sensed something special might materialize because of those Greeks and their diving boats.

Long after they'd sailed out of view, she remained on the dock, listening to the Anclote River lapping alongside the pilings and feeling an unexpected sense of peace. When at last she picked up her bag and headed toward home, the sun was above the horizon and the sky held promise of a beautiful day.

Before she could make out her features, Lucy caught sight of Zanna's familiar plaid skirt. Still sensing the peaceful mood she'd experienced at the dock, Lucy waved to her friend and hurried to meet her, eager to share the incident with Zanna.

Instead of stopping when she drew near, Zanna offered a quick greeting and continued walking. Lucy turned about and joined her. "Where are you off to in such a rush? I thought we could talk for a few minutes."

Zanna gave her a quick sideways glance and continued on her way. "If you want to talk, you'll have to do it while we walk. I must get down to the encampment."

"Whatever for?"

"I want to find out when Nico is going to take the crew out on their first run. When I talked to him yesterday, I couldn't get a straight answer, but I intend to get one today."

Lucy reached forward and grasped Zanna's arm. "Would you please stop for a minute?"

Zanna shook her head and tugged her arm from Lucy's hold. "I'm in a hurry, Lucy. I know you don't care about the business, but I need to give it my full attention. I can't do that by standing in the middle of the sidewalk visiting with you."

Lucy stopped and watched her friend take several more strides. "There's no need to go to the camp, Zanna. Nico isn't there."

Zanna came to an abrupt halt and wheeled around. "What? How do you know?" She marched back to Lucy's side.

"Because they sailed earlier this morning."

Zanna shook her head. "That's impossible. Nico wouldn't sail without telling me, not without gaining my consent. You must be mistaken."

"I think not. Atticus assured me the three boats at the end of Pier Two were my boats. I watched them set sail just as the sun was rising this morning."

"I'm sorry, but I'm confused. You were at the docks at daybreak, spoke to my brother, and watched all three boats set sail?"

"I did, and it was the most peaceful, serene experience, Zanna. I can understand how you could find pleasure in working near the water. It's truly peaceful, don't you agree?" She grasped Zanna's hand in her own. "I owe you an apology for my behavior and—"

"You don't owe me an apology."

"Please don't interrupt, Zanna." Lucy touched a finger to her friend's lips. "I want you to understand that ever since you told me about my father's investment—and the arrival of all those men—I just haven't been myself. I spoke harshly and I feel terrible about it. I took advantage of you and our friendship, and I need your forgiveness. Please say you'll forgive me."

"You're forgiven. Now can I talk?"

"If you truly mean it?"

"I do, Lucy." Zanna flashed her an indulgent smile. "There's no need for an apology. You're my friend and I love you, but right now I'm trying to take care of your sponging business. If I don't know what's going on, I can't do that. So, please detail for me what happened this morning. Why were you at the docks at daybreak?"

Step by step, Lucy recounted the morning's events. "There you have it, every detail."

Zanna frowned. "After Atticus told you about the boats and offered to introduce you to Nico, where did he go? I didn't see him at home this morning, and I didn't pass him on my way."

Lucy giggled. "Oh, I forgot. He said he was going out with Nico."

"What?" Zanna clenched her fists. "And you let him go? Oh, Lucy!"

"How was I supposed to stop him?" A train whistle hooted in the distance. "Come back to my office and let's talk. Nico and the rest of the men are gone, Atticus is gone, and other than commandeering a boat yourself, there's nothing you can do to bring them back. Besides, I don't think you'd get far in a canoe, and that's the most you could handle by yourself."

The comment was enough to gain a weak smile from Zanna. Right now, that was the most Lucy could expect. "Why don't we go to my office and chat? I don't have any appointments until this afternoon."

"You look tired, Lucy. Are you sure you are up to it?"

"I delivered Mrs. Faraday's twins last night, but I'll catch a nap later."

"Twins? Are they doing well?"

Lucy beamed. "They are absolutely perfect, and Mrs. Faraday is fine, too."

"Then congratulations are in order for all—including their tired doctor."

"Thank you, but do say you'll come to my office with me. I'm longing to chat with you."

Zanna agreed, then stepped behind her as a group of chattering youngsters sidled past them on their way to school. "Oh, to be young and without worries once again."

Lucy chuckled. "You sound as though you've one foot in the grave, Zanna. I didn't realize this job was taking its toll on you—and so soon. Perhaps I should devote myself to finding someone else. This is unfair to you, and I'm ashamed of myself for forcing you into this position."

"You didn't force me, Lucy. I offered. If you recall, I even listed the reasons why you should select me to take over. I will admit that sometimes I feel there is more to it than I imagined. Nevertheless, I'm up to the task. And I don't know that there's anyone else who would be more capable and available to do the job." Zanna followed Lucy into the office. "I'm merely concerned because Nico didn't let me know he was planning to depart this morning. As for Atticus, I know you couldn't have stopped him. Not even I could have stopped him once he'd gained Nico's permission. When they return, I'm going to have a long talk with both of them."

"If you're certain you want to continue, then I'm delighted to have you do so. But if it becomes too much for you, I want to know. Between us, we can come up with an alternative plan."

"Thank you, Lucy." Zanna scooted back in the chair. "Since you have a little while, I can tell you what's been accomplished so far, but if you have other things that require your attention, we can talk later."

"Absolutely not. I have time right now, and I'd like to hear whatever you want to share."

Lucy gave an affirmative nod once Zanna had recounted events of the past days. "You've done an amazing job, Zanna. I'm impressed that you took Nico grocery shopping, but I am a little surprised you invited him home to dinner. Has he captured your attention?"

"Lucy! Not in the way you're thinking, and I'm not the one who invited him to dinner. It was Atticus who extended the invitation, and now I understand why. He was intent upon befriending Nico in order to go out on the boat with him. He's enthralled with those diving suits, and it worries me that he'll be fool enough to try using one if given the opportunity."

"He did mention he was eager to see how the diving suits were used, but he never said he wanted to dive. I don't think he'd attempt anything so dangerous, and surely Nico wouldn't let him."

Zanna fidgeted with the ink blotter on Lucy's desk. "I'd like to believe Atticus couldn't convince Nico, but Atticus can be persuasive when he wants something."

"I'm sure he can. Still, don't those divers have to be trained before using the equipment?"

Zanna shrugged. "I haven't been able to obtain many answers about the equipment from Nico or the other men. I do think they'd need a great deal of training, however. I know it doesn't do a whit of good to worry, but I won't feel at ease until the boats return."

"Yes, I wish I would have asked when they were coming back."

Zanna pushed up from her chair. "It's fine, Lucy. I may go home for the noonday meal and see what I can find out from Papa. I'd like to know if he gave Atticus permission to go out on the boat. If so, he may know when they're due to return."

"Try to be careful how much you say. I know you wouldn't want to cause your parents concern." Lucy stood and rounded the desk. Although she longed to comfort her friend, she doubted anything other than the appearance of Atticus would bring her any peace. She wrapped her friend in a warm embrace. "Everything will be fine. Remember our favorite Bible verse."

"'Trust in the Lord with all thine heart; and lean not unto thine own understanding.'" Zanna turned toward the door. "I'll do my best."

Throughout the remainder of the morning, Zanna attempted to concentrate on setting up the necessary accounting schedules for the business, but the effort proved fruitless. She remained in her office until eleven and then walked down to the docks. She didn't expect to see the boats return until midafternoon, yet she couldn't stop herself from checking.

An old man with a fishing pole resting on his shoulder and a string of catfish in his hand walked toward her. He held up the fish, his weathered face creasing into a thousand wrinkles when he smiled. "Good day for fishin'."

Zanna smiled in return. "Have you seen any boats coming or going?"

"Naw, jest the three that left around dawn. Not many boats in and out on auction days. And me? I try to get off the docks afore noon when they begin all that hollerin' and scare off the fish."

She'd forgotten the sponge auction would begin at noon. She wanted to attend and learn how things worked—and meet Mr. Pappas if he happened to be in town.

She nodded to the old man. "Enjoy your fish dinner."

He tipped his hat. "I surely will, miss. I surely will."

Zanna half walked, half ran the distance home and was gasping for air by the time she entered the house. "Is Papa here?"

Her mother looked up from the stove. "Not yet. He should be coming in for lunch in a few minutes. Why have you been running? Your face is red, and your hair is wet with perspiration. Is something wrong?"

"No, I forgot about the sponge auction at noon and I wanted to come home and eat beforehand." She glanced around the kitchen. "Am I too early?"

Her mother pointed to a pita. "You can fill it with the minced lamb. There is some feta and spinach you can add if you like."

Zanna picked up the crusty pita and spooned the lamb mixture inside. "Are Atticus and Homer working with Papa today?"

"What kind of silly question is that? Don't they work with your papa every day?"

She crumbled the feta on top of the meat, then added spinach and leeks. "Most every day. Sometimes they do other things."

"Like what?"

Zanna hiked a shoulder. "I don't know. Go to town and purchase canvas from Mr. Fernaldo, or maybe go to the drug store for Yayá's medicine."

Her mother stacked several pitas on a plate and placed it in the middle of the table. "Your papa didn't need any canvas today, and Yayá has a good supply of medicine, so it only makes sense your brothers are working with your papa."

When the back door opened, Zanna looked up. Her father was followed by Homer, who closed the door after he stepped inside. She shifted in her chair. "Where's Atticus?"

Her father picked up a glass of water and drained its contents. "Out on one of Nico's boats."

She inhaled a deep breath. "They aren't Nico's boats. They belong to Dr. Penrose."

Her father sighed and dropped into his chair. "Excuse me. He's out on one of Dr. Penrose's boats. Is that better?" One of his eyebrows shot high on his forehead.

"You gave him permission to go?"

Her father nodded. "Things are slow in the shop right now, so I told him he could go. The boats are different from what we build. It will be good for him to see how they handle in the water."

"And Nico agreed?"

"He did. We talked when he was here for supper last night. Nico said if Atticus was at the docks when they sailed at dawn, then he could go." Her father frowned. "This is a problem?"

"No, Papa. It's not a problem as long as everything goes well while they're out in the Gulf." She hesitated a moment. "I didn't know they were going this morning until Lucy told me they had sailed."

Her father's eyes widened. "Ah, I see. You were left out and now you have the hurt feelings."

"This isn't about hurt feelings, Papa. I oversee the business. I should know when the boats are going out, and if Nico is taking anyone other than a crew member, he should get my permission."

"You should go easy for now. He is not used to asking permission, especially from a woman. If you want to make this business work, it will take cooperation." He patted her cheek. "You know I am right, do you not?"

She forced a smile. "I need to get down to the docks. I want to be there for the sponge auction."

Her father slapped his palm to his forehead. "*Oi!* My daughter at the sponge auction. You may find out women are not allowed."

"We'll see. When our crews start bringing in better sponges than anything that's ever been offered at the exchange, they'll let me in."

"Remember that a little honey will get you further than too much spice."

"Yes, Papa, I'll remember."

She hurried out the door before her father could offer any more advice.

CHAPTER
9

Once the three boats were well on their way down the Anclote River, Nico gestured to Atticus to move to his side. He'd told the young man he could come along on this first voyage if he didn't get in the way. So far, Atticus had been good to his word. He'd barely moved a muscle since they'd set sail.

Careful to step over the equipment, Atticus moved to Nico's side. "I wish I could spend more time out here on the river. It's so peaceful."

"These men would tell you that being on the water means hard work and danger. It's only peaceful when you go sailing for pleasure. And we don't ever have time for that." He pointed toward the horizon. "I have to admit there is time to admire that beautiful sunrise." He inhaled a deep breath, the scent of damp moss, fish, and river filling his nostrils. "I'm surprised your sister gave you permission to come along. I thought for sure she would object." When he turned to glance at Atticus, the young man looked away. Nico reached out and grasped Atticus by the arm. "You did ask her, didn't you?"

"No."

Nico cupped his ear and leaned closer. "Tell me I didn't hear you say no."

Atticus's jaw tensed. "I knew she wouldn't approve, but you don't have to worry. My father knows I'm with you, and he gave me permission to come along."

"Your father's approval isn't the same. I think you know that. Your sister will be ready to send me back to Greece if she finds out you're on this boat."

"I don't think she'll know. She never checks on my whereabouts, so I think we're safe." He remained by Nico's side. "Do all the diving crews sail with boats of different sizes?"

Nico shook his head. "No. The *Crete* and *Anastasi* are known as second class and manned by fourteen to sixteen men, but the *St. Nicolas* is a little larger and manned by a crew of twenty to twenty-two men. There are usually ten divers on first-class boats and five on second-class vessels. Divers on the first-class boats work from twenty-three to thirty fathoms, while the divers on the second-class boats dive from fifteen to twenty fathoms. I don't have as many trained divers with me. For now, we must make do with what we have."

Atticus let out a low whistle. "Thirty fathoms? That would be about one hundred eighty feet, wouldn't it?"

"Right." A gust of wind rippled the lateen sails, and the boat picked up speed.

"That's way deeper than I thought anyone could dive." Atticus shifted his attention to the air hoses and signal lines. "I guess all the equipment makes it easy."

A few of the men laughed at the comment. One of them pointed to the diving dress that looked like a canvas union suit. "Just wait until you see us get into our gear and what we must do to stay alive once we are underwater. You won't think it's so easy then."

They'd been sailing for over two hours before the mouth of the Anclote River opened into the Gulf. Nico stepped to the bow and scanned the open waters. Before setting sail, he and the boat captains had charted their course. Once they entered the Gulf, they would remain in sight of each other, but separate as far as possible so the divers could search a broader area on this first voyage. Nico removed the kerchief from around his neck and waved it overhead. Soon the *Crete* and *Anastasi* changed directions and began sailing to the north.

The *St. Nicolas* sailed in a westerly direction, until Nico gestured to lower the sails and called to Dyson, one of the crewmen, to help him get suited.

Atticus gasped. "You're going to dive? Why?"

"Because I would never ask my men to dive in a new location unless I, too, am willing to go down."

Nico moved to a different seat near the center of the boat and waited while Dyson set a heavy metal collar around his neck and shoulders. He then removed his shoes and shoved his feet into the wide-neck opening of the diving suit and tugged on the rubberized canvas until his feet were pushed into place. After wriggling his arms into the neck opening, he pushed until his hands emerged from the vulcanized rubber cuffs. He pointed to two cast-iron shoes. "Bring me those diving shoes, Atticus."

Atticus bent forward and grasped the top of the boots, but he grunted and dropped both shoes before they were more than two inches off the deck. He swiped at a hank of hair that fell across his forehead and chuckled. "I didn't think they'd be so heavy."

"They're made of iron. Each one weighs about twelve pounds. Look inside." Nico turned back the leather top of one of the shoes. "There's a cypress wood insert. The top is attached to the insert." Once Nico's foot was inside the iron boot, he tied heavy cord around the leather top to hold it firmly in place.

Atticus watched as another diver rigged the breastplate with a single line around the neck ring and secured it in front. "What's the line for?"

"One end is fastened to the cinch line to prevent the helmet from rising when Nico inflates the dress with air. The shorter end of the line is used to hold the signal line in front of the diver."

"You put air inside the dress?"

Nico chuckled. "The amount of air inflated or deflated into the diving suit will control my buoyancy. Too much air and the dress will blow up like a balloon and shoot me to the surface with no control. Too little air causes the dress to collapse, and the suit becomes very heavy. It's exhausting to move because you lose buoyancy. It takes much practice to control the air valve with accuracy. Once I have the helmet on, I won't be able to talk to you. Dyson will have to tell you what we are doing."

Next, Dyson lined up the holes on the rubber suit with those on the collar. He set a breastplate on top of the first collar before lowering the brass helmet in place. The helmet, fitted with four ports, now sealed Nico inside. Using a wood block, Dyson tightened each of the twelve brass nuts, securing the helmet to the collar. Nico's shoulders sagged under the weight.

Atticus pointed to the helmet. "How much does that thing weigh?"

Dyson cocked an eyebrow. "The breastplate and helmet together weigh thirty-four pounds. Once in the water, he has plenty of weight to take him down. He'll take a hook and net with him, and we will hope that he will fill the net with lots of large wool sponges. The signal line is used when he needs something. If he tugs with two quick pulls, that means he needs more air. Three pulls means his net is full and it is time to come to the surface. There is a signal for whatever he needs. Before he comes up, we will have another diver suited to go down."

Over the next half hour, Nico worked underwater, his excitement mounting as he explored these new waters. The sponge beds were full of the large wool sponges—the type buyers fought to purchase. He filled his bag and tugged on the line six times before making his ascent. To stay below any longer would be dangerous, and he knew his limits. He didn't want to take the risk of remaining under too long and becoming disoriented or unconscious due to poor air circulation in the helmet.

He pulled on the line to signal he was coming up. Soon he was reaching for the hinged ladder that had been lowered so he could climb back into the boat. A wave of thankfulness washed over him as the men greeted him with their cheers. This first dive was enough to assure him that his crews could earn enough money to live a better life in this new country and eventually have their wives and families join them. Since the day they'd boarded the ship in Greece, the responsibility for these men had rested on Nico's shoulders much like the heavy weight of his diving gear. As Dyson removed the helmet and lifted the breastplate, Nico released a shout of glee that echoed across the water.

He tugged to remove the diving dress, eager to tell the crew more of what he'd discovered. "The size and quality of the sponges are beyond what we could have imagined." He pointed to one of the net bags the men had already emptied. "Are they not the best we could have hoped for?"

The crewmen nodded their agreement. "As good as what we harvested from the Aegean," one of them said. "Perhaps better."

Nico's enthusiasm quickly spread among the crew. "There is more sponge here than I ever dreamed of. We could harvest for years and still there would be more sponge left over." He gestured to the diver who was preparing to descend. "Were you watching my air bubbles to see where I harvested?" When the man nodded, Nico pointed toward the water. "Continue moving in the same direction. I hit some unexpected drop-offs, so make sure you have plenty of line each time you move forward."

The diver signaled that he understood Nico's instructions before he straddled the bow and jumped into the water. Atticus stepped close to Nico's side and leaned forward to watch the diver's descent.

"I've never seen anything as exciting as this. Each man knows exactly what he has to do while the diver is underwater."

Nico nodded. "They had better. Otherwise the diver could die. The divers must trust that the men in the boat will stay alert, especially the hose tenders who operate the air pump. The constant turning causes exhaustion to the arms of the hose tenders. Sometimes they may not realize they have slowed the rate of air flow until the diver tugs on the line to signal for more air. There have been divers who have died because they become unconscious before they can signal the hose tenders. That's why I want the hose tenders to trade out every half hour."

"I wouldn't want that responsibility." Atticus shifted to watch the men on either side of the pump. Each man rotated a wheel attached to the two sides of the pump while also keeping a close watch on the gauges located in the center of the pump.

Nico patted his shoulder. "All the positions on diving boats require attentiveness. A mistake from any one of the men could mean disaster for all of us." He pointed at the oarsmen. "Even though we have three hundred feet of line, those oarsmen must keep the boat moving with the diver and be certain the diver's air bubbles are close to the starboard side when the diver breaks the surface. That way, his lines don't get tangled as he climbs aboard using the ladder." He gestured to the net bag of sponges the line tender and deckhand were pulling onto the boat. "Did you help bring in the bags?"

Atticus shook his head. "I think they wanted me to stay out of their way, but from the way they worked at it, I figure those bags must be heavy."

"Right. The sponges hold a lot of water, and lifting them onto the boat takes a great deal of strength. They should have used your muscles to help them." He stood. "I need to go help the next diver into his gear. We want to get as much diving done as we can before our return to land."

The three captains had agreed to remain in the Gulf until late afternoon before making their return to Tarpon Springs, where they would assess their catch. Nico was curious to learn whether the sponges gathered by the smaller boats would be of the same quality as those harvested by Nico's crew in the larger boat.

As the hours passed, the divers descended, each man filling several bags of sponges. Nico was assisting another diver into his diving dress when one of the men called out, "Nico! Look to the west!"

The urgency of the command caused Nico's stomach to tighten. He jerked around and stared at the dark flat base forming along a line of developing gray-and-white puffy clouds. "The wind has picked up." No sooner had he spoken the words than two huge waterspouts formed and steadily rose from the surface of the Gulf like giant, swirling sea creatures eager to capture their prey. "They're moving in our direction." He turned toward the line tender. "Signal Markos! He needs to surface!"

The line tender's mouth gaped when Nico shouted the order, yet he remained as still as a statue.

"Now!" Nico waved his arm in a wild gesture until the realization of danger sent the line tender into action. "We need to get Markos on board so we can turn the boat and get ourselves out of danger."

Atticus pulled his hat down on his head. "Anything I can do to help?"

"See if you can get the attention of the other boats. They're turned in an opposite direction and it doesn't look like they're aware of the danger heading our way."

One of the crewmen thrust two blue-and-white flags attached to wooden handles into Atticus's hand. "Wave these at them until they signal they see you. It won't take long for them to spot the danger once they look in this direction."

The line tender tugged on Markos's signal line and waited while Nico watched over the side of the boat for any sign of the diver's bubbles. "No sign of him. Signal again."

The line tender nodded and tugged five times in rapid succession, the signal for an on-board emergency. Nico stared at the churning water for what seemed an eternity.

"Markos signaled he's staying below." The line tender held the signal line in his hand and waited for Nico's direction.

A tight knot formed in Nico's stomach. Markos was putting all of them in danger. He understood the excitement of seeing the vast beds of sponge, but his men knew they were expected to follow orders, especially in an emergency. His anger mounted. He'd never had one of his men defy an emergency signal. "Signal him two times in quick succession."

The force of the wind picked up with each passing minute. "Nico!" the engineer barked. "We need to turn the boat. The waterspouts are coming directly at us."

Nico didn't miss the alarm in his engineer's voice, but he couldn't leave a man behind. He glanced over his shoulder. "Give Markos another few moments to surface."

The engineer raised a fist toward the oncoming spouts. "They wait for no one, Nico!"

Panic seized him. Should he jeopardize all his men for the life of one? Never before had he been forced into such a position. "Please, God. A little direction. A little help." His murmured prayer lifted on a massive gust of wind that sent him careening to the side of the boat.

His gaze dropped and settled on the churning water. "There!" he shouted while pointing into the water. "Look! Air bubbles!" He waved two of the deckhands forward. "He's coming up. Drop the ladder!"

Nico and the deckhands helped the diver up the ladder and onto the boat while the line tender struggled to hoist the heavy sponge-filled net. Atticus stumbled to the line tender's side and helped him lift the bag onto the boat while the two deckhands worked to remove Markos from his diving gear.

Organized chaos reigned until the sails had been hoisted. Nico shouted for the engineer to turn the boat. "We need to sail at a ninety-degree angle to the waterspouts' movement."

While Nico continued to shout orders to the crew, he silently prayed that the waterspouts would move toward shore. Most fair-weather spouts dissipated rapidly upon landfall, though there were no guarantees. These two were huge and could cause significant damage if they didn't quickly dissolve. Even at this distance, the water churned and roiled beneath the surface, rocking the boat like a child's toy.

Nico strained about and caught sight of the other two boats. Both had turned about, all three of them now turned away from the spouts in a ninety-degree angle that took them farther into the Gulf. Still, the waves heaved the vessel up and down like a cork.

On shaky legs, Atticus returned the flags to the storage chest fastened along the starboard side. He clutched the edge of his seat. One look was enough for Nico to see the terror in the younger man's eyes.

Nico signaled for him to come aft where he was manning the tiller. "Try to keep calm, Atticus. We're going to be fine. We're sailing opposite the waterspouts, and there's not a storm in sight. I'm sure you've seen your share of these things in the past."

Atticus nodded. "I have, but I was on land and they didn't come anywhere near Tarpon Springs. We did have that hurricane back in '96—the one my father told you about—but back then I was young enough to think nothing could hurt me. I'm a little wiser now."

"We'll be late making it back to Tarpon Springs, but I'll get you there safe and sound. If I let anything happen to you, your sister would find out you were with me, and we both know that wouldn't sit well."

CHAPTER 10

By the time Zanna arrived at the docks, the auction was already in progress. Men with pencils and slips of paper in their hands were advancing from one group of sponges to the next. They murmured to each other and didn't seem to notice her. The auctioneer called for all bids on Lot Number One. Several men scurried forward and shoved one of the papers in his hand before the auctioneer made the final call. After looking through the slips of paper, he announced Mr. Burgess the winner.

As the bidding continued, the skies began to darken in the distance. There'd been no sign of Nico or the boats. One of the buyers nudged another man and pointed to the sky. "Looks like a couple of giant waterspouts are forming out over the Gulf."

The other fellow nodded. "You're right. Hope none of our boats are out there right now."

Zanna's chest tightened. Not only were Lucy's boats and the spongers in danger, but so was her brother.

Lord, keep them safe. I trust in you.

The auction had ended hours ago, yet Zanna remained at the docks, watching and waiting, determined to be here when the boats arrived. Her father had come to the auction warehouse looking for her when he'd first spotted the waterspouts. He'd wanted to offer reassurance that the men would come back unharmed. His words had calmed her, but as the hours continued to pass without any sign of their return, she'd begun to waver.

Shortly after her father departed, the men at the auction house had exchanged stories of their experiences—times when they'd been out in the Gulf and waterspouts had arisen like huge serpents determined to chase their boats back to land. She'd wanted to cover her ears as they spoke of men pulled overboard and lost to the deep, but something inside caused her to listen. Now each of those terror-filled events raced to the forefront. What if the men hadn't seen the waterspouts in time to escape? What if their boats had been damaged and they were stranded, unable to make it back to shore? What if they were injured and unable to render aid to one another? What if the roiling waters had capsized their boats? What if, what if, what if . . . her mind raced with an onslaught of tragic possibilities.

"Sorry, Miss Krykos, but I'm closing for the night." Ned Francis, who owned the auction warehouse, stood beside her with several keys dangling from a leather strap. She looked up at him, but her feet felt bolted in place. He arched his brows. "Miss Krykos?" He waited a moment, and when she still didn't move, he stooped down beside her. "I really gotta lock up. If you want to sit out on the dock, I can let ya borrow that old wooden chair over there. You'll have a better view of the harbor from out there anyway." He gestured to a chair that looked like it might collapse if anyone sat on it. "Want me to put it out there for ya?" She nodded but still hadn't moved a muscle by the time he returned to her side. He leaned down and cupped her elbow. "Let me help ya up."

The gentle push at her elbow propelled her to her feet. She stumbled across the dock and dropped into the chair, her gaze still set upon the horizon. She reached for Mr. Francis's hand and grasped it tight. "They'll come back, won't they?"

His smile didn't lessen the worry that dulled his dark eyes. "You know the Greeks are some of the finest sailors in the world, Miss Krykos. If they can't make it back here, nobody could."

He gently tugged his arm from her grasp. His answer hadn't delivered the assurance she needed, but she released his hand. "Thank you, Mr. Francis. When the men return, I'll put your chair over by the door."

He touched the scarred wood. "Given the condition that chair's in, it won't matter none if it goes missing." Mr. Francis's footsteps echoed on the wooden planks of the dock, though she didn't turn to watch him go.

Zanna couldn't be certain how long she'd been sitting there, but the sun had set and a full moon now shone among the twinkling stars. The moonlight and stars would surely help the men navigate. She should be thankful for the moonlit night, but instead of thanksgiving, anger filled her heart. Why had this happened? Atticus was on one of those boats, and this was the first voyage for fifty strangers in a new land. It wasn't fair. She rested her elbows on her knees and cupped her face in her hands. Tears rolled down her cheeks, and she swiped at them with her sleeve.

"Zanna! What are you doing down here?"

She whirled around to see her father running toward her, his heavy footsteps resounding on the boards. "I'm waiting for the boats, Papa."

His breath came in short gasps. "You can't sit out here all night. Come home. We have been worried. Your mother thought you had gone to Lucy's for supper, but as the evening wore on, we became more and more concerned. I stopped at her office. There was a sign on the door that said she was out on a call." He reached for her hand, but she pulled away. "Come along, Zanna. Sitting here won't make them return."

"I can't leave, Papa. They're out there suffering. I can't go home and settle into a warm bed as though nothing has happened. Atticus may be in trouble. Aren't you worried?"

"Worry doesn't bring them home. Except for your brother, they are good sailors who have weathered storms in the past. They are in God's care, and we must trust He will bring them home."

"Trust in the Lord with all thine heart; and lean not unto thine own understanding." Her papa's words were a reminder of the Bible verse she and Lucy frequently recited to each other. Lifting her eyes toward heaven, she silently asked God's forgiveness. Her father was right. Her brother and the other men were in God's care. She needed to trust Him. Her fretting wouldn't provide them with any help. The men needed her prayers, not her worry.

She stood and grasped her father's hand. "Let's go home and pray for the men's safe return."

Zanna stood and shaded her eyes. She'd been at the dock all morning, and her fear had increased even more than the heat and humidity.

"Your mother was concerned when you didn't come home for the noonday meal."

At the sound of her father's voice, Zanna wheeled around. "I'm sorry, Papa. I told her I was going to keep watch for the boats."

He placed his muscular arm around her shoulder and pulled her close. "All the women in my life are worriers. My mother, my wife, my daughter—all of you." He shook his head. "The Bible tells us that our help comes from the Lord—not from worrying. Am I right?"

"Yes, Papa, but that's easier to say than to do, especially when you fear more than fifty men might be dead." She didn't add her concern over the loss of the boats and how that would affect Lucy. The loss of property was unimportant when one considered the tragedy of so many men having perished in the Gulf.

"If you remain out here on the dock for much longer, someone may try to charge you rent." He chuckled and tightened his hold on her shoulder. "You need to eat or I will start to worry about you."

Zanna knew her father's ways. He was doing his best to ease her fears and lighten the mood. She turned toward him, rose up on tiptoes, and kissed his cheek. "I'm not hungry right now. I'll go back to my office in an hour or two and then I'll stop by home for a quick bite to eat." She rested her cheek on his shoulder and remained in his embrace longer than usual, aching to absorb some of his strength.

With a suddenness that startled her, he jerked his arm. "Look, Zanna!" His voice was hoarse with emotion. "Over there." She pulled away as he stretched out his arm, pointing toward the horizon. "Do you see the boats?"

She squinted and shook her head, unable to see anything beyond the glaring reflection of sun on water. "I don't see anything, Papa. I think your eyes are playing tricks on you."

He moved behind her, placed his hands over each of her ears, and turned her head ever so slightly to the left. "Now do you see them?"

"No, Papa. I don't see anything that resembles a boat."

Her father blew out a sigh. "I am an old man. It is my eyesight that should be failing, not yours." He dropped his hands, turned toward the open door of the auction warehouse, and cupped his hands to his mouth. "Ned! I'd like to borrow your spyglass."

The warehouse owner appeared at the door, then strode toward them with the leather-encased instrument in his hand. "Think you saw the sponging boats coming in?" He shaded his eyes and pointed the spyglass in the same direction her father had indicated. "Sure enough, all three of 'em headed for home."

Frustration set in. Zanna still couldn't see them. She extended her hand toward the spyglass in Ned's hand. "May I?"

"Sure, just put it to your eye and look in the direction I pointed. You may have to adjust it a little."

Excitement swelled in her chest. "They're out there, I see them!" She moved the spyglass away from her eye and looked at the two men. "Can you believe it? Finally!" She couldn't hold back the smile that spread across her face. "Do you think any of them are injured?"

Her father reached for the spyglass. "No need to worry about injuries now. If any of the men need medical care, we'll know once they arrive at the docks." He lifted the spyglass and peered in the direction of the boats. "There's a good wind, and they're moving at a nice clip. They'll be here before we know it."

"Do you think I should go and see if Lucy's in her office? If any of the men are sick or injured . . ."

"My daughter, the worrier." He gently squeezed her hand.

"This isn't about worrying, Papa. It's about being organized and prepared. If anyone needs treatment, it would be helpful at least to know she's in her office."

Ned gave a nod. "She's right, Jurek. I can send one of the boys from the warehouse to see if Doc Penrose is in her office." He turned to Zanna. "Want him to tell the doc why he's checking on her whereabouts?"

"Only if she asks." Zanna didn't want to cause her friend needless worry.

"Are you going to wait until they arrive, Papa?" The wind whipped at her skirt and wrapped it tight around her legs.

He studied the river, then shrugged. "I won't accomplish much work if I leave. By the time I get home, I'd have only a half hour or so before I need to head back here. I want to be here when they arrive."

She arched her brows. "To make sure Atticus is safe?"

"To see that all the men are safe and if the boats have suffered any damage. I can lend a hand if there are repairs needed. I like Nico, and I want the spongers to succeed. It will be good for the town. Besides, it's nice to have Greeks living nearby, don't you think?"

She tipped her head in a faint nod. Having the Greeks in Tarpon Springs had proved far more difficult than she had imagined. If they hadn't arrived earlier than expected, she likely would have forfeited the position as manager. That had been her plan before her conversation with Lucy was interrupted by that fateful telegram. If only she'd spoken up a few minutes earlier, these worries and problems would belong to someone else. Then again, if she wasn't managing the business, she'd likely be on a ship to Greece with Yayá. She shuddered at the thought of her grandmother scouring the cities and hillsides of Greece to find her only granddaughter a suitable husband.

The clatter of running footsteps on the dock was soon followed by Lucy's arrival at her side and a quick greeting. "What's going on, Zanna? The messenger from the warehouse didn't seem to know why I might be needed on the docks." Her forehead creased with concern. She glanced about. "Is someone injured?"

"No. At least not that we know of." She pointed toward the boats. "Those are your boats approaching in the distance."

Zanna detailed her concern that bad weather had seemingly delayed the boats' return and her fear that some of the men might be injured. By the time she completed the tale, the boats were nearing the dock. The workers from the warehouse had joined them on the dock. The spongers waved and shouted, their voices filled with excitement. Zanna scanned the boats, uncertain where she would locate her brother—and Nico.

Her father stepped close to the dock's edge and called to the men in Greek. "Any injuries? We have the doctor here if anyone needs medical treatment."

The *Crete* and *Anastasi* were the first to dock. The *St. Nicolas* followed and maneuvered into position on the other side of the large dock, closer to the auction warehouse. Once the crews of the *Crete* and *Anastasi* had communicated all was well aboard their boats, Zanna rushed to the other side of the dock, where she caught sight of Nico and Atticus. A wave of relief washed over her. From what she could see, neither of them appeared to have suffered any ill effects from the voyage.

Her brother waved both arms overhead and grinned like an impish schoolboy. "We made it safe and sound." Atticus jumped onto the dock while the rest of the crew remained on board to perform their final duties. "You can't begin to know how exciting that was, Zanna. I got to watch Nico and the other divers." He pointed to the sponge-filled nets. "Look at all the sponges they brought back." He raked his fingers through his dark hair. "I'll be the first to say I was sure scared when those waterspouts came out of nowhere. Did you see them out there? They were huge. And the waves!" He took a gulp of air. "The boats took a beating. I don't know how Nico and the others were able to keep them afloat."

Zanna didn't miss a word Atticus said, but her eyes were riveted on Nico. She didn't know whether to thank him or pummel him. Her relief was overcome by the fact that he'd gone on this first expedition without her knowledge. And, even worse, he'd taken her brother along without her permission? Clearly he held no respect for her as manager, or he wouldn't have done either.

Then again, the safe return of the men was proof of Nico's abilities.

Her emotions continued to roil as her father drew near and patted Atticus on the shoulder. "You had a lot of excitement for your first time on a sponging boat."

"And his last time, as well." She glared at her brother. "You may have had Papa's permission to go out on the boat, but you went without my knowledge. You knew I wouldn't have agreed, so you went behind my back."

"Now, Zanna, take a minute to be thankful your brother is safe." Her father grasped her brother's arm. "We need to go home and let your mother and Yayá know you're safe. They have been worried about you."

Atticus grinned at Zanna. "And I know you were worried about me, too, little sister—even if you won't admit it." He squeezed her shoulder. "You won't have to worry about my going out in the Gulf again. This voyage was enough to show me that I don't want to be a diver. I enjoyed seeing how the crew handles things, but my future is going to be on dry land."

"I hope that's true, but if you ever . . ." Before she could scold her brother further, their father waved her to silence and led him toward home.

She watched the two of them with their heads close together as they walked away before she strode to the warehouse door. Mr. Francis had agreed the men could store the sponges in his warehouse until morning. The crew members had unloaded the sponges and their gear from all three of the boats and were scattering toward town when Nico finally climbed off the *St. Nicolas*. Zanna remained in place, watching and waiting, her mood wavering between anger and relief.

The corners of Nico's lips lifted into a broad grin when he saw her. "Zanna! I'm happy to see you. I thought everyone was gone."

She didn't return his smile. "You didn't think I would be waiting for an explanation as to why you took the boats out without letting me know, and why you let my brother accompany you? He could have died!"

Nico tipped his head to the side. "We all could have died, but that's the chance we take making our living on sponge boats. Atticus is fine. He's a young man and was eager for a taste of excitement and adventure. He got his fill of both while we were in the Gulf." He grinned. "When we neared shore, he told me he'd lost all interest in making his living as a seafaring man." Then his brow creased. "He had permission to go with me, so why are you angry?"

She folded her arms across her chest. "Don't make light of what you did. He may have had my father's permission, but you knew I didn't want him going out on the boats."

"Why, then, did you tell him he could come along with me?"

Her mouth gaped. "I never . . . did he . . . ? Oooh, I'm going to see that he pays dearly for that lie."

"I'm glad to hear your anger is directed at Atticus and not me." He lifted his hand and pretended to wipe nonexistent beads of perspiration from his forehead.

"Don't become too reassured. You're not out of trouble that easily. You still haven't told me why I wasn't informed you were taking the boats out on this first voyage."

He rested his hip against the weathered boards of the warehouse. "I can't work on a time clock or come looking for you each time the boats are going out. As long as the crews have enough food and water and the weather is satisfactory, they'll remain until they locate good sponge beds and harvest a full load—sometimes as long as two weeks." He shoved his cap back on his head. "Yesterday the weather appeared favorable, and the men and I were eager to see what we would find in the Gulf waters."

"From what I observed, the weather wasn't so favorable."

"The conditions were excellent when we left the docks. Fair-weather waterspouts can arise at any time. If you don't believe me, ask your father, or any fisherman."

A breeze tugged at her hair, and she brushed a strand behind her ear. "I'm sorry. I don't mean to sound abrupt, but you need to understand how worried I was when I realized the boats were out there and might capsize."

"And what about the men? Were you worried about us?"

"Of course I was worried about the men. I care more about their safety than I do the boats or the sponges."

He leaned in. "And what about me? Do you wish I'd have fallen overboard?"

Her pulse quickened, and her cheeks warmed at his nearness. His coal-black eyes held a hint of mischief, which made her want to smile. She forced her expression to remain neutral. He didn't need to know he had any sort of effect on her. But how could she tell this man that, besides having something happen to her brother, losing him was her greatest worry? She didn't want him putting himself in harm's way. She told herself it was a reasonable feeling. After all, without him, what would she do with the fifty spongers? Still, in their short time together, had she begun to see him as a friend? A business partner?

"Did you fear I might not return and that you would forever miss me?" He waved his hand in front of her face.

She blinked and swatted his hand away. "Don't flatter yourself, Nico."

He chuckled. "I have great respect for you, Zanna. I am proud to call you my friend."

Zanna's eyes widened. Friends? Was that what they were becoming? She straightened her shoulders. She'd have to be more careful. Naturally, two people working toward a common goal could become friends, but was that wise? This was Lucy's business, and what was best for it needed to come first.

CHAPTER 11

Lucy traced her finger down the calendar of today's appointments. Zanna was expected at nine o'clock. She'd asked to come by to discuss matters relating to the sponging business. Lucy's continued assurance that she'd given Zanna complete control to operate the business had seemingly fallen upon deaf ears. Still, Lucy had to admit she was somewhat eager to speak with Zanna and hear her news.

They hadn't spoken since the boats returned from their first voyage. Once Lucy had been certain none of the men needed medical treatment, she'd returned to care for the patients waiting in her office. However, Lucy was intrigued by Zanna's surprising anxiety each time she spoke of Nico. While Lucy had expected Zanna's concern over Atticus and his well-being, she was surprised by her friend's strong reaction over the safety of the Greek who, from all accounts, had been at odds with her since his arrival. There was no denying the man was handsome, but Zanna wasn't a woman whose head was turned by an attractive man. If so, she would have been married long ago. Lucy knew of at least three striking gentlemen who had attempted to pursue Zanna. All had been met with kind yet firm refusals. But Lucy had detected something in her friend's countenance when she spoke of Nico that day. There had been a tremor in her voice and a distant look in her eyes that wasn't apparent when she spoke of the other Greeks—or her brother.

Lucy was still mulling her thoughts when the bell over her office door jangled and Zanna breezed into the office. She removed her gloves as she crossed the room. Lucy grinned. "You must be intending on a long visit."

Zanna tucked the gloves into her bag. "I'll try to be brief, but I would like your approval on a couple of matters. And before you object, I know you've given me authority to make decisions, but one of them involves signing a contract, and I'm not going to forge your name."

"Not another contract. Contracts haven't served me well thus far."

"I know, but this one is fairly simple. After their first voyage, Nico and the other divers reported to me that the quality and quantity of sponges in the Gulf is far beyond their greatest expectations. All of that is good news. It also means we need a place to trim and store the sponges. According to Nico, a place much larger than I anticipated. We'll need to rent a warehouse close to the docks."

"Why do we need a contract to rent a warehouse? Can't you just verbally agree to a monthly rental?"

"Perhaps if we didn't need something so large and close to the docks," Zanna replied. "I do have a possibility, though, which is why I wanted to talk to you about the contract. Mr. Francis owns a large building next to the auction warehouse that he's willing to clear out and let us rent—if you'll sign a contract that binds the sponging company to rent it for at least a year. And he'll give us the option to extend the contract after the year is over. It's a wonderful solution to our problem, Lucy."

"While attending medical school, it never entered my mind that one of my future problems would be locating a warehouse to store sponges." She folded her hands atop the walnut desk. "I considered challenges such as being rejected by male patients or being unable to save the life of a child. But locating a sponge warehouse to rent?" Lucy shook her head.

"You don't have to locate the warehouse. I've already done that—and I've drawn up the contract." She reached into her bag, retrieved the paper work, and slid it across Lucy's desk. "All you need to do is sign at the bottom and the problem is solved."

Instead of reaching for her pen, Lucy leaned back in her chair. "Does the contract have a clause that permits termination if I sell the business?"

Zanna lurched back as though she'd been slapped.

"I know you don't want me to consider selling the business, but owning a sponging business, even one that may become profitable, continues to feel like an albatross around my neck."

"No, this contract doesn't permit termination. However, if you find a buyer and decide to sell the business, we could draw up a contract of sale that requires the buyer to assume the warehouse contract with Mr. Francis." Zanna sighed and reached forward to retrieve the paper work. "It may be best if I write that into the contract so there's no possibility of a dispute should you sell. You'll sign it with the additional clause?"

Lucy didn't miss her friend's look of disapproval. "Yes, of course, but I do hope my desire to sell isn't going to create a problem for our friendship."

"No, this is purely business. I'm trying to do my best for you, and I think the wise thing is to hold on to the business for several years—especially now that we know there are excellent sponge beds in the Gulf. But the business belongs to you, and whatever you decide isn't going to change our friendship." Zanna tucked the contract into her bag, then sat up and met Lucy's gaze. "I'm a little hurt you would question my loyalty to your business over our friendship."

Lucy tilted her head. "In truth, I was thinking more of Nico than the actual business when I questioned a possible fracture to our friendship."

"Nico? He would never come between us. How did that thought ever pop into your mind?"

"I was watching and listening to you down at the dock the other day when the boats were coming in from their first voyage. Your concern for Atticus was expected, but it appeared your worries over Nico were as intense as those for your brother."

"Lucy Penrose, that isn't true at all!" Zanna stiffened in her chair.

"Isn't it? Then why are you so defensive?" Lucy curved her lips in a soft smile. "There's nothing wrong with having feelings for Nico or any other man, but I was surprised you hadn't told me."

"Because there was nothing to tell. You're making a mountain out of a molehill. Of course I was concerned about Nico. He's the one who brought that group of men to Tarpon Springs. What was I going to do if he didn't come back? They won't listen to a word I say unless he repeats my orders as if they're his own. If he'd been injured and unable to issue orders, the men would have been off doing whatever they pleased."

Lucy chuckled. "I doubt that. If something had happened to him, they're intelligent enough to realize they'd need to listen to you in order to survive."

"You don't know Greek men, Lucy. Those spongers would rather return to Greece than take orders from me or any other woman. As for Nico, we may have begun a working friendship of sorts, but it's nothing more than that."

"You can say there's nothing between you and Nico, but the blush in your cheeks betrays you, my friend."

"That's because it's warm in here." Zanna pulled a glove from her bag and waved it in front of her face. "If we could talk about matters of importance, I wanted to tell you that Mr. Francis mentioned that Mr. Pappas—the sponge buyer from New York who knew your father—will be in town on Friday for the auction. You said you wanted to speak to him when he came to town."

"Thank you. I do want to meet him and ask why he didn't write to me after my father's death. And might I add that your ability to move the conversation from Nico to Mr. Pappas was quite skillful. Is that something you learned while studying the law with Mr. Burnside?" When Zanna's mouth gaped, Lucy waved. "I was only teasing you. I do want to—"

Before she could finish, the front door burst open and the bell above it rang with a vengeance. Bessie Rochester glanced up at the offending bell before scurrying toward Lucy. "Praise the Lord! I was worried you wouldn't be here." She gasped for breath. "Come quick! Sister is lying in a heap down at the ice-cream store."

Lucy pushed away from her desk and stood. "Let me get my bag." She hesitated a moment. "Which sister, Bessie? Is it Viola or Eugenia?"

All three sisters loved attention, especially from Lucy. They didn't mind the expense of a home visit, even if it wasn't necessary. Having Lucy attend to them at home meant they would receive her uninterrupted care. Unfortunately, they'd feigned emergencies on so many occasions, Lucy was becoming wary of their antics.

"It's Viola. She was enjoying a dish of ice cream when she got up to go back to the counter and request a glass of water. I think there must have been something slick on the floor. She slid and fell in a heap. You'd better hurry. I think she's broken something—a leg or an arm—I'm not sure, but she was wailing like a newborn when I left the store." Bessie patted Zanna's shoulder. "Sorry to interrupt you, my dear."

"Not at all, Miss Bessie. Your sister's emergency is much more serious than my conversation with Dr. Penrose." Zanna smiled at the older woman. "Is there anything I can do?"

Bessie bobbed her head. "Since you asked, it might be helpful if you came along. You can calm Eugenia while Dr. Penrose cares for Viola. There's no keeping Eugenia settled when Viola or I need medical attention. She does become distraught, doesn't she, Doctor?"

111

Lucy arched her brows. "She does, but I think all three of you tend to be a bit histrionic regarding medical problems."

Bessie clasped a hand to her lace fichu and gasped. "You think *I'm* histrionic?" She shook her head. "I'm like the calm before the storm."

Lucy grinned. "And Viola and Eugenia are the storm? Is that what you're saying, Miss Bessie?"

"Absolutely."

Lucy cleared her throat and touched a finger to her ear.

Bessie frowned. "Well, I suppose I was a little melodramatic when I thought I'd lost my hearing."

Lucy stepped close and whispered in Zanna's ear, "She was in hysterics. I thought I'd never get her settled. She insisted upon being seen before any of my other patients."

Zanna looked at the older woman. "So, what was the problem with your hearing, Miss Bessie?"

Bessie pursed her lips. "We don't have time to talk about this while Sister is lying on the floor at the ice-cream shop." She hooked her hand into the crook of Dr. Penrose's arm, then looked at Zanna. "Are you coming with us?"

"If Lucy thinks I can help." Zanna stood and looked at Lucy.

Lucy wanted to set things aright before the two of them parted. Zanna's discomfort had been obvious during their earlier conversation. The two of them had been friends for far too long to let anyone or anything jeopardize their relationship—especially a sponging business. If all went well, there would be a few minutes to finish their conversation after she tended to Viola.

"I'd appreciate having you come along, but if you need to go back to your office and rewrite the contract, I understand."

"The contract won't take long. Besides, I want to know what happened to Miss Bessie's ears."

Bessie wrinkled her nose and tugged Lucy forward. "You didn't need to tell her about my ears, Dr. Lucy."

Lucy chuckled. "You must admit there was no reason for all that hysteria." Lucy slowed her step and came alongside Zanna. "Bessie forgot she'd put small pieces of cotton batting in her ears the night before, and . . ."

Bessie leaned forward to make eye contact with Zanna. "Because I couldn't get any sleep, what with Viola snoring like she does."

Lucy nodded. "All I did was remove the batting from her ears."

Bessie sniffed. "It was a miracle. Pure and simple. One minute I couldn't hear a thing, and the next, everything was clear as a bell."

Lucy attempted to stifle her laughter. "I'm not sure pulling batting out of your ears qualifies as a miracle, but I won't argue with you, Bessie."

"You know you wouldn't win." The old woman gave a firm nod.

Bessie continued to chatter until they'd arrived at the ice-cream store. Lucy stopped short when she spotted Viola and Eugenia sitting at one of the wrought-iron-and-oak parlor tables, spooning ice cream into their mouths. "Looks like we have another miracle, Bessie."

The older woman closed the distance between the doorway and table in record time. "Viola! Why aren't you on the floor?"

Viola stared at her sister. "Why would I want to sit on the floor? I'd look like a fool."

"Because you were on the floor when I left. Do you recall falling down and shouting in pain? You said you needed the doctor." Bessie didn't wait for a response. "I hurried to fetch Dr. Lucy, and now just look at you. You're eating ice cream as if nothing happened."

"Now, Sister, don't get all worked up. You should be glad that I'm fine. Come sit down and have a dish of ice cream."

Lucy smiled at Bessie. "Go ahead and join your sisters, Bessie. No harm done. I'm glad Viola is fine." She glanced at Zanna. "We could have a cup of coffee and finish our conversation, if you'd like. Or if you enjoy ice cream this early in the day . . ."

Zanna shook her head. "No ice cream, but coffee would be nice."

After placing their order, the two of them sat down at a table located on the other side of the shop. Lucy stirred a spoonful of sugar into her cup. "Before we parted ways, I wanted to be certain nothing I said earlier had created ill feeling. I know I can be curt when it comes to any discussion of the sponging endeavor, but I'm afraid I still harbor some bitterness that I was caught off guard by the entire matter." She forced a smile. "I understand that none of this is your fault. If not for you, I'd be struggling on my own. But it's still difficult for me to accept my father left me in this predicament. Gambling his money on a business venture that he knew nothing about was out of character for him."

Zanna took a sip of her coffee. "There's no way to know why he did it, Lucy. Perhaps he'd reached a point in life where he wanted a bit of adventure. Who can say? Besides, even if we knew, it wouldn't change anything. Instead of wondering why he made the investment, we need to make his investment successful, and the only way to do that is to rent a warehouse and hire additional employees to trim, size, and package the sponges."

Lucy sighed. "I'll sign the contract for the warehouse if you make the change I requested. I'm not sure about employees. I don't have money to pay wages, and I'm sure they won't work without pay."

"I talked to Nico about the wages. He said the easiest answer is to explain we're a new business and they won't be paid until we begin selling at auction."

The two of them waved to Bessie, Viola, and Eugenia as the three sisters departed the shop.

"I suppose if you can hire anyone under those circumstances, I can't object." She leaned forward and touched Zanna's hand. "If I offended you when I questioned you about Nico earlier today, I'm sorry. I didn't mean to imply anything untoward. You likely depend upon him as much as I've been depending upon you, but I do see a glimmer in your eyes when you mention his name."

Zanna pulled her hand away and giggled. "Stop it, Lucy. The

only glimmer in my eyes is caused by the sun glaring through the front window. Nico may be a business friend, but nothing more."

Lucy grinned. "The lady doth protest too much, methinks, but I'll say no more." She pushed away from the table. "I must get back to the office, but remember I want to speak with Mr. Pappas. I still hold out hope he may want to purchase the business."

Zanna sighed. "I do wish you'd give it more of a chance. Nico says—"

Lucy leaned down and brushed a kiss on Zanna's cheek. "I know. Nico says everything will be fine."

With her heart full, Lucy strode toward her office thinking of Nico and the other spongers. Of course he'd told Zanna the business would be profitable. But would he feel the same if he'd had a roomful of ill patients dropped in his lap instead of a sponging business?

CHAPTER 12

Zanna quickened her step, hoping to arrive at Lucy's office before her first patient of the afternoon arrived. They'd seen little of each other since their conversation last week, and she wanted to speak with her. She'd redrafted the contract, and it now required Lucy's signature, although Mr. Francis had already allowed them to begin using the warehouse. His kindness had been unexpected and greatly appreciated since there was little doubt the boats would return with more than enough sponges to fill their current space.

She stopped short in front of Lucy's office door. A sign hung in the front window saying she would be out of the office until four o'clock. Strange. It didn't say where she could be reached. When leaving town, she usually added that piece of information.

While Zanna continued to stare at the sign, she heard the sound of footsteps on the sidewalk and looked up. She smiled at the sight of the Rochester sisters. They were attempting to walk three abreast on the narrow walkway, none of them willing to walk alone. "Good afternoon, ladies."

"Good afternoon, Zanna. The doctor isn't in this afternoon." Bessie spoke with an air of authority as she drew near.

Zanna pointed to the sign. "So I see. You don't happen to know where I might find her, do you?"

Viola giggled. "Well, of course we do. She's our speaker at Women's Club this afternoon. That's where we're going."

"And you should be attending, as well." Bessie's furrowed brow emphasized the censure in her voice. "That's one of the many problems with the younger generation. You have little desire to help your fellow man, whereas we older folks are attuned to the needs of others." She glanced at her two sisters. "Isn't that right?"

They bobbed their heads in unison.

Zanna frowned. "I don't know that I totally agree with your assessment, Miss Bessie."

Bessie tipped her head to the side. "Oh, so you *are* attending the meeting."

Why not? If she could secure Lucy's signature before the meeting, there was a possibility Zanna could sneak out without being noticed. At least that was her hope. Not that Zanna didn't want to help others. But, unlike the Rochester sisters, she had a job that required her time and attention. Besides, wasn't she helping fifty Greek men establish their lives in a new country? Didn't the sisters count that as helping her fellow man?

She gave the older woman a firm nod. "Yes, I believe I will attend."

Viola clapped her hands like a child at play. "Oh good. You can sit up front with us."

Zanna slowed her step and swallowed. "We'll see. I need to speak to Lucy before the meeting, if I can. Perhaps you should go ahead and be seated as soon as we arrive. I don't want you to be forced to sit near the back on my account."

Eugenia smiled. "We'll do that, and I'll be certain to save you a seat next to me."

Zanna sighed. If nothing else, the ladies were determined to make sure she had a front-row seat whether she wanted it or not. They were walking toward the Golden Crescent, so nicknamed because of the crescent-like shape of the bayou and the wealth of the early developers. Lucy's father had been among them, though he had chosen to build their family home a short distance from the crescent. "Who's hosting today's meeting?"

"Since I oversee membership and communication, I know that a meeting notice was sent to you. Do you read your mail, Zanna? I would hate to think the expense of sending postcards to our members is going to waste." Bessie's lips drooped into a frown.

Could she say nothing without incurring Bessie's condemnation? "I'm sure I read it when it first arrived, but I have been quite busy since the Greek sponging crews arrived, and the details have slipped my mind." She forced a smile. "Please forgive me."

"Today's meeting is once again at the Knapp home, so I know it will be delightful. Virginia is a gracious hostess who always exceeds expectations. When Jennie Brumfield had to unexpectedly return to Massachusetts, Virginia agreed to host another meeting." Bessie sniffed. "I know you young women don't agree, but society would be better served if you dedicated yourselves to hearth and home rather than taking over jobs better suited for men. I simply don't understand your desire to overstep society's boundaries."

"That was never my intention, Miss Bessie. I became a lawyer because I wanted to use my mind and help people with their legal issues. I'm sure Lucy would tell you the same regarding her medical practice. After all, you ladies rely upon her for medical treatment at every turn. Where would you be without her?"

"That's true enough, but she's the only doctor in town. We might choose otherwise if—"

Viola stopped short. "I wouldn't. I love Dr. Lucy and I'd go to her even if there were lots of other doctors in Tarpon Springs."

"Hush, Viola. I'm trying to have a private conversation with Zanna."

"I will not hush. You can't always speak for me, Bessie. I have a mind of my own, you know."

Zanna sighed. Dear me, what had she started by merely asking the location of today's meeting? She needed to do something before the sisters waged war against each other. She glanced at Eugenia, who had been dutifully silent. "That's a lovely dress, Eugenia."

Eugenia bobbed her head. "Thank you. Bessie said it was too late in the season to wear such a pale color, but I disagree, don't you?"

Zanna wanted to run. Perhaps she should have gone to her office, after all. "The color is lovely on you, Eugenia." She gestured toward the basket the woman carried on her arm. "What's in your basket? Are you helping with refreshments?"

Before Eugenia could respond, Bessie groaned. "Mrs. Knapp would never ask anyone to assist with refreshments. As I said earlier, she's a perfect hostess."

"She was talking to me, Bessie, so let me have a chance to answer." Eugenia glared at her sister. "Dr. Lucy said if we wanted to bring strips of cloth with us to the meeting, she would show us how to roll bandages so we can send them to Kenya. She's going to give us a list of projects that will help the people in Africa and tell us about two of her friends who are missionaries in Kenya." Eugenia's face was alight with excitement. "Can you imagine going to a place like Africa? Sister wants to visit France, but I would never venture that far from home."

The three sisters continued to quibble about the advantages and disadvantages of traveling abroad. Instead of older women, they sounded like schoolchildren arguing over who should win a penmanship award.

Zanna relaxed her shoulders as they neared the Knapp house. She'd never been so happy to arrive at her destination. A group of ladies were visiting on the front porch, and the sisters bustled forward to greet them. Zanna took the opportunity to slip off in search of Lucy. She'd made it no farther than the vestibule when Mrs. Knapp spied her and offered an effusive greeting.

Zanna peeked over the woman's shoulder while they exchanged

pleasantries. No sign of Lucy. "I was wondering if Lucy has arrived? I hoped to speak with her for a few minutes before her presentation."

Mrs. Knapp's lips curved in a generous smile. "Of course, my dear. She's going over her notes in the side parlor. Let me show you the way."

Zanna followed as Mrs. Knapp led her through the formal dining room and parlor before opening a pocket door into the small side parlor. Lucy was sitting at a corner desk and looked up when they entered.

"I'll leave you two alone. I need to attend to my other guests." The older woman exited and closed the door behind her.

Zanna watched Mrs. Knapp depart. She truly was the perfect hostess.

Lucy turned her chair. "I'm surprised to see you here, Zanna. Is anything wrong?"

"No, nothing wrong. I just need your signature on the redrafted contract. Mr. Francis has already signed. I stopped by the office, and the Rochester sisters told me you were speaking today. They insisted I come along." Zanna removed the contract from her bag.

Lucy chuckled. "They do have a way about them, don't they? I've cared for them since the first day I opened my office, and the sisters still leave me speechless at times."

Zanna handed Lucy the contract. "They may leave you speechless, but they certainly have no problem arguing among themselves. I thought they were going to come to blows before we made it here." She shook her head. "I know you're eager to speak with Mr. Pappas, but he didn't appear at the sale last week. I asked Mr. Francis if he had any idea why he hadn't attended."

Lucy looked up. "And did he know?"

"He said Mr. Pappas told him he wasn't going to be in Florida for a month or so due to some other business, so another buyer would be attending the Friday auctions."

"Then I suppose I'll have to wait until he returns. Perhaps his other business dealings won't take as long as he anticipated." She heaved a sigh. "At least I can hope."

Zanna's stomach tightened. "I'm pleased another buyer will be there in his place. That means the bidding should remain competitive. Any added income is a benefit. I'm hoping you'll agree to finance more suitable housing for the men once our income increases."

Lucy sighed. "It appears the expenses of operating the business are going to exceed profits for a long time if you continue to rent warehouses and build housing for the men." She turned back to her notes. "Let me know when Mr. Pappas is expected. I believe he's the best option to purchase the business."

Zanna winced at the offhand remark. Why couldn't she convince her friend to give the business more time? "I hope you don't mind if I sneak out before your speech. I have several matters that need my attention."

Lucy shook her head and offered a fleeting smile. "As long as you don't mind if I'm absent when the ladies ask you to speak at a meeting in the future."

Zanna nodded. "Agreed." She tucked the contract back into her bag. With a little luck, she could make it through the formal parlor before the ladies gathered to take their seats. She glanced over her shoulder at Lucy. "I hope all goes well with the speech."

Lucy grinned. "I hope all goes well with your escape."

She opened the pocket door far enough to slip through. If only she knew how to find the rear entryway, yet she dared not wander through the house. She'd have to take her chances going out the way she'd come in. Darting around groups of women, she'd almost made it to the vestibule when Eugenia jumped to her feet.

"Over here, Zanna!" Eugenia flapped a pamphlet overhead, her voice growing louder. "Zanna! I saved you a seat."

Zanna let out a sigh. So much for making an escape.

At midmorning the following day, Nico took note of the supplies needed in camp before heading into town to make the necessary purchases. If he timed things correctly, he could buy the items, return to the camp and put them away, and still be at the warehouse before one o'clock. And if he didn't linger along the way, he might even have time to eat lunch.

Over the past weeks, there had been several more trips to the Gulf, each for only a few days, but upon their return at the end of the week, the crews had encouraged Nico to let them remain in the Gulf for at least two weeks. He had agreed. The men could accomplish much more if they remained out for a longer period of time, and these men were accustomed to being at sea for six months while sponging in the Aegean Sea. For them, two weeks would be a simple feat. Of course, there would be no mother ship going along to carry supplies, so staying out for longer than a few weeks would be difficult. The three boats would need to carry enough food and water to sustain the crew for two weeks while allowing space for the sponges they would harvest.

Nico had considered sailing with the men, but in the end decided his abilities could be put to better use in Tarpon Springs. The living conditions for the men were inadequate, and he planned to use some of his time working with the few men they'd hired to reinforce the shanties in the camp. Thus far, they'd been slow to accomplish much of anything unless he was present, and Nico feared the huts wouldn't serve the men much longer—at least not without complaint.

In addition, they needed more workers to trim, sort, and pack the sponges, especially if the crews came back with full loads. Two days ago, Zanna mentioned there were itinerants who came to the area during the cold winter months, so they'd posted a sign in the train station advertising for seasonal workers. Interested employees were advised to report to Nico at the warehouse at one o'clock each day. Of course, Zanna would need to be present and interpret for him. She'd offered to perform the hiring without him, yet he was quick to point out that she knew nothing about the preparation of sponges for market.

A passing breeze tousled Nico's dark curls before he lifted his face to the warmth of the morning sun. He couldn't deny the beauty of this place that reminded him of home. Before they'd left Greece, he had prayed the men would adjust to this new country. This place, so reminiscent of home, had been an answer to that prayer. He was nearing the crescent-shaped bayou when his thoughts were interrupted by the sounds of arguing women. Though he could understand little of what was being said, one woman was clearly in charge. He heard her say something about "the springs" and guessed they were heading toward the mineral springs Zanna had pointed out to him on one of his first trips to town. Along with the warm winter weather, the springs were an immense attraction to the wealthy, who had constructed opulent homes surrounding the crescent.

Nico didn't know if the mineral springs would truly heal aching muscles or cure ailments, but he doubted he'd ever have time to personally test the waters. However, there was little doubt the ladies of Tarpon Springs took the cure seriously, for a large pagoda-style structure had been erected above the springs, where visitors could sit on benches before or after they'd descended the short stairway into the waters. He turned to cross the street when a startling shriek cracked through the morning quietude. He hesitated and looked over his shoulder.

"Help! Someone, help!"

The cries of a woman brought him to an abrupt halt. Another scream followed. The calls sounded as though they were coming from the area near the mineral springs. Someone needed help. He ran, retracing his steps and then veering off toward the springs. The sun shone in his eyes, and he slowed his step to gain a better view. Another cry for help drew his gaze. Two older women were in the pagoda, one quite buxom, and the other, who was much shorter, possessed a voice as shrill as a grosbeak. The larger woman was leaning over the side of the pagoda, swinging her closed parasol at something and yelling words he couldn't understand. Moments later, the shorter woman turned, spotted him, and screamed. She raised her arms and flapped about like a windmill in a storm.

The ladies were in distress, but from his vantage point he couldn't determine the cause of their problem. Perhaps the gyrating woman was having some sort of seizure. He'd seen men come up from the depths of the ocean and have seizures, but those men hadn't screamed and jumped up and down. The woman continued to shout and wave him onward. He picked up his pace and ran toward the pagoda.

The scent of rotten eggs filled the air. He wrinkled his nose in protest. What was the foul-smelling odor? Never before had he come this close to the springs, and never before had he noticed such a stench anywhere near the river. The old woman screamed once again, and he raced forward. As he drew closer, he caught sight of a woman thrashing in the water, her white head of hair bobbing up and down, while the larger woman continued to shout at her.

Nico decided the quickest way to reach the drowning woman was through the pagoda and down the steps leading into the water. The moment he entered the pagoda, the short gyrating woman, still screaming, rushed off toward town. The larger woman barked orders he couldn't understand.

Nico shouted back in Greek, "Be quiet!"

She took a backward step, placed her hand to her heart, and clamped her lips in a tight line. No doubt he'd offended her, but he couldn't keep his wits about him if she continued her constant screeching.

He raced down the steps and made a shallow dive toward the woman. Her skirts had ballooned around her, and the weight of the water-soaked fabric was pulling her under. He made several long strokes and then dove beneath the water. He grabbed hold of the woman and lifted her upward. Using the crook of his arm, he caught her beneath her chin and tried to swim toward the water's edge. She fought against him. With each movement, her head went underwater.

"Stop fighting me! I'm trying to save you." His Greek command likely meant no more to her than the shouts of the woman in the pagoda had meant to him. If only he could make her understand. She was going to drown if she didn't let him help her. He'd seen this before with men who'd been tossed overboard during storms at sea. Panic seized them and they wouldn't relax and cooperate.

Suddenly her body went limp in his arm. He needed to get her to shore. She'd likely stopped breathing. He dragged her to the muddy riverbank and dropped to his knees, surprised to see no more than a sprite of a woman. After the battle she'd waged when he was trying to save her, he'd expected her to be as large as the woman with the parasol. Placing his ear to her mouth, he listened. Nothing. He pinched her nose between his finger and thumb with one hand, tilted her head back, and placed his lips over her open mouth. He watched her chest for movement as he blew into her mouth.

He continued, determined to revive the woman, but then let out a yelp and turned when someone landed several sharp blows to his back.

The buxom woman who'd been leaning over the edge of the pagoda held her parasol in a threatening manner. "How dare you? Stop accosting my sister!"

He had no idea what she was saying. Had she been attempting to drown the woman and was angry he'd thwarted her plan? He could think of no other reason why she wouldn't want him to save a drowning victim. He gestured for her to leave him alone and leaned down to continue his ministrations. No sooner had he begun than she whacked him again. He ignored her, but with every ounce of his being, he wanted to grab that parasol and toss it in the river.

Finally, the woman coughed and then sputtered, and Nico knew what would follow. He moved aside as the woman turned her head and immediately lost the contents of her stomach. He stood and was met with another whack of the parasol. "Look what you've done!"

"Bessie! We're coming. How is Eugenia?"

Nico looked toward the sound. Dr. Penrose and Zanna were accompanied by the woman with the shrill voice, who had rushed off when he entered the pagoda.

"That man was kissing Eugenia!" The old woman standing beside Nico shouted the accusation toward Zanna and Dr. Penrose, then raised her parasol and struck him again.

CHAPTER 13

Nico raised his arms over his head to protect himself while Zanna and Dr. Penrose shouted. He wasn't sure what they'd said, but at least she lowered the parasol. Lucy hurried to Eugenia's side and knelt beside her and then quickly opened her medical bag while Bessie and Viola chattered like magpies.

"If you two don't quit fussing, I won't be able to listen to your sister's heart." She gave them a stern look that gained the requested result. "Thank you, ladies."

Nico leaned close to Zanna's ear and gestured to Bessie. "What was that woman shouting?"

"She said you were kissing her sister," Zanna responded in Greek.

Nico's mouth fell open, and he slapped his palm to his forehead. "She thought I was kissing her?" He shook his head. "I pulled that lady from the river. She wasn't breathing, so I did the rescue breathing on her. That is not kissing." He rubbed the back of his hand across his lips. "She really thinks this?"

"I believe that's why she was striking you with her parasol." Zanna grinned. "I didn't realize you were so eager to find a bride."

"The only bride I would want is not among the group gathered

129

around the doctor." He lifted the corner of his water-soaked shirt and gave it a squeeze, then nodded toward Bessie and Eugenia. "They do not look like sisters. One so large and the other so small."

"Viola is also their sister." Zanna gave a nod toward Viola.

"That one, too?" Nico glanced at the woman in question. "She has a voice so shrill, it hurt my ears." He wrinkled his forehead. "And that bigger one—she's dangerous with the parasol."

Zanna chuckled. "She was only trying to protect her sister from a passionate Greek."

He pointed his index finger at her. "You know that is not true." Gesturing toward the road, he added, "I'm going back to camp for dry clothes. I had planned to purchase supplies before going to the warehouse, but that will have to wait."

"Go ahead and get the supplies. I will go to the warehouse and interview anyone who answers the advertisement."

He shook his head. Deciding upon the right men to fill positions with the company was Nico's job. At least that was his opinion. He wanted to be certain they were men who would show up at work each day and give a good day's work. Preparing sponges for sale required long, tedious days of repetitious labor. He didn't want to take the time needed to train men only to see them leave a few weeks later.

"You stay and help the ladies," Nico suggested. "The doctor needs your assistance more than I do."

Her shoulders stiffened when he refused her aid. There was little doubt he'd angered her, but she needed to accept that he was going to oversee any decisions regarding workers and their jobs. She could make those decisions regarding finances and legal matters. He started up the muddy hillside.

"Stop him! You stop him right now, Zanna. I'm going after the sheriff." Bessie charged toward Nico while holding her parasol like a sword.

Lucy had been focused on Eugenia, but Bessie's shouts startled her. She called to the older woman, "Bessie! Come back here this minute." Lucy gestured for Zanna to join them. "I need to keep my attention on Eugenia. Please explain that Nico saved her sister's life."

"By kissing her?" Bessie wheeled around to make certain Nico was still nearby. She pointed at his back. "You! Don't you leave until this is settled."

Nico spun around, his brows arched, and looked at Zanna. "What other silly ideas does she have?"

"No new accusations, but she doesn't want you to leave until she understands. It will only take a minute. I'll talk fast so you don't miss any of your interviews."

Nico flinched at her final comment. Zanna knew how to make a point when she was unhappy. He glanced at the old woman, who glared at him in return. There was little doubt she would either scream or attack him with her parasol if he attempted to make a getaway, so he simply folded his arms across his broad chest and dutifully waited while Zanna detailed exactly what he'd been doing. He couldn't understand a word she was saying to the old woman, but from her deep-set frown, it didn't appear Zanna was making much headway.

When Zanna's conversation with the woman stopped for a moment, Nico stepped closer to Zanna's side. "Is it safe for me to leave now?"

Zanna shrugged. "You can try, but I still don't think she believes me. Maybe once Lucy tells her what you were doing is an accepted medical procedure, Bessie will trust that your actions saved Eugenia's life."

Nico turned his gaze toward Lucy. She was placing her medical equipment back into her bag. "It looks like she's done caring for the woman. Why don't you ask her to explain so I can leave?"

Lucy stood and turned toward Zanna, Nico, and Bessie. "I'm glad you're still here, Nico. Could you lend Eugenia a strong arm to lean on? I need to get her back to my office and I'm afraid she may fall."

Zanna immediately interpreted Lucy's request. Nico studied her for a moment. Had the doctor truly requested his assistance, or was this a trick so he wouldn't get to the warehouse before Zanna? He couldn't be sure, but if the doctor really needed his help, he'd appear to be an uncaring scalawag if he didn't help. Besides, he didn't want Bessie on the attack again.

"Looks like Lucy can explain while you help Eugenia to the office." Zanna strode toward the other women, Bessie close on her heels.

When he didn't move, Bessie glared once more and waved him forward. Now that Lucy wanted him around, Bessie was going to make sure he complied. He sighed and followed, careful to remain out of reach of Bessie's parasol.

Lucy gave instructions to Zanna, who then told Nico that once Lucy had Eugenia sitting up, he should help her to her feet. With Viola on one side and Lucy on the other, they lifted Eugenia into a sitting position. But before Nico could step forward and assist the woman to her feet, she fainted.

Nico's chest tightened, and he lifted his arms heavenward. Could nothing go right this morning? "Move aside," he said. "I'll carry her."

Bessie tugged on Zanna's sleeve. "What's he doing? What did he say? Tell him to get away from Sister. Dr. Lucy can care for her."

"Eugenia has fainted again. We need to get your sister to Lucy's office. Nico is going to carry her, so please step out of his way."

Bessie gasped. "It's unseemly. What will people think, Zanna, if they see him carrying Sister down the street?"

"I don't know, Bessie, but I don't think we need worry what others think right now. It's more important Eugenia receives medical treatment, don't you agree?"

Bessie tilted her head to the side and furrowed her brow. "Well, I suppose if . . ."

Nico didn't wait for the ladies to say anything further. He pushed between Zanna and Bessie, leaned down, and scooped Eugenia into his arms. He marched up the sloping hillside and slowed only once to catch his breath before arriving at Lucy's office.

Zanna kept pace with him and opened the office door when they arrived. "There's a bed in one of the rooms at the back. I think Lucy will want her there."

By the time Nico had placed Eugenia on the bed, Lucy, Bessie, and Viola arrived and soon entered the room. Nico found himself hemmed in on all sides. It seemed no matter how hard he tried, he couldn't escape. He was edging his way around the perimeter of the room when Eugenia groaned and opened her eyes.

Lucy hurried to her side and placed a damp cloth on her forehead. "I thought I was going to need smelling salts to bring you around."

A wobbly smile curved Eugenia's lips. "Was I dreaming or did a handsome man kiss me?" Her head lolled to the side and she looked at Bessie. "I rather liked it."

Bessie gasped. "Hush that shameful talk, Eugenia."

Eugenia frowned. "There's nothing shameful about enjoying a kiss from a handsome man."

Nico was pleased the woman was awake and able to talk, though it appeared her sister wasn't pleased with whatever she was saying. He'd almost made it to the doorway when Eugenia spied him and lifted a soggy handkerchief in the air. "There's the handsome man I dreamt about. I want him to come to tea, Zanna. Tell him to come to our house tomorrow at two o'clock."

"I don't think he will—"

"Just tell him," Eugenia insisted.

Zanna did as the older woman instructed, but after interpreting the invitation, she added that she would pass on his regrets since she was certain he wouldn't want to attend.

Instead, he said he'd be delighted—provided she went along to interpret. He smiled, nodded, and gestured while talking to Zanna, hoping Eugenia would gather some understanding from his actions. When the old woman clapped her hands, he smiled at Zanna. "It looks like we will be going to tea tomorrow, but right now I am going to find clean clothes and then hurry to the warehouse."

He opened the front door with Zanna's final comment in his ears. "I'll be there before one o'clock."

She was one strong-minded woman, and yet he needed her help. The men applying for jobs most likely would not understand Greek any more than he understood these three crazy sisters.

Zanna hurried home and downed her lunch while her grandmother chided her for being late. She couldn't eat and talk at the same time, so she offered a mumbled apology rather than take time to detail what had occurred at the mineral springs. If she started that story, her mother and Yayá would ply her with more questions than she had time to answer, especially if she was going to make it to the warehouse before one o'clock. She needed Nico to respect her, and she didn't want to give him reason to believe she couldn't do her job.

Yayá pointed at her shoes. "How come you have all that mud on your shoes?" She leaned to the side and touched the edge of Zanna's skirt. "And on your skirt." She *tsk*ed and ran her fingers along Zanna's jacket sleeve. "Your jacket is damp. Did you go for a swim with the alligators this morning?" She cackled at her question.

Zanna forked a bite of tomato salad into her mouth and shook her head. Why did Yayá have to notice everything? She swallowed and speared her fork back into the salad. "No. It's a long story. I'll tell you at supper. I need to be at the warehouse by one o'clock."

Her grandmother's eyes sparkled with curiosity as she dropped into the chair beside Zanna. "I like a good story. You can talk quickly and I will listen with both ears." She grinned and touched a finger first to one ear and then the other.

Her lunch was only half eaten, but Zanna knew she needed to make her escape. If she waited any longer, Yayá would insist on hearing the story this very moment. "Sorry, Yayá. I have to leave for the warehouse." She pushed back from the table, stood, and turned toward the door.

"You are going to leave here with mud on your shoes and dirt on your clothes? Disgraceful! What will people think?"

"I don't think they'll even notice, Yayá. I'm going to interview possible warehouse workers. A little dirt on my shoes will not matter to them."

Once outside, she swiped her hand down the side of her skirt and hoped the dried dirt wouldn't be noticeable. If there had been enough time, she would have donned a clean skirt and changed her shoes, but today that wasn't possible.

When she arrived at the warehouse, a cluster of men had surrounded Nico and were bombarding him with questions. Side-stepping them, she made her way to Nico's side. He shrugged and said, "Tell them to sit down and soon I will explain the work and then speak to each man individually."

Zanna quickly interpreted and gestured to some nearby chairs. Once they were seated, she smiled and cleared her throat. "Hello and welcome. Mr. Sevdalis and fifty experienced Greek divers and spongers arrived to this area a short time ago. This sponging business is owned by Dr. Lucy Penrose, who has appointed me as her business manager." There were several groans. "If any of you have a problem working for a woman, then you can leave right now." She folded her arms across her chest and waited.

Nico stepped close. "There is a problem?"

When none of the men got up to leave, she shook her head. "No, I don't believe so. You can begin now. If any others arrive, we'll have them wait until you've finished with the first group."

Nico, too, welcomed the men with a broad smile. "Preparing sponges for sale is tedious work. I want only men who are willing to be here every day and work hard. I'm going to tell you how we clean, trim, and pack sponges. When I'm done, you need to think about whether this is work you are willing to do for more than a few days or weeks. I don't want to teach men and have them leave me after only a short while. I don't have time to keep training new workers

135

every week. I know most of you have come south for the winter, and that's fine. But unless you plan to work for me all winter long, please leave now before you have been taught how to perform the job."

As soon as Zanna finished interpreting Nico's beginning remarks, one of the men waved at her. "You gonna be around all the time to be sure we understand what he says?"

"No. We have already hired some Bahamians who are experienced. They will be available to help you once you begin your work, but we want you to have a clear understanding of your job beforehand. We don't have enough men to keep up with the harvests the boats have brought in, and we're expecting a large haul in the next week or so."

The man shifted in his chair. "Them Bahamians speak English?"

Zanna nodded. "Yes. And they're excellent workers. Do any of you have experience working with sponges?" When none of them indicated any know-how, Zanna interpreted for Nico and asked him to continue.

He stepped to a table and picked up a large black lump. "Does anyone know what this is?"

A man sitting near the front of the group grinned. "Looks like coal to me."

Zanna shook her head. "It's sponge."

The men leaned forward, most of them frowning. "Don't look like no sponge I ever seen," one of them hollered.

"Ain't interested in washing myself with one of them things."

Zanna explained what the men had said and why the others were laughing. Nico nodded and smiled before he continued.

"I think it is important that you know about sponges before you begin to work with them. That is why I showed you this sponge." He held it up. "This is what divers learn is a good sponge. Before it is transformed into the sponges you see in a store, much work is necessary. When our boats are in the Gulf and the divers bring up bags of sponges, the men begin the first process of cleaning. The crew must vigorously press them with their feet or pound them with blocks of wood to get a white substance we call 'gurry' out of the pores and kill any elements the sponge has trapped in its canals as food."

"You make it sound like they're an animal or somethin'."

"They are. They don't have a brain or heart, or mouth, but they're a very simple form of animal."

"That don't seem right, to be killin' animals," another man said.

"Don't be a fool." A tall fellow elbowed the man who'd expressed his disapproval. "A sponge ain't like a dog or cat. She said it ain't got no brain or nothin'. Iffen you wanna work here, you need to shut up and listen."

Nico gestured for the men to be quiet and then he continued. "We will do things like we did in Greece when we were out at sea for months at a time. The crew will press out the gurry and then place sheets over the sponges to make sure any remaining living things inside the sponge will die. After that, the sponges are washed and strung onto lines that are returned to the water, where they remain overnight. The movement of the water continues to cleanse them. The next day we do the same thing. Finally, only the skeletal portion remains. That's when the men use their sharp knives, and while they strip off the skin, they squeeze the sponge to make sure all the gurry has been removed. Then they string the sponge on twine and they are hung on ropes on the boat to dry in the sun. After they are dry, they are stored in nets in the prow of the boat."

"Sounds like all the cleanin' is done before they return." The comment came from one of the men in the back row.

Zanna interpreted, and Nico acknowledged the man. "You are right, but once the sponges are returned to the dock, they must be off-loaded and brought here to the warehouse. You will examine the sponges to make certain they have been well cleaned. Then they must be trimmed with these shears." He held up a pair of heavy metal shears, much like those used in sheep shearing. "Your hands will become sore, but you must continue working. Each sponge must be free of any dark spots and trimmed to look like the ones you use when taking a bath. After the trimming is done, the sponges are then sorted by size and strung on couleurs."

A man waved his hand. "You say *colors*? What's that?"

"Couleurs." Nico pronounced each syllable slowly. "A couleur is a thin cord that is fifty-eight inches in length. It can hold twenty to sixty sponges, depending on the size of the sponges you are stringing."

After demonstrating the trimming and sorting process with a crate of sponges he'd placed nearby, Nico described the packing process. "Every man I hire will be trained to perform each of these jobs." He hesitated a moment. "And to do it well." He glanced around the crowd. "So, who is interested in becoming a sponge worker?"

Zanna arched her brows and gestured toward the table as she completed translating Nico's final comments. "You can come up here and give your name. Training will begin immediately."

Chair legs scraped against the wooden floor as the men stood. A number of them scurried out the door, but several stepped forward to apply. The interview meetings took longer than Zanna had anticipated, but by three o'clock, Nico had hired the men he believed would be reliable. He and Zanna introduced the men to the Bahamian workers before she departed. Now she needed to get back to the office and figure out how they were going to pay for their new employees.

Nico called after her when she neared the front door. "Don't forget you promised to go to tea at Eufemia's house tomorrow."

She turned on her heel. "Eugenia. Her name is Eugenia, not *Eufemia*. And you are the one who was invited to tea, not me. I never promised to go along."

"But you know you can't bear to be away from this handsome face for more than a day." He cupped his chin in his palm and grinned. "I'll come by the office for you."

Heat crawled up her neck and colored her cheeks. She wanted to tell him she could stay away from him for much longer than twenty-four hours. And she would have, if it had been true. Instead, she turned and rushed out the door.

CHAPTER 14

When she had finished her lunch the following day, Zanna hurried to her room and changed from her dark skirt and jacket to a lavender-and-white-striped chambray dress with lavender trim. She performed a quick pirouette in front of the mirror. Yes, this was much more appropriate for tea with the Rochester sisters. She pinned her hat trimmed with a small lavender flower atop her dark curls and then wriggled her fingers into a pair of white gloves.

Zanna listened at the open bedroom door, thankful to hear the voices of her mother and Yayá coming from the kitchen. She tiptoed around the corner, down a short hallway, and through the living room to make an unobserved departure out the front door. If either of them caught sight of her in different clothes, there would be far too many questions.

She'd seen little of Nico today. He'd left a note at the warehouse saying he was going to purchase the supplies needed in camp, the ones he'd been unable to purchase yesterday. When she'd completed her tasks at the dock, she returned to her office to pick up a file and then had gone home for lunch. Shortly before two, she glanced at the clock. Had he forgotten? Eugenia would be in a dither if he didn't appear. Perhaps he'd gotten busy working at the camp and tea had slipped his mind.

She went to retrieve her bag. The bell jangled over the front door, and she wheeled back around. "Nico! I thought you weren't coming, so I decided I should go without you."

He gave her an appraising look, then pointed at her dress and grinned. "I see you changed your clothes so you would look your prettiest for me."

She gasped and pressed a palm down the skirt of her dress. "I . . . I didn't change for you, I—"

He waggled his finger back and forth. "I know this dress is not what you were wearing this morning. I saw you going into your office when I was leaving the store. You were wearing one of those dark skirts and . . ." Using a brushing gesture, he moved his hand down his chest, then curled his lip.

"Jacket?"

He nodded. "Yes. Not nearly so pretty as this dress you are wearing." His dark eyes sparkled. "It pleases me that you wanted to look so pretty for me."

"Quit saying that. I didn't change clothes to look pretty for you. I thought a dress would be more appropriate for tea, that's all." He tipped his head back and laughed. "I don't know what you find so funny!"

"You should not get angry because a man tells you that you look pretty. I've never known a woman who did not like to hear such words."

Zanna furrowed her brow. "You didn't say I looked pretty. You said I changed clothes so I could look my prettiest for you." She took a step toward him. "First of all, you don't know if this is the prettiest I could ever look. And secondly, I'm not wearing this dress to make you happy. I'm wearing it because I'm going to tea."

He bobbed his head like a chicken pecking at feed. "So you said. Are you ready to go?"

She sighed. "I've been ready. You're the one who's late."

He held up a small net bag. "I had to return to camp. I forgot my gifts for the ladies."

"Gifts?" She eyed the net.

He opened the top of the bag and pulled out a sponge. "I'm giving each of them one of the sponges I brought from Greece. They're very soft." He traced it down her cheek. "Don't you think?"

She could feel his breath on her neck, and her skin tingled at his touch. "Yes, they're very soft." She swallowed. "But I think we should go or Eugenia will be worried. She won't want to serve cold tea."

He tucked the sponge back into the bag and followed her out the door. The moment she reached the boardwalk, he matched her step. "I think the sponges we are harvesting from the Gulf are as soft as these, but I thought the ladies would be pleased I brought these from Greece." He hesitated a moment. "Do you think it is a bad gift?"

"No, it's fine. I'm sure they'll be delighted." She didn't know what type of response he expected, but it seemed one day he was unhappy when she expressed her opinion, and the next day he wanted it. And what was she supposed to think about a man who would stroke her cheeks with a sponge? Was it common in Greece for a man to touch a woman in such an intimate way?

Her thoughts cascaded like a river rushing over a waterfall. She simply didn't know what to make of him. He wasn't like any other Greek man she'd ever met. Granted, she hadn't been around many, but still . . . he simply defied her suppositions.

For the remainder of the walk, he hummed a Greek tune she'd heard her mother sing, though she couldn't recall the words. Once they'd stepped onto the porch, Nico knocked and they waited, and waited, and waited.

He arched his brows and looked at her. "I should knock again?"

"Yes. I can't imagine where they are."

He lifted his hand and knocked with gusto. A few moments passed before the door opened and Eugenia stood in front of them, staring.

Finally, the older woman drew her gaze away from Nico and looked at Zanna. "Good afternoon. I wasn't expecting company." She lifted her fingers and patted her hair. "Were you two out for a walk?" Confusion shone in her eyes.

Zanna smiled at her. "Yesterday when Nico was leaving the doctor's office, you made him promise to come by for tea this afternoon, but we can come another time."

"No, I'm not going to turn away this fine-looking man." She grasped Nico's sleeve. "You come in here right now and I'll put the kettle on the stove." She smiled up at Nico. "I make a fine cup of tea, don't I, Zanna?"

Zanna wasn't certain whether Eugenia had ever brewed her a cup of tea, since Bessie was usually the one who took charge in the sisters' kitchen, but she didn't disagree. Instead she glanced about the house. "Where are Viola and Bessie? I thought they'd be joining us for tea."

Eugenia tugged on her earlobe. "I'm not sure. They went to town. I think Bessie needed eggs. Maybe she was going to bake cookies to go with our tea. I'm sure she'll be back soon."

Zanna didn't attempt to interpret for Nico. Rather, she merely told him that Bessie and Viola were in town and Eugenia hadn't yet prepared the tea. She'd barely finished explaining when Eugenia returned to the parlor.

"Sit down, sit down." Eugenia waved them toward a pair of fan-back wicker chairs. "The tea will be ready soon." She took a seat next to Nico and smiled at him. "Thank you again for saving my life. Dr. Lucy told me everything you did for me." She touched her fingers to her lips.

Nico looked at Zanna and hiked his shoulders.

"Eugenia is thanking you for saving her."

"Ahh." He smiled at the older woman and reached into the net bag at his side. "I brought you a gift from Greece."

She reached for the sponge, but her brow furrowed as she looked at Zanna. "Does he think I need to take a bath?"

Zanna chuckled and shook her head. "No. That's a sponge he brought from the Aegean Sea in Greece. He thought you might like it since it's from his home."

"Thank you." She formed her mouth into exaggerated shapes as she spoke. "I'm the one who should be giving you a gift for saving my life, but I didn't even remember you were coming for tea. I feel terrible, just terrible." Zanna had nearly completed interpreting the message for Nico when Eugenia jumped up. "I know! I do have a gift I can give him." She scurried out of the parlor, leaving the two of them alone.

Zanna sighed. "We should have left when it was clear she wasn't expecting us."

Nico leaned forward and glanced down the hallway where Eugenia had disappeared. "We can make an excuse and leave when she comes back to the parlor."

Zanna looked toward the kitchen. Surely the kettle must be boiling by now. She wanted to check, yet she didn't want to do anything to cause Eugenia further distress. Thus far this visit had been a disaster. And what on earth was Eugenia doing for so long?

When she couldn't bear to wait any longer, Zanna scooted forward on her chair. She was going to go and find Eugenia. She'd pushed to her feet when the front door burst open.

Bessie stepped inside, lifted her nose in the air, and sniffed. "Something's burning." She rushed past Zanna without a word while calling to her sister. "Eugenia! What have you done?"

Viola, eyes wide, hurried after Bessie. "Did she set the kitchen on fire, Sister?"

Amid her sisters' shouts and accusations, Eugenia appeared at the end of the hallway, waving a sock in each hand. "I found them, and I think they'll fit."

While her sisters busied themselves with the smoldering kettle, Eugenia placed one of the socks atop Nico's shoe and gave a nod. "Perfect." She shoved them into his hand.

Zanna stared at the socks and then at Eugenia. "Why do you have a pair of men's socks, Eugenia?"

Her chest swelled. "I knitted them myself. You don't need to tell Nico, but I made them for Bessie's friend, Mr. Pappas, who lives in New York. He comes to Tarpon Springs on business sometimes. I thought they would be an appropriate gift, but he said wool socks made him itch, so I put them back in my cedar chest." She frowned. "I hope Nico likes them." She stood close to his side and smiled at him.

"Eugenia! Didn't you hear me shout at you when I came in? You put the kettle on the stove and it boiled dry. You could have burned down the house." Bessie's gaze moved from her sister to the socks in Nico's hands. "And why have you given him those old socks you knitted two years ago?"

"He gave me a gift, so I gave him one in return." Eugenia jutted her chin and folded her arms across her waist.

Zanna's stomach churned. She and Nico needed to leave before the sisters entered into a melee that would detain them for the remainder of the afternoon. "If everything has been taken care of in the kitchen and we're not needed to help, I believe we'll leave now. Eugenia had forgotten she invited Nico for tea this afternoon. I apologize. We should have left earlier." Zanna forced a smile.

She gestured to Nico, who appeared thoroughly confused. Instead of making his way to the door, he removed the remaining two sponges from the bag and handed them to Bessie and Viola.

Eugenia clasped a hand to her chest. "You're giving them a present, too? That isn't fair. They didn't drown."

"Neither did you, Eugenia, but I do believe that tumble into the river has damaged your brain." Bessie scowled at her sister.

"We're going to leave, ladies." Zanna pushed Nico toward the door. "I apologize for disrupting your afternoon. We were attempting to keep the promise Nico made to Eugenia but had no idea it would create so much havoc."

They'd made it as far as the front walkway when Eugenia shouted and came scurrying after them. "You forgot your socks, Nico." She pressed them into his hand. "Thank you for saving me."

Nico looked at Zanna. "What did she say?"

"I'll explain it all later," Zanna said before she turned to Eugenia. "Nico said you are very welcome and thank you for the socks."

The old woman beamed at him before she turned and walked back to the house.

"I think you've won Miss Eugenia's heart, Nico."

"I think she's far too old for me, don't you?" He angled his head and looked down at her. "And it's not Miss Eugenia's heart that interests me."

Zanna stood on the docks with Nico at her side. She trained her eyes on the horizon, and when the first boat had come into view, she grasped Nico's arm. "There's one of our boats." She turned to him, a smile on her face. "It is one of ours, isn't it?"

He returned her smile and nodded. "Yes, it's one of ours." Lifting his hand, he pointed to a spot not far from the first boat. "And there come the second and third. Do you see them?"

"Yes." She rocked on the balls of her feet. "It's so exciting. I can hardly wait to see how many sponges they've harvested."

He turned his attention back to the water, his hand cupped above his eyes and his lips forming a tight line. "Let's hope they have done well."

"And that those men in the warehouse can get them ready for sale within a week to ten days. We need the money to keep things afloat." She stifled a giggle. "I'm sorry, I didn't mean to make light of the circumstances."

He chuckled. "You're right. We don't want the business to sink."

She laughed aloud at his witty reply.

His patience as they awaited the boats impressed her. Unlike her, he remained calm as the three boats sailed closer. "I'm going to see if I can borrow Mr. Francis's spyglass." When he didn't respond or move from his position, she crossed the short distance and entered the warehouse.

She caught sight of the older man and waved. "May I borrow your spyglass, Mr. Francis? Our boats are returning, and I want to gain a better view."

He gestured toward his desk. "Second drawer on the right. Just put it back once you're finished using it."

Zanna called her thanks, retrieved the spyglass, and rushed back to Nico's side. She lifted the glass to her right eye and stared out over the water. "Oh, look!" She pointed her free hand across the water. "I can see lots of sponges hanging from the masts." She hesitated a moment. "It looks like the first boat is full to overflowing with sponges." She extended the spyglass to him.

He shook his head. "I can see just fine without it. They've done well."

The wind caught her hat and threatened to send it sailing. Using her free hand, she held it in place while holding the spyglass aloft. "I'm going to return this to Mr. Francis." She squinted for one final look before turning toward the warehouse, uncertain how Nico could see the sponges without using the spyglass.

After stepping out of the sunlight, she hesitated and let her eyes adjust to the dim lighting inside the warehouse.

"All done?" Mr. Francis was at his desk, with a well-dressed gentleman sitting opposite him.

"Yes, thank you. From what I could see, it appears the men are bringing in quite a bounty." She handed the spyglass to Mr. Francis and nodded at the other gentleman. "I'm sorry to interrupt."

"No interruption. Mr. Pappas and I were just having a friendly chat." He grinned at the man on the other side of the desk. "It's been a while since he's been in town, so he was inquiring about the latest happenings around Tarpon Springs."

Zanna swallowed hard. So this was the elusive Mr. Pappas. She wasn't sure what she'd expected, but this man wasn't it. He looked like any other sponge buyer she'd seen on the docks. Dark trousers, white shirt, no tie, and a wide-brimmed linen hat he'd placed on Mr. Francis's desk.

Mr. Francis placed the spyglass in his desk drawer, then tipped his head toward his visitor. "Adelfo, have you met Miss Krykos?"

Mr. Pappas shook his head and stood. "I don't believe I've had the pleasure. I think I've met your father and perhaps one of your brothers. They're the Greek boat builders, aren't they?"

All thoughts of the arriving sponge boats fled from her mind. "Yes, they are."

Mr. Pappas returned to his chair and sat down. "They don't come down to the docks much, do they?"

"No. My father has a private launching area he uses for the boats he builds, and when there are boats in need of repair, it's much easier for my father and the owners to bring them to his launching area."

He withdrew a handkerchief from his pocket and wiped his forehead. "I should try to visit him. I enjoy spending time with other Greeks."

"Then you should be pleased to know there are fifty more Greeks in Tarpon Springs since you last visited." She stepped closer to the desk. "But I'm sure Mr. Francis has already told you of their arrival." She didn't wait for an answer. "I'm a lawyer here in Tarpon Springs and I represent Miss Lucy Penrose. I believe you and her father were well acquainted."

"Yes, we had spoken at length about his possible investment in a sponging business, and I offered my help."

She frowned. "You do know that Mr. Penrose died some time ago, don't you?"

He nodded. "Very sad—and very sudden, as I recall." He stroked his thin black mustache. "I sent letters to Greece for him and told him I would do everything I could to help him succeed if he decided to go ahead with the business." His eyes widened. "So those are the Greeks you mentioned? I didn't know he'd completed the arrangements for their travel before his death." He rubbed his hands together. "This is exciting news. My promise to Mr. Penrose holds true; I will help in any way I can. To have a prosperous sponging business in Tarpon Springs will be a good thing for the town—especially for us Greeks, eh?"

Zanna didn't know what to make of Mr. Pappas. He seemed a mixture of both knowledge and ignorance. Was this man truly as uninformed as he appeared to be? Perhaps a few questions were in order.

She pulled another chair close to the desk and directed a bright smile at Mr. Pappas. "Given how you've been in the area on several occasions since Mr. Penrose's death, I'm surprised you didn't make any attempt to inquire about the business proposal on one of your visits."

"You . . . you believe I should have gone looking for his relatives and poked my nose into their business?" He shook his head. "I'm sure they could have found my name among Mr. Penrose's papers and contacted me if they had any questions."

Zanna sighed. "The paper work wasn't immediately examined, but once I noted your name among some of Mr. Penrose's business contacts, I was interested in speaking to you. Even more, Dr. Lucy Penrose has expressed a deep desire to meet you. She is the only living heir of Mr. Penrose." Zanna leaned forward in her chair. "How long will you be in town?"

"A few days. I came for the Friday sponge sale and may remain until Tuesday's sale, depending on what I see." He lowered his voice. "Long ago I learned that sometimes the best sponges are held back for a higher price at subsequent sales. My customers prefer the best wool sponges. And now that the divers have arrived, I'm eager to see what they have found in the Gulf."

"So you could meet with Dr. Penrose tomorrow afternoon?"

"I suppose I could. I've told you all I can about my dealings with her father, but I'll keep my word and help the business in any way I can. I wouldn't want to see our countrymen fail here in America."

"Thank you for your offer." Zanna pushed up from the chair. "I know Dr. Penrose looks forward to meeting you."

He tipped his hat. "I don't think there is much I can tell her, but I'll meet with her nonetheless. However, it's the Greek spongers I'm truly eager to meet. I'll enjoy talking to them about the homeland."

Slivers of sunlight shone through the wood slats of the warehouse and danced across his white shirt. Zanna wanted to tell him she'd prefer if they never met. The last thing she wanted was Lucy selling the sponge business to Mr. Pappas. She took heart in the fact that he'd offered to help, yet he didn't appear to have much interest in the business itself. Instead, his excitement centered around meeting the new Greek arrivals.

She remained standing near the desk. "Say, one o'clock tomorrow afternoon? Would you like to meet at her office or would you prefer someplace else?" She wasn't going to leave the warehouse until she had a firm time and place set for the meeting. If Lucy discovered Mr. Pappas was in town and Zanna hadn't arranged a meeting, she'd never hear the end of it.

He removed a thick cigar from his suit jacket. "You may tell the doctor I'll be at her office at one o'clock tomorrow."

She tipped her head and smiled. "Thank you. Now, if you'll excuse me, our boats should be arriving any minute."

Mr. Pappas pushed to his feet. "The Greeks? They are coming in now?"

"They are. And it appears they've had a successful trip."

He strode to her side. "I'll go out to the dock with you. I want to greet them."

They hadn't yet made it to the door when Zanna turned to him.

149

"I understand you and Bessie Rochester are good friends. I'm curious how you and the Rochester sisters became acquainted."

He appeared momentarily befuddled, then took her elbow and directed her to the door. "That's a story for another time. Look! The boats are almost here."

CHAPTER 15

While Zanna, Mr. Pappas, and Nico waited for the boats to dock, the two men visited as though they'd known each other for years. Mr. Pappas was curious about deep-water diving equipment, and Nico was pleased to share his knowledge. Zanna understood every word that passed between the two men, but she paid little attention. She'd heard Nico describe the equipment and diving methods to her father and brothers, as well as to many of the dockworkers.

It wasn't until the first boat, heavily laden with sponges, had arrived at the dock that Mr. Pappas's unbridled enthusiasm captured her attention.

"I cannot believe my eyes!" Mr. Pappas lowered the brim of his hat to shade his eyes from the bright sun. "I've never seen so many large sheepswool sponge on one boat."

Nico chuckled. "You see? This is what can be harvested using diving equipment rather than the hook boats or old diving methods. We harvest more and better sponges using the diving equipment. And I believe the sponge in the Gulf is as fine, if not better, than what we harvested in the Aegean Sea."

Mr. Pappas twisted the tip of his thin mustache. "I'll have to examine them once they are ready for market. Then I'll tell you if I think these are equal to Aegean sponge." He pointed toward the second arriving boat. "Looks like they've all made an excellent haul. The sheepswool will bring the best price at market, so you should have your divers harvest as many of those as possible."

"I understand. The same is true in Greece, but I don't discourage my divers from harvesting yellow and grass sponge. It is better to hook what is in your path than to wander below water searching for only one kind of sponge. My men are expected to follow strict rules on the depth and length of time for each dive, so I want them to fill their nets with whatever sponge they locate." Nico hiked a shoulder. "Even wire sponge will sell, and I wouldn't want my men to remain underwater too long simply because I insisted upon only sheepswool sponge."

Zanna gave the older man a sidelong glance. She was pleased Nico had told Mr. Pappas that he valued the lives of his diving crew more than money. Judging from the frown on Mr. Pappas's face, Zanna wasn't certain he agreed, and then their discussion was cut short by the docking of the second and third boats.

The boisterous greetings and cheers among Nico and the men echoed along the waterfront and continued as the crew unloaded the sponge and carried it to the warehouse. When they'd finally completed the task, Zanna, Nico, and Mr. Pappas walked to the warehouse.

Mr. Pappas nudged Nico as they stepped inside. "Maybe I made a mistake by passing this opportunity to Mr. Penrose. If you continue these excellent harvests, I may have to see if I can arrange the finances should his daughter have an interest in selling."

"Who can say for sure, but I am hopeful we will be prosperous." Nico turned and strode across the warehouse to direct the men.

Zanna moved closer to Mr. Pappas. Now that he thought there was a handsome profit to be made, did he intend to take advantage of Lucy? It certainly sounded that way to her. "I didn't realize you were interested in owning a sponging business, Mr. Pappas."

He clenched the cigar between his teeth. "My interest is in making money, Miss Krykos. I don't care if I make it from sponges or grapes or olive oil. Whether I could own the sponging business remains to be seen. If Dr. Penrose wants to sell, and the business is making a profit, who can say? Financing can usually be arranged if a company is profitable, but I would need to seek advice from my banker if I wanted to make an offer."

Her jaw muscles tightened. "Then why didn't you invest when the opportunity was first presented to you, rather than passing it along to Mr. Penrose?"

He twisted the end of his mustache. "As I said, financing is simple for a profitable business. At the time Mr. Penrose revealed an interest in forming a sponging company, I didn't have adequate funds. Besides, I didn't know if diving in the Gulf would prove fruitful. But after what I've witnessed today, I would be inclined to seek funding to purchase the business."

The tightness in her stomach eased. "So, you're unable to make an immediate offer to purchase the business?"

"Only if Dr. Penrose would be willing to wait for her money." He chuckled. "And if she's any kind of a businesswoman, I doubt she'd agree. However, I've told you that I plan to keep my word to Mr. Penrose and help in any way possible."

Zanna forced a weak smile. "Since I'm her business manager and consider myself a capable businesswoman, I can tell you that I would advise Lucy against any arrangement where she wouldn't immediately receive payment. However, if you're ever financially able to purchase, you should present your offer to me. Lucy has no interest in dealing with the business."

"Since you are such a sound businesswoman, I am wondering how much you know about the sale of your sponges, Miss Krykos. Will you attend the sale tomorrow?"

She nodded. "Of course. Mr. Francis has explained a little to me, and I observed a sale last week. However, I watched from a distance since we weren't selling that day. Mr. Francis said only owners and buyers should attend the sales. Otherwise the dock would become too congested."

"Will you or Nico be the one who accepts bids on your sponges?"

"Dr. Penrose has placed me in charge, so I'll be the one who decides."

"That's good to know." He gestured toward the opposite side of the warehouse. "If you'll excuse me, I believe I'll go and visit with the men while they finish their work."

Before departing for her office, Zanna stared after Mr. Pappas. She hoped his offer to help was no more than a desire to honor his promise. If not, he might seek financial backing as soon as he returned to New York City.

Nico released the crews once they'd finished unloading. They'd worked hard and needed time to relax before heading out again. Though he had planned to remain behind, the men insisted he join them. One of the men looped arms with Mr. Pappas and insisted he come along, as well. Nico was pleased the older man accepted the offer. Visiting with a Greek who had been living in this country for many years would be helpful to all of them, and Mr. Pappas appeared happy to oblige them.

Having Mr. Pappas around would also provide Nico further opportunity to ask questions outside of Zanna's presence. Truth be told, she was sometimes quick to add her opinion, whereas Mr. Pappas answered questions and let Nico draw his own conclusions.

After they'd finished a hearty supper of fish stew and crusty bread, Mr. Pappas patted his stomach and sat down beside Nico. "I am surprised to find you living in such poor conditions." He nudged Nico in the side and arched his brows. "But what can one expect when a woman oversees a business?"

Nico shook his head. "I thought the same thing when we first arrived, but I soon changed my mind. I can't blame these conditions on Miss Krykos. She was assigned to manage the business the day we arrived. Dr. Penrose didn't learn that her father had sent money to bring us to America until a short time before we appeared. No man could have done better. Zanna has worked very hard to get the business functioning, and she learns quickly."

"Sounds like you may think of Miss Krykos as more than a business manager." Mr. Pappas winked at him.

"She has become a good friend, and I admire her determination to make the business a success."

Mr. Pappas grinned. "I won't force you to admit any more than you're willing, but I think there may be more than friendship between you two. I've seen the way she looks at you."

Nico's hearty laughter broke the nighttime quietude. "You mean that look when her eyes appear to be shooting fire? That means I've done something to anger her, nothing more."

"You go ahead and deny all you want, Nico, but I know what I've seen." He leaned closer. "Are you hoping to one day buy the business from Dr. Penrose?"

He shook his head. "I could never save enough money, but I do hope that one day the doctor will see I am able to take charge of the business and that Zanna can return to her work as a lawyer. I'm learning the language and the way things are done. That's why I'm glad you are here."

"I can tell you about what happens at the Exchange during sale days, and I can help with general business matters regarding the sponging business, but I don't know all the permanent residents who live in Tarpon Springs." He paused before continuing, "I've been coming here for many years to purchase the sponge harvested from the hook boats, so I know the other buyers and the captains who sell at the Exchange, but not many others. I would never have met Mr. Penrose had he not come to the docks seeking my advice about forming a sponge company. I had never even met Miss Krykos or Dr. Penrose before now. I'm pleased to say I'd never had need of a doctor or lawyer while in Tarpon Springs."

"Then you are a fortunate man." Nico gestured toward the other men. "While they finish their supper, tell me what I can expect at the sale tomorrow."

Mr. Pappas mentioned the names of several buyers and their penchant for locating the finest sponge at the lowest price and what to expect when the bids were announced. "Just remember that you don't need to accept any bid. If you believe it is too low, you can return your sponges to the warehouse and wait until the next sale."

The men joked and exchanged stories about their good fortune over the past days, each crew certain they had been the most successful. Laughter filled the air. A few of the men gathered their musical instruments while others surrounded the crackling campfire.

One of the men picked up his bouzouki and slowly turned the tuners while he plucked each string. He nodded to the other men. "As soon as I have this tuned, get ready to join in."

Mr. Pappas gestured to the musicians. "Do you have a *defi*?"

A crew member with a *klarino* motioned to the fellow holding a percussion instrument. "The *daouli* player has one."

The drummer passed the hand drum with hanging metal bangles to Mr. Pappas, then arched his brows. "You know how to play, Mr. Pappas?"

Mr. Pappas nodded. "I used to. It's been a few years, but I'll do my best."

A sharp metallic sound echoed through the campground, and soon the klarino player joined in and carried the melody. The men clapped along with the beat of the drummer and cheered when Mr. Pappas struck the defi. The metal jangles embellished the tune with a rhythm of its own. Some of the men jumped to their feet and danced while others clapped along with the music until most of the men finally wandered off to bed.

Only a few of the divers, Nico, and Mr. Pappas remained around the fire. The older man praised the divers for what they'd accomplished. "Those sponges you harvested will bring a fine price. You should be proud. Did you find it more difficult to dive in the Gulf than the Aegean?"

"No. The sponge is so dense that it is much easier," one of the divers said. "These waters will provide more sponge than we can ever harvest."

"That's good to know. My buyers in New York will be pleased to hear such news." Mr. Pappas leaned forward and rested his forearms across his knees as he looked toward the river. "You know, there once were reports of a vessel lost at sea not far from where you men were diving in the Gulf. It was rumored to have carried jewels and gold."

"We've heard those stories about ships being lost in the Aegean Sea, too. There are always rumors, yet no one ever finds any of those riches."

Mr. Pappas laughed. "You can't be certain. Maybe someone was lucky, and he was smart enough to keep his mouth shut so he didn't have to share with anyone."

"If I ever found a ship filled with jewels and gold, I'd be more than happy to share—after I'd purchased everything I wanted for myself," one of the divers replied.

The men continued to joke about what they would do with a chest of gold, until Mr. Pappas rose to leave. Before departing, he turned to the divers. "You men have already found your riches in those sponge beds. No need to worry about anything else. Just keep bringing in bigger and better loads each time you go out."

The men remained by the fire after Mr. Pappas departed. When he was out of earshot, one of the divers nudged the man beside him. "Mr. Pappas wouldn't think the sponges were equal to gold if he was sleeping out here in one of these shacks instead of on a soft mattress in the hotel."

The other man nodded. "Or if he'd had to leave his wife and children back in Greece."

Nico patted the diver on his shoulder. "One thing is certain: Mr. Pappas doesn't understand the danger of diving. He cares only about bigger and better sponges. He doesn't think about what can happen out there in the Gulf. That's why I'm always telling you not to do anything foolish. I promised your families to keep you safe."

The diver sighed. "We know, Nico—over and over, you announce those rules like a nagging parent."

"Because I care about you." He smiled at the other diver. "Besides, I don't want your wife to come after me with a rolling pin."

The following afternoon, Lucy removed a sheet of paper from her desk and carefully penned several questions. She didn't want to forget what had plagued her since discovering that her father had invested in the sponging business. Hopefully, Mr. Pappas would answer at least some of her queries. She was reviewing the list when the front door opened and a short-statured man with dark hair and a thin mustache entered the office.

She stood. "Mr. Pappas?"

"Dr. Penrose?"

"Yes," she said, smiling. "Please, have a seat." He sat down in the chair opposite her desk as she returned to her seat. "I'm glad to finally have an opportunity to speak with you."

He shifted in the chair. "As I told Miss Krykos, I have very little I can share that you don't already know."

She tilted her head. "Well, since you have no idea what I do or don't know about my father's dealings, please, indulge me."

He placed his elbows on the armrests, laced his fingers together, and tented them beneath his pointed chin. "That is why I am here, Doctor."

His lackluster smile said otherwise, but Lucy wasn't going to be deterred. "I was curious why you haven't been in Tarpon Springs for some time. Are you no longer a sponge buyer for your New York clients?"

He tapped his steepled fingers against his chin. "I said I would indulge your questions, but I didn't know you planned to inquire about anything other than my contacts with your father. Unless your questions are pertinent to issues surrounding your father, I find them rather intrusive."

"I apologize, but I've been eager to talk to you, and Mr. Francis indicated you came to Tarpon Springs on a regular basis. Your recent lack of an appearance made me wonder why you would stay away."

"And you immediately thought my absence had something to do with your father." He met her gaze with a hard stare. "Am I right?"

"The thought didn't immediately come to mind, but when others questioned your absence, I became concerned, yes."

He arched his brows. "Others? You mean Miss Krykos?"

"No, not directly." Lucy leaned back in her chair. "I asked Zanna to see if she could gain any information about why you hadn't been in Tarpon Springs. She merely passed along the information she gained from Mr. Vernaky, the proprietor of the hotel, and some of the other men who work at the docks. They all told her they hadn't heard from you lately and that they'd never known you to stay away for so long."

"Hmm, it's good to know I was missed." His words bore a hint of sarcasm. "I was attending to a personal matter, if you must know. I trust you won't expect me to go into the details, Dr. Penrose."

"No, of course not." Discomfort now plaguing her, she glanced at the sheet of paper on her desk. Before she could object, he reached forward and retrieved the document.

He glanced at the page and looked up. "These are your questions for me?"

"Yes." She folded her hands and placed them atop the desk and waited.

He pushed the paper back toward her. "I am sorry for your father's death, but you need to understand that we were not friends. I couldn't even say we were well acquainted. He came to me and asked for my help because he wanted to invest in a sponging business. I sent letters to Greece for him. He never advised me if he'd been successful in his business dealings and, quite honestly, I didn't even know he had a daughter. Though I would like to, I can't take credit for the wisdom of his investment."

"Wisdom? He's left me with an albatross around my neck, and you want to talk about wisdom?"

"In the future, you may be thankful for his wise investment. If I had the money, I would make an offer to purchase the business before nightfall. Perhaps one day I will be able to do so."

A flicker of hope quieted her doubts. "That's good to know, Mr. Pappas. I hope—"

The front door opened with a clatter, and Bessie Rochester bounded into the room with her sisters following on her heels. "Adelfo!" She bustled toward the Greek sponge buyer and reached for his hand. "You naughty boy. Why didn't you come by the house when you arrived in town?" She looked at Lucy. "Sorry to interrupt, but Zanna told me Adelfo was here, and I couldn't believe my ears." She tapped her index finger to her right eye. "But these eyes don't deceive me. Zanna was right."

Eugenia and Viola positioned themselves on the other side of Mr. Pappas's chair. With the desk in front of him, Bessie on one side and the other two sisters on the other, he couldn't have escaped if his life depended on it. And from the look on his face, Lucy thought he wanted nothing more than a quick getaway. At first blush, she'd been annoyed by the sisters' interruption, but this was proving far more interesting than anything she'd learned from Mr. Pappas thus far.

Lucy graced the imprisoned man with a bright smile. "I wasn't aware you were acquainted with the Rochester sisters. They are some of my very best patients."

All three women beamed at her while Mr. Pappas squirmed in his chair. "We became acquainted when I was in Tarpon Springs on one of my early sponge-buying trips. The ladies—"

"We were having tea in the hotel dining room, and Mr. Pappas joined us," Eugenia said.

Mr. Pappas sighed at the interruption. "If I recall, Bessie asked me to join you."

Viola placed a gloved hand over her lips and giggled. "Bessie thought he looked mysterious." She tapped her finger beside her right eye. "If I recall, she said his dark eyes and black wavy hair intrigued her."

"Hush, Viola." Bessie glowered at her sister.

Eugenia frowned. "Why does Viola need to hush? It's the truth. That's what you said."

Lucy forced a smile. "Did any of you need to see me, or did you stop by only to see Mr. Pappas?" If she didn't do something quickly, the ladies would end up in one of their disagreements, which could last for days.

"We came to invite him for supper this evening." Eugenia edged closer to Mr. Pappas's chair.

"Eugenia, I said *I* was going to extend the invitation." Bessie folded her arms across her chest and glared at Eugenia.

"Ladies! Ladies! Please." Mr. Pappas placed a finger to his lips. "I will be happy to join you for supper tonight, but only if you cease your arguing and promise there will be nothing but pleasant conversation once I arrive."

They all three bobbed their heads and agreed they'd be on their best behavior, but when Viola and Eugenia stepped toward the door, Bessie lagged behind. She leaned close to Mr. Pappas's ear and whispered.

Eugenia glanced over her shoulder as she neared the door. "Bessie!

Quit your whispering." She *tsk*ed and looked at Lucy. "Bessie thinks he cares for her more than either of us."

Bessie's ample figure blocked Mr. Pappas's view of the door, though he leaned forward to gain a look at Eugenia. "You are all lovely, and I am a friend to all three of you."

Viola straightened her shoulders, and Eugenia's nose lifted several notches. His comment had hit the mark and pleased them. Bessie, however, frowned and landed a quick jab to his shoulder—a gesture Lucy didn't miss. There was something more to this friendship. Something Lucy didn't quite understand, and she wasn't sure she wanted to find out what it was.

After the foursome had departed, Lucy barely had time to consider the curious happenings before Zanna appeared. She glanced around the room. "Didn't Mr. Pappas keep his appointment? I reminded him, and he promised he'd be here."

"He's been here and gone. He and the Rochester sisters. I'm surprised you didn't bump into them. They left only minutes ago."

"Oh no! That's my fault. They asked me if I knew where he was, and I mentioned his appointment with you." She hurried across the room and plopped down in the chair recently vacated by Mr. Pappas. "Can you believe they're friends?"

"You knew?" Lucy leaned forward. "How did you find out?"

Zanna related Eugenia's tale of having knitted socks for Mr. Pappas two years ago. "Since Mr. Pappas has some dislike or allergic reaction to wool, Nico is now the proud owner of a pair of wool socks. I doubt he'll find much use for them in the Florida heat." Zanna giggled and shook her head. "When Nico and I were on the dock with Mr. Pappas, I asked him about his friendship with the sisters."

"What did he say?"

"The boats were coming in, and he said it was a story for another day. I'm not sure what that means, but there wasn't opportunity to ask further questions."

Lucy pushed away from her desk. "I gathered the three of them were in the hotel for tea some time ago and Bessie asked Mr. Pappas to join them. A rather odd happenstance, since the sisters don't generally take up with strangers." She frowned. "Don't you think?"

Zanna nodded. "I do. Perhaps I can learn a bit more if I have a visit with them."

"I'm not so sure you should speak with them as a group. Bessie seems to have a genuine affinity for Mr. Pappas. You might do best if you direct your questions to Viola or Eugenia."

"Now that I think about it, Eugenia did refer to him as Bessie's friend."

"They all seemed pleased to see him, but Bessie whispered something in his ear once the other two were out of earshot." Lucy stood and picked up her bag. "I need to call on John Osgood. His wife says he's too sick to come to the office. Want to walk along?"

"I need to go to my office and then to the warehouse, but I can walk a short distance with you. I came to ask you if Mr. Pappas answered any of your questions."

Lucy sighed. She longed to tell her friend that Mr. Pappas had been a fount of information, yet his meager responses had been as stunted as a dried-up fruit tree. "He didn't explain things with any more clarity than you'd already surmised. His interest in purchasing the company was the only positive thing to come out of our conversation."

Zanna gasped. "He actually offered to buy the company?"

"No, not now, but he said he would if he had the money. It sounded as though he was going to try to secure funds so he could make a genuine offer. I know you don't approve, but I think it would be grand if we could both go back to the way things were before: me practicing medicine and you practicing law, and neither of us responsible for the welfare of fifty immigrants." Lucy stopped at the corner. "The Osgoods live on Read Street. I believe this is where we part ways."

Lucy's words rang in Zanna's ears like a death knell. Were they parting in more ways than one? When she reached the corner of Orange Street, she turned down Tarpon Avenue. While she'd done her best to convince Lucy that selling wasn't the best decision, the warnings continued to fall upon deaf ears. Lucy's excitement over a possible sale had been palpable.

A heaviness weighed on her. If Lucy sold the business, would Nico and the other men be treated well? Mr. Pappas was a man who knew the business, yet he only seemed interested in making money. She bowed her head against a stiff breeze and was pulled back when someone grasped her hand outside Alderman's Dry Goods.

"You look like you've lost your last friend." Viola Rochester's shrill voice cut like a knife.

"Viola! You startled me."

"Sorry. I didn't mean to frighten you, but I thought you might walk into Mr. Alderman's display if I didn't stop you." The older woman pointed to an arrangement of boxes sitting atop a table outside the store. "There would have been fruit everywhere if you'd bumped into that table." She tipped her head closer. "That table's as rickety as Bessie when she's using her parasol as a cane."

Zanna chuckled. "Thank you for saving me from certain disaster, Viola. I would have been here all day picking up oranges and apples."

"Tut, tut. We all get lost in our thoughts from time to time." Viola picked up several oranges and examined them. "Bessie sent me to purchase a few items. We're having Mr. Pappas join us for supper tonight." She sighed. "I don't think we really needed anything extra, but you can't argue with Bessie. I think she just wanted to get rid of Eugenia and me so she could be alone with Mr. Pappas."

"And where is Eugenia?"

"She said she wasn't interested in going anywhere except back home. Bessie did her best to send her along with me, but Eugenia wouldn't be persuaded. Sometimes I think Eugenia is as smitten with Mr. Pappas as Bessie is."

"Smitten? You think they view Mr. Pappas as a love interest?"

The older women lifted her gloved fingers to her mouth and tittered. "I do, but I don't think Mr. Pappas cares for either of them—at least not in that way." She glanced around as if she expected one of her sisters to suddenly appear. "Don't tell either of them I've told you any of this or I'll hear no end to it."

"Not a word." Zanna touched her index finger to her pursed lips. "And what about you, Viola? Do you care for Mr. Pappas, too?"

"Although he's a nice gentleman, I'm no fool. He doesn't call on Bessie because he has any thoughts of marriage—at least not to any of us. He's a businessman, and his interest lies in making money. That's all he talks about when he comes to visit."

Zanna frowned. Why would he discuss moneymaking ventures with the Rochester sisters? She wanted to quiz Viola further, but they were interrupted when Mrs. Alderman came to the front door of the store. "I have your order ready, Viola." Her focus dropped to the oranges in the woman's hand. "Did you want to add those to your account?"

The older woman nodded and scurried inside.

Zanna sighed. It seemed there was something more to Mr. Pappas's friendship with the Rochester sisters—or at least with Bessie—so what was it?

On Friday morning, Zanna and Nico were at the warehouse. The sponges harvested from their first excursions into the Gulf would be auctioned this morning. Their sponges were strung on couleurs and placed in piles at one end of the dock, while the sponges harvested by hook boats were displayed farther down.

Zanna strode outside as some of the buyers arrived. The comments were encouraging.

She straightened her shoulders and moved among the buyers, who were busy examining their sponges. Only a narrow wandering walkway remained among the heaping product.

With a reserved smile, Zanna gestured to several of the buyers. "These are from our first excursion into the Gulf. We will have many more cleaned and ready for sale in a short time, however. I hope you will become accustomed to looking first at what the Penrose Sponge Company has to offer."

The men didn't comment until Nico arrived at her side. Then they spouted one question after another. She offered another demure smile. "He doesn't speak much English. I'll be happy to interpret your questions."

Nico shook his head. "I am learning." He gestured for the men to continue. "Speak slowly and I will understand."

Mr. Pappas stepped out from the crowd of buyers. He placed an arm around Nico's shoulder but directed a hard stare at Zanna. "You should let him attempt to talk to the buyers himself. He won't become confident with the language unless you give him an opportunity."

Zanna frowned at him. "They speak too rapidly for him to understand."

"These men aren't accustomed to having a woman in their midst. Why don't you go inside? I'll be glad to interpret for him."

She stiffened at his tone. "Thank you for your offer, Mr. Pappas, but I think the fact that you, too, are a buyer might raise a few eyebrows." She wrinkled her nose. "We wouldn't want anyone to think you're involved with the Penrose Sponge Company as anything other than a possible buyer of our product, would we?" She gestured toward their display. "But I would be delighted to have you bid on our sponges."

He shrugged. "Suit yourself. I thought I might be of help. I trust you understand how the bidding process works."

"I had a long talk with Mr. Francis and the auctioneer earlier this morning. They've explained everything to me."

He tipped his hat, turned, and walked away.

Nico pointed after Mr. Pappas. "Where is he going? I wanted to ask him about the bidding."

"No need. I know how it's done." She directed him to the far end of the dock where she'd had the men move their sponges.

"Why did you have them move our strings to the end of the dock?" He frowned. "Everyone will make their purchases and leave before they come clear down to this spot."

"Not true. We drew for lots earlier this morning, and we were fortunate to get this spot. Mr. Francis said the sponges in the first lots bring a much lower price because the buyers tend to hold back at the beginning to see how the competition is bidding." She tipped her head to meet his eyes. "We're going to do well. Trust me."

"I'm trying, but sometimes you make it most difficult."

Before she could reply, the Exchange bell clanged to alert buyers the sale was about to begin. She grasped Nico's arm and squeezed. "It's time for the sale to begin. I've been praying this goes well. You should do the same."

The auctioneer stood near the first lot and announced there were ten strings with five wool, twenty yellow, and one glove sponge on each string. The auctioneer stepped away and allowed the buyers to further examine and feel the sponge. The crew and captain stood nearby, their eyes shining with anticipation. Once the buyers had completed their examination, the auctioneer shouted for bids. Several buyers scribbled on slips of paper and handed them in.

The auctioneer shouted, "Everybody in?" A few more men hurried forward to hand him their bids. Other buyers continued to examine the lot, and the auctioneer called out, "One more!" Finally, when all bids had been turned in, the auctioneer walked into the warehouse, read the slips, and quickly returned to announce the highest bid and price.

The captain stepped forward. "I'm refusing the bid. We'll put them back in storage and bring them back when there are buyers who can see what my sponges are worth." He stalked off, shaking his head.

Nico nudged her. "What happened?"

Zanna explained while the auctioneer moved on to the next lot. The process was slow, and by midmorning the auctioneer called for a break. They resumed the bidding at ten-thirty, and it was close to noon when the auctioneer called for bids on their Gulf sponges.

The auctioneer pointed to Nico. "These are some of the fine sponges our new Greek divers harvested from the Gulf. I think these deserve some impressive bids."

The buyers followed the same procedure, though Zanna noted bids were now being written on many more slips of paper. Her heart soared with excitement as the auctioneer read over the bids and then called out the highest bid and price.

Zanna waved back and forth and shouted, "I accept!"

Confusion shone in the eyes of the auctioneer as he looked first at Zanna and then at Nico. "The offer isn't made to you, miss. It needs to be accepted or rejected by him." He pointed at Nico.

"What did he say?"

She ignored him and took a step forward. "I am the business manager for Miss Lucy Penrose, owner of the boats. She has given me written authority to conduct all business for Penrose Sponge Company."

The auctioneer shook his head. "I don't care what she gave you. He's the one who needs to accept or reject the bid."

Zanna drew closer and rose on tiptoes to whisper in Nico's ear. "He won't let me agree to take the bid. The acceptance must come from you."

He smiled down at her. "And is it enough?"

She remained close to his side. "It is."

Nico bowed his head and whispered, "So I should accept?"

"Yes," she said.

"You know, all those men staring at us are likely thinking you have a romantic interest in me."

Her mouth dropped open. "That's what you're thinking about?"

"Not entirely. I was thinking you should tell me how much the offer would be in drachmas." He edged closer. "I think you are a good lawyer, but you don't know what price we should accept for our harvest. I think you are judging only by what you've heard on previous bids."

She knew he was right, but she wouldn't admit it. Instead she mentally converted the bid into drachmas and whispered the amount to him.

"We can get a higher bid if we hold out a little longer." He grinned. "You see how much we need each other?"

The twinkle in his eye and the intimacy of his words caused her insides to quiver. Why did Nico have that effect on her?

CHAPTER 17

Nico stood on the dock and raked his fingers through his thick black hair. Much had happened over the past few months. The men had continued to harvest excellent sponge, the quality far surpassing what they had anticipated when they left Greece. At auction, the competition among the buyers remained robust, with Mr. Pappas doing his best to win the bids each time he arrived at the docks. With his English much improved, Nico was pleased he no longer needed Zanna's assistance interpreting during the sales. Still, she attended as many of them as possible, insisting she needed to be mindful of progress with the business.

The men were now saving a portion of their earnings, and many of them anticipated bringing their families to America in less than a year. Now that they were beginning to experience some profit, Zanna had convinced Dr. Penrose to use part of the money to help begin construction of more permanent housing for the men. They'd been adjusting to this new country much more quickly than any of them had anticipated. Perhaps it was due to the similarity in climate and the richness of the harvests, or the fact that the Turkish authorities had proposed new taxes and restrictions, which had begun to paralyze the sponge industry in Greece.

Nico had been thankful for these past months, yet worry pinched the edges of his mind. He wanted to believe nothing was amiss with their new venture, but his gut told him otherwise. He stood on the dock, waiting for the boats and praying the *Anastasi* would bear a full load. The last three times out, the boat had returned with far fewer sponges than in the past. While Markos and Felix, the divers on the *Anastasi*, had blamed Demetrios, the boat's captain, for taking them into new waters that had yielded far fewer sponges, Demetrios had argued against their claims. The other crew members remained unwilling to take sides.

"Why the frown, Nico? Yesterday the bids for your sponges were higher than any that have ever been sold in Tarpon Springs." Mr. Pappas reached inside his jacket, withdrew a fat cigar, and tucked it between his lips. "At each sale I attend, my bids must go higher in order to purchase your sponges. If I were you, I would be smiling from ear to ear. Instead, you stare out at the water like you've lost your last friend." The cigar danced up and down as he spoke.

"To others it would appear I have no worries, but there are always problems that arise." He gave the older man a sideways glance. "Surely you must know this. You have been a businessman for many years."

Mr. Pappas pushed his straw hat off his forehead and swiped at beads of perspiration with a white handkerchief. The smell of dank water and fish permeated the air. The early morning hour and slight breeze did little to relieve the oppressive humidity that beset the area.

Nico inhaled the soggy air and blew it out in a sigh. He didn't know what weighed on him more—the diminishing harvests on the *Anastasi*, or the fact that his men wouldn't confide in him. Something was going on out in the Gulf, and the conflicting stories between the divers and captain left him looking to the rest of the crew for answers. Yet his frustration continued to mount since they refused to confirm one story or the other. If the *Anastasi* returned again with a small load of sponge, he would set aside his duties in the warehouse and at the auctions and go out with her crew the next time they sailed. He wanted answers. If his men wouldn't reveal the truth, he'd find out for himself.

Pappas held a match to his cigar and inhaled quick puffs until the tip burned bright orange. "Exactly what problems trouble you? The sponges are of excellent quality, and from what your men tell me, the sponge beds are vast. You have good boats and equipment. What more could you ask for?" He held the cigar a short distance from his mouth and smiled at the glowing ash.

There was nothing but truth in what the older man said. To anyone other than those within the business, everything looked perfect. Even so, he and the men knew something wasn't right. The crews on the other two boats had mocked the crew of the *Anastasi* before the three boats departed on their voyage. They'd even taken wagers, betting the *Anastasi* would come back with a small harvest. Nico had cringed at their raucous laughter, yet he couldn't fault them. The men had to take their fun where they could find it. There was little laughter to be had once they were in the Gulf.

"You can talk to me, Nico. Perhaps I can help." He arched his brows and grinned. "Or is it only the pretty little Greek girl that you trust."

Nico frowned at the remark. "Zanna is not a little girl. She's the manager of the business. And you're right, I do trust her. That doesn't mean I'm unable to trust anyone else."

"Glad to hear it." He clapped Nico on the shoulder. "I want you to know that you *can* trust me. I want to do everything I can to make sure my fellow Greeks are successful in their new home and that I have done what I could to honor my promise to Mr. Penrose." He flicked the ash from his cigar into the murky water that slapped at the pilings. "So, tell me what troubles you."

Nico momentarily considered the man's comments. He didn't

know Mr. Pappas well, yet had it not been for Adelfo Pappas and his willingness to aid Mr. Penrose by writing those letters to the Greek Sponge Exchange, Nico would still be in Greece. There was no denying Mr. Pappas had been instrumental in bringing Nico and his crews to their new homeland, or that he wanted them to succeed and remain in America.

Though he doubted there was anything Mr. Pappas could tell him that would be of assistance, Nico desired the opinion of another man.

The cigar smoke wafted toward him when he turned toward Mr. Pappas. "It's the *Anastasi*. The last three times they've gone out, they brought in fewer sponges each time. The divers blame the captain, and the captain blames the divers. I don't know who to believe." He went on to detail what little he'd discovered after questioning the crew. "I suspect there's something more to all of this, I just don't know what it is. But I plan to find out."

Adelfo nodded thoughtfully. "And how will you do that if the men won't confide in you?"

"If they don't return with a good harvest this time, I plan to go along with them on their next voyage and dive myself. I'll see then who is speaking the truth and who is not."

Mr. Pappas took a long draw on his cigar, sucked in his cheeks, and attempted to blow smoke circles, his mouth opening and closing like a banked fish. Weighed down by the stickiness in the air, the puffs of smoke resembled nothing more than the haze that enveloped them. "Seems as though you don't need my help after all. You've already worked out a solution to your problem."

"We'll see. I'm not as confident as you. I'm praying I'll discover my worry was uncalled for and they will return with an overflowing harvest." He shaded his eyes with one hand. "We should know soon. I see the *St. Nicolas* on the horizon."

Though the boats were in sight, it seemed to take forever before they finally docked. Nico knew it was because of his own concerns. They'd truly taken no longer than normal. The *St. Nicolas* was first to dock, and as usual the sponges were strung and piled in every available space. The same was true of the *Crete*. Nico held his breath as the *Anastasi* pulled alongside the dock.

The moment they'd cast their lines to the dock, he cupped his hands to his mouth. "How was your harvest this time?" he called.

Only the screech of gulls broke the silence, until Markos shook his head. "Not as good as we hoped, but the sponges we harvested are good ones."

Nico's shoulders sagged. "That's not the report I hoped for."

Markos shrugged and held out his open palms. "We do what we can."

"Where is Felix?" Nico scanned the deck.

"He's below. I don't think he's feeling well."

The hairs on the back of Nico's neck stood up. "What's wrong? Did he stay down too long?" Two of the men secured the boat to the moorings, and in one long stride Nico jumped onto the deck of the *Anastasi*. He went to the captain. "I want to see him, and I want to see the logbook."

He descended the narrow steps and came alongside the man's makeshift bunk. Felix's eyes appeared to be mere slits, but when Nico spoke, the diver's eyes popped wide open. Nico knelt beside him to gain a better look. "Markos tells me you're sick. Were you down too long, or did you make too many dives in one day?"

Felix rolled his head back and forth on the pillow. "It's not the bends, Nico. As soon as one of us is ill, you think we're breaking your rules."

"My rules are in place so I can keep you alive. Did you lose consciousness while you were underwater? Were you breathing too rapidly? You may have pushed beyond the crew's pumping limit. Remember, they can't sustain more than thirty revolutions a minute, and if you dove too deep, they can't even maintain that rate."

"No, I told you, I followed the rules."

After looking at Felix's eyes, Nico could tell that the man hadn't received enough air at some point during the dive. The whites of his eyes were nearly as dark as the pupils, evidence the outside water pressure had suddenly become greater than the air pressure inside his helmet and suit. Something had happened to create the imbalance of air and water pressure, and Nico guessed Felix had descended too rapidly and the pump crew hadn't been able to build up air pressure quickly enough. Felix's diving suit likely compressed and pushed his body upward into the rigid helmet where there was less pressure, thus causing the injury to his eyes. Either that or he'd allowed himself to sink into deeper water while below so that the crew couldn't maintain adequate pressure. Either way, there was no doubt in Nico's mind that Felix was withholding the truth.

He fisted his hands. "Don't lie to me, Felix. Your eyes reveal what happened down there. The skin surrounding them has already turned dark."

"I didn't want to place blame on the crew. They couldn't help it. I accidentally dropped into much deeper water, and the pump crew couldn't build up the air pressure quickly enough to keep up with the increasing water pressure." He reached for Nico's arm. "It isn't their fault. They turned the flywheel as fast as they could once I signaled the line tender. The drop wasn't so deep that I suffered permanent injuries. My sight will return. Nothing happened that will keep me from diving again."

Nico arched his brows. "You think not? I'm sure your wife would disagree if she was out there on the dock, and you can't be sure you will regain your eyesight."

"Diving is my life, Nico. Once I can see again, I must return. This was an accident that could happen to any one of us."

"If what you told me is true, then I can't fault you. We'll talk about diving once the doctor says you have fully recovered. I am planning to go out on the *Anastasi* the next time she sails, so I will take your place." He stood, staring down at Felix lying in the bunk. "Stay here. I want the doctor to examine you before you leave the boat." He reached down and grasped Felix's arm. "If you ever want to dive for me again, don't move from this bunk until the doctor gives permission. Is that clear?"

Felix offered a mock salute. "Aye, aye, Captain."

Nico frowned. "This isn't a joke, Felix. You could have died down there."

"But I didn't," the sailor muttered.

Nico ignored the remark. He'd been around divers all his life. He was one of them, and he understood them—at least most of the time. Felix's argument came as no surprise. Every diver he'd ever known was filled with a daring bravado, a willingness to push the limits. They'd stay underwater just a little longer, ascend or descend a little faster than was prudent, overlook signs of the bends, dive to unsafe depths, remain underwater far too long, each one certain nothing would happen to him. They were men eager to show their mettle while flirting with danger and placing their lives at risk. Nico had seen too many of them die. The wails of their widows and children echoed throughout the Greek islands. He didn't want the same outcome here in Tarpon Springs.

After returning to the deck, Nico sent one of the men in search of Dr. Penrose, then gestured to Markos. When the man drew near, Nico pinned him with a hard look. "I thought you said Felix was ill. You knew he was suffering from the squeeze, yet you lied to me. If he lay down there and died, would your conscience bother you at all, Markos?"

"Only his eyes were damaged. He wouldn't have died." The diver shoved his hands into his pockets. "He begged me not to tell you. He begged all of us." Markos hollered the last remark and looked at the men unloading the sponges. "Didn't he?"

They nodded their agreement.

"Just because he asked, doesn't mean you should do it." Nico stood in the midst of the crew. "I think it's shameful you'd all agree to keep such a secret. What's come over you men?"

One of the crewmen who turned the pump's flywheel stepped forward. "I wanted to tell you what happened. Once we knew he needed more air, we turned the flywheel as fast as we could, but we couldn't get enough air to him quick enough." He bowed his head. "What happened is our fault."

"If what Felix told me is true, it was an accident and nobody is to blame. If there's any fault here, it's that you men didn't immediately come forward and tell me after you docked. You've all seen what the squeeze can do. Did you think I wouldn't notice that Felix couldn't see?"

The pump handler nodded. "I understand, but you know how it is for us. We need to be in the water sponging so we can support our families still in Greece. Felix can't give up sponging. He said he was sure his sight would return, and he was fearful you'd never let him dive for you again."

"I need every man if we're going to be successful, but I won't put money before the lives of my crew. I'd like to think you value your own lives as much as I do." Nico shifted his attention to the captain. "What news can you give me regarding the harvest?" He glanced at the sponges remaining in the boat and those on the dock. "It doesn't look as though you've fared any better than the last few trips."

The captain shook his head. "The divers will tell you the same tale they've given you the last three times out, but I can tell you that the waters they were diving in are where the divers of the *Crete* and *St. Nicolas* have harvested large yields. Felix and Markos don't fill their baskets with the same speed of other divers. Maybe the *St. Nicolas* should send me some of their divers, and I'll give them Markos and Felix."

"Felix won't be going out on the next voyage. I plan to take his place."

The captain straightened his shoulders and tipped his hat. "Now, that would please me very much."

Nico's head snapped up at the clatter of feet on the wooden dock. He heaved a sigh when he saw Dr. Penrose hurrying toward the boat. He held out his hand and helped her onto the deck and gestured toward the stairs. "Felix is below. I'll wait up here unless you call for me." Thankful his English had improved enough to be understood, he offered the doctor a faint smile.

Lucy started toward the stairs. Before heading down, she glanced over her shoulder. "He may need to be moved to my office. Walking could be harmful, even if he's able. I admit, I don't know much about diving injuries."

Nico nodded. "If so, the crew will help move him. But I think it is only Felix's eyes that are injured. With time, such injuries usually heal." He hesitated, then added, "Sometimes the squeeze paralyzes divers for life. Some even die." He signaled to two of the crew members. "You are to remain by the stairs, and if the doctor calls for you to move Felix, help her do so at once."

Once the crewmen were in position, Nico jumped off the deck of the *Anastasi* and surveyed the sponges that remained on the dock. The harvests from both the *St. Nicolas* and *Crete* were bountiful. For that he was grateful. He'd need to make some decisions about future voyages. His presence was needed for the sales at the Exchange, but he'd have to determine if his diving skills were of greater importance. Unless he changed the schedule, the boats were to sail again next week.

"How is your diver faring?" A hand clasped his shoulder, and the familiar scent of cigar smoke wafted toward him. Mr. Pappas nodded toward the men carrying the sponges to the warehouse. "The crew of the *Anastasi* believes you've lost confidence in them."

Nico hiked a shoulder. "I haven't lost confidence. I just don't know what exactly is going on, and they refuse to be honest with me. They even lied about Felix." His disappointment in the men outweighed any concern over their limited harvest.

"Let me talk to them. I'll come to the camp tonight and play music with them. Afterward, perhaps I can discover who is telling the truth."

The offer came as a surprise, yet Nico didn't have a better plan at the moment. The crews enjoyed the company of Mr. Pappas, and the older man could weave an interesting story. On his last visit, he'd promised to tell them how a poor Greek had become a success in New York City. Perhaps an encouraging story and a bit of entertainment was what they all needed right now. It certainly couldn't hurt, could it?

CHAPTER 18

Rather than go to the docks and wait for the boats to come in, Zanna quickly changed her plans when she caught sight of Viola Rochester strolling along Pinellas Avenue. Seeing Viola out and about by herself was a rare sight. Truth be told, seeing any Rochester sister on her own was an unusual occurrence.

Besides, other than lending moral support or cheering for the crews, there was little she could do during the unloading process. She did wonder if the *Anastasi* would return with a full load, but one look at Nico would be enough to relay that news. And who could say when she might have another opportunity to visit with Viola when her sisters weren't in tow?

The peacock feathers adorning Viola's hat waved like children in their Sunday finery. Always on the lookout for a way to appear taller, Viola had likely chosen the hat because of its towering height. No matter if her chapeau wasn't in style. If it added a few inches to her stature, she would purchase and wear the item. She held the same belief with shoes—at least she had until two years ago, when she'd broken her ankle wearing a pair with extremely high heels. Bessie had avowed the shoes were made for ladies of the night, not the ladies of Tarpon Springs, but Viola hadn't listened. Ultimately, she'd suffered the consequences of a broken ankle and, even worse, was required to listen to Bessie say "I told you so" until the ankle finally healed.

Zanna flashed a smile and waved as she strode toward the older woman. A moment passed before Viola's features softened with a look of recognition, and she waved in return.

When she drew near, her shrill voice pierced the morning quietude with an overly loud greeting. "Good morning, Zanna. Out for a bit of fresh air?"

"I need to go to the docks a little later, but when I saw you approaching, I thought it might be nice to ask if you'd join me for a cup of tea or coffee at the bakery. We seldom have an opportunity to visit. If you have time, of course." She hesitated a moment. "Or are you busy with errands of your own?"

"I'm busy with errands, yes, but not for myself. You may recall the Women's Club is scheduled for our quarterly cleanup chores at the cemetery this afternoon." She drew herself up to her full height. "I'm in charge of the Cemetery Committee, you know."

"I do recall you were elected to that prestigious position during last year's election. However, I didn't realize the cleanup was scheduled for today."

"Tut, tut, you younger ladies are busy with your own work. Unlike my sister Bessie, I admire you and Lucy Penrose, as well as the school-teachers and a few other young ladies who have attended college and aren't afraid to step into businesses usually controlled by men." She shook her head. "Just look at my sisters and me. If our father hadn't been wealthy, where would we be? All three of us spinsters and no training to work outside the home. We'd be in a real pickle. I've said as much to Bessie, but she just shushes me." Viola lowered her voice. "She thinks she knows everything, but she doesn't."

"I certainly don't want to interfere with your cleanup duties, Viola. Perhaps we can have coffee another time?"

Viola checked the timepiece pinned to her bodice. "No reason we can't go now. I can gather up the tools and take them to the cemetery after we have our coffee." She grinned. "And a cinnamon roll. Mrs. Caldwell bakes the best cinnamon rolls in the entire state."

They turned east onto Tarpon Avenue, and once inside the bakery, settled themselves at one of the small wood tables. The mouth-watering aroma of every imaginable yeasty confection wafted out the front door and drew customers inside like bees to honey. Mrs. Caldwell and her daughter bustled through the shop, filling coffee cups and committing orders to memory rather than taking the time to write them down.

Nora Caldwell stopped at their table. "Ladies, what can I get for you this morning?"

After they'd placed their orders, Viola licked her lips in obvious anticipation of the sugary treat. "How are you enjoying your work with that fine-looking young Greek that saved Eugenia's life?" She leaned forward and winked. "He might make a good husband for you. From what I've been told, he's a hard worker and really knows the sponging business."

"And who has been filling your ears with tales about Nico?" Zanna asked.

"Adelfo Pappas. He says a wise person would use their money to purchase the business from Dr. Lucy."

Zanna's heart pumped a rapid beat. She'd wanted to question Viola about Mr. Pappas but worried there wouldn't be a proper opportunity. Viola had opened the door even wider than Zanna had hoped. The older woman's words had sent a sliver of fear coursing down her spine. What was Mr. Pappas up to? While he'd expressed an interest in buying out Lucy, she had no idea he might be encouraging others to do so.

"What else has Mr. Pappas said about the business?" Zanna's voice broke, betraying her.

Viola reached across the table and covered her hand. "Do you need a drink of water, dear? Your complexion is pale, and your voice warbled when you spoke." Without waiting for a response, Viola pushed away from the table and hurried to the counter with her peacock feathers flapping overhead. She soon returned with a glass of water. "Drink this. Dr. Lucy says water is good for everything."

Zanna didn't argue. She downed the glass of water and thanked Viola. "I'm fine. I think the heat overwhelmed me for a moment."

"Let's move to a table near the door where we'll get a breeze." The older woman gathered her gloves and pocketbook. Zanna stood and followed her. Viola pulled out a chair and motioned Zanna to the opposite side of the table. "This will be much better, don't you agree?"

"Yes, thank you," Zanna said, sitting down again.

Nora then arrived with their orders. Once the waitress scurried away, Zanna turned her attention back to Viola. "Let's see now . . . what were we talking about?" She lifted a finger in the air. "Oh, I know. I asked you what else Mr. Pappas had told you about the sponging business."

Viola's forehead creased into tiny lines. "I think he's up to his old tricks again."

"When we recently spoke at Alderman's, you did mention that Mr. Pappas talks about money a great deal. Has that continued?"

She nodded. "He knows we inherited our father's wealth, and while I don't believe he's interested in marriage, Bessie thinks differently." Viola *tsk*ed. "She says she's the one who got the brains in our family, but that's not true when it comes to men. Both she and Eugenia think he'd make an excellent catch. Yet I don't think either of them has a hook that's big enough to hold him." She giggled until tears traced down her cheeks and fell onto her bodice. She withdrew a lace-edged handkerchief from her pocket and patted her eyes. "I know it isn't kind to laugh at them, but they're making fools of themselves."

Zanna took a sip of her tea and nodded. There were other questions she wanted to ask but worried that if she interrupted, Viola would decide she'd already divulged too much private information.

After cutting a bite of her cinnamon roll, Viola forked it into her mouth and sighed. "I could eat these every day."

Viola continued to extol the delights of her cinnamon roll until Zanna could no longer remain silent. "In what way is he making fools of them, Viola? If he simply calls at the house and his company is enjoyable, there's no harm done, is there?"

"He wants more than company. He wants *money*. I told you before that all he talks about is investing money in this business or that business and how he's going to make a fortune, and how he'd do the same for the three of us if we'd only follow his advice." She wrinkled her nose. "Well, that isn't going to happen. At least not with my share of the inheritance. I suppose Bessie and Eugenia can do as they like, but if they give their money to him, they'd better not come running to me to support them when they don't have a penny to their names."

"Now, now. I know that isn't true, Viola. You're too kindhearted to turn your back on your sisters." Zanna poured more tea into her cup.

"That's probably true enough. Still, you'd think Bessie would have more sense. She hasn't seen any profit from the money she's already given him to invest for her." She leaned in. "On top of that, she made him a loan. She's asked for repayment, but she hasn't seen a cent."

"Oh dear." Zanna's mind reeled. "Well, let's hope that he does repay her." Her stomach twisted in a tight knot. To hear that Bessie Rochester had given Mr. Pappas money to invest on her behalf, and that she'd also loaned him money, was difficult to believe. Zanna had never pictured Bessie as a woman who could be easily deceived. And perhaps Mr. Pappas hadn't been deceptive. Yet, she marveled at the fact that Bessie would continue to listen to his investment schemes when the man had never repaid his outstanding debt.

Viola finished the last bite of her confection and wiped her lips.

"Do you recall when Dr. Lucy was wanting to speak to Mr. Pappas and he stayed away from Tarpon Springs for so long?"

Zanna inwardly shuddered at the question. How could she forget? Lucy had been at her office on more than one occasion, inquiring after Mr. Pappas, before he finally appeared on the docks. "Of course I remember."

Viola pursed her lips. "I think he stayed away all that time because he didn't want to face Bessie. Mr. Pappas had told her that the next time he was in town, he'd have her money." She shook her head. "Of course, he didn't, but did that stop Bessie from inviting him to dinner and acting like an enamored schoolgirl? Not for a minute. And she's still hanging on every word he says."

Zanna wasn't certain how to react. Investing in the sponging company would likely be a wise choice for the three sisters. However, if they wanted to purchase the company, they didn't need Mr. Pappas. Was he hoping to use their money to purchase the business and then keep a share of the profits? Her thoughts churned as she attempted to sort through what Viola had told her.

Viola pushed aside her empty plate. "I don't mean to sound harsh. Mr. Pappas is good company. There's nobody who can tell a better story. But sometimes that's what worries me. I believe what he tells us about investments is no more truthful than those make-believe stories he shares with us." The older woman leaned back, folded her arms, and waited. There was little doubt she expected some sort of response.

Zanna remained uncertain how she should reply. She chased the crumbs of her cinnamon roll around the plate with her fork. Finally, she looked up and met Viola's stare. "There's likely reason for concern, Viola. Especially since Mr. Pappas hasn't repaid Bessie's loan. At this point, my only suggestion would be to pray and follow God's leading."

Viola finished the last sip of her tea and gave a firm nod. "Praying is always good advice, and I'll see where the Lord leads me on this one. But if He has plans on my following Mr. Pappas's financial advice, it's going to take a thunderbolt to move me." She chuckled as she picked up her gloves and carefully inserted her fingers into them to avoid tearing the lace edging.

"Thank you for joining me, Viola. We don't get to visit often enough." Zanna enjoyed spending time with all three of the Rochester sisters. They were as different as day and night, yet each one possessed admirable qualities. Together they could be quite a handful, but alone, each was a delight.

After bidding Zanna good-bye, Viola pushed up from her chair and turned toward the door. She'd taken only a few steps when she stopped and returned to the table. She leaned close to Zanna's ear. "Promise me you'll not repeat a word of our conversation to my sisters—or anyone else, for that matter. I don't want Mr. Pappas to think I'm speaking ill of him until I'm completely certain he's a scoundrel."

Zanna grasped the old woman's hand. "Your secrets are safe with me."

Yet if he were indeed a scoundrel, did she dare keep such information from Lucy, or perhaps more importantly, Nico?

CHAPTER
19

Markos and several other men had carried Felix to the doctor's office on a makeshift stretcher and then returned to help unload the three boats. Once they'd completed the task and the sponges had been delivered to the warehouse, Nico, Markos, and two of the pump handlers headed off toward the doctor's office again. The pump handlers repeated their apologies as the four of them strode through town. As for Markos, he appeared quite sullen.

Nico slowed his step and came alongside the diver. "Is it Felix's condition that has you brooding? You haven't said two words since we left the warehouse."

Markos kicked at a pebble and sent it skittering down the sidewalk. "No. I mean, I hope he doesn't have any lasting effects from the dive, but that isn't what I've been thinking about."

"Care to tell me what's troubling you?" Nico gave the man a sidelong glance.

Nico and Markos had never been close—not like Nico was with some of the other divers—but Markos and Felix seemed to share a bond. One that would have caused Markos to be overwrought by what had happened to his fellow diver.

189

"I feel like you don't trust the crew of the *Anastasi*. You worry more about the size of our harvest than anything else. We don't go out to the Gulf with thoughts of failure. You may not believe me, but we want to do as well as the crews on the *Crete* and *St. Nicolas*."

"All right." Nico rubbed his jawline. "Try to put yourself in my position, Markos. During your initial sailings, the harvests your crew brought back were excellent. Then something happened. Something I don't understand. When I ask questions, I receive conflicting answers from the divers and the captain. The rest of the crew won't give me any answers at all. What am I to think? How am I to trust? Who am I to believe?"

Markos frowned. "Felix and I have spoken the truth. It's the captain who's misleading you. He goes off in a different direction every time we sail."

Nico remained skeptical about whether he was hearing the whole truth, though he'd become doubtful of the captain, as well. "I think the only way to gain a better understanding of what's happening is for me to go out with the *Anastasi* on her next voyage. And with Felix unable to dive, I can take his place."

The diver's mouth fell open. "B-but . . . you shouldn't be diving. If something happened to you, who would take charge of the business? None of us would want that woman ordering us around. There would be a mutiny—we'd return to Greece if she insisted on operating the company. You shouldn't consider going out in the Gulf, Nico."

"I need to stop here. Miss Krykos must accompany us in order to interpret. I don't think any of us will be able to understand the doctor."

Moments later, Nico returned with Zanna at his side. As they continued onward, he nudged Markos. "What were you saying?"

Markos shook his head. "Not now. We can talk later."

Nico didn't argue. Instead he detailed for Zanna what had happened to Felix as they hurried to the doctor's office. Once they arrived, Nico led Zanna and the men into the office.

The bell over the front door jangled, and Lucy stepped from an adjoining office. She smiled at the group. "Thank you for coming along, Zanna. I want the men to understand what I have to tell them." She directed her attention to the men. "I'm pleased you have come to inquire after your friend."

Nico peered over Zanna's head, attempting to gain a view into the examination room, but to no avail. "What can you tell us? Will he regain his sight? Was his hearing affected?"

Though Felix hadn't mentioned any pain in his ears, Nico knew the increased water pressure could have caused his eardrums to rupture.

Lucy shook her head. "He complains of no problems with his hearing, and I didn't note any, although I'm not certain he's being forthright with me. His primary concern is whether he can dive again, not that he can hear." She frowned at Nico. "A fact I find most disturbing."

Nico took a backward step as Zanna related what had been said. The doctor glared at him as though he were responsible for instilling such an idea among his men. "I find that information worrisome, as well. Ask any of my crew members and they will tell you I have placed them under strict rules regarding their diving habits. I discourage any behaviors that would put my men at risk."

One of the pump handlers bobbed his head. "That's true, Doctor. I've never worked for another sponger who enforces as many rules as Nico." He glanced about. "For all of us, not just the divers. He wants us all to be safe."

"That's good to know, and I hope that Felix truly experienced an accidental drop-off and that he wasn't jeopardizing his own health to meet some quota or other expectation."

Nico swallowed hard. Had something he said caused the men to believe he'd placed an unobtainable expectation upon them?

Had Felix remained underwater and then accidentally fallen into deeper waters because he had hoped to meet that expectation? Nico didn't want to believe that was the situation, but the thought gave him pause.

Nico did his best to push the thought aside for the moment. "How does Felix fare? Is he able to return to camp with us, or does he need to remain in your care?"

"I've put ointment on his eyes and bandaged them, though I don't know whether what I've done will be of any help. He has complained of some pain in his ribs, so I've bound them. The most I can say is that my treatment won't hurt him in any way. I've never encountered a medical condition such as this, so I relied upon prayer, God's guidance, and an old medical book that proved to be of no use at all." She pressed her palms down the front of her skirt. "I do hope I'm not going to be presented with other medical conditions such as this."

"Oh, it can get lots worse than what you saw this morning, Doctor." The pump handler tightened his lips into a thin line. "My pa was a diver, and he got a terrible case of the bends. He was paralyzed and died a month after. He made me promise to never become a diver."

Nico waved the man to silence. "That's enough. I don't think the doctor needs to hear all the details." He forced a small smile. "That's why I tell my men to follow the rules. If they don't, they can end up with the squeeze or the bends, and most times there's no recovery. Being out on the boats isn't for those of faint heart."

"Or those who are wise and wish to live a long and fruitful life." The doctor folded her arms across her waist. "In answer to your earlier question, I think Felix should remain here—at least for a time. I must be certain he doesn't develop further problems." She hesitated a moment. "I don't know what will happen to his sight, but rest and prayer would be beneficial."

By the time Nico returned to camp, the other crew members were either fishing or relaxing in their makeshift cabins. The men had developed a routine since they'd begun their new life. While at the camp, they divided up the chores. There were those who went out and fished and those who prepared the meal once the fishermen returned. For his part, Nico made certain to purchase the necessary staples the men would need for their meals.

Several men were returning from the beach and held aloft the fish they'd caught. "Time for the cooks to get out of their beds and fix our supper while we sleep," one of the men called.

Upon catching sight of Markos, the fishermen came running. Their inquiries about Felix and his well-being rained down like hail in a storm.

Markos nodded toward Nico. "You can give the men the doctor's report. I'm not so good with words."

Nico didn't argue, though he was taken aback. Markos had never been one to avoid stating his opinion or speaking in front of others. Perhaps the accident weighed more heavily upon Markos than he'd exhibited at the doctor's office. For sure, Markos was a man who would never want to show any emotion to the other crew members.

A somber mood pervaded the camp while Nico gave the medical report. He followed the report with a request that the men pray for Felix, along with another warning to follow the rules. The men agreed to pray, while his words about the rules only resulted in a host of groans from the men. "Following the rules won't change things when it's an accident, Nico," one of the men called out.

Nico didn't want to argue with the man. Instead he settled on a roughhewn bench and let the men talk among themselves while he wrestled with his own thoughts. Before sailing from Greece, he knew they would be faced with unforeseen difficulties, but they'd been fortunate and he'd become complacent. This was the first tragedy he'd encountered. There had been the waterspouts on their first venture, yet that hadn't resulted in injury to any of the men.

This was different, however. If Felix didn't recover, his family would have no source of income. Had he made a mistake bringing the men to a place so far from their families?

He didn't know how much time had passed before he felt a nudge and one of the men handed him a bowl of fish stew. Moments later, Mr. Pappas sat down beside him. "No sense letting one incident make you question your decision to come here."

Nico startled. "How did you know what I was thinking?"

"Just a guess. You seem to assume responsibility for everything that happens to these men. A fine attribute for a man so young."

"I don't feel young, especially when something like this happens." He took a bite of the stew and savored the rich flavor. The men had become excellent cooks over the past months. "I've many decisions to make. On our way to the doctor's office, Markos confided that the crew of the *Anastasi* thinks I don't trust them." He shrugged. "Yet how can I trust a group of men who will not tell me the truth?"

"Sometimes it takes an outsider to unearth the truth. I told you earlier that I would speak to them. I want to help. Besides, in some ways, my future rests in your hands, too."

Nico's stomach clenched at the comment. The last thing he wanted was another human being dependent upon his ability to operate this sponging business. "What do you mean? How is that possible?"

Mr. Pappas shrugged. "Now that my New York clients are stocking your sponges, they want nothing else, and neither do their customers. So you see, I need your men to continue harvesting the same quality sponges my customers have become accustomed to receiving." Mr. Pappas wiped the corners of his mouth. "I don't promise I'll be able to solve the problem, but I'll do my best."

"Thank you. I'll be grateful for anything you can do." Though he tried to calm his fears, the humidity wrapped around him like a thick blanket that threatened to suffocate him. "Please help me, Lord." Nico's prayer was no more than a whisper on the wind, yet it was the most he could offer right now.

Throughout the evening, Mr. Pappas worked his way through the men, particularly those who sailed on the *Anastasi*. Nico had taken note that Mr. Pappas took a seat beside Markos, and they talked in hushed tones.

Later in the evening, when the men pulled out their instruments, Mr. Pappas once again joined them, although he didn't appear to be enjoying himself. In truth, he clenched his jaw until it twitched. Nico raked his fingers through his unruly hair. It was obvious Mr. Pappas hadn't fared well in his discussions with the crew.

As the night wore on, the men took to their beds, and Mr. Pappas bid them all good-night. Nico remained by the campfire, praying for Felix, praying for the men and their families, and praying for a resolution to his problems. His head was throbbing when he finally strode toward his cabin. Without sleep he'd be of no use come morning.

Nico neared his lean-to, then stopped at the sound of a hissing noise. He held his breath and listened. A snake? He hesitated. There it was again. He glanced around.

"Nico. Over here." The urgent whisper came from a stand of oaks draped with low-hanging moss. "It's me. Adelfo."

Nico narrowed his eyes. Shafts of moonlight wove their way through the moss and outlined the shadowy figure of Mr. Pappas. Nico wended his way across the path and into the stand of trees. Strange, he thought Mr. Pappas had already gone back to the hotel. He hoped the older man had been on the lookout for alligators before selecting this spot for a private chat. It bordered the marsh and wasn't particularly free from danger.

When he neared the older man, he leaned close. "I'm surprised to see you out here. When you departed a short time ago, I thought you'd seek me out tomorrow and we'd talk."

"It's better we speak tonight. The men will be around town until they sail again. Any one of them could overhear us talking and I wouldn't want that to happen." He shifted his weight. "Besides, you may need some time to consider what I'm about to tell you."

Nico inhaled a deep breath and leaned against one of the oaks. "Go ahead. I'm listening."

"I spoke with Markos at length—and other members of the crew, as well."

"And?"

"They're unhappy about you taking over for Felix on the *Anastasi* the next time she sails."

"Why would they be unhappy? I want to go along and examine the sponge beds in the area."

Mr. Pappas nodded. "From what I could gather, both Markos and Felix had given their word to Theo, Markos's brother, that when a diving position opened, he'd be next in line. If you step in and take Felix's place, Theo will believe they lied to him. Markos knows his brother will be angry with him."

The stew that had tasted so good a short time ago now roiled in Nico's stomach. "I don't know how they think they would decide who was next in line for any job. They aren't in charge of assigning positions, or anything else for that matter. I can't believe they'd tell Theo such a thing."

"You know how men can be," Mr. Pappas said with a sigh. "They want to act as though they have some authority. It makes them feel important. And now with Felix unable to dive, Theo is ready to take his place." The older man stayed him with his hand. "Before you oppose the idea, Nico, give it some consideration. Markos tells me that Theo is experienced and was diving in Greece, but that he gave up his position as a diver so he could come to America."

Nico nodded. "I had already filled the diving positions, but there isn't a better lifeline tender than Theo. Both Felix and Markos trusted him more than anyone else, but now Markos wants him to dive?"

"That's what he told me. I didn't ask about the—" he hesitated— "what did you call it? Life tender?"

"Lifeline tender. A signal line or lifeline is attached to the end of the diver's waist cinch. It's the only means of communication between the tender and the diver. The diver can tell the tender what he needs by specific pulls on the line. The tender is also careful to make sure the line doesn't get tangled when the diver is moving along the bottom. A good lifeline tender is as important as any diver."

Mr. Pappas tipped his head to the side. "From what you've explained, I would have to agree. But Markos tells me that the wages received by divers are greater than the wages paid his brother—is that right?"

"The payment system here is the same as in Greece. The men are paid a percentage of what we get at auction. Divers receive a higher percentage than line tenders. Theo knew his wages would be less than his brother's when he signed on to come here. If he didn't want to accept the lesser wage, he should have remained at home where he could dive."

"He's young and eager. I think it would be wise to let him dive the next time the *Anastasi* sails. It would create goodwill among the men and show you trust them. If you insist on going on their next outing, it may emphasize your lack of confidence in the crew." Mr. Pappas tugged at the tip of his mustache. "The decision is yours, of course, but I've listened to the men and believe my advice is sound."

Nico thanked him for his efforts. "I'm not completely convinced, but I'll consider what you've told me before I make my final decision."

The moonlight revealed a sheen of perspiration on the older man's face. "Give your decision careful thought, Nico. A content crew can prosper your company, while a discontent group can create chaos and failure."

There was more truth in the comment than Nico cared to admit. He must weigh his decision with great care.

CHAPTER
20

Nico dropped into a chair near the doors of the warehouse. He bowed and rested his forehead in his cupped palms. "Please, Lord. I need an answer." The days had passed all too quickly. His prayers had been fervent, yet he'd still been unable to decide if he should sail with the *Anastasi* or assign Theo to Felix's diving position. If only the men would be honest with him, he would set aside the past and they could begin anew.

A part of Nico believed the crew's trust in him as their leader would be restored if he remained onshore and assigned Theo as a diver on the *Anastasi*. Yet how was Nico's trust in the crew to be restored if they wouldn't speak the truth?

In his hope to discover what was happening during their voyages in the Gulf, Nico had privately spoken to each member of the *Anastasi*'s crew. Other than the captain and the divers, not one member of the crew would offer an opinion as to why their harvests had lessened. He didn't know if they'd been threatened by the captain or the divers—or if they simply desired to remain neutral—but it was strange they chose to remain silent.

He'd appealed to each man's conscience and duty as a provider to their families back in Greece. After all, when the sponges were sold, the crews' wages were a percentage of the harvest. Surely they wanted to increase their wages so they could save money and bring their families to America. Thus far, nothing he'd said had unlocked their lips or their consciences.

"There isn't much time, Lord. The boats sail tomorrow at dawn."

A hand pressed on his shoulder. He startled and whirled around.

Zanna smiled down at him. "Have you begun talking to yourself?"

He shook his head. "I was praying. I need to decide who will replace Felix when the *Anastasi* sails tomorrow."

"The men continue to withhold the truth from you?"

Like a sword swooshing through the air, her words hit their mark. "Other than the captain and divers, they choose to remain silent."

She looked down at him, her eyes revealing sadness—or was it pity? He didn't desire pity. He wanted an answer. Until now, Zanna had withheld any opinion on the matter. He'd not asked for one, and she'd remained as silent as his spongers. He wasn't certain why he hadn't asked . . . perhaps a matter of pride? Yet he'd come to value her ideas and judgment over these past months.

He gestured to an empty chair. "What about you? What do you think? Should I take Felix's place or should I assign Theo?"

She tipped her head to the side and met his gaze. "I don't know if I should offer my opinion. I'm a bit biased."

His mouth dropped open. "So you've talked to Mr. Pappas and think he's right?"

"Mr. Pappas?" She frowned and shook her head. "No, I've not spoken with him. What part does he play in all this?"

Nico detailed his recent conversation with the sponge buyer. Though her brow had furrowed several times while he spoke, Zanna hadn't interrupted. When he'd completed the tale, Nico's eyes darkened. "So? What do you think? Should I take his advice? I noticed you appeared concerned several times as I spoke. Do you have questions?"

She offered a delicate smile. "I do." She tapped her index finger on the arm of her chair. "First, I'm curious why the crew members were willing to talk to Mr. Pappas when they don't seem to want to express their feelings to you. They know you, while he's practically a stranger to them."

Nico returned her smile. "You're right, but I think it's because he is an outsider. He doesn't have anything to gain no matter what is decided. Besides, they didn't tell him what was happening out in the Gulf, which is what I truly would like to know. Instead they told him what Markos had already said to me—they think I don't trust them."

She frowned. "So they believed that by having Mr. Pappas argue their case on behalf of Theo, it would carry more weight than speaking to you on their own?"

"I think so. In some ways, it does help to have the opinion of an outsider like Mr. Pappas." He gestured back and forth between Zanna and himself. "We oversee and make decisions for the business, so the crew likely believes all decisions are for the benefit of the company, not for them. Mr. Pappas doesn't have a dog in the fight, so they think his words will carry more weight with me."

"And do they? Carry more weight? Because I don't think they should. Mr. Pappas doesn't know everything about the business or about sponging. The two of us are the ones who know what profits are made on the harvests from each boat." She nodded toward the water. "And you're the one who has knowledge about diving as well as the life-and-death situations the crews face out there."

"That's true, but I still think an outsider can be more objective."

"Perhaps. Although you can't be certain Mr. Pappas is truly objective."

There was a ring of anger in her words. What did that mean? She was speaking in riddles. Was she angry because he'd considered the older man's opinion before he asked for hers?

"Why wouldn't he be? Other than being able to purchase more sponges for his clients, what gain is there for him in any of this?"

She shrugged. "I don't know. Even so, you need to make your decision based upon your own knowledge rather than anything Mr. Pappas says. Is Theo a good diver? Do you trust his abilities? Is he known to follow the rules you've put in place? Would he take your direction above that of his brother or the other crew members? Is your presence needed on the boat more than in Tarpon Springs? Do you think that your questions will be answered if you're on board the *Anastasi* on her next sailing?"

Nico massaged his forehead. "I wanted answers, not more questions, but let me see if I can answer all that. Then perhaps the two of us will arrive at a solution. In answer to your first questions, yes, Theo is a good diver. Well trained, though he doesn't have quite as much experience as his brother. Second, I want to believe he would follow my rules and directions above those of any other crew member, but I want to believe that of all my men. I have no way to be certain. As to where I am needed the most, well, I'm not certain of that, either."

She nodded. "And if you sail with the *Anastasi*, do you think you'll finally discover who is telling the truth?"

"I have my doubts. The captain could tell me he's taking the boat to the same place he's always sailed, yet Markos could say the opposite." He ran a hand through his hair. "There's no easy answer. What do you think is best?"

"You could let Theo go with the boat when they sail tomorrow and see what kind of harvest they bring in. If it goes well, Theo could continue with the crew. You'll be giving them what they've asked for. If it doesn't go well, then you can go with them the next time. Before they depart, tell the crew that if their harvests remain poor and they continue to withhold the truth from you, you'll have to accompany them on future sailings."

"You continue to amaze me, Zanna." He met her gaze, his lips curving in an affectionate smile. "I believe God sent you at just the right time in answer to my prayer."

Her eyes widened. "My answer wasn't inspired, Nico. I simply weighed the possibilities of what might happen if you did or didn't assign Theo to the position."

He grasped her hand and gave it a gentle squeeze. "Perhaps that's true, but I believe God was at work when He sent you here this morning." He lifted her hand and pressed a kiss to her fingers. "Thank you."

The following morning, Zanna stood by Nico's side while the men prepared to sail. Throughout the night, she'd dissected the advice she gave Nico. She wanted to believe it had been God's will for her to speak to him, but she wasn't as certain. Still, if she'd been willing to break her promise to Viola, she would have told him that Mr. Pappas might have several dogs in this fight. Had her promise to keep Viola's disclosure secret been a mistake?

While she believed her advice to be sound and that Theo should dive, the fact that Mr. Pappas had provided the same advice gave her pause. She now questioned everything the man had ever said. Had he been attempting to raise funds and buy out Lucy even before he returned to Tarpon Springs? Viola thought he'd stayed away because he owed Bessie money, but now Zanna wasn't sure. Lucy would have taken a huge loss on the business if she could have sold it to him before that first harvest. Truth be told, she was still willing to rid herself of it. The thought nagged like an itch that needed to be scratched.

"Nico!"

Zanna shaded her eyes and caught sight of Mr. Pappas waving his hat and hurrying toward them. "Why is he here? The sale isn't until Friday."

Nico shrugged and waved at the white-suited figure. "I don't know. Maybe he had some other business." He grinned. "Maybe he's in love with one of those Rochester sisters."

Zanna gritted her teeth. "I don't think so. More likely he's come to see if you're following his advice."

Nico frowned at her. "Who can blame him for that?"

Zanna didn't like that Mr. Pappas was becoming more and more interested in the business—not just their day-to-day activities but the overall success of the company. Before she knew it, he'd secure funding and make Lucy an offer for the business. While Zanna knew it unfair to pass judgment on Mr. Pappas, something smelled fishy—and it wasn't today's catch.

"I'm glad I got here before the men sailed." Mr. Pappas gestured toward the boats.

His smile faded when Zanna leaned forward and pinned him with a hard stare. "Why was your arrival of such importance, Mr. Pappas? Our boats can sail whether you're in Tarpon Springs or not."

"Well, I wanted . . . I mean, Nico and I had discussed . . ." His words died on the wind as he directed an expectant look at Nico.

"I'm sure he was interested in knowing whether I was going to sail with the *Anastasi* or if I would be at the Exchange for Friday's bidding."

Mr. Pappas bobbed his head at Nico. "Exactly. I was hoping you'd remain in town."

Zanna frowned. "And why is that, Mr. Pappas?" Irritation soured her tone.

He cleared his throat. "There were a few things I wanted to discuss with Nico. Nothing that would interest you, Miss Krykos."

She looped her hand into the crook of Nico's arm. "Anything that interests Nico is of interest to me, Mr. Pappas, but right now neither of us has time to visit with you. As you can see, we're preparing for the departure of our boats."

He gave a slight nod before returning his hat to his head. "Good day, then, Miss Krykos. And, Nico, I'll talk to you later. I'm pleased to see you took my advice." That said, he turned on his heel and marched off.

Zanna squeezed Nico's arm. "If he comes to talk and it's about the business, I'd like to know what he has to say."

Nico smiled down at her. "He's likely more interested in gaining a look at the sponges before the other buyers than talking to me about anything that would interest you." He didn't give her an opportunity to respond before pulling from her grasp to untie one of the mooring lines. He glanced over his shoulder. "The boats are casting off and I need to help. We can talk another time."

Zanna forced a smile. "I'll be in my office." She offered a quick wave to Nico and the departing crew, although Nico was the only one to return her gesture. "They'll never accept me," she muttered before turning away.

But right now, that was the least of her problems.

Mr. Pappas sat down in the chair that Zanna had occupied a few hours earlier. "I don't think your young lady likes me very much."

"She is cautious and dedicated to making this business a success for Dr. Penrose." Nico did his best to avoid giving a direct answer, but Zanna's abrupt comments to the older man hadn't left him with much wiggle room.

"You are very diplomatic, Nico."

"I'm not sure what that means."

The older man chuckled. "It doesn't matter. First, I wanted to tell you again that I am heartened you took my advice." He patted his palm to his chest. "It's good to know that you trusted my counsel and understand it is my desire to help you and your men succeed in this new business venture."

"Thank you. I appreciate all you've done to make us feel at home in this new country."

Mr. Pappas removed a cigar from his jacket pocket. "Think nothing of it. Having the opportunity to spend time with you and the men has been a pleasure for me. Especially the music making." He grinned and rolled the cigar between his palms. "I have some exciting news, but I'd like you to keep it between the two of us until I am certain it's going to work out."

Nico's stomach clenched. He didn't want to keep secrets—not from Zanna, not from Dr. Penrose, and not from his men. "I'm not fond of secrets. Perhaps you shouldn't tell me until the news can be shared with others."

"I trust you to keep a secret for a short time. Anyway, I can't move forward with this unless you're interested in the idea." He didn't wait for Nico to object before he plunged forward. "I have several investors who are willing to put up a large sum of money toward purchasing additional boats and equipment. They want you to manage the operation."

Nico lifted his chin. "I couldn't possibly take such a position. It wouldn't be fair to Dr. Penrose. Working in two positions would create a conflict."

Pappas tapped the tip of his cigar on the desk. "If you're to become a success, you may need to set aside some of your high-minded principles. There are ways around most everything. Legal ways. I'm sure your lawyer lady friend knows all about finding ways in and out of such situations."

"Zanna would never agree to such an arrangement. Don't you see the problems that would arise in such a venture? Look at what has happened with the three boats I now oversee. Two are doing much better than the third. Even though it's untrue, one could argue I'm forcing the captain to take the *Anastasi* to poor sponge beds. Think what would happen if the boats were owned by different companies, with myself as manager of both." He shook his head. "No, it would never work. Besides, I would not be a part of creating competition for the doctor. I want her business to succeed."

Mr. Pappas crossed his arms over his chest. "Would you rather someone else come in and manage the competition?"

Nico shrugged. "I am not going to worry about such a thing.

First you need to have enough money. Then you would need to go through the same process as Mr. Penrose. Our arrangements took almost two years, and he had the funds. In two years, this business will be established and I'll be able to withstand any competition that comes into Tarpon Springs."

"I think you're making a mistake, Nico."

"Who can say for sure? Not me, but I do know I cannot accept your offer. If you have interested investors, why not buy out Dr. Penrose? She may still be willing to sell. Wouldn't that be the best option for you and your investors?"

"I'll pass along your suggestion, but I doubt they'll be interested. These are men who enjoy competition."

Nico arched his brows. "More than making money?"

"When you're already wealthy, it's competition rather than money that feeds the soul."

Nico shook his head. "Then they need to look elsewhere. I would never be a good fit for such business partners."

CHAPTER 21

As had become his custom, Nico stood on the dock awaiting the return of the boats. The crew had been out seven days, and he was eager to discover how they had fared. Before their departure, Nico had argued against a longer time in the Gulf. With a new diver on the *Anastasi*, he didn't want the boats out for too long. He had acquiesced and assigned Theo to Felix's diving position, but he'd refused the men's request to remain at sea for fourteen days. He wanted to be certain Theo could handle the diving position, and he wanted assurance the captain and crew of the *Anastasi* had followed his orders.

Against the objections of the captain and Markos, Nico had insisted the *Anastasi* remain within sight of the *Crete* or *St. Nicolas* while in the Gulf. He'd given the captain a choice, yet he didn't want the *Anastasi* off on her own this time—partially because this was the first time Theo would dive with this crew, and partially because the sponge beds would be similar for both boats.

The captain of the *Anastasi* had chosen to remain within sighting distance of the *Crete*. Nico hoped the captain had made that decision because the vessels were both second-class boats with the same number of divers and crew members, and not because the two captains were close friends. The wives of the two captains were related, and there was a family bond as well as a friendship between the men. Neither of them was friendly with the captain of the *St. Nicolas*. Nico thought they might harbor a tinge of jealousy since the *St. Nicolas* was a first-class boat. In Greece, the captain of a first-class boat commanded greater respect, although Nico doubted anyone in Tarpon Springs was aware of such a distinction.

He'd been on the dock only a short time when Zanna and Lucy approached. He waved in greeting and hoped the doctor's appearance didn't signify Felix's condition had worsened.

"I was certain I'd find you here." Zanna's cheerful smile encouraged him.

"My favorite position when the boats are due to return." He tipped his cap to the ladies, then directed his attention to Lucy. "I hope your appearance is only because you are curious about your sponging business and not due to any worsening in Felix's condition."

"Felix is doing a little better than I'd expected. All things considered, he's very fortunate." She glanced at Zanna. "Zanna stopped by my office and said she was on her way to the docks, so I decided to come along. I believe Felix could return to the camp, but he'll need someone to assist him. Although he wanted to try it on his own, I was against that idea. I pointed out he might stumble or fall and that could cause further difficulty with his recovery. He was unhappy with my decision, yet he agreed to wait until someone could come and aid him."

"Of course. I'm pleased for the good report. Once the boats have arrived and are unloaded, I'll send Markos to fetch Felix. They're good friends."

"No need to do that. I'm more than willing to lend a hand."

All three of them turned to see Mr. Pappas standing behind them on the dock. But it was Zanna who frowned and took a step in his direction. "You certainly make a silent approach."

His smile didn't quite reach his eyes. Nico was certain Zanna's words had struck a chord with the older man. Nico moved to her side and lightly grasped her arm. He'd prefer she say nothing more right now. An argument would serve no purpose, and the boats would soon arrive. Yet he, too, wondered at the sudden appearance of the older man. Of late, Mr. Pappas was in Tarpon Springs far more often than in the past, perhaps because he was gathering more information for his investors.

Nico met the older man's gaze. "Did you speak with Dr. Penrose about your investors?"

Mr. Pappas gave a dismissive wave. "They've rejected the idea of investing in the sponging business, so there's no need to trouble the doctor with details of our discussion."

Nico pushed his cap to the back of his head. "So soon? Even before asking for a selling price?" He shook his head. "They're going to miss a good opportunity. If she decides to sell later, I'm sure the price will go much higher."

Mr. Pappas shrugged. "What can I say? These wealthy men are quickly distracted by every opportunity that comes their way. Yesterday it was sponges; today it's something else."

Lucy tugged on Zanna's sleeve. "What are they talking about? I heard Nico mention my name, but then he and Mr. Pappas started speaking in Greek, even though Nico's English is much improved. I don't think they want me to understand what they're saying."

"I'll tell you later. It's not important." Zanna turned toward the water. "Look! The boats are in sight."

"I hope the report of this harvest will be as good as the news you gave me about Felix." Nico looked at Mr. Pappas. "If you want to assist Felix from the doctor's office down to the camp, I'm sure he'd be thankful. Otherwise I'll have Markos help him after the boats return."

"Of course," Mr. Pappas said. "We fellow countrymen need to stick together and help one another whenever we can." He withdrew a cigar from his jacket. "I'll be back a little later. I'm curious to see if the *Anastasi* had a successful harvest."

Lucy nudged Zanna as the older man departed. "He certainly has an interest in the business. Maybe he'll soon gain the necessary financing to purchase the company."

A short time later, Nico caught the line one of the crew members of the *Anastasi* tossed to him on the dock. From the smiles and cheers, he wanted to believe it had been a successful journey. Still, he hesitated to celebrate just yet.

When he caught the attention of the captain, Nico cupped his hands to his mouth. "Do you have a good report for me?"

The captain bobbed his head up and down. "You will be very pleased!" His shouted response was music to Nico's ears.

He glanced at Zanna. "Finally. A good report."

Lucy smiled when Zanna repeated the news. "In that case, I believe I'll go back to my office. Even if I don't have any patients waiting, there's always something that requires my attention."

Zanna chuckled. "Watch out for the Rochester sisters. I'm sure they'll whisk you away to some committee meeting if they see you out and about."

"No doubt you're right about that." Lucy waved and bid them both farewell before she hurried off.

While the crew tied off the boat, Nico stood by Zanna's side. "I'm most thankful for the good news, but the *Anastasi*'s success does raise some questions."

"I thought the same thing," Zanna said. "Do you think Felix might have been the cause of the problem? Perhaps his diving abilities aren't as good as they used to be. I doubt Markos and the other men would have wanted to tell you that."

"Possibly, but I myself trained Felix several years ago. He's been diving longer than some of the other men. Then again, he may have suffered some injuries he's hiding from me. If that's the case, his success would be more limited. Rather than cause problems for the entire crew, I'd like to think he would speak up if he'd been suffering from some physical problem before that last dive." Nico hiked a shoulder. "Instead of a problem with Felix, I wondered if my order to remain near the *Crete* was the reason they were successful on this voyage."

"Ah, but who can say for sure?" Once again Mr. Pappas appeared behind them without a sound. "You worry too much, Nico. Just be thankful your boats have all three come in with a good harvest."

Nico gave the older man a dismissive wave and headed toward the other boats. "I am paid to worry. Making this business a success is why I am here." He turned to Zanna. "I'll see you later. Your mother has invited me to supper this evening." He saw the surprise register in her eyes and grinned. Apparently, Mrs. Krykos hadn't mentioned the invitation to her daughter.

She tipped her head and met his eyes. Her brow furrowed ever so slightly as though she thought perhaps he was joking with her. When he said nothing further, she gave a nod. "Yes, of course. I'll see you at supper." She lifted her hand in a quick wave and strode off.

As Nico neared the *St. Nicolas*, he glanced over his shoulder to see if Mr. Pappas had followed him, but the man was deep in conversation with Markos. Odd. If Mr. Pappas was going to form a friendship with one of the men, wouldn't he prefer one of the captains who was more his own age? Nico stared at the two men. They stood with their heads close together and furtively glanced around when anyone drew near. Perhaps the investors Mr. Pappas had spoken of hadn't backed out after all. Maybe the older man thought Markos could take charge of the new operation his investors had wanted to form. Nico exhaled a long breath. Were Zanna's suspicions wearing off on him? Maybe Mr. Pappas simply wanted Markos to know Felix was doing well and could return to the campsite.

Nico pushed thoughts of Mr. Pappas from his mind and headed

toward the *St. Nicolas*. He took bundle after bundle of sponges from the men, hefting them onto the dock. Sweat trickled between his shoulder blades. He'd need to wash up before supper.

A smile tugged at his lips. Delicious food with delightful company. Perhaps he'd have time to pick a bouquet of flowers for Mrs. Krykos—and for Zanna. Or maybe that would be too presumptuous. Zanna wanted everyone to believe she was a no-nonsense, tough businesswoman.

But he knew the truth. There was more to her than just a lovely lawyer. There was an intelligent, beautiful lady who would do anything she could to help her friends.

Deciding she should change out of her walking suit before dinner, Zanna hurried home earlier than usual. Her mother was dicing vegetables into an iron kettle when she entered the house.

Her mother glanced at her and then at the clock. "Zanna! You're early." She blew out a breath that caused a loose strand of hair to ripple over her forehead. "Seeing you made me think I was behind schedule with my supper preparations." Her brow crinkled into tiny worry lines. "Why are you home already? Is something wrong? Are you ill?"

"No." She shook her head. "Nico told me you invited him to supper tonight. I . . . I thought you might need an extra pair of hands to help."

"She already has two extra hands to help." Yayá rested her elbows on the table and wiggled her fingers in the air. "Right here. Two hands that help prepare the meals every day. Am I right, Halina?" She pinned Zanna's mother with her dark eyes.

"Yes, of course. You help me with everything. I don't know how I would manage without you." Zanna's mother smiled at the old woman.

Yayá shook her head. "You might fool your mother, but you

don't fool me. You came home to make yourself pretty before that young Greek arrives for supper." She tapped her finger alongside her right eye. "I can see that look in your eyes. You want him to notice you." She cackled. "Your mother didn't invite him so he would take notice of you. Your mother and father have already said they want you to marry a good Greek man who will be at home by your side every night. Not one who is out diving for sponges."

She wanted to argue with her grandmother that Nico seldom was out at sea and that he was a good Greek man, but such a remark would only cause an argument. Besides, there was no reason to create a problem where one didn't exist.

Zanna stepped to her mother's side and folded her arms across her waist. "There are fifty Greek spongers at the campsite, so why did you invite Nico to supper?"

Her mother shrugged. "Because your papa asked me to."

Her mother's reply only begged more questions, but Zanna knew that anything further on the subject would need to come from her father. Not because her mother wouldn't divulge the information, but because she wouldn't have inquired. Over the years, her parents had developed many routines in their lives, and this was one of them. Her father would make his request known, and her mother would set an extra place at the table without any discussion.

Zanna stepped around the wooden table. "Since you don't need my help right now, I'll go and change out of my suit."

"Aha!" Her grandmother's shout brought Zanna to an immediate halt. "I told you she had eyes for that diver. Now she goes to change into something she thinks will make her prettier for him. Maybe a bow in your hair or a dress with ruffles, ya?" She pointed her paring knife at Zanna's mother. "I told you she would think the Greek was coming to call on her."

Zanna hurried from the kitchen before her grandmother could say anything more. The revelation that her father was the one who had invited Nico dashed any romantic thoughts she might have had. She knew her father. This offer of supper had something to do with business. Perhaps Atticus had changed his mind and was once again expressing a desire to go to sea. If so, her father might ask Nico to discourage Atticus. One thing was certain: Her father wasn't interested in matchmaking—he'd leave that to Yayá.

When she returned from her room, wearing a dress of white-dotted swiss with a lace-trimmed bodice, her grandmother grunted and bobbed her head. "I told you so. She's got more lace on that dress than you had on your wedding gown, Halina."

Zanna could feel the heat rise in her cheeks. "I change into a dress for supper every evening, Yayá. Don't make this into something more than it is."

"You don't change into a fancy dress to eat supper every night. You wear that dress when you go to church or for a special occasion. So, I am left to think you have decided tonight is special." She pursed her lips together and patted her white hair. "And I see you fixed your hair, too."

Thankfully the door burst open before she was required to respond. One by one, Atticus, Homer, her father, and Nico stepped inside. She was surprised to see Nico with her father and brothers. She'd expected him to arrive alone. Had her father asked Nico to meet with him before supper? If so, it was strange that he had mentioned receiving an invitation for supper only from her mother.

Zanna was quick to notice he'd donned a clean shirt and pants, and his curly hair had been recently combed. Moments later he looked up and caught her staring at him. Was that a wink or only her imagination? An unexpected rush of heat raced up her neck.

Her father lifted his nose and sniffed. "I am guessing we are having lamb and vegetables. Am I right?"

Her mother gestured toward the other room. "The table is set. It won't take me much longer." She glanced at Zanna. "Fill the bowls and carry them to the other room, please."

The talk around the dinner table was jovial, and Nico was especially pleased to tell about the latest harvest. "All three of the boats carried full loads this time. Now I must pray they continue to do so." He nodded at his plate. "A wonderful meal, Mrs. Krykos."

Zanna's mother smiled. "Thank you. I'm glad you like it. I only wish Zanna would learn to cook."

He nodded. "Every man hopes to marry a good cook, but love is most important, don't you think?"

Yayá cleared her throat. "Love is good until the stomach rumbles for food. Right, Jurek?"

Her father chuckled. "Right. Pass me the lamb, Zanna."

Nico looked across the table at Zanna. "We had other good news today, didn't we, Zanna?" She bobbed her head, and he continued. "Felix, one of our divers who suffered a diving injury, is doing better."

"What kind of injury? Zanna told us nothing about a hurt diver." Her mother gave her a suspicious look. "Were you trying to hide something from us?"

Zanna shrugged. "No, but I don't think to tell you everything that happens on the docks. You don't know Felix, and it slipped my mind."

Nico met her fleeting gaze. "An injury to his eyes, but Dr. Penrose is encouraged by his progress. He returned to the camp today."

She'd been holding her breath while he answered, and now slowly exhaled. Thankfully he'd realized she didn't want him to dwell on Felix's injury. Her parents already considered sponging dangerous work, and discussing Felix's injury would only reinforce their belief. Besides, if Nico ever asked to court her, the danger of diving would provide her father with an excuse. Even though Nico seldom went out with the boats, the risk involved still existed.

She needed to change the course of their conversation to a neutral topic. "Did you have something special you wanted to ask Nico, Papa? Something I couldn't have answered about the business? Is that why you invited him to supper?"

"I wanted to talk to him about building sponging boats." He took a bite of lamb, chewed it, and swallowed. "It is not important."

Using her fork, she pushed the roasted vegetables to the side of her plate. She knew her father. Even if she pursued the matter, he'd say nothing more. She decided to ask Nico later.

During the remainder of the meal, they talked of Greece and questioned Nico about the town where he had lived. Afterward, the men gathered outside and talked some more while Zanna, her grandmother, and her mother cleared and washed the dishes. When they'd finished, Zanna excused herself and went outside.

Her heart plummeted when she stepped outdoors. As her eyes adjusted to the darkness, she saw Atticus and Homer, then her father. Had Nico already left? Without saying good-bye? When she turned to go back into the house, she heard his voice. He'd been leaning against a tree, his body shadowed by the overhanging branches. She crossed the short distance and stopped near her brother's side.

Atticus, sitting on a tree stump, looked up at her. "Come to ruin the fun, have you?"

"Only if you've been attempting to convince Nico and Papa to let you go out on the boats again."

He tipped his head back and laughed. "No chance of that. I may be Greek, but I'm not the seafaring type."

Her father stood and gestured to Atticus and Homer. "Come on, boys. If I know my daughter, I think she wants to question Nico about those boats I mentioned at supper."

Once they were out of earshot, Nico stepped close to her side and grinned down at her. "Was your father right? Is it the boats you wanted to know about, or did you just want to be alone with me?"

Her breath caught at his nearness, and she willed her heart to quit beating so quickly. "I do want to know about the boats."

"Nothing to worry over. Mr. Pappas came and talked to your father about the cost of building several sponging boats; then today he came back and said he wasn't interested after all. He said his investors had backed out. I think it must be true. Besides, I can't worry over what he might or might not do. He's a strange man. One minute I believe he's my friend and has my best interests at heart, the next minute I'm not so sure."

A breeze filled the air with a sweet honeyed scent. "I don't know what to make of him, either. I do agree that it's difficult to know whether he has your best interests at heart."

He lifted her chin with his fingertips and looked into her eyes. "What about you, Zanna? Do you have my best interests at heart?"

Zanna's pulse beat like the waves against the shore on a windy day. She opened her mouth to answer him, but the words were slow in coming.

"Zanna!" Yayá shouted from the doorway. The older woman pressed a hand to her forehead and peered into the dim light, searching. "Where have you gone? Has that handsome man left yet? Did he tell you that you look pretty?"

Heat rushed up Zanna's neck and into her cheeks, and she thanked God for the dim light. "I'm so sorry."

Nico chuckled, cupped Zanna's cheek for a moment, and then let his hand fall to her wrist. "You do look pretty, Zanna." He grinned. "And the ability to cook isn't really that important to me."

With that, he slipped away into the night. She pressed her hands to her lips and sucked in a breath. Had Nico really implied what she thought he had?

Practicality told her she shouldn't make too much of his words, yet her heart didn't seem willing to listen to reason. She leaned against the tree's rough bark, relishing the warmth bubbling inside her. Everything would have to return to normal between them tomorrow, but tonight she could simply be pretty.

CHAPTER 22

Nico settled at the desk with Zanna near his side. Since his arrival in Florida, he'd been diligent in his study of the English language, but Zanna insisted it was important he acquire even greater skills. Already he could speak and read more than the other men. His accounting skills, however, still needed attention. Zanna wanted him to become knowledgeable enough to review the ledgers and understand if they were working at a profit or a loss and also know the financial changes occurring within the company week by week.

Going over the accounts made him long to hear the squawking of gulls and the lapping of waves against the side of a sponging boat. Not that he minded sitting next to Zanna. Her appearance could rival any view of the rising sun over the Gulf. Yet staring at these figures made his head ache.

Since their time together after supper the other night, Zanna had softened. She seemed less determined to prove herself at every turn, but when she felt strongly about something, she remained relentless.

Nico sighed when Zanna tapped the page with her fingertip. "I know you don't find this interesting, but try to concentrate. Otherwise we'll be here much longer."

He rested his elbow on the desk and cupped his chin in his palm. "I find these figures tedious. I don't ever plan to take charge of this part of the business, so why do you think it's so important that I learn?"

"You must understand the financial condition of the company, Nico. How will you know if you can afford to purchase another boat or hire more men and expand the company? Or how will you know when costs exceed income and you must decrease the size of the business?" She placed her hand atop the page she was studying. "If you don't know the company's finances, you can't make sound decisions. You need to be able to speak with knowledge and authority to anyone who wants to conduct business with us."

"That's why I have you, isn't it? When I arrived, you told me Lucy placed you in charge of the business. I oversee the boats and my men, and you are responsible for the books and contracts." He leaned back and raked his fingers through his hair. "I don't ask you to go out on the boats and learn to dive or operate the pumps, and you shouldn't expect me to learn how to write numbers in a book."

"But how will you know when—"

He waved a dismissive hand. "If I want to know whether we have enough money for a new boat, or if we can purchase more diving equipment, I will ask you."

"And what if I'm not here?"

His brow furrowed. "Where else would you be? This is your home. If you are gone visiting for a while, then I will wait for your return. There is nothing so urgent that I can't wait to ask you." He tilted his head. "At least nothing I can think of at the moment." When it appeared she could think of no rebuttal, he leaned across the desk. "But since you are here right now, there is one question I want to ask about the money."

"You see? This part of the business is important."

She straightened her shoulders as if she'd bested him, and he laughed—a loud belly laugh. "I never said it wasn't important. I said only that I don't want to learn about it. However, I do want to know if there's enough money that I could promise the men a celebration of some sort. All three boats have brought in full loads each time they went out this month. I think this is something to celebrate. Don't you agree?"

Zanna nodded. "I think that's a good idea. A celebration would be a wonderful way to show how much you appreciate their hard work."

"How much *we* appreciate their hard work—not just me, but you and the doctor, too. She owns the business, and even though she doesn't come around much, I think it would be wise if she attended, as well."

A smile spread across Zanna's face. "I'm sure Lucy would be happy to attend, and even help us prepare." Her eyes shone with excitement. "Why don't you tell the men that if they return with a full harvest the next time they go out, there will be a celebration waiting for them? That way, there will be plenty of time to prepare something special."

There was little doubt that Zanna was thinking of something much larger than what he'd had in mind. The thought pleased him. Knowing she was eager to do something special for the men warmed his heart.

"I can see you already have some ideas." He grinned. "I didn't miss that look in your eyes."

"What look?" She widened her eyes until they were the size of two saucers, then pointed at them. "You mean this look?" She dropped her hand onto the desk and laughed.

He nodded. "Yes, that look."

"Well, I was thinking it would be great fun if we went out to the lighthouse at Anclote Key and had a picnic. We could enlist my mother and Yayá to help cook. The men could bring their instruments so there would be music and dancing. There's a nice beach for those who want to swim, or they could fish off the dock. It could be a day of good food and relaxation." She smiled and pushed the ledger toward him. "And there is enough money that if you wanted to give each man a small bonus, we could afford to do so."

"Only if the doctor agrees. The money we would be using for a bonus belongs to her."

"You're right, of course," Zanna said, "although I think Lucy would agree to it."

"I'm not so sure. The only time she speaks of the business is when she thinks she might have the opportunity to sell it. A picnic and extra money for the workers might not appeal to her."

"I'll talk to her. Lucy is very generous. If her father had confided in her so that she hadn't been taken by surprise, I believe she would have been more accepting of what's happened."

"That isn't our fault. And even you said she should have taken care of her father's estate much earlier. I understand she wants to use her time healing sick people. But I hope she'll be careful about who she sells the business to. I won't work for an owner who isn't honest."

"I don't think that's anything we need to worry about right now. If any buyers had made an offer, Lucy would have told me, so set your mind at ease and let's finish going over the ledgers. Later I can think about the picnic and celebration party."

Nico leaned back in his chair and crossed his arms over his chest. "I'll go over these ledgers again on one condition."

"What condition?"

He lifted his brows. "That you'll dance with me at the party."

"Oh, the things I must suffer through to keep Lucy's business afloat." Her eyes sparkled. She put on a stern face and tapped the books. "Now, no more distracting me with waggling eyebrows. I'm too smart for that."

He did his best to concentrate, but his focus kept shifting from the page to Zanna's ruby lips. Then she leaned close and their arms would brush or he'd feel her breath on his cheek. It was maddening.

At last, Zanna shoved the ledgers aside. "We'll study these again another day. You're not even paying attention."

"I . . . I tried." He rubbed the back of his neck and drew in a long breath. He had no intention of admitting her proximity had driven him to distraction. They had to maintain the ability to work together. That was paramount. If Zanna thought for a minute that his feelings could put Lucy's business in jeopardy, she'd squash any possibilities between them. "I promise to study the ledgers more—when I'm alone."

The offer of a celebration had been met with the men's promises of more sponges than they'd ever before harvested. In addition, Lucy had lauded the idea as a great way to show her appreciation for all the men had done since arriving in Tarpon Springs. She'd even talked about higher bonuses for the men than Nico had suggested. The men set sail with high hopes.

As their days at sea passed, anticipation onshore mounted. The men were expected to return in four more days. Zanna, her mother, and Yayá had been hard at work deciding which foods should be served and what preparations could be completed in advance. Even Lucy had agreed to lend a hand on several occasions, although Yayá had dismissed both Lucy and Zanna from cooking duties. She'd declared their lack of skill in the kitchen would only delay the preparations. Neither Lucy nor Zanna argued the point. Instead, Yayá put them to work locating and collecting tablecloths, blankets, and other items to make the festivities comfortable. Nico decided they could use all three boats to transport the men and food to the island on the day of the festivities.

Lucy, Nico, and Zanna met and agreed upon the bonus that would be given to each man. Zanna had withdrawn the funds from the bank, and this afternoon she and Nico would divide the money into individual envelopes that would be distributed among the crews. She was eager to begin. Few things gave her more joy than handing someone an unexpected gift.

A smile graced her expression as she entered the warehouse with the money tucked into her bag. She raised the bag and gestured to Nico. "I stopped at the bank on my way. There should be enough envelopes in the desk, so I think we can get to work."

"This will be the most enjoyable work I've done in a long time." He slid open the lower desk drawer and pulled out a stack of envelopes.

Zanna sat down in the chair beside him, and while Nico printed each man's name on an envelope, Zanna counted out the money. "Lucy said she would be more than happy to attend the picnic and offer her own thanks to the men."

He looked up from the envelope he was personalizing. "The men will be honored to have her attend. She's the owner of the company. Without her agreement, none of this would happen."

Minutes later, Zanna handed him a sealed envelope. "That's the last one."

Nico pushed up from his chair. "Let me put these in the safe and then I'll walk you to the dock. I need to stretch my legs."

Once the envelopes had been secured in the safe, the two of them exited the main doors of the warehouse. Instinctively, Zanna looked out over the water. She squinted against the reflection of the sun glistening on the dark river.

Her breath caught. "Is that . . . ?" She shaded her eyes with one hand and pointed to the water with her other. "Nico! That's the *Anastasi*. She's coming in."

He ran to the end of the dock, his eyes trained on the horizon. "She's alone. There's no sign of the *St. Nicolas* or *Crete*." He turned his gaze toward her. "You don't see any other boats, do you?"

She shook her head. "Do you want me to borrow the spyglass from Mr. Francis so we can be certain?"

He nodded. "If the *Anastasi* is alone, the other boats may have been caught in a storm."

She hesitated. "But none of them are due in yet. You think the

Anastasi is coming to get help or to let us know the other two boats are lost in the Gulf?" She slowly backed up toward the warehouse.

"I don't know, but you can be sure this isn't good. They wouldn't be coming in early unless it was bad news of some sort."

She rushed to locate Mr. Francis. When she returned a few minutes later, Nico was pacing the dock. She handed him the spyglass. He lifted it to his eye, slowly searched the distant waters, then shook his head. "No sign of the other two boats."

Mr. Francis came alongside Nico and patted his shoulder. "Don't believe all is lost just yet. The skies have been clear. Maybe there's a problem with the equipment on the *Anastasi* so they decided it was better to come in early."

Zanna wrung her hands. "Or maybe someone is ill. Do you think it's possible another diver might be injured?"

Nico frowned. "After all the talks we've had about the rules since Felix was injured? I don't think so."

"But Markos and the others said his injury was caused by an accident. It's possible another accident could have happened, isn't it?"

Once again Nico lifted the spyglass to his eye. "I suppose it's possible." He lowered the spyglass to his side. "Do you know if the doctor is in her office today?"

Zanna shrugged. "Unless she's been called out for some emergency, she should be there."

Mr. Francis glanced toward the end of the dock. "Why don't I go and fetch her just in case?"

"That might be a good idea," Zanna told him. "In the meantime, we'll pray we won't need her."

Time crawled as the boat made its approach. One of the men stood on the deck with his hands cupped to his mouth and shouted something neither of them could understand. Nico shouted for the man to repeat his message, and the sailor called out again. Over and over, the sponger shouted the same garbled words.

Nico's jaw clenched, the tendons along his neck tightening like two pulsing ropes. Zanna grasped his arm. "What is it? What's he saying?"

"I think he's telling us that one of the men has got the bends." She shook her head. "Are you certain? I didn't hear that."

"Listen. He keeps repeating the same two words: 'the bends, the bends.'"

If only the wind would quiet for a moment, she might be able to hear. As if on cue, a moment of silence surrounded them and she heard the crewman's words with clarity. Her stomach tightened. No. This couldn't be happening. Everything had been going so well. They were planning a celebration. There must be some mistake.

"We'll need the doctor," Nico said.

The urgency in his words jarred her back to the present, and Zanna turned toward the other end of the dock. There were two figures in the distance, but she couldn't be certain if Lucy was one of them. Snatching the spyglass from Nico's hand, she held it to her eye.

"Lucy and Mr. Francis are on their way." After returning the spyglass to Nico, she waved them forward. "I do wish they would hurry. They look like they're out for an afternoon stroll."

Nico looked toward the twosome. "They will be here before the boat arrives. Besides, if one of the divers has the bends, he'll need to be moved from the boat."

"Do you think it's Theo or Markos?"

"I don't know. But if it's Theo, Markos is going to regret that he argued with me to let his brother dive. The guilt would be difficult to live with, I think. No matter which one is injured, both brothers will need our prayers."

Moments later, Lucy hurried to Zanna's side. "Tell me what's happening, Zanna. Mr. Francis said he didn't know if I'd be needed, something about a problem with the *Anastasi*." Lucy's lips were drawn tight with worry.

"One of the divers has the bends. A crewman called from the boat to tell us, but that's all we know."

Lucy moved closer to Nico. "I don't know anything about an ailment known as the bends. I didn't study any such condition in medical school." Her fingers tightened around the handle of her black bag. She nudged Zanna. "Did he understand what I just said?"

Nico looked at her. "You don't know how to fix such a sickness."

Lucy nodded. "I located a few books and I've read about nitrogen narcosis, but what I found wasn't promising. There seems to be no cure. What can I do to help him?"

"We need to wait and see how bad it is." Nico waved to the captain as the boat neared the dock. He cupped his mouth and shouted to one of the sailors, "Who is it?"

"Theo." The crewman shook his head. "He's in bad shape."

Lucy tugged on Zanna's sleeve. "What did he say?"

"It doesn't sound good." Zanna's stomach churned as she repeated the report to Lucy.

Lucy turned to Mr. Francis. "Is there a piece of canvas we can use as a stretcher to carry him if needed?"

"Yes, I'll get one from the warehouse." He scurried off and returned before the men had completely tied off the boat.

Lucy didn't wait for Nico or the other men to offer a report before she stepped forward. "Come on, Zanna. I want to check his condition before they move him, and I need you to interpret."

One of the crewmen offered a hand to the doctor while Zanna spoke to Nico. "Do you want to come with us?"

Nico waved them onward. "The two of you go below and examine him. There won't be room for me, and I'll only be in the way. I'll talk to the crew and find out all I need to know."

Zanna followed Lucy down the steps and stopped for a moment as her eyes adjusted to the dim light. Slowly the figure lying on the cot became clear. He groaned, and Lucy motioned Zanna closer. "Ask him if he can tell you where he hurts."

Zanna asked the question, but Theo didn't respond. His arms remained in a rigid position at his sides, and his knees twisted at an awkward angle. He stared straight ahead with his hands clenched into tight fists. "Theo, can you talk? The doctor wants to help you, but she needs to know where you hurt."

"Everywhere. I was down too long. The bends . . ." His mouth clamped shut, and he closed his eyes.

Lucy turned to Zanna again. "Tell him we need to move him where I can care for him." Zanna repeated the message. Theo's only reaction was to grimace.

"I'll go up and tell Nico." Zanna hurried up the few steps and called to him. "Mr. Francis has a canvas we can use as a stretcher. He needs to be moved to the room in Lucy's office. He's much worse than Felix."

Nico nodded. "Two different injuries. Both can be deadly, and from what the men have told me, it doesn't sound as though things will go well for Theo." He called for several men to help with the stretcher. None appeared desirous of the duty, yet they did as Nico ordered.

Canvas in hand, they descended the steps. The pained screams and guttural groans from below soon obliterated the screeching of the gulls flying overhead. Zanna covered her ears, but Theo's cries continued to shatter her very being. Her body trembled at the sight and sound, and she clung to Nico's arm.

"Why has this happened? Everything was going so well." Unbidden tears rolled down her cheeks. She swiped them away with the back of her hand.

Nico leaned closer. "I don't know, but I intend to speak with Markos and find out. I'm sure Theo must have stayed down too long or he went deeper than he should have—or both." He shook his head. "He's young, and I'm afraid he was trying to prove he could bring up a larger harvest than his brother. Divers can become prideful and want to prove they're the best, especially the young and inexperienced ones who have never seen a man suffer and die from the bends. They hear the stories of how many have died, but they don't think it can happen to them."

The men ascended the steps and moved onto the dock with care. Even so, each movement of the makeshift stretcher caused Theo to cry out in agony. Markos moved to his brother's side and murmured something in his ear, then signaled to the men to move slowly.

Word of the incident spread, and soon a crowd began to gather. Men from the warehouses and buyers in town for the coming sale mingled together, straining to catch sight of the injured man.

Nico gestured to Zanna. "You should go with Lucy. She may need your help. She will surely need you to interpret."

Nico stepped to Markos's side and placed his arm across his shoulder. "I'm so sorry, my friend. You go with your brother. Later, we will talk about what happened out there."

Markos nodded, his eyes glazed with pain. "Yes, later. I need to be with Theo." He looked Nico in the eye. "I fear Theo is going to die."

Nico swallowed hard as he squeezed Markos's shoulder. "I'll be praying for both of you."

CHAPTER 23

Once Theo had been placed on a bed in one of Lucy's examination rooms, the men made a quick exit into the waiting area. All except Markos, who remained at his brother's bedside. Before the other crewmen could leave, Lucy and Zanna rushed after them. Zanna glanced over her shoulder and shuddered at the sight of Theo's paralytic form lying on the bed. How could Lucy possibly do anything for him?

Lucy nudged her. "Ask them to wait. I need to know if they've ever seen a man in this condition healed and what was done to help. Tell them I know little about nitrogen narcosis. Ask if any of them have knowledge that might help me care for their friend."

Zanna quickly conveyed Lucy's concerns. They'd all seen cases of the bends in varying degrees but were quick to add that severe cases such as Theo's usually resulted in death. "There is nothing to do for him. In Greece, many divers were not even brought home to their families. They died on the boat, and we would bury them on any nearby island in the area where we were sponging."

The other men had already backed out the front door, and the remaining sailor was eager to make his escape, as well. Before he

233

could do so, Zanna grasped his arm. "What happened out there? Did Theo stay down too long?"

The man hesitated, then hiked a shoulder. "He went too deep and stayed down for almost half an hour." He gave a quick clap of his hands, then thrust his arm upward. "Then he shoots up from the bottom too fast." He nodded toward Theo's examination room and shook his head. "Not good to come up so fast like that. But when they stay down too long, they lose their minds. That's what a diver told me. He said he couldn't get enough air and couldn't work the valves. Who can say, though, what happened to Theo. Maybe Markos can tell you more."

Zanna didn't miss the troubled look in Lucy's eyes. Even though her friend had understood nothing of what the sailor had related, his expression had spoken volumes. "Thank you for telling us what you could."

"I hope the doctor has something special in that black bag she carries. If not, Theo's life is in God's hands."

Zanna offered a fleeting smile. "Theo's life has always been in God's hands. We just don't know His plans for Theo. You and the other men should pray for him—and for Markos."

The man gave her a quick nod. "I can leave now?"

"Thank you again for your help. Yes, you can leave." She waited only a moment before interpreting for Lucy. "I don't think there's medically anything to be done for him except to keep him as comfortable as possible."

Lucy tucked a loose strand of hair behind one ear. "That's what I was afraid of, but even trying to keep him comfortable isn't going to be easy. I need you to stay with me. I won't understand what he or Markos might say." She grasped Zanna's arm as they stepped into the examination room. "Ask Markos if he knows of any medical procedures that might help Theo, or if there's anything I should do to aid in his comfort."

Markos sat at his brother's bedside and looked up when they

entered. Zanna offered an encouraging smile as she pulled a wooden chair next to Markos and related Lucy's questions.

Tears shone in his eyes as he stared at his brother's rigid form. "I know of nothing that will help him. None of the doctors in Greece could do anything for this. They just wait for death to come." Markos clasped his hands together and looked toward the door as Theo continued to groan in pain. "I want to go back to the camp and get the prayer rope our mother sent with Theo." He looked up at Zanna. "She sent one with each of us, and we promised we would pray the Jesus Prayer each night. She promised to do the same." Fresh tears dampened his cheeks. "But I didn't keep my promise. If Theo could see or feel the rope, it might give him some comfort."

Zanna patted Markos's arm. "The doctor and I will remain at your brother's bedside. If you think it will comfort Theo to have the prayer rope, you should bring it to him."

Once Markos departed, Lucy retrieved her stethoscope. "I'm glad Markos is out of the room for a while. I want to listen to Theo's heartbeat again to see if it has weakened any further. I'll need to move him a little, and I was afraid Markos would become upset. It's always more difficult to administer an exam or treatment when a loved one is in the room." She gestured to Zanna. "Go to the other side of the bed and move his arm away from his chest so I can listen."

Zanna took a backward step. "Me? I can't do that. It will hurt him. I know it will."

Lucy leveled a hard stare at her. "I need your help." She pointed to Theo. "More important, he needs your help. Please, Zanna, do as I ask."

Zanna nodded slowly, then went over to the opposite side of the bed and attempted to pull Theo's arm from his chest. The instant Theo's agonizing cry filled the room, she released her hold and jumped away from the bed.

Lucy glared at her. "Lift his arm again, but this time don't drop it if he cries out."

Zanna returned the glare. "You mean *when* he cries out, don't you?" she whispered. She didn't wait for a response. Gritting her teeth, she stepped forward and gently lifted Theo's arm.

When he cried out, she turned her face away but held fast to his arm while Lucy bent over him with her stethoscope. Zanna stared at the wall and wondered how the crewmen who had seen their fellow divers in this condition could ever consider breaking the rules? Why would they chance such an excruciating death? It was beyond her comprehension.

"Zanna!" Lucy nodded toward Theo. "He's trying to talk. Come back to this side of the bed and listen. See if you can understand what he's saying."

Zanna released Theo's arm. Each step around the bedside was like slogging through thick mud. She avoided looking into Theo's eyes. Theo wouldn't want to see her here. If he was conscious, he'd want Markos.

Lucy pushed a chair close to the bed and pointed downward. "Now sit." Zanna followed the doctor's command and lowered herself onto the seat. Lucy touched her shoulder. "Lean forward so he can see you. Say something in Greek. It may help if he hears something familiar."

Zanna tipped her head to the right and looked into Theo's glassy eyes. Her chest tightened with unexpected pain, and she forced back tears. "Theo, it's me, Zanna. I work with Nico in the warehouse." He blinked his eyes. She didn't know if that meant he understood her or if it meant nothing at all. "If you understand me but don't feel you can talk, blink one time."

He blinked once. She turned and glanced at Lucy. "Do you have any questions you want me to ask him?"

"Ask if he can swallow. I want to give him some pain medicine, but I don't know if he's able to drink."

Zanna did as Lucy requested, and Theo blinked once. "I think you should try to give it to him."

Quickly, Lucy prepared the medication and stepped to Zanna's side. "Tell him you're going to lift his head from behind the pillow while I hold the glass to his lips."

"What? Now you want me to lift his head? You know how it hurts him to be moved."

Lucy sighed. "He's going to hurt for a little while, but then the medicine will help. If the pain's too great, he'll lapse into unconsciousness."

Zanna frowned. "That doesn't make me feel any better."

"Zanna! I'm not trying to make *you* feel better. I'm trying to relieve Theo's pain. Are you going to help me or not?"

This was not what she'd planned for today. Truth be told, this was not something she would ever plan for herself. "I don't have a choice since there's no one else here." Turning to Theo, Zanna forced a smile and explained what they were going to do.

Zanna didn't miss the fear that shone in Theo's eyes when she said she was going to raise his head. "I'll do my best to be gentle. The medicine will help ease your pain."

She moved to the head of the bed and carefully slid her hands beneath the pillow. When Lucy nodded, Zanna lifted. Theo screamed in pain.

"Theo, you need to drink this," Lucy said, which Zanna swiftly translated. The doctor held the glass to his mouth. The liquid gurgled in his throat and trickled down the sides of his mouth. Lucy wiped his face with a soft towel and told Zanna to lower his head. The movement brought another shout, followed by a string of words that caused her to blush.

Lucy arched her brows. "What did he say?"

"Nothing I would repeat." Zanna returned to the side of the bed, though she didn't sit down. If the medicine caused Theo to drift off, perhaps Lucy would dismiss her.

Zanna watched as the injured man quieted. She was about to ask if she might leave when Theo's eyes popped open, and his legs and arms tightened into an even deeper rigidity. He exhaled a groan and muttered something.

Without being told, Zanna dropped to the chair and leaned close to him. "What did you say, Theo? Tell me."

"S-sunken ship. Must find the treasure. Only a little . . ." He exhaled a long breath, and his eyes closed before he finished the sentence.

Zanna jumped up from the chair and backed away from the bed. "Is he . . . ?" She waved Lucy forward. "I think he stopped breathing."

Lucy moved closer to Theo's side and checked his pulse. She turned to Zanna and gave a pained sigh. "He's gone. But I think we can count it a blessing he didn't continue to suffer in this condition for any longer since there was no helping him."

Zanna gasped. One diver dead, with another still recovering from a diving illness. What would this mean for Nico? Would he consider taking over the position? She prayed not.

"What did he say to you?" Lucy asked.

Zanna blinked at her friend. "What?"

"Right before he died—what did Theo say?"

"He said he had to get to the sunken ship and find the treasure." Zanna let the words seep into her consciousness. "Lucy! Do you think that's what happened to Felix and Theo?"

"What are you talking about?" Lucy's eyebrows pinched together.

"Do you think the divers may have located a sunken ship out in the Gulf, and they were staying down too long looking for some sort of treasure?"

Lucy slowly shook her head. "No, of course not, Zanna. All sailors dream of finding sunken treasure, don't they? He was delusional. That often happens before people die. They say all kinds of irrational things that have no bearing on actual circumstances in their lives. I'm sure that's the case with Theo, as well."

"I'm not so sure you're right, Lucy. Both of the injured divers were on the *Anastasi*, and it's the boat gathering the smallest harvests. What if Theo was looking for a sunken ship and stayed underwater for too long? It's possible."

Lucy's expression was one of disbelief. She patted Zanna's shoulder.

"I know how that lawyer mind of yours works, Zanna, but this isn't a puzzle you must solve. What happened was clearly an end-of-life episode. I've seen it numerous times. My dying patients have made utterances that made no sense to their family members or to me." She retrieved a medical book from a nearby shelf and flipped through the pages while she continued to speak. "Doctors have found that these deathbed utterances mean nothing. As the internal organs cease working, the brain doesn't function properly. And when you combine that with strong doses of pain medication, the result is a delusional patient."

"But I . . ."

Before Zanna could say anything more, Lucy tapped a page in her medical book. "Look, here is a case where a man spoke of murdering twenty-five people in England. He was born in this country and never set foot in any other." She turned the page, obviously prepared to read every instance recorded in the book.

"You need go no further, Lucy. I ask you to accept my legal opinions, so I should certainly do the same and accept your medical opinion."

Zanna hadn't expected a lecture, yet she understood Lucy's need to prove her point. In that respect, the two of them were alike, possibly because their chosen professions were dominated by men. Early on, both of them had learned they must substantiate their opinions if they were to be taken seriously.

"I must go." Zanna turned toward the door. "Markos is going to be devastated that he didn't make it back here before Theo died."

Lucy offered an encouraging smile. "I know it isn't easy being the one to tell him, but I'm sure he'd prefer to hear the news directly from you."

She'd been longing to leave Lucy's office since the moment they arrived, but she hadn't wanted to depart bearing news of Theo's death. Then again, perhaps it was better Markos was away when Theo died. Not being there to witness his brother's final agony might make it easier for Markos to continue diving.

She hurried toward the docks, certain Markos would take the

shortest route from the camp. If she didn't see Markos along the way, maybe she should tell Nico and let him bring the sad news to Markos. When she neared the dock, her stomach churned. She wanted to turn and go home rather than face either Nico or Markos.

The smell of river water and fish assailed her like unwelcome friends as she continued along the dock. The familiar odors usually had no effect on her, but today her stomach rose in protest. She scanned the figures still on the pier. No sign of Markos. Where could he be? Surely he wasn't still at the camp. She stepped into the dimness of the warehouse. Once her eyes adjusted to the low light, she saw Nico and Markos standing near the back of the building.

Waving in their direction, she hurried toward the two men. Markos took a halting step toward her and then stopped. His eyes reflected an undeniable fear. "Is there some change? I shouldn't have stopped to speak with Nico."

She bowed her head, unable to look at him. "I'm sorry, Markos. Theo didn't make it. There was nothing the doctor could do for him." She took a breath. "Dr. Penrose will help you with any arrangements you want to make for Theo's burial. I can go with you to interpret if you like."

He shook his head and opened his hand to reveal the knotted silk rope in his hand. "Not yet. I need a little time."

Zanna nodded. "I'll be at the desk near the front of the warehouse." She glanced at Nico. "Nico could go with you, if you'd rather."

He gave a slight nod and walked away.

Nico reached for her hand. "Thank you for staying with Theo. Markos stopped to tell me Theo's condition wasn't good and that he'd returned for the prayer rope."

"Seeing Theo in so much pain was horrible." Tears burned at the back of her eyes. "Promise me you won't ever consider going back to diving again."

He met her gaze. "I can't make that promise, Zanna."

"I know you wouldn't go unless you believed it necessary, but you need to think about the business. How could we succeed if something happened to you?"

"You could carry on with the business." He smiled. "You're the manager."

"Yes, but you know the business would fail without you. The men would never listen to me. I may know how to keep ledgers, and I could hire a man to help at the sponge sales, but who would oversee the boats and the crews?" She paused, then sighed. "You know it's true, Nico. You think going out with the men will change things, but in your heart you know you must remain behind. This business needs you—and so do I."

"I promise you that before I would dive again, I will first consider the welfare of the business. But that isn't a promise I will never dive again, only that I will weigh all the circumstances. And if I do decide to dive, I will take all the precautions I can to be safe." He gently squeezed her hand. "In my heart, I don't believe either Felix or Theo was following the rules I set out for the divers. There's no way to prove or disprove what I've been told, but something simply isn't right. Going out with them and diving may be the only way I will discover the truth."

Her heart plummeted. She couldn't bear to lose him. Not now. Not when she'd just begun to realize how much she cared for him. She parted her lips to speak but then stopped short before recounting Theo's final words.

She'd told Lucy she believed her—and Lucy was far more knowl-edgeable about dying patients and deathbed remarks. Besides, the medical scholars quoted in that book of Lucy's substantiated her explanation. Repeating Theo's deathbed words would only create upheaval and give the men further cause to ignore and mistrust her.

Adelfo Pappas was waiting among a stand of trees near the camp-site when the crew of the *Anastasi* returned late in the afternoon.

His conversation with Markos had been brief and worrisome. Grief over his brother's death had muddled Markos's thinking, and Adelfo needed to speak to the crew—at least those who were aware of what had been taking place on the *Anastasi*.

There was no doubt he would need to be firm with the men. He didn't plan to tell them that Markos had spoken of giving up their venture and even coming clean with Nico. Although he felt confident he'd dissuaded Markos from doing anything until they talked further, the older man couldn't afford to wait until the crew did something rash. Adelfo needed this scheme to work if he was going to survive the creditors beating down his door. This plan needed to succeed because, short of marriage, it didn't appear Bessie Rochester was going to loan him any additional funds, and he'd run out of options.

He leaned against the thick trunk of a palm tree and pictured himself boarding a train to New York with cases full of the recovered gems and gold coins. He would sell them to wealthy collectors and jewelers who would beg to keep company with him. His name would be known among all of New York society. Of course, he'd take more than his share of the money he gained from each sale, but the crew would never know that. Within reason, they would believe what he told them. Besides, they needed him. They didn't have the necessary connections or wherewithal to sell any of the treasure they salvaged.

He startled at the sound of voices and stooped down. Until he was certain Nico wasn't with the men, he didn't want to be seen. Words of condolence drifted on the breeze, and one of the men was humming a haunting dirge as they trudged into the camp. Instead of going to their individual shelters, the men gathered around the fire pit. Markos sat on one of the surrounding logs with his arms resting across his knees, his back hunched forward, and his head bowed low.

"I'll get some wood." Demetrius pushed to his feet.

Several of the men looked surprised by the captain's offer, but none offered to take his place. For that, Adelfo was pleased. He watched as the captain circled one direction and then another, slowly wending his way near the stand of trees where Adelfo was secreted. As soon as the captain was close enough to hear, Adelfo called to him in a low voice. The captain startled and looked in his direction.

"Over here." His words were no more than a hoarse whisper. He immediately placed his index finger to his lips and gestured the man forward.

The captain glanced about as he approached. "Why are you hiding out here, Mr. Pappas?"

"I need to talk to all the men who know about the ship."

The captain shrugged. "And? What do you want me to do?"

"Tell them to gather here in the trees with me. Think of some excuse to keep the others away. Tell them Markos wants some privacy to plan his brother's funeral."

The captain reared back. "Have you no decency? You would even use Theo's death to your own advantage?"

"Theo's death is no advantage to any of us, but it is an issue we need to discuss. Tell the men we must talk."

The captain spat on the ground near Adelfo's shoe. "I didn't like you before, and now I like you even less. You pretend to be a Greek brother, but you are nothing to us."

The blood rushed in Adelfo's ears. He wanted to strike the man, yet he dared not lose his temper. "It doesn't matter what you think of me. We all made an agreement, and I plan to hold every one of you to it or you'll all be without jobs. Now get them over here and do it without alerting the others that there's anything going on."

A short time later, the group of men drifted toward the stand of trees while the other men wandered to the shore to catch fish for supper.

Anger flashed in Markos's eyes. "We already talked. My brother is dead. What do you want?"

"I want you men back out on that boat the next time the other boats set sail, and I want you to bring back more from the sunken ship than I've seen so far." He glared at Markos. "I have a feeling you're holding out on me. I'm guessing Theo must have found something worthwhile or he wouldn't have stayed down so long."

The line tender shook his head. "There was nothing in his basket. I'm the one who brought it up—only sponges. I don't think we were close enough for him to locate the ship."

Adelfo directed a dismissive wave toward the line tender. "And you think just because you tell me there was nothing in the basket, I'm going to believe you?"

Markos shoved forward. "What do you want us to do, Adelfo? Use some sort of magic and make a basket of jewels appear for you?" He didn't wait for an answer. "Well, we can't do that. Besides, this is the first time we've been able to sail anywhere close to where we found that ship. Nico gave orders for the *Anastasi* to stay in sight of the other boats. We can't disobey his orders, and we've decided we don't want to keep on with this. Theo's death is too much. There isn't any treasure worth a man's life."

Beads of perspiration popped up across Adelfo's forehead, and he struggled to hold his temper in check. He clenched his jaw until he thought it might crack. "You men listen to me and you listen well. If you don't do as I say, I'll tell Nico what you've been doing out there without his knowledge. What do you think he's going to say when he finds out half the crew of the *Anastasi* has been lying to him and caused injury to one of his divers and death to another? None of you will ever work on a boat again. And if he doesn't see to it, I will." He poked his index finger in Markos's chest. "You do what you're told." He glanced around at the other men. "That goes for all of you. Now get out of here before the others come looking for you."

Every muscle in his body tensed. He didn't know if he'd convinced the men or not. Adelfo hurried out of the trees and headed back toward town. Maybe he should pay a visit to Bessie Rochester.

CHAPTER
24

His heart heavy, Nico stood on the dock watching the *St. Nicolas* and *Crete* return to Tarpon Springs on schedule. The two boats carried full loads of sponge, and he could imagine the excited crews were prepared to celebrate.

One of the line tenders on the *Crete* shouted as they tied off at the dock, "What time is the party, Nico?"

Nico waved in response. He didn't want to shout back the news of Theo's death.

The men would learn soon enough that instead of dancing and singing at a celebratory party, they would be paying their respects to Markos and mourning the loss of a friend. Although Markos had suggested the celebration go on as planned, Nico wouldn't hear of the idea. A few of the men had come to him and requested that he reconsider, yet Nico remained adamant in his decision. To honor the life of Theo was more important than celebrating a harvest of sponges.

After the funeral, Theo was buried in a small cemetery plot, the land donated by Lucy and designated as a cemetery for the Greek community. She'd told Nico she hoped it wouldn't need to be used again until all the men reached an old age. He'd agreed, but if the men continued to take risks, they might need the cemetery far too often.

Later that same day, Nico gathered the men and once again emphasized the need for safety. He didn't want to lose another man. A few of the men, especially Markos, might have considered his comments harsh, but he had to make them understand that they'd end up alongside Theo if they didn't heed the instructions that had been laid out for them.

The food that had been planned for the celebration was served after the funeral, and though the men ate well, later that night the mood remained somber around the campfire. Nico hadn't been surprised to see Mr. Pappas at the funeral, though the man's appearance at the campsite later in the evening was unexpected. Nico watched and wondered as the older man took a position alongside Markos and other crew members of the *Anastasi*. Was he simply there to offer condolences, or was there something deeper going on between some of the men and the Greek sponge buyer? If so, what could it be? Mr. Pappas possessed a great deal of knowledge about buying and selling sponges, yet he knew little about harvesting them.

Nico strolled to the side of the fire where Mr. Pappas and Markos were seated. He nodded toward an empty space. "Mind if I join you?"

Markos motioned for Nico to sit down. "Thank you for arranging the funeral and for the good food. I appreciate all you did for Theo and me."

"The food had already been planned for the celebration, but when I canceled the party, Zanna's mother and grandmother asked if they could prepare it for the funeral dinner. I'm sure they would appreciate your thanks. I can take you to where they live if you want to go over there tomorrow."

He offered a brief nod. "We're still going out tomorrow, aren't we?"

Nico's mouth dropped open. Before Theo's death, the boats had been scheduled to sail tomorrow, but Nico had planned to wait several more days to allow the men time to grieve and rest before making another trip. The men sitting closest to Mr. Pappas all leaned forward as if anticipating Nico's response.

He shook his head. "No. I think we'll wait a few more days yet." He patted Markos on the shoulder. "It's the least I can do right now. You need to rest and take time to mourn. You can't do that out in the Gulf."

"I don't want to mourn, and I don't need to rest. We all want to get back to work. What am I to do sitting around the camp? I am a man. I don't plan to beat my chest and wail like a woman who has lost her child. I loved my brother, but crying for him won't bring him back. Harvesting sponge is what I need to do." Markos gestured toward the other men around him. "It's what we all need to do." Several of the men bobbed their heads in unison and murmured their agreement.

Mr. Pappas nudged Nico. "You should let the men go out if it's what they want. After all, you won't make any money with the men sitting in camp."

Nico frowned at the older man. "Everything isn't about making money. There are some things in life that are far more important."

"Not many, my boy, not many. And as you grow older, you'll discover I'm right." Mr. Pappas glanced at the captain. "Am I right, Demetrius?"

The captain's eyes darted between Mr. Pappas and Nico. The usually outspoken captain gave a shrug and nodded his agreement.

Nico exhaled a long breath. "If that's what you want to do, then I'm not going to argue. We can set sail tomorrow."

"We?" Markos cocked an eyebrow. "You mean all three boats?"

Nico gave a firm nod. "All three boats—and me. I'll dive in Theo's position."

"No." The strangled word escaped Markos's lips, and he shook his head.

247

Nico jerked back. "What do you mean, no? Who else did you think would dive in that position?"

Markos nodded toward the crew members of the *St. Nicolas*. "They have two extra divers on the *St. Nicolas*. You could send one of them with us. You shouldn't dive, Nico. If something happens to you, then what happens to all of us? It isn't wise."

"You may not think it is wise, but I am in charge. The additional divers on the *St. Nicolas* have little experience. They have worked mostly as line tenders. Until one of them is better trained, I'll be the second diver on the *Anastasi*." He shrugged. "I'd like to think I will bring good fortune to the boat. Besides, I may find some problem the rest of you have overlooked in the past. We'll take a different route than the other two boats and see what we discover. Who knows? We may locate even finer sponge beds."

"Dr. Penrose might disagree with you, Nico." Mr. Pappas puffed on his cigar. "She may not want to take a chance on losing the man who is in charge of this crew. After all, she's got a lot of money invested in you."

Nico frowned. "Not in me—in the sponging business."

The older man flicked ash from the cigar. "All the same thing, isn't it? Don't let pride cause you to make foolish decisions."

"Pride? This isn't about my pride. It's about keeping these men safe." He glared at Mr. Pappas. "The operation of this business is none of your concern, so it would be best if you kept your opinions to yourself."

Mr. Pappas shrugged. "Just trying to help, Nico."

Demetrius leaned forward. "I know you have the final say in this, Nico, but if something does happen to you, what will become of us?" He gestured toward the other men. "We need you to manage the business. To take such a risk—do you think it is wise?"

Had Zanna talked to the captain? His words echoed what she'd already said to him. Or was this a warning from God that he shouldn't go out with the men? Nico couldn't be sure, but he'd promised Zanna he would carefully weigh his decision about diving. Perhaps he needed to spend some time in thought and prayer before the boats set sail.

Adelfo breathed a sigh of relief when Nico stood and announced he needed time to think and departed for town. Once certain Nico was out of earshot, Adelfo nudged Markos. "We need to talk. Alone."

"You're right, we do." Markos nodded and started walking to a spot on the far side of the camp.

From the tone of Markos's voice, Adelfo feared he was going to have a disagreement on his hands. He'd need to strike the first blow in this verbal sparring match if he was going to gain the upper hand.

Before they'd come to a halt, Adelfo grasped Markos by the arm. "Don't think you're going to tell me what you will or won't do, Markos. We've already had that discussion. The thing we need to talk about is Nico going out on that boat with your crew. We need to make sure he doesn't go."

"If you don't want him coming along, why'd you antagonize him? You likely made him even more determined to sail with us. Why didn't you just keep quiet until we had a chance to talk in private?"

"Because I didn't know if there'd be a chance." Adelfo poked his finger against Markos's chest. "Listen to me. If he sails on the *Anastasi* and acts as the second diver, the easiest thing to do is let him die out there in the Gulf."

Markos gasped. "You want me to commit murder?" He shook his head until his hair whipped back and forth against his forehead. "No! I won't do it."

"It can be an accident. You can take over for the line tender and make sure he doesn't get enough air. It will be easy."

"Easy?" Markos's voice trembled. "Killing someone would never be easy, and I won't do it. Even if I agreed—and I never would—there's no way I could take over for the line tender and not raise suspicion. You know nothing about being out on the boats, so don't try to tell me how I can cause someone to die out there." He looked toward the water. "This has gone too far. The other men and I just want to go back to sponging and forget we ever found that sunken ship."

"Here's the thing, Markos. You can do as I say or I'll go to Nico. I can make this bad for all of you. I can even tell him that you intentionally killed your own brother because he didn't want to go along with the rest of you to try to find the ship."

"There's more of us who would tell him the truth. He'd believe us. I know he would."

Adelfo shrugged. "Even if he did believe you, would he ever trust you after this? Your crew disobeyed orders and began treasure hunting before I ever got involved. He can look at the logs and see when the harvest shortages began. After that, you'll never find work on another sponge boat."

Lines of defeat etched the young diver's face as he leaned against the trunk of a palmetto tree. "Give me a chance to see if I can convince Nico to remain in Tarpon Springs. But if he decides to sail with us, don't expect anything to happen to him. To have an accident so soon after Theo's death would raise too many questions. Besides, Felix will soon be able to dive again."

Adelfo took a step closer and looked Markos in the eyes. "Three sailings and then you need to have Felix back out there with you, or Nico needs to spend eternity in a watery grave." He went to leave, then turned and glared at Markos over his shoulder. "Do not discuss this with the other men until I tell you."

He stalked off before Markos could respond. His hands trembled as he removed a cigar from his jacket. His reasoning with Markos hadn't been as strong as he'd wanted. Still, Markos obviously feared having the wrongdoing of the crew exposed to Nico. No man wanted to jeopardize his livelihood, otherwise he would have walked away. At least, that was what Adelfo wanted to believe.

After leaving Nico at the warehouse earlier in the day, Zanna returned to her law office. Though her work for the sponge company consumed most of her time, she'd continued to see occasional clients. Of late, her work had fallen behind schedule, and she'd taken the remainder of the afternoon to review a detailed and lengthy railroad contract Mr. Burnside had sent to her. He wanted her opinion and had asked that she also cite the legal precedent to support her decision. She'd returned to the office after supper, hoping to complete her research. Then she could begin writing her opinion tomorrow morning and send it off to Mr. Burnside. She wouldn't meet his requested deadline, but she'd be only a few days late.

She glanced up when the bell above the front door jangled and Nico stepped inside. "What a nice surprise. What brings you back to town this evening?" She glanced at the clock that sat on a wooden filing cabinet. "By now, you and the other men have usually returned to camp for the night. Did you have some work to complete that I didn't know about?"

He sat down across from her and shook his head. "Not work, but I need to make a decision and thought if I took a walk, it might help."

"And did it?" She tilted her head and looked into his coffee-brown eyes.

"No." He shrugged. "So I continued walking, and when I saw you were here, I thought you could help." His forehead creased with wrinkles, and he pointed to her desk. "What is all of this? You're having to take care of your legal work at nighttime? Why didn't you tell me? This is not good."

"It's nothing I can't handle. A bit of research I need to complete. Besides, it's quiet in the evening and there are no interruptions."

"At least if I would stay away."

She leaned back in her leather chair. "I'm glad you're here. I've been reading too long and my eyes are tired." She smoothed a wrinkle from the skirt of her green-and-gold plaid dress. "What is it you want to discuss?"

"You remember we talked about moving the sailing schedule so the men could have some extra days to rest and mourn?"

"Of course. What of it?"

He detailed the conversation he'd had with Markos and the other crew members, but made no mention of Mr. Pappas. "Since they want to remain on the old schedule, I agreed."

She jerked back. "I thought one of the reasons you were waiting to sail was so that Felix could return to the *Anastasi* and dive."

"I never said that." He frowned and shook his head. "I don't think Felix will be ready for several more weeks, if then. I'm not sure we can count on using him as a diver in the future. I pray he will recover enough to dive, or at least be able to work in another position on one of the boats, but his future remains uncertain. Only God knows for sure."

Her mind reeled as she tried to sift through what he told her. "But if you've already told the men they can sail, who's going to take the position as second diver on the *Anastasi*?"

He clasped his hands together and rested them in his lap. "That's the decision I must make. I think I should be the second diver. The men have expressed concern about my decision and—"

"And I have some concern, as well. I don't want you to go with them, Nico. I've already told you I don't want you to dive."

His lips curved in a playful smile. "I know, I know. You don't want to lose me. I'm too important to you."

"To the business, Nico. There isn't a man in that crew who could take over for you, and you know that's true. If I agreed you should go with the men and something happened, I'd never forgive myself."

He chuckled. "Of that I am sure. I may be the only one who can help you with the business, but I'm also the only man who would marry a woman like you."

Heat scalded her cheeks. "What does that mean—a woman like me?"

"That means I am a man who wouldn't object to having his wife work alongside him in his business. Of course, I am also a man who wants his wife to give him beautiful babies, too, so maybe you couldn't handle all of that, after all." His eyes, though weary, twinkled when he spoke.

"You talk out of both sides of your mouth. Not so long ago you told me you wanted a wife who would stay home, cook, and have babies."

He shrugged. "We are all allowed to change our mind sometimes."

Every nerve in her body tingled when he leaned forward and rested his forearms on the desk. She could no longer deny the rush of emotion she felt in his presence, yet she needed to guard her feelings.

Nico was a man who one day said he wanted a wife who would remain at home and tend babies, and another day said he would not object to his wife working alongside him. Which was it? Would he say one thing before he married and another afterward? Of course, he'd not even come close to actually asking her to marry him. Truth be told, he'd never even kissed her—though recently he seemed as though he'd wanted to—so what was she to think of these comments? Was he using them as a ploy to change the topic now that she'd voiced opposition to his plan? She'd told him before she didn't want him to dive, so why would he think she'd change her mind now? Was that why he made that final comment about being allowed to change one's mind sometimes?

She forced her practical side to the forefront and sighed. "I think we need to use our time deciding who is going to dive when the boats sail. Even though you told the men they could sail tomorrow, I think you should tell them you've changed your mind. Blame it on me. Tell them I need you here to help with problems in the warehouse or to oversee at Friday's sale. You know the buyers don't like to talk to me."

Nico shook his head. "I won't lie to the men."

She placed her palms on the desk. "Nothing I've said is a lie. I do need you here. The workers in the warehouse don't think I know anything about cleaning and packing the sponges."

"And you don't. You should spend more time back there. This would be a good opportunity for you to learn more." He flashed that smile of his—the one that made her heart flutter, even though now it also made her angry.

"And what about the sale on Friday? Are you willing to take a chance that all will go well with that if you aren't here talking to the buyers before they place their bids? We need every penny we can get on sale days."

"We are doing fine. I studied the ledgers you showed me like I promised."

"Yes, but if we're to keep Lucy happy, we need to continue showing growth and profit. The only way to do that is to continue selling at high prices and, Nico, the buyers like you. They want you here to answer their questions."

He shrugged. "They like me, but it usually ends up with Adelfo Pappas gaining the highest bid for his New York clients. Most of the other buyers can't compete with what he offers. Still, Pappas agrees with you. He doesn't want me to dive."

She straightened her shoulders and lifted her nose high in the air. "You confided in Mr. Pappas? You asked his opinion before you came to me?" She paused and drew a deep breath. "Why would you seek his advice?"

"You are taking offense when there's no reason to do so. I didn't seek his advice. He came to the campsite tonight—uninvited, as far as I could tell. No one asked for his opinion, but he voiced it just the same. And not in a particularly considerate way."

"What do you mean? Was he surly or forceful?"

"I would say a little of both. It wasn't what he said so much as his tone and attitude. I may have misunderstood his intent, but some of his statements sounded almost like threats." Nico's smile appeared as if forced. "What reason could he have to threaten me or care whether I dive or not? It makes no sense. I must have misunderstood."

Zanna weighed his words. She was pleased the older man agreed that Nico should remain behind, yet she wondered if this had anything to do with his desire to own the sponging company. If so, she couldn't imagine what it could be.

She stifled a yawn with her hand. "Pardon me."

Nico stood and held out his hand. "You're tired. Let me walk you home."

Glancing at her paper-littered desk, she considered his offer. She really should stay and finish her work, but perhaps she could persuade him not to dive on the way to her house.

She placed her hand in his and allowed him to pull her to her feet. After locking her office, they walked along the deserted boardwalk.

Nico cleared his throat. "How would you have gotten home if I had not come?"

"I'd have walked, just as I'm doing now."

"Unescorted?"

"I've done so many times. Other times, my brother comes to fetch me." When Nico grew quiet, she slipped her hand into the crook of his arm. "What's wrong?"

"I don't like to think of you putting yourself in danger."

She pulled him to a stop near some palm fronds. Beyond them, a light was flickering inside her home. "Now you know how I feel about you diving."

"Ah, but you said it was because you don't want the business to suffer." He grasped both of her hands. "Is it more, Zanna? Will you tell me now or will you, like my men, hold the truth from me?"

Truth.

In Zanna's life, she'd had a few moments when she knew the next thing out of her mouth could change the course of her life, and this was such a time. If she said one thing, Nico would return to being her business partner only. If she said another, he would become something more. Nico deserved the truth, but could she summon the courage to tell him?

Early on, she'd realized her respect for Nico had been growing every day. What she hadn't realized was that her love had been only a step behind. Her father wouldn't approve, especially if Nico began diving again, but she'd fought her father before and she could do it again.

She swallowed hard. "I don't want to lose you, Nico, because I believe you have taken hold of my heart."

He grinned. "Your anchor holds fast in mine, as well."

"So you won't dive?"

"I didn't say that." He chuckled. "I still must do what I think is best." He pressed a kiss to her forehead. "But I will be careful, and I promise to come back to you."

"You'd better or I'll kill you."

"If I'm dead, how will you—?"

The front door opened, and her brother stepped out. Nico swiftly pulled Zanna behind the fronds.

"I need to go. He's coming to get me," Zanna whispered.

"Then I'd better make this quick." Before Zanna could process Nico's words, he pressed a sweet, tender kiss to her lips.

"Sweet dreams." He squeezed her hand and slipped away seconds before Atticus rounded the corner.

Atticus stopped short when he spotted her. "Zanna, you walked home alone? What were you thinking? Father will be furious."

She didn't answer. For a lawyer, she had certainly been finding herself speechless an awful lot lately. As if she were walking on clouds, she followed him inside. Her feelings zipped and dived like the gulls over the bay.

Sweet dreams?

Guaranteed.

CHAPTER
25

Nico stood near the bow of the *Anastasi*. A month had passed since Theo's death. Against the wishes of Mr. Pappas and Zanna, Nico had sailed with the crew of the *Anastasi* during the month-long period. After much prayer, an idea had come to him—a compromise of sorts—one that could prove long lasting and good for everyone. He assigned Peter Kamis to the crew of the *Anastasi*. Peter was a diver who had completed his apprenticeship only weeks before sailing from Greece. Since arriving in Tarpon Springs, he'd worked as a lifeline tender and deckhand on the *St. Nicolas*, and the young man had been eager to begin diving again.

Yet before making the assignment permanent, Nico advised the captain and crew of the *Anastasi* that he would be sailing with them until he was certain Peter would be safe. Some members of the crew were insulted by Nico's decision, while others seemingly welcomed his presence. The journeys had gone well, and they'd harvested massive loads of sponge on each of their ventures. Today the boats would sail without him.

A twinge of regret knotted in Nico's chest. He would miss the camaraderie of the crew and the rush of excitement that overtook every inch of his body when he descended into the depths of the Gulf. Diving was a challenge, a way divers proved their worth, and unfortunately the reason many ended up losing their lives. He wanted one last talk with Peter before the men departed. He'd expected to find him waiting on board, eager to sail, yet he wasn't on the boat.

He moved closer to the captain. "Any sign of Peter this morning?"

Demetrios pointed toward the warehouse. "Last I saw him, he was in the warehouse talking to Markos and Adelfo Pappas." The captain barked an order at one of the crewmen before turning back to Nico. "We won't sail for another hour. I never expect the divers on board until a half hour before sailing time. You know that."

Nico gave a nod, for he knew the rules. Still, the younger divers, unable to contain their enthusiasm, usually boarded early. And why would Mr. Pappas want to speak with Peter and Markos before they sailed? The question niggled at him as he jumped from the boat and crossed the dock. He strode from the bright sunlight into the dimness of the warehouse and was momentarily blinded, but then an animated discussion captured his attention.

His sight now restored, he turned toward the voices and caught sight of Markos, Mr. Pappas, and Peter huddled in conversation behind piles of sponges that awaited final cleaning, packing, and shipment. If he didn't know better, he'd think they were hiding. But why would they need to conceal themselves in order to talk togther? And why did their voices sound so frenzied?

Their conversation ceased when a warehouse worker hollered a greeting to Nico. He waved in return and stepped around the pile of sponges. The conversation among the threesome had come to a halt.

Nico approached the men. "Good morning. I need a little time with Peter here before he boards. I hope you two will excuse him. I'm sure there's nothing of great importance you need to discuss with him." He arched his brows. "Am I right?"

Mr. Pappas dropped the stub of his cigar and ground it out with his heel. "We were just wishing him good luck on his first dive without supervision."

Peter's features tightened into an angry frown. "This isn't my first dive without supervision. It's my first time diving without Nico on the *Anastasi*."

"Right. My apologies, Peter. I meant no offense. I'd forgotten about your diving experience back in Greece." Mr. Pappas tugged on the end of his mustache.

Nico gestured toward the floor. "Be sure that cigar is out before you leave. We don't want a fire in here." He didn't wait for a response before heading out the door, with Peter scurrying to catch up.

Peter panted for air as he came alongside Nico. "I'm sorry, Nico. I didn't know you wanted to see me or I would have refused Markos when he said he wanted to talk to me alone. But then when we got inside, Mr. Pappas joined us."

Nico gave the young diver a sideways glance. "From the little I heard, it didn't sound like a pleasant conversation."

Peter shoved his hands in his pockets and looked away. "You know how Mr. Pappas can be. He gets loud whenever he's excited. He said he wanted to wish me well on my diving."

"Did he? Well, that was kind of him." The young man was being evasive, but Nico wasn't going to push him. Forcing Peter to relay information would only cause him to become nervous, and he needed to be calm when the *Anastasi* sailed for the Gulf. "I know I've gone over all my rules with you, but I want to be certain you understand that, although I want a good harvest, safety is the most important thing. I don't want harm coming to another diver—or any other crew member. Understood?"

Peter gave a firm nod. "I'll do my best. You've taught me things I didn't learn in Greece, and I'll put them to good use."

Nico clapped him on the shoulder. "Good. If all goes well, I want you to continue working on the *Anastasi*, since Felix's recovery hasn't proved as successful as we had all hoped."

"What's that? Did I hear you mention Felix's name?" Both men turned toward Markos. "Did you talk to the doctor, Nico?"

"Not since you returned, and you know everything she had to say. I hope the doctor's predictions are wrong, but Felix hasn't recovered much further since he returned to the camp. Short of a miracle, I don't think he'll ever return to diving."

Markos grunted and then grasped Peter by the arm. "Come on, Peter. The boats will be sailing in half an hour. We need to board." He directed a sour look at Nico. "Don't want to be caught breaking any of the rules."

Nico heard the mockery but simply shrugged. "If you don't break the rules, you don't have to worry about being caught, Markos." He hesitated a few seconds. "It's just like lying. If you don't lie, you don't have to worry about what lie you've told. The truth is always easily remembered." He smiled at the diver. "Don't you agree?"

Markos tugged on Peter's arm. "C'mon, Peter. We don't have time for another sermon."

Adelfo Pappas stood at a distance and watched the *Anastasi* slowly sail down the Anclote River toward the Gulf. The talk with Peter hadn't gone the way he had hoped, but Markos believed the young diver would come around once he discovered other members of the crew were as eager as the divers to find treasure on that sunken ship. And while Markos could be convincing, Peter didn't appear to be a risk taker. Nico had been on the boat with Peter long enough to convince him that he'd be discharged if he didn't abide by the rules. Of course, Nico had said those same things to the other divers, but a few lies here and there could take care of Nico and his incessant questions.

Adelfo believed he could become a rich man if the divers continued to explore the sunken ship and discovered a wealth of treasure. However, he was a man who didn't rely on one plan if he could arrange for two. As he hurried along the dock toward town, he worried neither of his plans would come to fruition. He needed one or the other to work out if he was going to have enough money to purchase the sponge company. While immediate money from sunken treasure was a good thing, a long-term business could reap huge benefits over the rest of his life. The doctor would be easily enough convinced if he could hand her a bundle of cash.

His last conversation with Bessie Rochester hadn't gone well. He'd need to up his game if he was going to get her to loosen her purse strings. The woman held no appeal, and sacrifice was going to be required if he was to realize true success.

He heaved a sigh and climbed the steps leading to a wide front porch that skirted the large house. He lifted the heavy clapper and watched it fall against the brass plate. Viola's shrill voice carried through the solid front door and was followed by the sound of footsteps. The moment the doorknob turned, he pasted on a bright smile and extended a bouquet of flowers.

"For me?" Viola's piercing tone caused him to take a backward step.

"I thought all of you lovely ladies could enjoy them." The three sisters continually vied for his attention. Long ago, Adelfo had learned to be careful with his words.

Bessie hurried from the kitchen, wiping her hands down the front of a large frilly apron. "Adelfo, what a treat to see you. I didn't know you were going to stop by." She quickly glanced in the hallway mirror, then tucked a loose strand of hair behind one ear. "Dear me, I do look a mess. If I'd known you were going to call, I would have set aside my baking for today."

He lifted his nose in the air. "I believe I'm delighted you didn't. What delicious delicacy have you prepared?"

Viola wriggled past her buxom sister. "I'm going to put these in water. Excuse me for a moment, would you?"

Adelfo nodded and smiled at Viola, then stepped closer to Bessie.

"I would enjoy a cup of tea, and I do hope you've been baking something even sweeter than you—though I doubt that's possible."

Her cheeks blossomed bright pink, and she lightly swatted his arm. "Oh, Adelfo. You do know how to make a woman blush." She gestured for him to follow her. "Do sit down in the dining room and I'll put the kettle on."

He did as he was told. His chest constricted when both Viola and Eugenia followed Bessie into the dining room a few minutes later. Now what? He needed to speak to Bessie alone. His mind whirred. Viola continued to prattle in her shrill voice, and Eugenia, though quiet, appeared to be settled in for the remainder of his visit.

Bessie pushed to her feet to retrieve the now-hot kettle. From the kitchen, she called to her sisters, "Don't forget you both volunteered to help at the library this morning. You'd best hurry or you'll be late."

Adelfo blew out a long breath. Saved by the ladies' penchant to make certain the library remained open for at least several hours every day. He graced them with a smile. "You are true gems. I don't know what Tarpon Springs would do without your devotion to charity work. Even though New York is my home, my admiration runs deep for all you do to make Tarpon Springs a better community."

Eugenia leaned forward, her face flushed as she clung to his every word. Today, Viola appeared less attentive, but he cared little. Though he sometimes enjoyed his ability to captivate the women, today it was only Bessie he wanted to charm.

He pushed back from the table. "I don't want to delay you, ladies. Let me see you to the door."

They each stood, disappointment filling their eyes. Their feet rose and fell at a snail's pace as they closed the distance to the front door. Bessie grinned like a Cheshire cat when she strode into the hallway to bid Viola and Eugenia good-bye. A smug smile played at her lips before she turned toward the mirror and began to preen.

"I do hope you'll still be here when we return. Perhaps you'll stay for lunch. I'm sure Bessie won't mind preparing a delightful meal while we're gone." Eugenia directed a scowl at her. "Will you, Sister?"

"We'll see. Adelfo and I may need to complete our visit out at the pagoda or in town. I wouldn't want anyone to think I'm exhibiting improper behavior. Entertaining a man without a chaperone just isn't proper."

"Oh, pshaw, Bessie. At your age I don't think anyone is going to give a whit." Viola arched her brows. "Besides, we both know you'd rather entertain Adelfo than cook for him—or us."

Bessie narrowed her eyes and glared at Viola while Eugenia pinned on her hat and picked up her gloves. Moments later, Viola followed suit. The last thing Adelfo needed was one of the sisters riling up Bessie. It could take hours to calm her, and he needed to get down to business the minute Viola and Eugenia departed.

He stepped in front of Bessie to block Viola's view. "Don't fret, ladies. If Bessie can't prepare a meal, I'll take you all to the restaurant. It will be a delight for me."

Viola thrust back her shoulders and peeked around Adelfo's shoulder. She looked like the cat that swallowed the canary. "Enjoy yourself, Bessie. We'll join you soon." That said, both Viola and Eugenia, heads held high, took their leave.

Bessie sighed and stepped near Adelfo's side. "I thought they'd never leave." She curved her lips in a flirtatious smile and blinked several times.

Her behavior reminded him of a schoolgirl attempting to gain her first suitor. He returned her smile. "Shall we go sit in the parlor?"

"Oh, no, Adelfo. I meant what I said to Viola. I don't want to tarnish my reputation. While it's possible nobody would know you're here and that we're alone, I wouldn't want to take a chance." She pressed her hand to his arm. "You do understand, don't you?"

"Of course. We'll do as you suggested. The pagoda will provide a proper place to visit, so long as there aren't other people there. I do want to speak with you privately."

Anticipation shone in her eyes. He knew what she was thinking. And if worse came to worse, he'd propose. He would never marry her, but a proposal might be enough to gain her trust—and her money. Truth be told, if he intended to retain her trust, he'd need to be careful. The proposal would need to come before the request for money, and he had a plan he hoped would work.

While he waited, she removed her apron. "I'm going to take along a couple of my scones for us to enjoy while we talk."

"Delightful idea, my dear." His words hit the mark, and the color heightened in her cheeks. This should be easy.

He carried a small basket with the scones in one hand while Bessie clung to his arm as if she feared he might escape. When they neared the pagoda, he quickly surveyed the area. Thankfully no one was in sight, and he escorted her to one of the benches. He didn't have much faith in the mineral springs that rippled below the pagoda, which had brought visitors to the city long before he'd begun traveling to the town.

After they sat down side by side, Adelfo turned to her. "I know I haven't been very attentive of late, but my work has kept me busier than usual. Each time I planned to pay you a visit, some emergency would come up that needed my immediate attention. The businessmen in New York whom I work for have been quite unreasonable over the past months. One minute they want me to buy more sponges, and the next minute they want cheaper yet the same quality. It is impossible." He held his palm to his forehead and shook his head.

"Oh, my dear man. I didn't realize you'd been under such pressure. I do wish you would have let me know. Of course, I doubt there's anything I could have done to help you, but it breaks my heart to know you've been struggling so. I could have at least provided you with a listening ear."

"I knew you would be compassionate, Bessie, but I didn't want to burden you. Even now, I don't want to speak of my problems. I came because I've decided what I need is joy and fulfillment in my life." He reached for her hand. "And I believe you are the woman who could provide that enrichment."

"Oh, Adelfo." She pressed her open palm to her chest. "Do you mean what I think you mean?"

He nodded. "I'd like you to be my wife, Bessie." For a moment he worried she might swoon.

Bessie listed toward him, then straightened her shoulders and met his gaze. "Did I hear you correctly? You've asked me to marry you?"

He nodded and steeled himself to catch her full weight should she faint. "Yes, my dear. I would be proud to call you my wife, if you'll have me."

"If? Of course I'll marry you! Our wedding day will be the happiest day of my life!" She fluttered her lashes. "I hope you don't want to wait long. We're no spring chickens."

He forced a chuckle. "You're right, and I would very much like to wed you tomorrow, if only it were possible. However, I fear we can't marry right away. At the moment I can't give you a date that's certain, but I love you and I hope you'll agree to wait for me."

Her brows dipped low, and she squinted against the sunlight. "But why must we wait, Adelfo? I don't understand."

Adelfo massaged his temples with his fingers before he looked at her again. "I'm embarrassed to tell you this, Bessie, but I'm financially ruined at present. I have incurred extensive debt. I won't marry you and bring that burden into our marriage. It simply wouldn't be fair to you. Once I'm able to erase my indebtedness, then we will marry."

Bessie leaned toward him and rested her head on his shoulder. "My dear man, if that's the only thing holding us back, you needn't worry any longer. I have more than sufficient funds to clear any obstacle that threatens our wedded bliss."

He placed his arm around her shoulder and smiled. "As soon as I have the funds, I'll go to New York, pay off my creditors, and return to you, my love. Then we can begin our lives anew."

Bessie patted his hand. "I won't have you going off to New York now that we're engaged. I much prefer having my banker, Mr. Larson, take care of paying the debt. He would never approve of any other arrangement. Besides, this way you can remain in Tarpon Springs." She beamed. "We can marry without waiting."

A knot fisted in Adelfo's chest, and he clutched the lapel of his jacket. "No, no." He shook his head. "I need to go and personally pay the debts myself, dear."

Bessie's lips drooped into a frown. "Don't be foolish, Adelfo. We both know that creditors don't care if their payments are delivered personally or through a third party. I believe this is the safest method—for both of us." Her frown faded. "Using Mr. Larson as our liaison will give us peace of mind and allow us to wed much sooner."

His stomach churned, but then a sliver of hope pushed to the forefront. "I'll still need to travel to New York and speak with my employers. They may want me to train in a new buyer to take my place."

She shot him a brief smile. "Letters to those New York business-men will suffice. You'll not be working for them in the future, so there's no reason for a personal visit." Her voice quivered with excitement. "You can stay here with me forever." The words gushed forth like a spring freshet. With a sigh, she lifted her head. "I think we should seal our love with a kiss."

He might be able to wiggle out of most things, but there was no way he could escape kissing Bessie Rochester.

CHAPTER
26

At the jingling of the bell on the front door, Zanna looked up from the sheaf of papers strewn across her desk. Her full lips instantly curved in a welcoming smile. "Nico! What a nice surprise. I was going to come down to the warehouse later this morning, but I wanted to go through the remainder of these papers first."

His dark curls fell across his forehead, making him look more like a schoolboy than a seasoned diver and businessman. He flashed a broad smile, yet it was his tender expression that caused her heart to race.

He dropped into one of the chairs opposite her desk. "I no longer expect you at the warehouse every day. We agreed you would work on the new project Mr. Burnside sent to you." He leaned forward. "But I do miss seeing your beautiful smile each morning, so I decided to stop by on my way to purchase some cordage."

Heat crawled up her neck and into her cheeks. "No problems with the ledgers this week?"

He shook his head. "You trained me well. Everything is—" he hesitated a moment—"balanced. That's the word, is it not?"

"Yes, and I'm amazed how well you've done. Soon you won't need me at all."

He reached across the desk and captured her fingers with his. "I will always need you, Zanna. You must know that by now. It is only in the operating of the business that I don't need you as much. And that is a good thing. Now you are able to work on these papers for Mr. Burnside. Before, you would have had to tell him you were too busy." He rubbed his thumb across her fingertips. "You will be earning much more money from him than at the docks."

She couldn't argue that point. The offer from Mr. Burnside had come as a surprise. He'd personally come to Tarpon Springs to ask her if she would be willing to examine a stack of contracts for the railroad. With the need to travel so much, he'd fallen behind and the company had agreed he could hire an assistant he trusted. Zanna had been flattered by the request and also the fact that the work would provide her with funds she could save for the future.

Lucy had voiced no objection when Zanna approached her. In fact, she'd encouraged Zanna to accept the offer. Lucy had been delighted to hear her friend was going to spend a portion of her days practicing law. After all, Zanna would be available to support Nico if he needed help, though Lucy had expressed doubt he'd need much assistance.

While at first Zanna felt affronted by Lucy's comments, she knew they were true. Nico was more than capable of operating the business without her. His command of the language had consistently improved, and he seldom needed to ask her to translate a word. And now that he could manage the ledgers, she wasn't needed as much.

Instead, she'd begun helping the men in purchasing individual plots of land on which to construct homes, working with two local builders to make certain the men weren't cheated. Even though the men had never warmed to her when she wanted information about the sponging boats or their voyages, they'd more than welcomed her assistance when they were ready to begin securing land and building homes. Most were eager to move out of the cramped huts and establish permanent homes where eventually they could welcome their wives and start raising families. However, Zanna didn't relish the tedium of haggling with the agents and builders. The work didn't bear the excitement of being on the docks and watching the boats sailing in and out of the Anclote River. She'd missed seeing Nico every day, and although he spoke with her regarding progress of the purchases and building of homes, his real interest remained with his men in the Gulf.

So when Mr. Burnside had come calling, his offer had piqued Zanna's interest and her desire to return to her first love—the law. With Lucy and Nico both expressing their approval, there'd been nothing to hold her back.

Yet faced with Nico's ability to get along without her, a feeling of loss now enveloped her.

"Anything interesting in all those papers?" Nico's eyes sparkled in the morning sunlight that slanted across the room.

"I believe I've found a few issues that will interest Mr. Burnside. The lawyer who prepared the contract has attempted to slip in a few clauses the railroad won't like." She smiled. "And what about the *Anastasi*? The last you told me, Peter was doing well and there had been only two voyages when their harvest was lower than expected."

He sighed. "You need to keep your attention on those papers from Mr. Burnside and quit worrying about the boats. If the harvest is not what I expect, then I will take care of it. Eventually I will discover what is the cause of the shortage on the *Anastasi*."

"So there *are* still problems. Why didn't you tell me? I thought we agreed you would keep me informed if the losses continued."

He tipped his head to the side. "And I thought we also agreed you would be working for Mr. Burnside and your time was too valuable to worry over fluctuating harvests on the *Anastasi*."

Zanna shook her head with such gusto, the cotton padding holding her pompadour hairdo nearly escaped. "I never said my time was too valuable, and you know I have a deep interest in the problems with the *Anastasi*." She folded her arms across her chest. "I'd like a full report."

He chuckled. "And I have work that needs my attention. If you want a full report, perhaps I can give you one over dinner tonight? I think there's a good special at the Tropical Hotel restaurant. How about I call for you at, say, six o'clock?"

She gave a nod, and a thrill of anticipation shot through her—a sense of joy she experienced each time she was with Nico. And if she couldn't get the information she wanted right now, she was certain he'd tell all before they parted company tonight. "Six o'clock will be fine. Maybe you should call for me here. I need to keep working on these contracts. I'll let my mother know I won't be home for supper when I go home at noon."

"It will be a long day for me." He stood and flashed her a charming grin. "I'll spend the day counting the minutes until I get to see you again."

She laughed. "Well, you'd better spend the day counting sponges instead."

Nico departed Zanna's office with a spring in his step. He'd told her he needed to purchase cordage, but that wasn't the only reason he'd come into town today. In truth, he was intent upon speaking to her father. He knew Mr. Krykos didn't like the idea of Zanna marrying a man who spent his time at sea, and although Nico was seldom on the boats, he couldn't promise he would never dive again. He prayed Mr. Krykos would overlook his occasional diving and consider him a man worthy of his daughter's hand in marriage.

He stopped to order the cordage from Mr. Fernaldo and arranged to pick it up on his way back to the docks. Next, he strode toward Krykos & Sons, considering each word he would say—just as he'd done on three other occasions. On each of those visits, he'd been unable to deliver his speech. On two of the calls, Mr. Krykos was busy negotiating with customers. Both times Nico had waited for nearly an hour but then needed to return to the docks before speaking to Zanna's father. The third time, Mr. Krykos wasn't at the shop. Atticus had told Nico there was no use in waiting, for his father wouldn't return until late afternoon. Today, Nico hoped he would meet with success. He wanted Mr. Krykos to give him his blessing before he spoke of marriage to Zanna.

With the words fresh in his mind, Nico stepped inside the large building that housed the boat-building business. Atticus stood on the bow of a nearly completed boat that rested on wooden scaffolding. Nico waved to Zanna's brother. "I've come to speak with your father. Is he busy?"

Atticus shrugged. "I can't say for sure. He's not here."

Nico's shoulders sagged. If he didn't know better, he'd think Mr. Krykos had some foreknowledge of when Nico planned to arrive and ask for permission to wed his daughter. "Do you know when he will return?"

"Not until late tomorrow," Atticus replied. "He took the train to Tampa to meet with some men who want to hire him to build several boats." He swiped his forehead with a handkerchief. "Anything I can help you with?"

"No. I'll talk to him after he gets back." Nico mumbled his thanks before turning and exiting the building.

He kicked a stone lying in his path and watched it tumble along the wooden sidewalk until it hit a fence. It made a sideways hop, then settled in the dirt beneath the fence. He felt much like that rock. Kicked, battered, and bruised, even though no one had said or done anything to him. Still, his plans had been thwarted at every turn. He'd prayed about his future with Zanna and also prayed before each attempt to visit Mr. Krykos. Nico believed God had sent Zanna into his life, so why had it been so difficult to meet with Mr. Krykos?

He blew out a sigh, trudged to Mr. Fernaldo's store, and picked up the cordage before returning to the docks. At least he'd have this evening with Zanna. He had hoped to speak to her of his love and the possibility of marriage, but now . . . now he must wait for another day.

With her hand nestled in the crook of Nico's arm, Zanna's heart warmed. Their dinner at the hotel's restaurant had been filled with an exchange of information and pleasant conversation, but now, as Nico walked her home in the late evening, she felt an even deeper intimacy arise between them.

At the corner, only doors from her home, he paused beside a dramatic angel's trumpet, its honeyed scent filling the air. Her Yayá called it the queen of the garden. Personally, Zanna thought the plant was a bit of a show-off with its pendulous floral bells swaying gracefully from sturdy branches in the sultry evening air.

Nico snapped a flower from a branch and held it out for Zanna. "Something almost as sweet as you."

Her cheeks grew hot as she took the flower. Did Nico notice her blushing in the fading light? She had no trouble seeing the depth of emotion in his dark eyes.

"Zanna." He cleared his throat and took her hand. "I hope you know how much I care about you—so much more than you could ever imagine." He sighed. "But timing has not been our friend, my sweet lady."

My sweet lady. He'd just called her his. Her heart soared at his declaration. "I care about you, too, and we have all the time in the world."

A smile reached his eyes, crinkling the corners. "I'm glad to hear that." His gaze dropped to her lips.

Zanna drew in a quick breath, her pulse racing. They shouldn't kiss. Nico should speak to her father first. She shouldn't want something this badly.

But she did.

Before she could draw back into the sensible recesses of her mind, he brought his mouth to hers, kissing her until she had a taste of his love, and she realized one kiss would never be enough.

Two days after Zanna's dinner with Nico, Lucy stopped by the office for a visit. The two of them were deep in conversation when the door opened and Zanna's father appeared. He glanced back and forth between the two women before stepping inside.

"I was on my way to the store when I saw you through the front window." He gestured toward her office window. "I was surprised to see you in here. I thought you were in the office at the warehouse all the time."

She shook her head. "No, not as often anymore. I had some legal work that needed my attention."

Lucy bobbed her head. "And Nico is very capable now. His English is good and he can even balance the ledgers." She glanced at Zanna. "Isn't that right, Zanna?"

Zanna gave a slight nod. "Yes, he's catching on."

Her father leaned against the doorjamb. "I'm pleased to hear that. And the business is doing well? You are pleased with the progress, Doctor?"

"Oh, indeed. Zanna was correct. I'm not inclined to sell anymore. She and Nico have created a business that will show large profits far sooner than I could have ever expected." Lucy's smile broadened. "Of course, Nico's knowledge of diving and his ability to learn the business operation so quickly have made the business flourish. I couldn't be more pleased."

Zanna's father nodded. "This is good news. I am happy for you, Doctor." He turned to his daughter. "I'll see you at supper tonight, Zanna. Don't be late. I will have a big surprise waiting for you."

Lucy turned around and grinned. "Do you think he brought something back from his trip to Tampa?"

"I don't think so. If he'd purchased a gift, I think he would have given it to me upon his return. It's not my birthday, so I have no idea. But, knowing Papa, it will be something very special."

"Promise you'll stop by in the morning and tell me." Lucy gathered her gloves and stood. "I hate to rush off, but I need to go and visit Bessie Rochester. She said there was a matter she wanted to discuss with me."

Zanna's lips curved in a feeble smile. "I wish you well. I think I'd rather go through all of these documents than listen to Bessie seek sympathy for her nonexistent ailments."

Lucy nodded. "That's why you're a lawyer and I'm a doctor." She then breezed out the door, while Zanna attacked the remainder of the contracts with a vengeance.

Lucy accepted the cup of tea from Bessie—whose gray hair was perfectly coiffed for their visit—then settled back in the brocade-upholstered chair. "Tell me what's so important that you needed me to come to the house." Her gaze traveled up and down the older woman. "You appear to be feeling quite well, Bessie."

"Yes. I am quite well—for a change." Bessie paused to clear her throat. "Let me rephrase that remark. I am physically quite well. Emotionally I am in deep distress."

Lucy swallowed a sip of her tea. Already she feared this was going to be a long afternoon. "How so?" Though Lucy knew she'd likely regret the question, she'd agreed to come and visit with Bessie. The only way to offer any help was to discover the problem.

"As you know, my sisters and I have counted Mr. Pappas a friend for some time."

"I'm aware of that, yes." She set the teacup on its china saucer. "So you want to discuss your friendship with Mr. Pappas?"

Bessie sighed. "My engagement to Mr. Pappas."

Lucy's eyes flew to Bessie's ring finger. "I don't see a ring."

"A ring isn't important to me, but I do have a few doubts about Mr. Pappas. I know you've had dealings with him, and I thought you might share your insights regarding his honesty and trustworthiness."

"I doubt I know him well enough to make such a judgment. You've had far more contact with Mr. Pappas." Lucy traced her finger along the swirling pattern on the chair's cushion.

"Surely you can judge a man from his business dealings. You've been negotiating the sale of your business with him. Hasn't that provided you with some idea of his integrity?"

Lucy inhaled a quick breath. Sale of the business? Whatever was Bessie talking about? She gave a slow shake of her head. "I'm not considering a sale of the sponge company, Bessie. Early on, when I first learned of my father's decision to invest his funds in the business, I spoke of selling. Back then, Mr. Pappas didn't appear to have much interest. I believe he told Nico that he was content with his employers in New York and that he enjoyed living in a large city." She shrugged. "If he has pursued some further offer to purchase, he must have spoken to Zanna or Nico, but he hasn't sought me out on the matter."

"Perhaps I misunderstood." Bessie stroked her forehead with the tips of her fingers. "Maybe he isn't going to speak with you until he has all the money available to make the purchase."

Lucy reached forward and touched the woman's hand. "How could he have the money necessary to purchase my business when it isn't for sale?"

"You're right, I suppose." She poured a splash of milk into her teacup. "You don't think Nico or Zanna would try to sell the business without telling you, do you?"

Lucy chuckled and shook her head. "No, Bessie. Even if they wanted to, they couldn't do such a thing. Besides, I trust them—although I'm beginning to develop some concerns about Mr. Pappas if he's told you he plans to buy my sponging company." Lucy leaned forward as a troubling realization struck. "Has he attempted to borrow money from you?"

Bessie busied herself pouring more tea and straightening the napkin that lay across her lap. "He has borrowed money in the past and hasn't repaid it, which has caused quite a rift between my sisters and me since I forgave the loan when we became engaged." She sighed. "He admitted to a large amount of debt and wanted to wait to marry me until he could pay his creditors, but I agreed to pay those debts, as well."

"Oh, Bessie, I'm not sure that was wise. Did you give Mr. Pappas a large sum of money?"

Bessie quickly explained she'd gone to Mr. Larson at the bank and arranged for him to pay the debts rather than give Mr. Pappas the money directly.

"Mr. Larson wasn't any more pleased with my decision than Viola and Eugenia. But I love Adelfo. At least I think I do, and I didn't want him to go back to New York." A tear formed in Bessie's eye. "You probably think I'm a foolish old woman, yet I've always wanted to have a husband and children. I'm too old for children now, but I could still have a happy marriage."

Lucy moved to the sofa and placed her arm around Bessie's shoulder. "If it's with the right man who wants to marry you because he loves you, then you're absolutely right. But you don't want to marry a man who will take advantage and break your heart, do you?"

She shook her head. "That's why I decided I would pay another visit to Mr. Larson. I wanted a full accounting of the debts he'd paid for Adelfo, to make certain all was in order before I talked to the preacher about our wedding."

Lucy squeezed Bessie's shoulder. "Was it your visit with Mr. Larson that caused you to question Mr. Pappas's intentions?"

"Yes. Mr. Larson told me that Adelfo had been to the bank a few days ago and was inquiring about his rights to my money once we're married."

"What?" Lucy clasped both of Bessie's hands in her own. "This isn't good. He shouldn't be asking about your assets before you've even set a wedding date. And he certainly shouldn't be going to your banker behind your back. That alone should let you know he's not trustworthy."

As Bessie bobbed her head, the tears began to flow. "I know, I know . . ." Her voice warbled like a baby bird chirruping for sustenance. "He asked if the money would be considered his to do with as he chose." She hiccupped. "When I confronted him, he said Mr. Larson had exaggerated the conversation. Adelfo said his only concern was that if I became ill and unable to take care of my affairs that he would have the ability to do so for me."

Lucy curled her lip. "And you believe him?"

"I know it's foolish, but I want to believe him. I trust your opinion, Dr. Lucy. That's why I asked you here today. I already know what my sisters and Mr. Larson think, but I think you can be more objective."

Lucy didn't want to disappoint the woman, yet Bessie needed to accept the truth. Adelfo Pappas had only his own best interests at heart. He was a man bent upon gaining financial success at the expense of those around him. Bessie needed to send him packing.

"I know you don't want to hear this, Bessie, but you've asked for my opinion." Before taking a final sip of tea, Lucy outlined the many reasons Bessie should end her engagement with Adelfo. "And if I were in your shoes, I would see if Mr. Larson is able to rescind any of those payments to Adelfo's debtors. In fact, we could go to the bank right now."

Bessie removed a handkerchief from her pocket and wiped her eyes. "You're right. In my heart, I knew he wasn't in love with me, but I wanted to believe it so badly."

"I understand, Bessie. Everyone needs to be loved, but once we've put our faith in Jesus, we find we are truly loved—for now and for eternity." Lucy helped the older woman to her feet and offered her a warm smile. "You're going to be just fine, Bessie. Just fine."

upon to bring in a full harvest each time she sailed. He'd questioned Peter at length, but to no avail.

Her fingers rested atop one of the stacks while she recalled the entire conversation. Nico said Markos had clung to Peter's side like an added appendage whenever Nico came around. And though he'd talked to Peter, there hadn't yet been an opportunity to speak to him alone. Whether in the warehouse, on the dock, or in camp, Markos always remained close by. Zanna had dismissed the comments when Nico mentioned them, but now she wondered if Markos was afraid Peter had discovered some sort of information that would prove damaging to Markos should it become known. The lawyer in her wanted to get to the truth. Yet the truth seemed more and more difficult to uncover.

She shook the thought from her mind and returned to the papers on her desk. She transferred them into separate folders. When she was lifting the final stack, a paper fluttered and landed on the floor. She captured the document between her fingers, placed it on her desk, and pressed it flat. Her breath caught. *L. D. Vinson, Undertaker and Embalmer.* In neat script below the engraved heading, Zanna read the words *Embalming and Funeral Arrangements for Theo Hatzidakis. Paid in Full by Penrose Sponge Company.* During one of her trips back and forth between the warehouse and her law office, Zanna must have inadvertently left the proof of payment in Lucy's paper work.

She folded the receipt in a reverent manner, as if doing so paid homage to Theo and his untimely death. He'd died far too young, and for what? Because he'd wanted to prove he could collect more sponges than Markos? Or was it something more? His dying words pierced her memory. He'd said he needed to find the treasure on the sunken ship. Had it been true? Was that why Theo died? Was that why Felix would remain an invalid the rest of his life? Was that why the *Anastasi* continued to reap unpredictable harvests?

If there was any truth to what she was thinking, the spongers aboard the *Anastasi* would continue to suffer injuries and possible death. Would they really be so foolish? Perhaps she should speak to Lucy again. And yet Lucy had dismissed the matter, saying Theo had been delusional prior to his death. She'd even pulled out a medical book to prove her contention. No doubt she'd be offended if Zanna questioned her further. Maybe it would be better to talk with Nico. But if she mentioned it to him, he'd surely confront the men. If there was no merit to the deathbed confession, it could stir up problems among Nico and his men, and she didn't want to be the cause of trouble with the crewmen.

Zanna glanced at the clock. She'd be going home for supper in less than an hour and could discuss the matter with her father. He would be neutral and judge the matter solely on its merits rather than feeling any need to take sides. Unless of course he believed anyone might be placed in danger. In that case, he would insist action be taken—and she would be in total agreement. She didn't want another man to lose his life hunting for sunken treasure simply because she feared it might cause problems between Nico and the crew.

She tucked the receipt into her pocket. Tomorrow she'd return it to the files in the warehouse where it belonged. After locking the front door behind her, Zanna walked toward home, pleased with the decision she'd made. Her father was the perfect person to help her decide how she should handle this situation.

While she trod the familiar path, she organized her thoughts and questions. She wanted to be clear in her presentation so that she wouldn't sway her father's thinking. By the time she arrived home, she was prepared. Now all she'd need was time alone with Papa. She didn't want to discuss this in front of Atticus or Homer. And for sure she didn't want her mother or Yayá hearing the conversation with her father. Yayá would be voicing an opinion before Zanna had finished even the first portion of her story.

The scent of her mother's spanakopita greeted her like a warm embrace when she stepped inside the house. She could almost taste the savory spinach and feta cheese pastry. She had hoped for a moment to tell her father that she wanted to speak with him privately after supper, but when he arrived, both Homer and Atticus were nearby.

The spanakopita melted in her mouth, and she complimented her mother at least three times on the flakiness of the crust. Zanna leaned back and patted her stomach. "This is the best spanakopita you've ever made."

He grandmother nodded toward the sideboard. "Look what else your mother has made for you." Zanna clapped her hands when she spied the plate heaping with kourabiethes, the almond shortbread cookies her mother baked for family celebrations. "What are we celebrating?"

Her gaze traveled around the circular table and finally rested on her father's smiling face. "You remember when I stopped by your office today and said I would have a surprise for you this evening?"

Zanna nodded. Confusion assailed her. For some reason, neither her mother nor her brothers would look at her. Instead, all three of them stared at their dinner plates as though attempting to memorize their colorful design. Her stomach now tightened around the large helping of spanakopita she'd finished only minutes ago.

Her father tapped the china plate with his fork. "After we finish our dessert, I will tell you what it is."

Though her father spoke of a surprise, and the food her mother had prepared was often served at family celebrations, no one appeared in a celebratory mood. She glanced at her grandmother. No one except Yayá.

Her father's words had been enough to excite the older woman, and she soon gestured for the rest of the family to finish their meals. She frowned at Homer, who was chasing pieces of spinach around his plate. "Never have I seen you eat so slowly. What is wrong with you?"

Homer looked up from his plate. "I guess I'm not very hungry." He shifted in his chair and shot a fleeting look at Zanna.

Her father pushed away from the table, stood, and went to the sideboard. He picked up the platter of cookies and extended it toward Zanna. "Since this is your celebration, you should have the first cookie."

Zanna carefully chose one of the cookies and laid it on the edge of her plate. "But what are we celebrating, Papa?"

"One more minute, please. Let me finish passing the dessert." He smiled, but the smile didn't reach his eyes. And when had she ever before seen her father pass dessert like this?

When finally her father returned to his chair, he reached into his pocket and withdrew an envelope. "This is your surprise, Zanna. Two tickets to Greece. One for you and one for Yayá. You and Yayá will sail to Greece to find a husband for you." He lifted the cookie from his plate. "Two of you will depart, but three will return."

Zanna's mouth gaped, and she feared she might swoon. She clutched the collar of her shirtwaist in an attempt to gain more air.

The next thing Zanna saw was her grandmother's ancient face peering down at her. "We're going to have such fun, Zanna. Just you wait and see. I will find you the perfect man. We will sail in a couple of weeks."

After Zanna regained her composure, she pushed up from the divan and returned to the kitchen where she sat opposite her father.

"I didn't expect such a reaction to my news," he said. "Perhaps we should go and sit in the parlor where you'll be more comfortable." She followed behind him and sat down again. He dropped into his favorite chair and leaned back against its thick cushion. "To be honest, I thought you would figure out the surprise long before you returned home." He tapped his finger to the side of his head. "That lawyer mind of yours usually knows what's going on long before anyone else." His lips curved in a crooked smile.

"No . . . I had no idea." Her response was a mere whisper. She was taken aback, engrossed in her plans to discuss the possibility of sunken treasure with her father, her thoughts focused on Theo and the reasons for his death. "I would also add that I don't understand why you believe I should sail for Greece when I'm still working for Lucy."

"Ah, but are you really, daughter?" He wagged his finger back and forth. "Do you not recall the conversation the three of us had earlier today?"

"Yes, of course, but—"

"But? There are no excuses, Zanna. I hope you remember our discussion when you first convinced me I should give you my blessing. In case you've forgotten, I said you could help your friend until it was clear the business would either succeed or fail. Those were my exact words." Once again he tapped his finger to his temple. "Those words are etched in my memory. And now it is clear that the business is considered a success by both you and Dr. Lucy."

"Not yet, Papa. There are still problems with one of the boats and—"

He held up his hand. "Problems with one of the boats is not what determines success or failure. We both know that, Zanna. I listened closely to what Lucy said in your office. She's certain her father made a sound investment, and she's reaping enough profit so that she's no longer seeking a buyer for the company. That proves the company is a success."

She must think quickly, but her brain had become muddled by this unexpected turn of events. And fainting hadn't helped matters. She silently chided herself, then pushed aside the thought in order to dwell on matters of greater importance. "Papa, the company is beginning to show a profit, and I believe one day it will be of great value. But that time has not yet arrived."

He shook his head. "It is close enough for me. You gave your word, Zanna."

Though she'd agreed to his terms, she was certain she would be able to change her father's mind when the time arrived. And she hadn't planned on falling in love with Nico. How could she go to Greece and search for a husband when she was already in love with the man she now wanted to marry? Her nerves grew taut at the idea of another man courting her. How could she possibly do this? She shivered at the thought.

"You are cold?" Her father eyed her with concern.

"No. I'm troubled by your plan." As soon as she'd murmured the words, she was struck by a thought. "Tell me, Papa, how were you able to purchase the tickets today? Nobody in Tarpon Springs could sell you tickets on a vessel sailing for Greece. Train tickets that will take us to port, yes, but not tickets aboard a large ship." She leaned toward him, her hopes escalating. "May I see the envelope with the tickets?"

"Yes, of course." He withdrew the envelope from his pocket and offered it to her.

She stared at the envelope, willing herself to reach out and take it from her father while fearing she was wrong. Yet it would have been impossible for him to purchase the tickets this afternoon. Her stomach roiled as she extended her hand, took hold of the envelope, and lifted the flap. Carefully she removed the sets of tickets. On top were tickets for rail transportation, part of the journey in a Pullman sleeping car.

His eyes settled on the Pullman vouchers. "Yayá will need her rest or she will become a difficult traveling companion."

Zanna drew in a deep breath. At the bottom of the stack lay two tickets for passage on a Cunard sailing vessel. "But how . . . ?"

"How did I get them this afternoon?" He arched his brows.

She nodded. "Yes, it would not have been possible to make the arrangements so quickly."

"I agree. These tickets were ordered the day you and I made our agreement. You have never broken your word, so I purchased the tickets so they would be here when needed." His chest thrust forward, and he pinned her with a satisfied smile. "I may not be a lawyer, but I am smart enough to understand tickets from Florida to Greece cannot be purchased in one day."

His words stung. Did he truly think her arrogant because she'd become a lawyer against his wishes? "I have never considered myself to be more intelligent than anyone else, Papa, so your answer troubles me. That matter aside, I must tell you that I have no desire to travel to Greece to look for a husband." She let her gaze drop to her folded hands. "I already care very deeply for a man. I've found love here in Tarpon Springs, so there's no need for a voyage to Greece."

"What? How can that be? There has been no man seeking my permission to court or marry you." His eyes simmered with anger. "This is a ploy so that you can stay in Tarpon Springs and remain single, but I will not have it." He pointed his finger at her. "And I am surprised you would tell falsehoods to your father. I'm ashamed of you, Zanna."

"I'm telling the truth, Papa. I'm in love with Nico, and I'm sure he feels the same about me."

Her father's mouth tightened into a thin line, and his face reddened. "How can you be speaking the truth? Nico has never spoken to me. He's never asked my permission to call on you. And if he'd asked me for permission to wed my daughter, I wouldn't keep it a secret." He shook his head. "A man who truly loves a woman would talk to her father. I live in the same town as Nico. It would not be difficult for him to come and talk to me if he wanted to court you."

"There have been problems with the divers, and Nico has been attempting to discover what is happening on the *Anastasi*. I know he wants to talk to you, Papa. If he knew you were going to send me to Greece to find a husband, he would be here this minute."

"Baah!" He waved her to silence. "If he loves you, he should have said something before now, and he certainly shouldn't need to hear I am sending you to Greece to find a husband before he declares himself."

Zanna pressed a hand to her stomach. This couldn't be happening. Not now. She felt so trapped that she could scarcely breathe. Questions pummeled her mind. How was she going to get out of this trip? What would her father say if she flatly refused? Worst of all, was her father right about Nico? Why *hadn't* he asked her father for permission to court her?

CHAPTER 28

The following morning, Zanna lay in bed staring at the ceiling. She'd been awake most of the night, trying to arrive at some argument that would sway her father. One thing was certain: She did not want to go to Greece. Granted, she'd made an agreement with her father, but that was before Nico had turned her world upside down. For all her life she'd been obedient—except of course that one tiny incident of becoming a lawyer. Otherwise she'd been dutiful and respectful of her parents' wishes. Besides, becoming a lawyer hadn't occurred until after she was of legal age to make such decisions on her own. And now, faced with the threat of a voyage to Greece with Yayá, she must find a way to convince her father that his attempt to send her in search of a husband was inappropriate. Yet dissuading him once he'd made a decision was usually impossible.

Her feet hit the bedroom floor with a thud. Whether she felt like it or not, she needed to get out of bed and face the day. After she'd completed her toilette, she donned a gray skirt and white shirtwaist, then pinned her straw boater into place. She wasn't going to sit down at the breakfast table and make small talk. Not this morning. Not with this weight of despair.

The moment Zanna stepped into the hallway, Yayá called for her to eat breakfast. "Not today, I'm late." Zanna hurried out the door before the older woman had an opportunity to argue further.

After her father's surprise last night, Zanna had pushed aside all thoughts of speaking to her father about Theo's deathbed remarks. But she could at least talk to Lucy again. After all, Lucy knew only what Theo had said; she didn't know all the circumstances.

Zanna stepped inside Lucy's office and immediately removed her dove-gray gloves. Lucy smiled and arched her brows. "Appears you're planning to stay awhile."

Zanna glanced at her gloves that she'd placed on the side table. "It's too hot for gloves. Why do women feel we must tolerate such nonsense?"

"For the sake of proper etiquette and civility, I suppose." Lucy sat down at her desk. "What brings you to the office so early?" Her brow furrowed. "Your color isn't good. Are you feeling unwell?"

"I'm fine. Just tired. I didn't sleep well last night." Zanna didn't want to dwell on her father's unpleasant surprise at the moment. Right now, she wanted Lucy's opinion regarding Theo.

Lucy's frown deepened. "You're sure?"

Zanna nodded. "I want to discuss Theo's deathbed statements with you." Before Lucy could stop her, Zanna hurried to continue. "I know we talked about his comments at the time of his death, but you don't know everything that's been happening on the *Anastasi*."

Lucy straightened in her chair. "Go on."

That was all the encouragement Zanna needed. When she'd completed the tale, she leaned back in her chair. "Well, what do you think?"

"I think there may be some merit to what you've told me, especially since only the *Anastasi* is bringing in smaller harvests. I believe you should tell Nico and let him be the one to decide whether he should approach the men. There's a good possibility they're behaving recklessly because they hope to find some sort of sunken treasure. If so, more lives could be lost. None of us wants that to happen. Besides, Nico may have already heard rumors circulating among the men."

"I doubt that has happened. They talk only business to Nico, while the crew of the *Anastasi* seem to enjoy the company of Mr. Pappas during their time onshore."

"Mr. Pappas? Really? How interesting. I've been hearing his name a good deal lately."

Zanna startled to attention. "How so? Has he offered to buy the sponging business from you again?"

"No, but he's apparently told Bessie Rochester he plans to purchase it, even though it isn't for sale." Lucy leaned forward. "Did you know they're engaged?" She whispered the question as though the room were filled with patients.

Zanna reared back in her chair and clapped a hand to her chest. "No! You're kidding. Please tell me this is a joke." If Zanna hadn't given her word to keep Viola's promise, she would have told Lucy that Mr. Pappas owed Bessie money.

"I wish I could tell you there's no merit to it, but unfortunately it's true. She doesn't have a ring, however. Somehow the man got her to pay off some of his debts, and she's also forgiven a loan she made to him some time ago. I do believe he's only after her money, and he's convinced her he loves her."

"Humph! I don't think Mr. Pappas loves anyone other than himself." Zanna sighed. "I don't know if I can abide another day like these past two days. Can nothing good happen?"

Lucy came around the desk and sat down in the chair beside Zanna. "Has something else happened? Something you haven't told me about?"

Zanna nodded. "Yes, and it's terrible. Even worse, I don't know how to fix it." Lucy remained attentive while Zanna detailed for her what had occurred the previous evening. When she'd finished, Zanna leaned back in her chair. "I was awake most of the night attempting to arrive at a solution, but there's nothing up there." She pointed to her head. "I haven't even one good idea."

Lucy grasped Zanna's hand. "You need to have a long talk with Nico. You need to discuss Theo and the problems with the *Anastasi*, and then you need to tell him about your father's plans to send you to Greece. There is no doubt in my mind that as soon as he hears what your father has done, he will be at your family's doorstep begging for your hand in marriage."

Zanna hesitated, trying to process what Lucy had suggested. Telling Nico about Theo's deathbed comments wouldn't be overly difficult. He might be unhappy she'd withheld the information for so long, but once she explained it had been her hope to avoid causing any trouble among Nico and the crewmen, he'd surely understand. Telling him about her father's surprise was another matter. Would he think she was trying to force him into proposing? The mere thought of professing her love for him before he'd spoken of love or marriage caused her cheeks to warm.

"If you don't think you have the courage to tell him what your father has planned," Lucy continued, "perhaps you could ask him a few questions about love or marriage that would cause him to ask for your hand." She paused and added, "I don't know, Zanna. I'm certainly no expert when it comes to these things. We were the ones who were going to remain single for years, remember?"

Zanna lifted her head and met Lucy's eyes. "I know, but thoughts of being his wife overwhelm me when I'm around him. I think God has changed my mind about marriage and, strangely, I have no objection. Perhaps I'm beginning to learn His ways are far better than my own."

Lucy released Zanna's hand. "That may be, but right now you need to speak with Nico." She suddenly pushed to her feet. "Wait! I have an idea. You write Nico a note, telling him your father is sending you to Greece to find a husband. Then I'll go to the warehouse and tell Nico what Theo said prior to his death. After all, I was the one who thought his statement was only delusional muttering, so it makes sense that I tell him. Before I leave, I'll place the note on his desk. You wait a couple of hours before you go down to the warehouse." Lucy clapped her hands together. "I think this is going to work."

Zanna stared at her for a minute as she attempted to sift through the idea. She slowly nodded. "I'll write Nico a letter, you tell him about Theo and deliver the letter, and then I go to the warehouse in a couple of hours. And you think he'll be prepared to propose after that?"

"Of course he will. I'm sure he loves you. You're sure he loves you. It's time he voices his love for you." Lucy beamed. "It's a perfect plan, isn't it?"

"I suppose so." Right now, Zanna was still attempting to grasp the idea. Could it possibly work?

Before she could give it further thought, Lucy tugged at her arm. "Come around the desk and sit in my chair." Lucy opened one of the drawers and removed a piece of paper. "You can't write while you're standing up." Zanna dropped into the chair, and Lucy immediately pointed to the pen. "Write, Zanna, write. It need not be eloquent. Just a note stating what happened in the fewest words. That way he'll want to ask questions the minute he sees you."

Zanna reached for the pen, looked up at Lucy, and offered it to her. "Would you like to write the note?"

Lucy perched her hands on her hips. "No, I would not. The message needs to be written by *you*. And there's no need to be grumpy. I'm only trying to help."

"I know, and I appreciate it, but I'm feeling completely overcome." Zanna's voice quivered. "I'd like a few minutes to gather my thoughts if I'm going to write a love note to Nico."

"You're not writing a love note. Just tell him that your father is sending you to Greece to find a husband. You can add that he's already purchased the tickets for your voyage. It's as simple as that.

There's no need to fuss over each word. If I'm going to deliver the note and talk to Nico, I should go soon. I have appointments later this morning. If I'm not in the office when my patients arrive, they'll be unhappy. Besides, the sooner I speak to Nico, the sooner he can speak to you and your father."

Lucy crossed the room, picked up her straw hat, and pinned it in place while Zanna penned the note. She'd written what Lucy instructed, but what should she use as her closing? She gripped the pen, uncertain if she should write "love" or "sincerely" or perhaps "yours truly" before adding her signature.

"Zanna!" She startled and looked up as Lucy marched across the room and tapped her finger on the page. "Finish the note."

Without further thought, she scratched the tip of the pen across the bottom of the page, folded it in half, and placed it in the envelope Lucy handed her.

Lucy took it from her and placed it in her bag. "Come on. We can walk together to your office, and then I'll go on to the warehouse and speak to Nico."

A short time later, the two of them parted in front of Zanna's office. She watched as Lucy continued down the street. Had she made a mistake? Was the note a good idea? Her stomach cinched. Would Nico ask for her hand? And if he did, would her father still insist on sending her to Greece to find someone other than a seafaring man? Her fingers trembled as she unlocked the office door and stepped inside. She leaned against the door and murmured a prayer. "Please, God. If you intend this man for me, make our path smooth and straight."

Adelfo Pappas tugged on the tip of his mustache before knocking on Bessie's front door. She'd sent word she needed to speak to him. Since he'd proposed to her, he'd done his best to remain at a distance. One kiss had been one too many, yet he needed to keep her happy. She was his safeguard if things didn't work out with the sunken treasure. The thought of marrying Bessie was distasteful, but he needed her. No, he needed her money—he didn't need her. Unfortunately, he couldn't have one without the other.

She pulled open the door and bid him come in. He was surprised to see there was no tea cart waiting along with his favorite desserts. Perhaps she hadn't had time to bake. He arched a brow. "No pastries? Not even a cup of coffee or tea?"

"Sit down, Adelfo. I don't think you'll be here long enough for coffee. I'll be brief with what I have to say."

His mouth went dry. For some reason, he felt as though a noose had been slipped around his neck. "I'm here for as long as you want me, my dear." He gave her a generous smile. "And may I say you look lovely today? That shade of blue is most becoming on you."

"Thank you." She finger-pressed the pleats of her skirt and straightened her shoulders, though she didn't smile.

His flattery was usually more impactful. There was something amiss, though he wasn't sure what it might be. "Are you feeling unwell, my dear?"

Her lips tightened into a thin line as she folded her hands in her lap. "As a matter of fact, I feel quite well. Would you like me to tell you why?"

He nodded. Finally she was warming up. "Of course. I'm eager to hear anything you have to tell me."

She nodded, her gray hair bouncing with the gesture. "Because I've been back to the bank and had another conversation with Mr. Larson."

He stiffened. "Now, Bessie, I've told you there's no need to worry over your finances."

"That's true. There's no longer a concern. You see, Mr. Larson was worried over that list of debts I'd given him to pay. You do recall the list you gave me?"

"Yes, of course. Why did the list worry him if it is your money and you asked that the debts be paid?"

She tapped a finger to her pursed lips. "Well, you see, Mr. Larson knows me much better than you, and he was concerned you might take advantage, so he hadn't yet paid those debts." She clasped a hand to her chest. "Believe me, I was so relieved when he told me my money was still safe in my bank account."

"But, I don't understand. You were the one who wanted to pay the debts so I wouldn't have to go to New York."

"Yes, but that was before I came to my senses and realized the only reason you want to marry me is so you can be freed from your debts and have access to my money, so that you can then purchase Dr. Lucy's sponging company—which, I might add, is not for sale."

His anger mounted with each word that came from her mouth. "It sounds as though you've been going about town spying and spreading rumors about me."

"I've been single and on my own for a long time, Adelfo. I'll admit you swept me off my feet and I thought I was in love with you, but after a lot of prayer and thought, it became clear that you don't love me. The only thing you desired was my money. Thankfully, Mr. Larson saved me from my foolishness. Your debts remain outstanding, so I suggest you go back to work." She leaned toward him. "I think the only person you love is yourself, and that's a sad thing, Adelfo."

"So you invited me here to insult me." He clenched his teeth. If she were a man, he'd challenge her to a bout of fisticuffs or perhaps a duel. But she wasn't. His only choice was to fight her with words. "There have been a few women I have truly loved, Bessie. Unlike you, they were women of beauty and charm."

She chuckled. "If they loved you in return, they have my pity. And you, Adelfo, have my prayers. Please leave."

He stormed from the house, his hands clenched into fists. That ungrateful woman! To think that he had actually kissed her. He punched at the air. That noose he'd felt slip around his neck had tightened a notch. Those divers had better find that treasure soon because his debtors wouldn't wait forever.

Nico looked up at the sound of clicking footfalls outside the warehouse door. His jaw dropped when Lucy stepped inside. He could count on one hand the number of times she'd come to the warehouse since he'd arrived in Tarpon Springs. She disliked the docks, and unless she was needed for a medical emergency, she typically stayed away.

Lucy smiled. "Your reaction to seeing me down here doesn't surprise me."

"I heard the footsteps and thought Zanna would appear in the doorway. You don't come here often, so . . ." His chest tightened. "Is Zanna ill? Is someone injured?"

"No. At least no one that I know of. I wanted to visit with you, if you have a few minutes." She glanced around. "I'd like our conversation to be private."

"I think it's fine to talk here. There's nobody around right now, although I expect a few of the men from the *Anastasi* to come to the warehouse and help with the trimming and cleaning." He gestured for her to take a seat. "Their boat returned earlier than the others. Problems with some of the diving equipment, but it will be repaired by the time they are due to sail again." He inhaled a deep breath. "In the meantime, I plan to keep them busy in the warehouse. Maybe then they'll remember to check their equipment before they sail the next time."

She scooted forward in her chair. "The *Anastasi* is what I want to talk to you about."

He arched his brows. "What about her? She's a sound boat. There are no reasons for concern, Dr. Penrose."

"I have no doubt she's a seaworthy vessel, but I understand the harvests have been unreliable when she sails. From the records, it appears sometimes the harvest is excellent, while other times it's far below average."

"That's true. There is something not quite right. I keep trying to discover what it is, but I haven't yet figured it out."

Lucy nodded. "That is why I feel I should talk to you about Theo."

"Theo? What more can be said about a dead man?" Nico placed his hand on his chest. "My heart aches for his family back in Greece, and I know Markos grieves for his brother, but there is nothing we can do to change what has happened."

"No, but maybe there's something going on that will prevent such a thing from happening in the future."

His brow furrowed. "What do you mean?"

"Right before Theo died, he made a comment. At the time I thought he was hallucinating and his words meant nothing."

Nico leaned toward her. "What did he say? Please—tell me."

She repeated Theo's remarks about the sunken ship and treasure. "I don't know if there's any truth to it, of course, but it's odd that the only injuries or death have occurred on the *Anastasi*, and the only problems with reliable harvesting are with that same boat. After considering all that's happened, I wonder if one of the divers discovered a sunken ship and they're taking chances staying down too long."

Nico stared at her, momentarily unable to comprehend what she'd just told him. A knot of anger formed in his chest. "Why did you wait so long to tell me this?"

"I've already said that I thought he was hallucinating. The death-bed ramblings of dying patients aren't taken seriously—at least not by physicians. Besides, don't all sailors dream of finding some sort of sunken treasure? Before dying, many people say things that make no sense." She rested her elbow on his desk. "I'm sorry I didn't tell you before now. You may discover there's no connection between the unreliable harvests and the injuries on the *Anastasi*. However, if telling you saves another man from injury, then Theo's words weren't in vain."

Nico nodded. "I apologize for lashing out at you, but I have been discouraged in my attempts to figure out the problems on the *Anastasi*. Now perhaps I can find answers to my questions. Thank you, Doctor."

Lucy stood. "You're most welcome." She started to leave, then stopped and turned back to Nico. "I almost forgot. I was at Zanna's office earlier today and she asked me to give you this note." She reached into her bag and withdrew the envelope containing the note. "Please let me know what you discover about the *Anastasi*. Just because I don't come down to the docks doesn't mean I have no interest in my business."

He gave her a mock salute. As Lucy departed, he slid his finger beneath the sealed flap of the envelope.

"Nico! Come quick—I need help." Ned Francis's panic-stricken voice echoed from the dock only seconds before he appeared in the warehouse doorway.

Nico tossed the note onto his desk and rushed outside, where Ned was pointing toward the water. "A young boy fell off the dock. I think he's lodged under there. I tried to get a pole to him, but he couldn't reach it." Ned's features tightened. "I can't swim or I'd go in myself."

Without a word, Nico yanked off his shoes and jumped into the water. Shaking the water from his head after he surfaced beneath the dock, Nico spied the boy clinging to one of the thick pilings. Each time his grip failed, the boy's head went underwater.

Nico swam close and lifted the boy to keep his head above the water. "You need to quit fighting me so you don't go under. You're going to be fine. Just do what I tell you."

Once the boy ceased struggling, Nico easily managed to rescue him from beneath the dock. Several men had gathered on the pier and hoisted the child into the arms of his frightened mother, who thanked Nico until he finally gestured to his wet clothes.

"I'm glad I was here and could help your boy, but now I need dry clothes." A small pool of water had formed beneath his socked feet. He leaned down and picked up his shoes in one hand and motioned to Ned with the other. "I'm going to the camp to change my clothes."

Water dripped from Nico as he strode to the end of the dock, his thoughts returning to Lucy's earlier revelation. For sure, he wanted to discover if Theo's deathbed remark held any truth, and some of the men should still be at the camp. One by one he planned to question them, and he wouldn't stop until he got to the truth.

CHAPTER
29

Zanna's nerves tingled as she made her way to the docks to see Nico. An involuntary warmth spread through her chest, spiraled up her neck, and spread across her cheeks. She shouldn't have signed the letter "Love, Zanna." If she'd signed using something more formal, she wouldn't be embarrassed to see him now. On the other hand, she wanted him to know she cared for him and didn't want to marry anyone else.

The sound of loud voices as she neared the docks pulled her from her private thoughts. She slowed her pace and attempted to gain a better view. Lifting one hand to shade her eyes, she caught sight of Mr. Pappas and the divers from the *Anastasi*, yet Nico was nowhere in sight. From what she could tell, they were in the midst of a heated argument. But why would the divers be arguing with Mr. Pappas?

Hoping she wouldn't be seen, she circled around the back of the warehouse, then slowly moved along the side of the building until the men were within sight. At this angle she was hidden from their sight yet could see and hear the men.

Though she couldn't be certain, it sounded as though Mr. Pappas was telling the divers they needed to remain underwater longer.

When someone shouted that he wasn't going to die in the Gulf, the others shouted their agreement.

"You better do as I'm telling you. It won't be long before Nico figures out what's going on, and you can believe he's going to want a share of whatever comes from that sunken ship."

Zanna clapped her hand over her mouth. Now she was certain Mr. Pappas was the one doing the talking. So what Theo had said was true. The men were trying to retrieve treasure from a sunken ship, and Mr. Pappas was in on the deal. In truth, it sounded as though he'd somehow taken charge, with the divers following his lead. How could that have happened? Mr. Pappas had never set foot on a boat, yet he was ordering the divers to risk their lives? It didn't make sense.

"You know we've found nothing but a few worthless trinkets. Do you think we're going to continue risking our lives for more of the same? My brother is dead. Do you hear me, Pappas? Dead! And Felix will never be the same. How many men do you want to sacrifice with your greed? You can have your share of the lousy trinkets. In fact, you can have all of them—they're worth nothing. But you can't have any more lives."

Zanna's breathing came in short bursts as she listened to Markos. So what they'd been doing had been intentional, and Mr. Pappas was trying to force them to continue by threatening to tell Nico.

"Don't you tell me what you will or won't do! I'll make sure none of you ever dives again if you don't do as I say. You know Nico won't keep divers who don't follow his rules. What will you do? Go back to Greece? Do you have the money to pay for your voyage? Maybe you'd like to work on one of the hook boats and make only enough money to feed yourself and never bring your families to this country. You have no choice in the matter."

The voices ceased and were replaced by heavy footfalls on the dock. She straightened, and when she was certain the men were gone, she peeked around the corner. There was no one in sight, but the scent of cigar smoke drifted into her nostrils. She wheeled around and came face-to-face with Adelfo.

She gasped as he roughly gripped her arm. His eyes were wide, and his nostrils flared like a frightened horse. He pulled her into a nearby boathouse and pushed her onto a rickety wooden chair.

His eyes darted around the room before he kneeled in front of her. "Listen to me. All that talk back there with the divers was only a joke. We were having a good time, making up stories about sunken treasure and the like. We do that all the time down at the camp. It's nothing at all."

Zanna shook her head. "I heard what was being said, and that was no joke—it was a terrible argument."

Eyes narrowing, Adelfo yanked a gun from his jacket pocket and pointed it at her. "Put your arms behind your back!" When she hesitated, he pushed the barrel of the gun into her back. "I'm not playing games with you, lady. Do what I said."

She slowly moved her arms behind her. "Why are you doing this if it was all a joke?"

He grabbed a coil of rope from the wall of the boathouse. "I want to talk to Nico before you have a chance to poison his mind. The only way I can be sure you won't do that is if I keep you in here."

"I don't believe you. You don't care about anyone but yourself. You need to ask for God's forgiveness."

His jaw tightened. "Don't you tell me I need forgiveness. You don't know anything." He pulled a handkerchief from his pocket and used it as a gag. "Looks like this is the only way to shut you up!"

Nico's visit with the few crew members he'd located at the campsite yielded no more information than he'd received in the past. One of the men commented that the person who could give Nico the most answers was Markos, and the last time they saw him, he said he was going to meet with Mr. Pappas.

Determined to gain some answers, Nico headed back toward the warehouse. If he couldn't find Markos, he would corner Mr. Pappas and see what information he could provide. Approaching the dock, he shaded his eyes, hoping to see either Markos or Mr. Pappas. Neither was in sight, but perhaps Markos had gone into the warehouse to clean sponges.

Once inside, Nico glanced at his desk and caught sight of the cream-colored envelope bearing his name. The note from Zanna. He pulled the piece of paper from the envelope and unfolded it, then dropped into his chair. The words jumped off the page and seared his mind: *My father is sending me to Greece to find a husband.* How could that be? He wanted to marry Zanna. She couldn't go to Greece and wed a stranger, not when he was in love with her.

He shoved the note into his pocket and ran out the door and down the dock. His breathing labored, he pushed on. When had she written the note? Lucy hadn't said when Zanna gave it to her. What if she was already on her way here? His heart pounded with such fury that he thought it might explode.

When he finally arrived at the Krykos home, Nico doubled over, breathless. He startled and spun around when the front door creaked open. A rush of fear, excitement, and regret wound together and cinched his chest in a grip that rendered him momentarily speechless. He had hoped to see Zanna appear.

Instead, her father stood at the threshold. "Nico. What brings you here this afternoon?"

"I was hoping to see Zanna. I didn't know you would be here at this time of day, but I want to speak with you, as well."

"Come in and sit down," Mr. Krykos said. "I have some time before I must return to work. We can talk in the kitchen."

Nico removed the note from his pocket and pressed the wrinkles from the paper. He tapped the neatly scripted words. "Zanna says in this note that you are sending her to Greece to find a husband, but I must tell you that I love your daughter, Mr. Krykos. I have loved her for a very long time, and I can tell you why I haven't yet spoken to you about courting her if you will permit me."

Mr. Krykos nodded slowly. "I'm listening."

"Since I arrived here, your daughter has enchanted me, and I soon fell in love with her. She is bright, caring, and—"

Mr. Krykos stayed Nico with his outstretched palm. "I know Zanna's qualities and also her faults, Nico. Now tell me why you haven't come and spoken to me before today."

"Yes, of course. You might remember that when I came to dinner at your home shortly after my arrival, your family made it clear you did not want Zanna to marry a diver. Because of that, I wanted to wait until I was certain I would become capable of operating the sponging business without the necessity of going out on the boats each time they sailed."

"That's encouraging, but my plan for Zanna has always been that she would meet and marry someone—a Greek man, for sure—who didn't make his living from the sea."

Nico inhaled a deep breath. "In all honesty, Mr. Krykos, I will tell you that I might have to dive on a few occasions in the years to come. I can't predict what the future will bring. Even so, it is not in my plans to be a diver. Rather, I want to operate the business for Dr. Lucy."

The older man's brow furrowed. "I'm thinking you must have arrived at this conclusion before now. From what Zanna has told me, you haven't been diving except to train another diver, is that right?"

"Yes, but I also wanted to be certain that my livelihood in Tarpon Springs was assured. I didn't want to ask for Zanna's hand before I knew I could provide for a wife. That, too, was known to me before now, and while you may find it difficult to believe, I have recently come to your business on several occasions to speak to you about my feelings for Zanna. Yet each time I came, you were not there. So when I read Zanna's note a little while ago, I came running here to beg her to remain until I could speak with you. I love your daughter very much, and if you would give me permission to marry her, I will do everything possible to make her happy." He looked into the older man's eyes. "You have my word as a man of faith."

Zanna's father studied him. Instead of attempting to further convince Mr. Krykos of his love for Zanna, Nico remained silent and prayed that God would soften the older man's heart. The two of them sat facing each other, neither of them speaking or moving. Then, without warning, Mr. Krykos reached for Nico's hand and pulled him into an embrace. "I have liked you since the first time I set eyes on you, Nico. I would be proud to have you as a member of my family. But I think you must first ask Zanna what she wants."

When the tightness in his chest finally subsided, Nico grinned at Mr. Krykos. "I would very much like to do that. Do you know where she is?"

"I haven't seen her since she left this morning. I am guessing she's either at her office or down at the warehouse. If you don't find her at either of those places, you might check with Dr. Lucy." Mr. Krykos reached out to shake Nico's hand. "You will have to deal with the wrath of Yayá when she hears the trip to Greece is canceled. She was looking forward to her visit to the homeland."

Nico took the older man's hand, pumped it, and grinned. "Maybe Yayá could still go. I'm sure she could find a beautiful wife for Atticus, if you could do without him at your business for a while."

Mr. Krykos tipped his head back and laughed. "I don't know if I'll do that, but at least the threat might frighten him enough to make him listen when I say he must work harder."

After thanking Mr. Krykos profusely for granting permission to court Zanna, Nico bid him good-bye. He strode back toward town but slowed when he neared Dr. Lucy's office. He didn't stop, however. A sign on the door said she was out of the office on a call. He continued on toward Zanna's office—but there was a sign on her door, too, saying she would return at three o'clock. It was already near four. She'd probably gotten busy at the warehouse and lost all sense of time.

The candid conversation with Mr. Krykos had granted Nico a feeling of joy and freedom. There was a bounce to Nico's step when he entered the warehouse, but his gait slowed and his smile faded when he realized Zanna wasn't there to greet him. He quickly surveyed the main room for any sign of her, then strode to the cleaning and trimming area. The men shook their heads in unison when he asked if they knew her whereabouts.

He exited the warehouse and stared down the dock. The *Anastasi* remained tied nearby. Surely she hadn't boarded the boat, for she knew the crews believed a woman on their boat would bring bad luck. While Nico didn't hold to such superstitions, he'd long ago given up on changing the minds of his sailors. Besides, why would she board the boat? All the sponges were in the warehouse, and the damaged equipment that had brought them back early was in the shop. He walked toward the boat, his gaze fixed on the bow, still uncertain if he should check there. He shrugged and jumped onto the boat, but a quick look revealed she wasn't on board.

Where could she be? Had she stopped in town to purchase something? Had he turned at Lime Street and she at Orange Street? Even if that had occurred, she would be at the dock by now—unless she'd departed just as he was arriving. His mind whirred as he stepped across the dock toward a row of boathouses.

As he approached the last boathouse, a banging sound and muffled cry captured his attention. He stepped closer to the boathouse, listened, then carefully pulled open the door. In the dim light he saw the outline of a woman as she lifted up and bounced the legs of a chair against the wooden floor.

He squinted and hurried forward. "Zanna! What's happened to you?" He yanked loose the ties that held her wrists to the chair and untied the handkerchief that had acted as a gag. He knelt in front of her and grasped her hands. "Who did this to you?"

A tear rolled down her cheek, and he brushed it away with his thumb. "Adelfo Pappas!" She detailed the conversation she'd overheard between the divers and Adelfo. "He said he was going to find you and tell you not to believe anything I said to him. He says what I heard is a lie and that he didn't know anything about the divers looking for a sunken ship—but he did, Nico. He was forcing the men to stay underwater for too long."

They both startled when the boathouse door creaked. A shaft of light zigzagged across the wood floor, and Nico jumped to his feet.

Adelfo stopped short, his mouth gaping as he sucked in air. "Don't heed what she says, Nico! She has believed lies and half-truths about me and the crew. Just listen to what I tell you. Don't let her poison your mind against me."

Nico moved to stand in front of Zanna. "An innocent man wouldn't tie and gag a woman. To put the lives of other men at risk for your own financial gain is beyond belief. What kind of man does such a thing?"

"I should have known you would side with her." Adelfo's lips twisted in a snarl, and he reached inside his jacket. Zanna screamed. Adelfo flashed his revolver back and forth between Nico and Zanna. "If the two of you are smart, you'll stay where you are. I'm leaving town, and unless you want to die, you won't follow me."

He backed toward the door, but before he could escape, Markos, Peter, and the sheriff burst into the boathouse. Before Mr. Pappas could take aim at them, the sheriff grabbed him by the arm and wrestled to gain control of the weapon. The weapon discharged, and the bullet struck a beam in the ceiling. While the sheriff held Mr. Pappas's arm against the floor, Markos seized the gun.

The sheriff jerked Pappas to his feet. "Come on, you! You're going to spend some time inside a jail cell, and then we'll see what the court has to say about all of your recent activity. I don't think you'll be doing much business in Tarpon Springs—or anywhere else for that matter."

Nico wrapped Zanna in a soft embrace. "Are you all right?" He tucked a loose strand of her hair behind her ear and gazed into her dark eyes. "You were so brave. If you hadn't made that noise, I never would have found you."

She looked up and gave him an unsteady smile. "I'm fine now that you're with me and Adelfo is gone. I can't believe he threatened us with a weapon. The man is a true chameleon."

Markos snorted. "I can think of worse names than that to call him."

Nico chuckled and patted Markos on the shoulder. "How did you know we needed help?"

"We didn't know until we heard Pappas yelling. He had been at the warehouse a short time ago and was looking for you. He was acting crazy, making all sorts of threats. We didn't know what he might do, so we went and asked the sheriff to come to the docks and see if he could reason with Adelfo. When we went to the warehouse, a couple of the men told us he'd left just minutes earlier. That's when we walked toward the boathouse and heard him."

Zanna sighed and leaned her head against Nico's arm. "There's no telling what he might have done to us. He was angry because I overheard the conversation you men had with him about the *Anastasi* and looking for a sunken treasure."

Markos nodded. "We need to have a long talk, Nico. I became obsessed with that sunken ship and the possibility there might be jewels, gold, or silver waiting to be discovered. The thought of riches caused me to lose sight of what is truly important. I feel responsible for what happened to Felix and to my brother, but when I attempted to stop searching for treasure, Pappas threatened to tell you what we had been doing and that he wasn't a part of it, that he'd heard us talking in camp. He said if you found out, we'd never dive again."

Nico frowned. "You must know that I would have given you an opportunity to explain, Markos."

Markos shrugged. "You always talk about the rules, Nico. You told us if we didn't follow them, we would be fired. I know you to be a man of your word. And that is a good thing, but I didn't think you would listen to my excuses."

"I don't know what I would have done, Markos, but I think it is time we wipe the slate clean and begin fresh. I need you and the other men. If you give me your word you will be diving to harvest sponges when in the Gulf, then I want you to continue working for me. But if you want to hunt for treasure, you need to seek work elsewhere. It is your choice and the choice of each crew member to decide what he wants for his future."

Once the men departed the boathouse, Zanna lifted her head from Nico's shoulder. "Shall we go back to the warehouse?"

He shook his head. "Let's go out to the end of the pier. I want to talk to you alone."

Her heart quickened at his words. "That sounds intriguing." Her cheeks turned warm when he placed his arm around her waist as he walked alongside her. Was anyone standing on the dock and watching? Would her father learn of Nico's behavior? Would her father be angry? She would have pushed his hand away, but she wanted to feel his touch, wanted to feel that she belonged to him.

After they'd stopped at the end of the pier, Nico reached into his pocket and withdrew her written note to him. "This is what brought me looking for you." He cupped her cheek in his palm and looked into her eyes. "I went to your house and spoke with your father. He has given us his blessing. If you agree, I would very much like to court you, Zanna Krykos."

She smiled at him and recalled how many times she'd vowed to remain a single woman. How much she'd changed since meeting Nico. God had brought this man into her life, and now all she desired was to become his wife. "I would be very happy to have you court me, Nico."

"And after I have courted you for a short time, I would like to marry you." He traced her lips with his thumb. "You're my lady. You are the only woman I will ever love, and you're all the treasure I could ever need."

He closed the distance between them, sealing his declaration of love with an unhurried kiss so sweet, so true, so possessive it made her heart feel as if it would burst. She was his—his lady of Tarpon Springs—and soon she would be his forever.

NOTE TO THE READER

My daughter first mentioned the sponging history in Tarpon Springs a couple years ago. She'd lived in Florida and was acquainted with the area. After visiting with her, I did a bit of research and was captivated by the idea of a story set in this lovely community. Tarpon Springs is located on the Anclote River, less than a mile from the Gulf, and was settled back in the 1870s. The town continued to grow, and by 1887 the first railroad, the Orange Belt Railway, arrived to the city. Later, Tarpon Springs became a popular winter resort because of the mild climate and the mineral springs there, which were thought to be rejuvenating.

The town of Tarpon Springs was already in existence when, in 1905, a Greek sponge buyer from New York introduced the first mechanized sponge-fishing boat. At that time, he also hired five hundred deep-water helmet divers who emigrated from the Greek Islands that had become famous for their sponging industries. More Greek immigrants soon followed, and businesses thrived as a result.

My story is fiction. Neither Zanna nor any other woman managed a sponging company in the early 1900s, and the number of divers who first arrived to America in 1905 was five hundred rather than fifty. The fatalities and injuries to the divers, whether in Greece or in the Gulf, were numerous. In that regard, the incidents I've depicted in the story are true. Although none of my characters actually existed, I hope they'll remain in your memory long after you've read about them.

And if you find yourself in Florida, do stop in Tarpon Springs. Take a walking tour of the city, visit the history museum and the docks. Partake of the Greek cuisine and pastries and visit the sponge shops located in the old Sponge Exchange. Take a boat ride to watch a diver jump into the deep while wearing one of those ancient helmets, heavy boots, and canvas suits. He'll drop over the side like a rock and then reappear with a black sponge on the end of his hook!

Thank you for choosing to read *The Lady of Tarpon Springs*. I hope you enjoyed the voyage.

Blessings,
Judy

Special thanks to . . .

My editor and the entire staff at Bethany House, for their devotion to publishing the best product possible. It is a privilege to work with all of you.

The staff at the Tarpon Springs Heritage Museum.

The staff at the Tarpon Springs Library.

The staff at the Tarpon Springs Area Historical Society.

The staff at the Safford House Museum, Tarpon Springs.

Mary Greb-Hall, for her ongoing encouragement, expertise, and sharp eye.

Lorna Seilstad, traveling companion extraordinaire and wonderful critique partner.

Mary Kay Woodford, my sister, my prayer warrior, my friend.

Justin, Jenna, and Jessa, for their support and the joy they bring to me during the writing process and throughout my life.

Above all, thanks and praise to our Lord Jesus Christ, for the opportunity to live my dream and share the wonder of His love through story.

Judith Miller is an award-winning author whose avid research and love for history are reflected in her bestselling novels. Judy makes her home in Overland Park, Kansas. To learn more, visit *www.judithmccoymiller.com.*

Sign Up for Judith's Newsletter!

Keep up to date with
Judith's news on
book releases and events by
signing up for her email list at
judithmccoymiller.com.

More from Judith Miller

Hope Irvine always sees the best in people. While
traveling on the rails with her missionary father, she
attracts the attention of a miner named Luke and a
young mine manager. When Luke begins to suspect the
manager is using Hope's missions of mercy as a cover
for illegal activities, can he discover the truth without
putting her in danger?

The Chapel Car Bride

You May Also Enjoy . . .

Amid the glamour of early 1900s New York, Dr. Rosalind Werner is at the forefront of a groundbreaking new water technology—if only she can get support for her work. Nicholas Drake, Commissioner on the State Water Board, is skeptical—and surprised by his reaction to Rosalind. While they fight against their own attraction, they stand on opposite sides of a battle that will impact thousands of lives.

A Daring Venture by Elizabeth Camden
elizabethcamden.com

In 1772, Lady Keturah Banning Tomlinson and her sisters inherit their father's estates and travel to the West Indies to see what is left of their legacy. On the island of Nevis, every man seems to be trying to win Keturah's hand and, with it, the ownership of her plantation. Set on saving their heritage, can she trust God with her future—and her heart?

Keturah by Lisa T. Bergren
THE SUGAR BARON'S DAUGHTERS #1
lisatbergren.com

Vivienne Rivard fled revolutionary France and now seeks a new life for herself and a boy in her care, who some say is the Dauphin. But America is far from safe, as militiaman Liam Delaney knows. He proudly served in the American Revolution but is less sure of his role in the Whiskey Rebellion. Drawn together, will Liam and Vivienne find the peace they long for?

A Refuge Assured by Jocelyn Green
jocelyngreen.com